A PRAYER BEFORE KILLING

THE COLIN BUXTON SERIES
BOOK 3

CC GILMARTIN

CCGILMARTIN.COM

READERS' REVIEWS OF THE COLIN BUXTON SERIES

"This series is unique."

"Another fantastic crime thriller series to get into."

"The breadth of this author's writing is just awesome."

Copyright © 2024 by CC Gilmartin

All rights reserved.

No part of this book may be reproduced in any form or by any electronic or mechanical means, including information storage and retrieval systems, without written permission from the author, except for the use of brief quotations in a book review.

Without in any way limiting the author's exclusive rights under copyright, any use of this publication to "train" generative artificial intelligence (AI) technologies to generate text is expressly prohibited. The author reserves all rights to license uses of this work for generative AI training and development of machine learning language models.

This is a work of fiction. Names characters, businesses, places, events and incidents are either the products of the author's imagination or used in a fictitious manner. Any resemblance to actual persons, living or dead, or actual events is purely coincidental.

ISBN 978-1-7391362-5-3

❦ Created with Vellum

CONTENTS

PART 1

Chapter 1	3
Chapter 2	9
Chapter 3	15
Chapter 4	21
Chapter 5	28
Chapter 6	38
Chapter 7	44
Chapter 8	50

PART 2

Chapter 9	61
Chapter 10	67
Chapter 11	75
Chapter 12	83
Chapter 13	94
Chapter 14	99
Chapter 15	105
Chapter 16	112
Chapter 17	117
Chapter 18	124
Chapter 19	132

PART 3

Chapter 20	141
Chapter 21	148
Chapter 22	155
Chapter 23	163
Chapter 24	174
Chapter 25	180
Chapter 26	186
Chapter 27	194
Chapter 28	198
Chapter 29	204
Chapter 30	209
Chapter 31	221

Chapter 32	226
Chapter 33	230
Chapter 34	234

PART 4

Chapter 35	243
Chapter 36	250
Chapter 37	255
Chapter 38	260
Chapter 39	269
Chapter 40	276
Chapter 41	285
Chapter 42	290
Chapter 43	295
Chapter 44	299
Chapter 45	309
Chapter 46	315
Chapter 47	324
Chapter 48	330
Chapter 49	338

PART 5

Chapter 50	347
Chapter 51	352
Chapter 52	358
Chapter 53	364
Chapter 54	371
Chapter 55	375
Chapter 56	380
Chapter 57	385
Chapter 58	390
Chapter 59	397
Chapter 60	403
Chapter 61	411
Chapter 62	415
Chapter 63	421
Chapter 64	428
Chapter 65	436
Chapter 66	440
Chapter 67	446
Available now	457
Available now	459

Coming soon	461
Available for free	463
Acknowledgments	465
About the Author	467

PART 1

CHAPTER 1
FRIDAY 3RD NOVEMBER 1995

Rain lashed the ground as Colin approached the offices of the Glasgow archdiocese. A crude block from the 1980s covered with mirrored windows, it sat overlooking the River Clyde next to the Georgian cathedral, as if trying not to be noticed. A perfect reflection of the church's diminishing role within Scottish society, thought Colin. Then again, he was biased – it had been a long time since he'd cared about Catholicism or its doctrines.

Sprinting the final few yards to the entrance, he paused to catch his breath before pushing open the door. His mother's warning that the building would burst into flames as he crossed the threshold, rang in his ears. 'Do they know you're a heathen?' she'd remarked as he raced from the house.

Advised by the receptionist to take a lift to the top floor, there was no sign of spontaneous fire. However, his heart skipped a beat as the lift came to a shuddering halt with the faintest whiff of burning rubber, and the doors juddered open. If there was a God, this was surely a sign that he was less than welcome.

As he exited, a woman wearing a grey trouser suit and clutching a Louis Vuitton briefcase shouted, 'Please hold!' Her accent had a French lilt and Colin wondered how someone so elegant had found themselves in the blandest of offices, let alone the toughest of cities; her appearance seemed more suited to the boulevards and smart cafés of Paris.

Colin pressed the button to keep the doors from springing shut and the woman brushed past him in a cloud of expensive perfume.

'*Merci*,' she said, without a smile, as the doors shut.

Bishop Trocchi beckoned from the entrance to his office. He greeted Colin with a weak handshake and closed the door. Taking his place at a wide wooden desk, the bishop sighed, settling his ample frame into a huge leather chair. Behind him a floor-to-ceiling window looked down on the river below, its leaden surface whipped by the wind. He crossed his arms. 'Your parish priest – Father Traynor – speaks highly of you.' He fixed Colin with a practised stare, no doubt learned from years standing in front of congregations, holding their attention, gauging their mood, assessing their character. 'He says you're ideal for the role.'

Clearly he had failed to mention he was lapsed.

'Father Traynor's been very kind,' Colin replied.

He'd met the priest once or twice on visits home, but they'd only ever exchanged pleasantries. He was 'The best priest ever!' according to his mother, and it was through him that Colin's name had been suggested for a job at the exclusive Catholic boys' school, Holy Trinity College. That Father Traynor had provided a reference was over and above what he'd expected; for it to be so flattering, was way beyond his expectations. But rather than an endorsement of Colin's suitability, perhaps Father Traynor's real motivation was to make sure his sick mother had someone living with her; maybe then she wouldn't need to pester him quite so much.

'And it's good to be back home, spending quality time with my mother,' Colin continued. 'I brought a copy of my CV for you.' He'd rushed back from travelling in India to help take care of her. However, he'd given little thought to work; a part-time position, even temporary, would ease money worries. Interestingly, there had been a hint that the role might involve more, that Colin's police background might be useful; quite how, remained to be seen.

'The bond between mother and son is the most precious of all.' The bishop selected a small key from a bowl and unlocked the top drawer of his desk. Retrieving a manila folder, he opened it and considered the contents. Putting on a pair of reading glasses which were far too small for his face, he studied each sheet of paper intently.

In the silence, Colin allowed his eyes to wander. Though the furnishings were plain, their heaviness suggested quality. Expense. Surfaces had been polished to within an inch of their life; even in the autumn gloom every wooden tabletop and pane of glass gleamed. He dragged the soles of his shoes across the luxurious carpet, leaving a distinct trail in the thick pile. It was a room of quiet contemplation, where the ticking of a clock might be the only sound heard in a day.

The bishop looked up. 'Forgive me. I've only just received this file from the rector, Dr Charlie Murray, and I haven't had a chance to skim through it.' He shuffled the papers together and placed them back in the folder. 'So, Mr Buxton, how much do you know?'

'I know the job's part-time, with a Wednesday off, and that it's primarily coaching sports, but with some pastoral care and oversight of study periods. Oh, and I'd have to do the occasional overnight to cover housemaster shifts. Father Traynor explained it's similar to a role he once had.'

The bishop raised an eyebrow. 'I was alluding more to one of our nuns, poor Sister Oran.'

'Right.' Colin's mouth went dry. 'I'm not really familiar with what happened.' Regarding the case, he only knew what his mother had told him. Two years ago, a nun attached to the school had disappeared. Six weeks later, her body had been discovered, bricked up in a hidden chamber on the grounds, her skull smashed in. An investigation quickly pinpointed a suspect, a priest – Father Young – who taught at the school, and who was subsequently charged and convicted of her murder.

Colin had been living in Berlin when the case was splashed all over the tabloids. His mother had relayed various far-fetched theories: a conspiracy involving high-ranking clergy, a scurrilous suggestion that the nun had been used as a sex-slave, rumours of ritual sacrifice. The red-tops had had a field day coming up with headlines to embarrass the church: *Orgies on the Altar, Slave to God, Nympho Nun*. So excited had his mother been about the case, he'd had to ask her to stop talking about it. Following on from his own treatment by the press in the aftermath of the Lawrence Delaney case, he was all too familiar with their desire to cast people in the worst possible light.

'We were in the eye of a storm for some time. Thankfully, that all disappeared with Father Young's conviction.' A smile flickered at Bishop Trocchi's lips. 'Not one of my appointments, I hasten to add.'

Colin vaguely remembered that Father Young had been a newly qualified priest who'd been sent to the school to teach Speech and Drama. Only there a couple of months, the police had quickly established his sexual interest in the nun, and the fact he'd led them to her body hadn't helped. 'The case is closed, isn't it?' he asked. 'He was sentenced to—?'

'Thirty years.' Within a split second, the bishop added, 'And if it was up to me, life would mean life. Throw away the key, I say. Let him suffer the same as that poor innocent girl.'

Colin resisted the urge to question the bishop about forgiveness. Instead, he nodded; this was a job interview after all.

With some effort, the bishop crossed to a tall cabinet and retrieved a second folder from within. 'This is background

A Prayer Before Killing

information for you.' Bulkier than the first, a thick elastic band securely held a ream of papers. 'I couldn't ask you to —?' he wheezed. Carrying the bundle appeared more than he could handle.

'Of course.' Colin sprang up and took the folder from him.

Breathless, the bishop returned to his seat and handed Colin the first folder. 'Also, for you,' he explained. 'Before you read through these, I should update you on recent events. Stuff and nonsense, but it needs to be dealt with.'

Colin sat and examined the folders.

'Recently, something – an object – appeared in the school chapel.'

'An object?'

The bishop cleared his throat. 'Our nuns are stripped of any personal possessions such as jewellery, but Sister Oran had kept a bangle hidden, which belonged to her aunt. When her body was found, her aunt thought it strange there was no sign of the bangle. Yet a few weeks ago, out of nowhere, it appeared around the wrist of a statue.' He glanced over to gauge Colin's reaction. 'A statue of the Virgin Mary.'

'A prank?' Colin asked.

'Whether it is or not, it's got tongues wagging, as everyone imagined Father Young had disposed of it. Which obviously, even I concede, cannot be the case.' He shuffled a few papers to the side. 'Anyway, we'd like to nip certain theories in the bud.' He stared at Colin. 'We were relieved that the Sister Oran story had finally been laid to rest, but with this, and talk of Father Young's intention to retract his confession—'

Colin noted the bishop's deliberately unfinished sentence. 'I wasn't aware of that.'

'Hopefully it will come to nothing,' he blustered. 'So I must ask for your discretion.'

'Of course. And what do the Church believe?'

'That there's no one less trustworthy than a disgraced

7

priest. That the appearance of the bangle is by no means a sign from God and certainly not – as some would have us believe – a miracle. Mischief. That's all.'

Colin fiddled with the elastic band. 'Are you saying this is part of the job?'

'Not officially, but while at the school, if you could use your skills to identify the person, or people, who placed the bangle around Our Lady's wrist, the archdiocese would very much appreciate it. It shouldn't be too difficult for a professional such as yourself.' He gestured to the first folder. 'Your contract's inside. I'm sure you'll find the terms more than favourable.'

'I've got the job?' Father Traynor had hinted that the interview might be a foregone conclusion, but the bishop had barely asked him a question, let alone glanced at his CV.

'There's been far too much adverse publicity of late. I need a rapid end to this nonsense before it gathers momentum. And I believe, Mr Buxton – having heard good things from others – you're the man to achieve that.' He held out his hand and Colin shook it. 'Father Bryce will see you out,' he said.

Out of nowhere, a young priest appeared at Colin's elbow, and politely escorted him downstairs to reception. As he tucked the folders into his rucksack and contemplated the rain outside, Colin wondered what he'd just signed up for.

CHAPTER 2
TWO YEARS EARLIER

The brightness of the spring sunshine cutting through the trees blinded Father Young, distracting him from the map of the school grounds he held in his hands. He was sure he'd followed the correct route up from the imposing entrance gates but was starting to worry he'd taken the wrong path where it forked halfway up.

Instead of retracing his steps, he continued onwards, imagining that the paths must surely reconnect further up the hill. Given his atrocious navigation skills, there was always the possibility he'd find himself miles from his intended destination. Considering he had little desire to teach, that didn't sound too awful a proposition. And he had even less interest in the spiritual welfare of a bunch of overprivileged teenage boys. The post had been thrust upon him, with little option to refuse. 'It'll do you good to experience a bit of the real world,' his parish priest and mentor, Father Mahon, had insisted. The upside was the contract was just for a year, making it a stopgap before his real aim, to work as a missionary in Africa.

To his right, a red-brick wall – about eight feet high and overgrown with greenery – emerged from among the trees.

Though there was still no sign of a school building, he cut off the main path and followed a narrow, muddy track towards the wall. As he approached, he could hear the soft murmur of someone praying on the other side. Spotting a wooden door half hidden by trailing ivy, he prised it open to reveal a small kitchen garden set out with neat hedges and freshly sown vegetable beds. At the centre of the plot sat a nun on a tiny patch of lawn, hands clasped together in prayer. He didn't want to interrupt her, but before he'd the chance to leave, she looked up. The creak of the door had obviously broken her concentration.

'Can I help, Father?' she asked, glancing up and fixing him with clear, innocent eyes. Her tone was direct, and judging by the thickness of her accent she was from the south of Ireland.

He averted his gaze. 'I'm sorry. I'm completely lost.'

'Where is it you're looking for?' As she spoke, she delicately touched the rosary hanging from her belt; her pale fingers turning small beads, shiny as blackcurrants.

'Sorry, I've disturbed you,' he said. 'If you could point me in the direction of the school, I'll be out of your hair.' He blushed at his reference to what lay concealed beneath her veil.

'Don't worry yourself, I wasn't doing anything important.' She stood and brushed the grass from her knees.

He noticed how young she looked – she must have been no more than twenty but could easily have passed for fourteen. And her build was childlike too. With tiny wrists jutting out from the thick sleeves of her dun-coloured habit and legs like sticks, she reminded him of a sparrow.

'I'm looking for the school. And the rector – Dr Murray.'

'Well, you've found the perfect girl to put you on the right track. I'm Sister Oran.' She vigorously shook his hand.

His face flushed again as she held him in a tight grip. 'Father Young.'

A Prayer Before Killing

'Pleased to meet you, Father Young.' As she manoeuvred him back out of the door, words tumbling from her mouth, her voice grew louder. 'This place is a maze. My first year here, so help me God, I couldn't find my own bed some nights!' She guffawed, holding a hand to her mouth. 'But you get used to it. I can take you the scenic route, or if you like, we could go through one of the tunnels.' Wide-eyed, she nodded to the ground. 'Right under our feet, they are, criss-crossing the estate. Creepy as hell though. You don't want to be caught down there on your own. Another time,' she winked. 'C'mon now, enough dilly dallying.'

Despite being small, she'd a firm grip, and Father Young felt himself swept along by her enthusiasm.

After a minute, she paused at a gap in the trees and pointed. 'Do you see it now?'

A few yards ahead, the woods opened out onto manicured lawns from which the silhouette of a concrete building rose, sharp and intrusive. 'How could I have missed that?' For a third time since meeting her, his face flushed. 'I've made myself look like an idiot, haven't I?'

'Then you'll fit right in,' she laughed, revealing crooked teeth. 'I'll show you,' she continued, taking his wrist again.

'There's no need,' he protested, wriggling free. 'I should be fine from here.' Her familiarity was beginning to grate. 'Honestly. I can see where I'm going.'

She smoothed down her tunic. 'I know who you are,' she said, her tone softening. 'You're the new Speech and Drama teacher, aren't you? The one who was on the telly before he got the calling.' She thumped his arm, as though this was the most bizarre story she'd ever heard.

'Yes,' he sighed.

'I used to love acting and singing when I was young. I was Oliver in the school show. I was the only one who could reach the high notes – I still can. Then *Calamity Jane*. I bet you know loads of famous folk. Do you? Tell me which ones you know.'

He felt her scrutinising him. 'Sorry, I don't,' he said. 'It was just the one show. Years ago. I was just a boy.'

'What was it called?'

'You won't know it,' he mumbled. 'It was a children's TV show – a Scottish production. *Skooch*.'

'No way, we had that at home.' She peered at him as though he were a stuffed animal in a glass cage, then screamed, 'I do know you! I know you! I really do!' She danced around him. 'You were a skinny wee thing with glasses, weren't you?'

Father Young nodded, embarrassed.

'I'd such a crush on you when I was about six, I swear to God I did. Me and my auntie used to watch you religiously. You were grand. Always up to high jinks, weren't you? Such a wee rascal!'

He tried to smile. 'As I said, it was a long time ago. I was a child. The priesthood is my true vocation.'

'Sure. Sure.' In a flash, her whole demeanour had changed towards him – her grip was now a tender touch, her gaze admiring, almost flirtatious. 'I hope you don't mind me saying,' she said, dragging him up the clearing towards the school, 'but you're way more handsome than any of the old farts round here.' She squeezed his hand. 'But you're awful glum. Why's that?' She turned to face him.

He'd no idea how to reply. 'It's just how my face is. I can't do anything about it.'

'Well, I reckon you'll be happy here. I really do. I can feel it.' She smiled broadly. 'Don't forget, God is love. I tell myself that every day.'

'You're Irish, aren't you?' he said, delicately releasing himself from her hold.

'The accent's a pure giveaway, isn't it? From Silvermines, County Tipperary. D'you know it?'

He shook his head. 'I've never been to the South.' Disappointed, she muttered something he couldn't catch and strode

A Prayer Before Killing

past him towards the school. 'But I'm hoping to go this autumn. I've family there.'

'Where?' She turned to hear his answer.

'Near Belfast. The suburbs.'

More utterances under her breath suggested this didn't impress. 'Come on.' She surged forward as they finally emerged from beneath the trees. 'This is it.'

Sitting on the far side of the grass, as if the massive hull of a battleship had somehow run aground in the middle of the Scottish countryside, stood Holy Trinity College. Built over several floors, slabs of thickly textured concrete cantilevered out towards the woodland, defying gravity. Ribbons of dark windows cut across the walls in all directions, making it appear as if the whole building was in motion.

'Wild, isn't it? They say it's a rip off of some French guy's church.'

'It's inspired by Sainte Marie de La Tourette, a monastery near Lyon that was designed by the architect Le Corbusier,' Father Young explained. He gazed up at the building. 'A couple of years ago, I was lucky enough to go there on a retreat. As I arrived the heavens opened, and the rain poured down. It was magical. Biblical. It made me feel like I was home.'

'Well, there's plenty of rain here – you don't get grass this green without a shedload of it.'

'The top floors are where the boys sleep?'

'Yes. For somewhere drowning in cash, it's an awful place to live. Their bedrooms are like cells,' she said. 'And there're leaks everywhere. I don't know why they don't just put a normal roof on it.'

He shook his head. 'I think it's beautiful just as it is.'

'You're joking, right?' Before he could answer, she ran across the lawn and held open a huge glass door. 'C'mon. I've something to show you.'

As kind and energetic as she appeared to be, something

about Sister Oran made him nervous. She was certainly eccentric and definitely not like any nun he'd ever met before. Perhaps it was him; for seven years at the seminary, he'd had little contact with any women, let alone a young woman. Maybe he just needed time to adjust.

Together, they entered, and immediately Father Young began to understand the architecture. The whole school was organised around a huge central space which ran the full height of the building. At the top level were the boys' rooms, and on the two floors below there appeared to be classrooms and a library. Communal spaces occupied the ground level – close by was a dining area set out like the seminary, with refectory tables and benches. But his eye was drawn to the far end of the space, to where Sister Oran was leading him, and a monumental pair of ornately cast bronze doors. Though their scale was more suited to a cathedral, this had to be the entrance to the church.

'Enjoy the quiet while you can,' she said. 'It'll be a mad house as soon as the bell goes, just you wait and see.' She opened one of the doors and let him step inside.

'Wow,' he said, sensing his voice reverberate around the deeply shadowed space. 'This is exactly like La Tourette.'

'Here,' she said. Once more, she took his wrist and drew him over to a side chapel. She pressed her face against the grille. 'Can you see?'

'What am I looking at?'

She pointed her finger at the portrait of a saint hanging above the altar. 'Can you really not see?' She grinned, making her face look even younger. 'It's you.'

Sure enough, the painting of a young man about his age looked remarkably similar to him: dark reddish hair, fair skin, brown eyes cast heavenwards, hiding his emotions.

'What do you think?' she asked. 'You and Saint Oran could be brothers.' She stared at him. 'Fate's brought you here.'

CHAPTER 3
FRIDAY 3RD NOVEMBER 1995

Colin's drive back from the city centre had been challenging. A torrential downpour had caused flooding, bringing traffic to a standstill, so what should have been a twenty-minute journey had taken over an hour.

He let himself in through the back door, which, as usual, was unlocked. 'Mum,' he called, expecting to hear her harsh Derry accent yell back 'Here!' but the house was completely still. Placing the folders the bishop had given him on the smoked-glass kitchen table, he went through to the hall and popped his head into the living room. His mother and Jeanie, a neighbour from the opposite house in their cul-de-sac, sat side by side on the sofa in prayer, their eyes closed and lips silently moving. An earthquake wouldn't have stirred them.

Tearing off his coat, he collapsed into an armchair near his mother and stared at the TV. Flickering brightly in the corner, a healthy young couple from one of the Aussie soaps frolicked across the screen, half naked on a beach. It felt like a world away from his mother's house.

Colin had always liked Jeanie but she had a reputation as a bit of a do-gooder. Until very recently his mother had regularly referred to her as a complete eejit, saying she'd been nothing but a skivvy to her husband. The man in question was Alec, a bully who his mother loathed with a passion and who had died less than a year ago after a long, debilitating illness. 'Good riddance,' Moira had crowed on hearing of his death. Quite how Jeanie and his mother had become such bosom buddies in the intervening months had never been fully explained to him. All of a sudden Jeanie was a saint and the only person who truly understood her.

Jeanie opened an eye and held up a finger, suggesting they'd be finished soon. Despite being in her late seventies – at least fifteen years older than his mother – she was sprightly on her feet and had the strength of a small army. Several times he'd watched her manoeuvre his frail mother from the sofa and upstairs to bed with all the patience of a team of nurses. But Colin wondered how his normally cantankerous mother could tolerate someone being around her so much, especially someone who exhibited such unwavering kindness.

He flicked through the channels. A quiz show he knew his mum enjoyed – *Fifteen to One* – was halfway through, and he considered turning up the volume to gain her attention. But just as the thought crossed his mind, his mother's eyes opened, peering at him suspiciously. 'Why've you not turned on the side lamps? It's pitch-black outside.'

One by one, he switched them on, filling the grey room with a warm glow.

'The display cabinet too,' his mother barked. A coughing fit followed, fierce and relentless, which he'd only previously heard during the night.

'Let it all out, darling,' Jeanie said, rubbing her back till she finally stopped.

Colin leaned down to turn on the socket. With a buzz, the bulb popped into life, showcasing a large, framed photograph of him, his sister and brother, all in their school uniforms, and all grinning maniacally. He hated it; all he could see were the

A Prayer Before Killing

battles which raged behind the smiles, tensions which they'd carried into adulthood.

'Curtains too,' his mother snapped, 'or do I need to get up and do them myself?'

'I'm doing it – give me a chance,' Colin replied.

Jeanie perched on the edge of the sofa, wrestling the cellophane from a packet of Benson & Hedges. 'I've made you a lovely casserole, Moira,' she said, her voice the texture of rough sandpaper. 'Brisket, onion, potatoes and a few carrots. Nothing fancy.'

'Thanks. I'll try to manage some later.'

'No rush. Just whenever you're ready. I'll tell Colin what to do.' She winked at him and lit a cigarette. 'I'll be off.'

'Give me a wee drag of that before you go, will you?'

'Mum!' Colin shouted.

'Get off your high horse.' His mother scowled. 'It's not like it's going to kill me.'

Colin shook his head. 'Don't let her browbeat you, Jeanie.'

'Where's the harm, son?' Jeanie smiled. 'There you go, love.'

'Thanks.' His mother savoured a long drag and blew a plume of smoke in his direction.

Taking the cigarette back, Jeanie kissed his mother on both cheeks and whispered, 'God bless.' For a moment, they stared at each other like a pair of young lovers, before Jeanie grabbed her coat from the end of the sofa, then her handbag. In a split second, she was fully buttoned up. 'Now son, you can have the casserole any time – I've left it in the oven on low – but mind and check on it. Stir it every half an hour to make sure it's not sticking.'

'You're too good to us.'

'Not at all. It's all for this woman here.' Jeanie squeezed Moira's hand. 'I'll see you tomorrow.'

'Night,' Moira replied, her attention switching to the quiz programme. 'The capital of Argentina? *Buenos Aires*.'

Colin rolled his eyes. 'I'll see you out,' he said, following Jeanie into the hallway.

'Your ma's had a dreadful afternoon,' she whispered once out of earshot. 'And she's barely eaten all day. Half a slice of toast, that's it. See if you can persuade her to have some casserole?'

'I'll do my best.'

She seized his hands. 'Bless you.'

'I don't think the new pills are working.' Colin had noticed how gaunt and pale his mother had become. 'And her hands shake constantly.'

'But she swears they're working just fine,' Jeanie replied. 'And I'm making sure she's taking them religiously.'

'I'll try and have a quiet word with Dr Hendry. I think she's in more pain than she's letting on.' He opened the front door, letting a blast of cold wind howl through the hallway.

'Night, love,' Jeanie edged past him.

'Good night.' He watched her scurry down the pathway, no doubt off to visit the next sickly neighbour on her list. She was quite something; from dawn till dusk, seven days a week she was out helping people. Plus, she never missed a funeral.

'Mum, can I get you anything?' Colin asked, re-entering the living room.

'Weesht!' She shook her head, which brought on another coughing fit, though mercifully shorter this time. 'It's the final round. *Remington Steele.* Oh, what's his name? *Pierce Brosnan.*'

In the kitchen he checked on the casserole. It smelled delicious.

Picking up the folders, he flicked through them. His plan was to spend the rest of the evening going through the individual files; the sizeable fee stated in the contract suggested the investigative work was more important than he'd initially thought, but why such a fuss over a bangle?

'Did you get the job?' Despite being frail, his mother's

voice still managed to soar over the sound of the quiz show's theme tune.

'Seems like it,' he yelled back.

'What does that mean? You either did or you didn't. Father Traynor will want to know.'

Despite her ill-health, his mother's instinct was still to argue, whatever the subject matter.

He popped his head back into the living room. 'I got the job.' He kept his voice calm, refusing to rise to the bait. 'Bishop Trocchi seemed happy with me.'

'So, it was the bishop himself you spoke to?'

He knew this would appease her. 'It was.'

'At least it'll keep you out from under my feet.' Her focus returned to the TV where a coiffed news presenter was interviewing a sad-looking woman. 'What an eejit! Where do they get these dafties? Pass me a cushion, will you?'

He offered her one but she struggled to take a grip of it and it fell to the floor.

'Look what you've done,' she barked.

'Here. Let me.'

'Stop fussing.' She shooed him away, then attempted a stretch to retrieve the cushion.

'Careful!' Colin grabbed it and handed it to her.

'You know you're worse than Jeanie. I'm not a bloody invalid.' Brandishing the cushion, she stared at him, her face tight as a drum, daring him to disagree.

'If you're wanting to eat later, I can do a bit of work now. We can have dinner with Annemarie when she gets back.' His sister had been staying for a few days. 'Did she say what time she'd be home?'

A casual shrug told him there'd been another disagreement. While relations between him and his mother had thawed in recent years, Annemarie continued to be at loggerheads with her. Any truces were brief and their relationship was mostly characterised by endless sniping. He admired his sister's tenacity. While he had run away to London, Berlin and then India, Annemarie made the effort to visit regularly, despite living over 150 miles away in Newcastle. The arguments, however bitter, seemed to tie her to their mother – a never-ending test of his sister's loyalty which she stubbornly refused to fail.

'Does that mean she won't be back tonight?'

'In the mood she left? I doubt it.'

He knew not to enter their battleground. And never to take sides. 'Okay. Well, I'm going up to my room. I'll be down in half an hour.'

'Said she was driving back to Newcastle.'

'So she's actually left?'

'Took the wee fella with her. Said he's missing his friends.' She shook her head. 'She's making him soft, pandering to him like that. I told her as much.'

Again, he'd learned not to interfere. The 'wee fella' was his fifteen-year-old nephew, Liam, football-mad, who Annemarie had dragged up from Newcastle in the hope that his presence might bring out the best in their mother. But Moira eyed her own grandson with the same level of distrust she reserved for any child over the age of twelve, and he was soon on the receiving end of the familiar critique they'd all been subject to as teenagers. Liam had quickly retreated outdoors and had spent the whole of the previous day kicking his ball against the gable-end of the house. A thumping rebuke to his mother's family.

'Well, you'll be glad to know I'm not going anywhere.' The frenetic theme tune of another quiz show drowned out his words. He was certain his mother wouldn't have replied even if she'd heard him.

CHAPTER 4

Colin placed the folders from the bishop on the yellowing candlewick bedspread. Since leaving home in 1987, his bedroom had changed little. Only a fresh coat of paint – magnolia – had been added. Of course, all the posters of bands he loved as a teenager – Blondie, Soft Cell, The Human League – plus pictures ripped from Smash Hits and Melody Maker had been removed, though not destroyed. They'd been folded up and neatly piled in a cardboard box at the bottom of his wardrobe. He found it hard to believe his mother had taken the time to do that; perhaps it had been Annemarie. The temptation to risk his mother's wrath and pin them back up hovered, but he hadn't been much of a teenage rebel then and his acceptance of a job from the archdiocese suggested he wasn't much of a rebel now. Bela – an eccentric librarian he'd dated after arriving in Berlin – had once called him the least transgressive gay man in the city. Maybe he'd had a point.

Removing the elastic band, he opened the first folder. A sealed white envelope addressed to him sat on top of a small pile of documents. The letter inside – an offer of employment typed on crisp paper, embossed with the school's gold crest –

came from the rector, and had been flamboyantly signed in red ink.

24th October 1995

Dear Mr Buxton,

Thank you for accepting the temporary position of Sports Coach at Holy Trinity College; the pursuit of physical excellence plays a fundamental part in the continuing development of our students and the wider scholastic community. Your start date will be Monday, 6th November.

Besides the aforementioned role, you will also provide pastoral support to students who continue to wrestle with the challenges of recent events; we sincerely hope that your guidance will offer boys an informed perspective on their religious duties and moral responsibilities.

We trust your time with us will be fulfilling, offering opportunity for professional growth and, of course, time for your own spiritual reflection.

Our school is a family, and like a family we seek to nurture and support our members. Should you ever need assistance, please remember that we are always here to help.

Yours sincerely,

Dr Charles Murray (DPhil, MA)
Rector

This was typical of the church. Though the bishop had interviewed him, it was the school that was actually employing him. And, given that the letter from the rector was dated ten days ago, it appeared he'd been interviewed for a job that was already his. Not only that, the letter made no mention of an investigation. Like much of his experience of the Catholic hierarchy, everything was opaque; you never knew who was pulling the strings. He was being appointed on an understanding – the main points tiptoed around – as if simply stating the facts outright might be too much for anyone to bear.

Was this really what he wanted to be doing?

When he'd left Berlin nearly a year before, he was a physical wreck, psychologically scarred from the trauma of exposing two killers. In the fallout from the case, his boyfriend Klaus had cut all ties. Newly single and emotionally exhausted, his decision to go to India was an escape to a far simpler life. For months he'd travelled alone, exploring the landscape, visiting historic temples, and practising yoga, determined to make what little savings he had left last as long as possible. Perhaps all he'd been doing was delaying a return home.

At the start of the summer, his friend Hannah from Berlin had joined him in Mumbai and together they'd travelled overland to Delhi. Her big plan was for them to finish their trip at an ashram in Agra. But the major revelation had been the type of meditation practised there – it had reinvigorated him. Having befriended one of the yoga teachers, he'd found out about another ashram, off the tourist trail, in the foothills of the Himalayas. This had offered a more intensive programme and he'd made a snap decision to go there on his own, despite Hannah's insistence that he should travel onto Thailand with her. 'You're such a killjoy,' she'd moaned. 'We should be partying together. We deserve it.'

But, back in Delhi, a telegram from Annemarie had been waiting for him at the main post office:

Phone home ASAP. Mum's not well. We need you here.

Annemarie had been tearful when he managed to get through to her. 'How ill?' had been his first question.

'It's lung cancer,' she'd said. 'That bloody woman didn't go to the doctor until it was too late. There's not a lot they can do now. She's got months, maybe a year.'

The words rushed to his head, making him feel dizzy. 'It's that bad?'

'Yes.' Annemarie had regained her composure. 'Mum's asking for you constantly. "I need my baby" she keeps saying.'

'That doesn't sound like her. You sure it's not a brain tumour she's got?'

'Not funny!' Annemarie's default position was always to scold him, but deep down, he knew she understood his need to make light of the situation. 'She has changed though. Well, slightly. She's still the same monster we know and love, just a little bit more sentimental.'

'And she does remember she doesn't actually like me?'

'She doesn't like anyone. It's all relative; she dislikes you the least. But seriously, she wants you home. She needs you. I need you, too. Another week of playing Florence Nightingale and I swear I'm going to throttle her.'

Thirty-six hours later he was on a flight to Glasgow; landing in a city he'd had no desire to return to and had long since left behind. Gone were his plans for calm reflection and spiritual enlightenment in the Shivalik Hills; that would have to wait.

COLIN PULLED a Polaroid from the second folder. It showed a young nun with a moon face standing in a garden holding a basket of laundry against her hip. Squinting in front of a rhododendron bush with pale pink flowers the same colour as her cheeks, one hand was raised as if reluctant to be photographed, though she appeared to be having fun. Sister

A Prayer Before Killing

Oran's name had been scrawled on the back, with a date – 1st June 1993 – two weeks before she disappeared. Several newspaper clippings were attached with a paperclip to the photo. Screaming with lurid headlines, a couple of stories were from national newspapers, but most came from the local press. Their headlines were factual, and somehow more sad. *Irish Nun Lay Undiscovered for Weeks; Sexual Motive to Nun's Killing; Mourners Gather for Tragic Nun*. The articles were accompanied by other images of Sister Oran – mostly in the laundry room where she worked – always smiling.

But what struck Colin most was how thin and physically fragile she looked. If reports were accurate and she had been locked away without food or water, she surely wouldn't have had the reserves to last a week, let alone six. However, that was not the cause of death – at some point her skull had been crushed by the priest who'd been holding her captive.

A single headline revealed the final verdict on Father Young: *Priest Guilty of Murder*. A formal portrait sat beneath this bleak sentence, most likely taken at his ordination. Staring into the lens with a serious expression, Father Young appeared hesitant, a reluctant sitter. As Colin lay the article aside, he realised he recognised him. Sure enough, at the end of the story there was more biographical detail: Simon Young, star of the Scottish TV show for kids, *Skooch*. Even as a child, Colin had been perplexed by the show's popularity; with its shaky sets and even shakier storylines about a precocious little boy wanting to take his pet dog Skooch to Crufts, he'd found it deathly dull.

The rest of the file consisted of a variety of photocopies: reviews of Father Young's teaching performance, some similar, shorter notes on Sister Oran's time at the school, what appeared to be transcripts from the court case and updates from the police on the progress of their investigation. At the end were a few more press clippings, which all repeated the same sorry tale.

Colin returned to the first folder. There was some general information included about the school and the history of the estate on which it was built; these looked like they'd been photocopied from the school prospectus. Right at the bottom, stapled together, were four final sets of photocopies – each from a pupil's file. Thinking it must be a joke, Colin smiled; the documents had been ordered so that the names almost corresponded to the four apostles: Matthew, Garr, Luc and Johnny. They offered general information on the background of each of the boys. Matthew came from Cornwall and was the son of a multi-millionaire playboy; Garr was brought up in Glasgow, and his father was an esteemed surgeon, his mother a lawyer; Luc came from a wealthy French family; and lastly, Johnny, from Lanarkshire, who'd been awarded a scholarship to the school. There was nothing to suggest why their details had been included. Perhaps it was an oversight, and the rector had added their files to the bundle by mistake.

Colin looked at his watch – it was almost eight. He was famished; maybe his mother could be persuaded to eat some of the casserole now.

He gathered the papers together – there'd be plenty of time to read them more thoroughly tomorrow. As he picked up the folder, he noticed ink had bled through to the inside. Turning the folder over, he found a note scrawled across the back:

DRAW COLIN BUXTON'S ATTENTION TO:
Sister Oran's bangle!
The 4 Apostles!
The questions over their relationship!

It didn't sound like the message was meant for him. Written boldly in red ink, it seemed more likely it was a message from the rector to Bishop Trocchi, but the bishop hadn't mentioned the four boys.

A Prayer Before Killing

Colin closed the folder and set it aside. Laying back on his bed he stared up at the ceiling, where a damp patch was spreading. He made a mental note to check the roof for loose tiles at the weekend, then wondered what the coming months were going to bring. Instead of meditating in the Himalayas, he was a part-time teacher-cum-investigator of holy miracles and carer to a not very compliant patient. Christ, what had his life become?

Downstairs, the phone began to ring.

'I'll get it,' he yelled, but before he reached the top of the stairs, he heard his mother answer with an abrupt, 'What?'

'It's for you,' she shouted. 'Someone calling themselves Charlie Murray.'

CHAPTER 5

The conversation with the rector, Dr Charlie Murray, had been brief.

'I can't go into detail, Mr Buxton, but it's essential you meet me at the school first thing on Monday morning. I've a few things I'd like to discuss with you.'

'Of course. I wanted to head in early anyway, get my bearings.'

'Is 7.30 AM good with you?'

Just as Colin was about to suggest 8.30 as a more realistic time, the receiver was put down and the line went dead. So, 7.30 it was.

ON THE FOLLOWING MONDAY, he left home at 6.30 AM in his mother's aging Fiat Panda, which she'd grudgingly agreed to let him borrow. Besides the occasional taxi and delivery van, the rain-spattered roads were deserted.

Joining the empty motorway, with only the radio for company, Blur's *Country House* bellowed out as he snaked through a city centre bathed in the sodium glow of streetlights. Reflected in the dank waters of the River Clyde, the

A Prayer Before Killing

moonless sky was bereft of stars as he drove over the Kingston Bridge, singing along to a haunting duet by Nick Cave and Kylie Minogue.

Heading west past Glasgow Airport, the motorway became quieter and darker as the suburbs gave way to open countryside. A line of tollbooths glinted in the dark as he approached the Erskine Bridge. He stopped to hand over his change to a shivering attendant who avoided making eye contact. The first glimmer of dawn kissed the sky as he swept up onto the bridge and over the Clyde, where the estuary began to widen.

Initially driving west in the direction of Loch Lomond, he took a left fork towards Dumbarton. Tenements were stirring into life as he passed through the town centre, catching a glimpse of Dumbarton Rock, the castle ramparts resolutely black against the lightening sky.

On the lookout for the turning to the school, he skirted the north shores of the Clyde as he drove onwards through villages, hamlets and low-lying farmland.

A large sign finally emerged from the shadows, announcing *Holy Trinity College*. Braking carefully, he turned into a single-track road and was plunged back into night as he navigated away from the river through a thick canopy of trees. Passing through a pair of elaborate, wrought-iron gates, he parked the car.

Outside, the morning air was cold and drizzly. An unlit path led up the hill from the carpark. Zipping up his parka, he grabbed a torch from the glove compartment and began to walk. Either side of him, the forest was silent.

Coming to a junction, the torch beam picked out a wooden arrow pointing left, which had the words 'Holy Trinity College' painted on it. The pathway continued to rise, and as the forest thinned, the wind began to lift, whistling through the trees and creating an odd, wailing noise that sounded almost human.

Though he'd visited the school many years before, he couldn't remember anything about the journey and there was nothing familiar about the grounds. That time, he was being considered for a scholarship. At his mother's insistence, Father McIlvanney, their parish priest, had nominated him. Moira had been adamant it was the perfect stepping stone to the priesthood, saying that the school had already produced two cardinals and that it would be the making of him.

The fact he'd deliberately flunked the entrance exam still filled him with guilt. It seemed odd to think of the different life the school might have offered him, the other friends he would have made, the other choices he would have had. But the idea of leaving home to come to live in the middle of nowhere with a bunch of privileged rich boys was too far out his comfort zone.

Emerging into the dawn light, the path turned and the trees opened up into mature gardens with stacked terraces of formal flowerbeds and lawns. At the brow of the hill, a solid wall of concrete soared skyward. This was a view Colin vividly remembered – the brutalist masterpiece they'd talked about that day, more than a decade ago. A single dark opening indicated where the entrance was, and above, cast into the concrete was the name of the school – Holy Trinity College – the gilded letters large and deep-set.

Like an alien craft had crashed into a Victorian park, nothing about the architecture should have worked, but somehow in its isolated location, with its tiers of floating concrete, twisting columns and dark, gleaming windows, it was thrilling and inspiring.

As he drew closer to the entrance, more of the building revealed itself, and in a corner room on the top floor, a light was turned on. Then another, followed by two more. A boy appeared at one of the windows, but as Colin looked up, he withdrew back into the room and one by one the lights turned off.

A Prayer Before Killing

'Can I help you?' A smiling face emerged at the top of the stairs leading down to a sunken garden which ran between the main building and a smaller wing. A man in his late thirties with stubble and tousled brown hair walked towards him. Handsome in a rugged way, he was noticeably fit despite the bulky fleece he wore.

'I start work here today,' Colin said.

The man tapped his wristwatch with a grubby finger. 'You're keen. I take it you're the new sports coach?'

Colin nodded. 'Colin Buxton. I've a meeting with the rector first thing.'

'Pleased to meet you.' The man wiped his palms against his jeans and offered Colin his hand. 'I'm Brendan, the caretaker round here, for my sins! Did you park down by the gates?'

'Yes. I didn't want to wake anyone.'

'There's a sneaky spot much closer.' He pointed to the far side of the main building, where a few cars were already parked. 'But here, I'll take you to the main office.'

Colin followed him round to a more modest side entrance with glass doors etched with scenes from the bible.

'You find the place okay?' Brendan asked. 'Folk often miss the turning and end up halfway to Faslane if they're not paying attention.'

'I've been here before,' Colin said, following Brendan inside where the temperature was noticeably colder.

'This isn't right,' Brendan muttered, hugging his arms to his chest. 'I can see my breath.'

A smart young woman with a perfect black bob and tortoiseshell glasses, stood behind a reception desk. 'There you are,' she snapped. 'Didn't I tell you last week this place has been freezing first thing in the morning?' Her focus momentarily rested on Colin before returning to Brendan. 'Have you even bothered to check the boiler?'

'Colin, meet Sarah, my wife and the school secretary,' he said. 'Though not necessarily in that order.'

Sarah tutted, picked up a scarf and wrapped it around her neck. The gesture caught the light, revealing a dazzling diamond ring on her finger. 'You need to do something about it and now, or it won't just be me complaining.'

Brendan turned to Colin, his expression that of a child caught with his hand in the cookie jar. 'She's not always this grumpy.' He leaned over and kissed her on the cheek. 'Are you, darling?'

Caught out by his sudden display of affection, she blushed. 'You've two minutes to get down to that boiler room.'

Brendan gave Colin a salute. 'I shall make my exit.' Heading outside, he shouted back, 'Colin's the new sports coach by the way. He's here to meet Charlie.'

'What? At this time?'

'Is there a problem?' Colin asked.

She shook her head. 'No, not at all, it's just I didn't know.' She opened a large diary, but before she could confirm or deny his appointment, a figure appeared behind her.

'Colin?' A man in his late-fifties, tall and tanned, with the air of a greying matinee idol approached.

'Yes?'

'You're timing's perfect. I'm Charlie.' He shook Colin's hand enthusiastically.

'You've not put it in the diary,' Sarah complained.

'It's fine,' Charlie said, waving her away. 'It was a last-minute invitation.' He tapped Colin's arm. 'Come with me. I'd like to chat somewhere quiet, without any distractions.'

Colin sensed Sarah bristle at this.

'Come on, I'll show you our church,' Charlie continued, ushering him through a door and along a corridor. 'It's a masterpiece, much underrated. This way.'

A heady smell of candlewax, incense and highly polished

A Prayer Before Killing

wood catapulted Colin back to his previous visit at the age of fifteen. Then, as now, the interior was impressive, with the capacity to make you feel small and insignificant. Its thick walls were punctured by tiny stained-glass windows and a scattering of gilded niches housed a myriad of religious artefacts, making the space feel cavernous. High above, the walls curved over, jutting out towards the centre to form the roof of the church. Instead of meshing together, they left a void which ran the length of the nave and through which daylight cascaded. At the far end, this illuminated the apse which housed an enormous steel crucifix and a spartan, stone altar. He recalled how the drama of this space had contrasted with the grim accommodation he'd been shown as a prospective student. Though each pupil had had a private room, these were uniform and cell-like, with only one small window, a wash-hand basin, and a single bed, chair, desk and wardrobe. Devoid of personality, not a single boy it seemed had been allowed any posters.

Charlie indicated a pew. 'Shall we sit?'

They turned to the altar and genuflected before sitting. For Colin, it was a reflex action; he'd barely stepped inside a church since cutting ties years before. For Charlie, it appeared more considered, the time spent on his knee a moment for spiritual reflection. Colin envied this purity of conviction.

'Is there a reason you wanted me here so early?' he asked as they sat.

Charlie bowed his head. A few moments passed before he looked up, leaned forward and whispered, 'I'm being sent to Aberdeen – to our sister college.' He checked nobody was around. 'They say it's a promotion but believe me it's not. The church want rid of me; I've no doubt about that.'

Colin had imagined Charlie would be his main point of contact; that's the impression Bishop Trocchi had given. 'I'm confused. The school's independent of the church?'

'In theory, but not in practice. The elite of the Scottish

clergy are former pupils almost to a man. Bishop Trocchi, the Chair of our board, was head boy.'

'But why would the church want you out of the way?'

Charlie stared at the floor. 'Let's just say I ask too many questions about all the wrong things. Then again, I'm forever tainted – don't forget Sister Oran died under my watch. And while most people have been supportive, I know behind my back some think my failure to keep my staff safe brings into question my ability to care for the boys, and by extension protect the legacy of the college.' He sighed. 'Perhaps they're right.'

Colin could see guilt – the lifeblood of the church – etched on his face. 'When are you leaving?'

'Today. I was informed on Friday evening – just before I called you. My office is being packed up as we speak.' Charlie lowered his voice. 'You need to be careful who you trust in this place.'

'Is that why you wanted to speak to me?' The shadowy machinations of the Catholic church were familiar to Colin: the sudden promotion overnight, a relocation halfway across the country, all conducted under a veil of secrecy. And almost always leaving rumours of misconduct in their wake – problems never to be solved. Add God, Jesus and the Holy Ghost into the mix, and everything the church touched became part of one huge obfuscation.

On the upper floors a piercing bell rang twice in quick succession and was followed by the sound of movement. Charlie glanced down at his watch. 'The boys will be coming down for their morning prayer before heading off to breakfast.' He stood. 'Follow me.'

Charlie crossed to the far transept and ducked through a narrow opening. Colin followed. A short passageway led into a small, circular chapel at the centre of which, in almost total darkness, stood a statue of the Virgin Mary, her face lit by a narrow beam of daylight. Colin looked up to the high,

A Prayer Before Killing

shadowed ceiling, but was unable to work out the light's source.

'She's stunning, isn't she?' Charlie lit some candles. 'Late medieval, most likely from the Low Countries.'

As Colin's eyes adjusted to the gloom, he could see that the statue stood on a plinth and was a little smaller than life size. Carved from wood, the painted blue robes had faded, and her arms were outstretched, with bone-white palms turned heavenwards. Like every other image of Our Lady he'd ever seen, her eyes were downcast and her face displayed a pensive expression.

'This is the one,' Charlie said. Sensing Colin's confusion, he added, 'Look closely.'

Colin stepped forward, and immediately spotted a gold bangle sitting round the left wrist of the Virgin Mary. 'Why's it not been removed?'

Charlie shrugged. 'At our last board meeting, the members of the clergy agreed it should remain until the culprit is discovered. A compromise between those who want to believe it could be a miracle and those who don't.'

Colin touched the bangle, a solid oval with no clasp or hinge, from which six small charms hung. At first glance, it wasn't clear how it had become attached to the statue's wrist. 'And you're sure it's not been here all this time?'

'Absolutely not. The cleaners would have noticed, or one of the boys. Or any number of people who pray here every day of the week.'

'You think it's a miracle?'

'I think it's a mystery.' Charlie sat on a stone pew and indicated for Colin to join him. 'There's a rumour circulating that Father Young plans to retract his confession and seek a retrial. This has very much put the wind up the high-heid yins, let me tell you. I never believed the poor man killed her, and there are others who think this too. But, at the highest level, the church decided long ago it was definitely him. It's the same with miracles, they'll do or say whatever suits them. Call me a cynic!' The noisy chatter of boys spilled in from the main church. Charlie rose and quickly genuflected. 'I need to go.'

'Could you leave me a contact number?' Colin asked as they emerged from the chapel, unsure how all of this added up.

'Of course. I'll tell Paddy – Father Traynor – to give it to you. He knows this place and its workings like the back of his hand and knew Father Young, and I think Sister Oran, a little.' He looked to either side again, and whispered, 'I need to be frank with you, the bangle has been a pretext for bringing you here. I knew the church wouldn't take much persuasion to agree to that. No, the real issue that needs investigated – and the reason I wanted you here – is Father Young's conviction, and whether or not it's safe. The idea of an innocent man wasting away in prison horrifies me.' Across the nave a group of teenage boys about sixteen years old sat on a pew playing a hand slapping game of chicken. 'Keep an eye on that lot,' he muttered. 'Matthew, Garr, Luc and Johnny – slippery little buggers.'

Colin glanced at the boys whose names he'd seen on the piece of paper.

As he did so, Charlie leaned closer as the boys collapsed into a fit of giggles. 'Those four were very close to Sister Oran. Too close. It wouldn't surprise me if they were involved in the reappearance of her bangle.'

Bored with the game, the two smaller boys had shifted their attention to the rector and his conversation with Colin.

'Have you spoken to them about it?' Colin asked.

'I wouldn't dare,' Charlie murmured. 'Luc's from a very influential French family and Garr's family would kick up one hell of a fuss at the merest suggestion their son was involved in anything untoward. You know, those four escaped all scrutiny during the original investigation.' He pressed his finger against his lips. 'But I can't say anymore – the school has a reputation to uphold, and it seems the boys are untouchable.' He paused for dramatic effect. 'But don't let that stop you.'

Colin looked over at them. They appeared unremarkable, an ordinary group of teenage boys.

'I need to go,' Charlie announced. 'Lots to do! If you find your way back to the main desk, Sarah will sort you out.' As suddenly as he'd first appeared, he strode down the nave and exited the church.

More pupils started to shuffle in, and the pews began to fill. Finding his bearings, Colin crossed to the side door. Passing the four boys, he felt their watchful eyes on him as he left.

CHAPTER 6
TWO YEARS EARLIER

From his drama studio, Father Young had a perfect view of the gardens below; trees thick with blossom, and spring flowers carpeting the lawns. A sweet fragrance drifted in through the open window and there was a hint of heat in the air.

Dramatically positioned on the floor below the boys' dormitories, the room thrust out from the main building and hovered, wing-like, in mid-air, as though about to take off. An architectural wonder. On closer inspection, however, Father Young noticed large cracks in the ceiling and a damp patch that was beginning to creep down the wall.

The rejection of his application to the prestigious East African missionary programme still stung. In his heart of hearts, he knew he was ready, so the Church's recommendation that he take this position grated. It felt like a sideways move or, worse, a demotion. And while he was struggling to see the value in being there, he vowed to make it work. Besides, this time next year, he would be in Kampala; he had no doubt.

At 9.15 a shrill bell rang to indicate the start of class. Father Young braced himself as a group of around a dozen

A Prayer Before Killing

fourteen-year-olds appeared, skulking in the doorway. 'No need to be shy,' he said, trying his best to sound upbeat.

They scrambled in, dragging seats across the floor to create a rough semi-circle in the centre of the room.

After a few seconds, the door was thrown open with a bang and three more students entered, grinning from ear to ear. He remembered boys like this from his own schooldays: disengaged, arrogant, bristling with an agenda. So, he was a little thrown when one walked towards him and shook his hand confidently.

'Pleased to meet you, Father,' the boy said. 'I'm Matthew.' Athletic and classically handsome, he towered above the other boys, who by comparison looked crude and unformed. There was little doubt who was in charge.

'Good to meet you, too.' Father Young picked up a chair and sat facing the class. 'If you could take your place.'

Matthew remained standing. 'Sister Oran told us you were on the telly. Is it true?' Eliciting some sniggering from his classmates, he looked Father Young up and down, as if determining whether he measured up.

'A long time ago. But yes, it's true.'

'Did you get paid loads?'

The question surprised him and in truth, he'd no idea – not once had he seen a payslip. After his agent had taken her cut, to the best of his knowledge his parents banked the rest 'for a rainy day'. With so much time having passed, it would have felt odd to ask them about it now. 'Plenty,' he lied.

One of the other boys – scrawny and wearing an oversized blazer – stepped out from behind Matthew and offered his hand, too. Father Young shook it. Unlike his friend, this boy's grip was gentle. Avoiding Father Young's eyes, he mumbled something before taking a seat at the furthest end of the semi-circle.

'That's Johnny,' Matthew said. 'Our little pet.'

The class erupted in laughter, but Johnny remained motionless.

Father Young turned to the third – tall, chubby, his face an explosion of acne – and joked, 'So you must be either Mark or Luke?'

'No, I'm Marie Antoinette,' he said, his French accent lingering on the final hard consonant as he collapsed into the nearest chair with an exasperated sigh. 'Of course I'm Luc, who else would I be?'

Deciding to play along with the joke, Father Young asked, 'So, where's Mark then?'

'He'll appear soon enough,' Matthew said, taking a seat next to Luc and folding his arms. 'Give him a few minutes.'

The rest of the boys, as if under instruction, nodded in agreement.

'So, we've a Matthew, Mark, Luc and Johnny? Any takers for Jesus?'

The class were silent.

'That's offensive,' Luc said with a scowl.

'I was joking. Just like you.'

'But we're *not* joking,' Luc whined. 'Those are our names. It's on the register. See for yourself.'

Father Young returned to his desk and scanned the list of names. Matthew, Luc and Johnny were definitely there but he couldn't find a Mark. 'Right, well I'm sorry. Let's get on with things, shall we?' Slightly flustered, he re-took his seat in front of the class. Stony-faced, the boys stared back at him. Starting to sweat, he got to his feet.

He'd been told that Speech and Drama would be unfamiliar to the students; however, they'd be excited to take part. His lesson plan had been to keep it fun and simple – lead with a few warm-up games, followed by some improvisations. But one look at their body language suggested there was no way these exercises would work. 'You might wonder why drama is an important skill,' he started, 'but just think of

A Prayer Before Killing

the many priests around the world who have to perform in front of hundreds of people every week.'

'Are you going to make us dress up?' Matthew butted in.

'I'm not wearing a dress,' one of the smaller boys said.

'You're an altar boy – you wear one every day, you fud!' Matthew snapped back. 'And Father, this one,' he said, pointing at a red-haired boy with freckles and glasses. 'He's got his granny's shawl stuffed at the back of his wardrobe. Haven't you? We all reckon he's a tranny.' Matthew stood and gave a slow handclap, chanting *tranny* over and over.

'That's not appropriate language,' Father Young said. 'Please sit down.'

Matthew ignored him.

'Much like the entire clergy,' Luc interjected. 'They're all transvestites, no? Those old men in their fancy smocks.'

'What does that make us?' Matthew laughed. 'We're all planning to be priests'

'It's not the same,' Luc protested. 'Personally, I would do it with style.' He got up and twirled. Everyone hooted with laughter.

'Anyway, is that not how your family make their gazillions?' Matthew continued. 'Supplying dresses to the Vatican?'

'Vestments. We make vestments, you ignorant twat,' Luc cried, giving Matthew a punch to the kidneys.

'Fat fucker,' Matthew growled, slapping Luc's head.

The rest of the boys, apart from Johnny, stamped their feet and banged the sides of their chairs.

'Quiet!' Father Young yelled. He hadn't been prepared for this sort of behaviour in a prestigious Catholic school. 'Matthew, I'd be grateful if you'd sit down. And Luc, less of the insults.'

Matthew made a signal with his hand and the class immediately fell silent. He nodded to the red-headed boy, saying, 'I'm sorry, Danny. No hard feelings, eh?'

Danny smiled broadly, as though touched by the hand of God.

'It's just banter, Father, nothing serious,' Johnny volunteered. 'It's the way we are. You'll get to learn soon enough.'

'Of course; it's forgotten already,' Father Young smiled, trying not to sound rattled. 'Okay, let's get down to work. Where was I?'

He picked up a piece of chalk and wrote on the board: INTRODUCTIONS. When he turned back round, a small boy with a shock of blond hair and NHS glasses, who hadn't been in the class before, was sitting between Luc and Matthew. Pretending nothing was untoward, but determined to draw attention to himself, he made a show of staring up at the ceiling then around the room, a smirk hovering on his lips.

'Excuse me,' Father Young said, 'but where did you come from?'

Immediately, the class descended into chaos as boys howled with laughter and rocked back and forth in their seats.

Above the cacophony, Father Young shouted, 'I asked, where did you come from?'

Feigning innocence, the boy replied, 'I'm Mark, Father. The fourth apostle. I've been here since the lesson started.' Raising his arms like an evangelist, he appealed to his classmates, 'Haven't I?'

Apart from Johnny, the rest of the boys chorused, 'Yes.'

Father Young knew this was a lie; if he'd just arrived, he would have seen him enter through the door. 'Were you here before the lesson started? Have you been hiding all this time?'

'Are you even a teacher?' the boy muttered in reply.

Father Young's instinct told him not to rise to the bait, to ignore the insolence, but the boy exuded an air of entitlement he didn't care for. 'Wait outside. I'll speak to you later.'

Scraping his chair across the floor, the boy stood, and with his hands held up in surrender, left the room.

A Prayer Before Killing

'That's Garr,' Johnny said. 'There's no Mark.'

'He was waylaid in the toilets,' Matthew explained. 'Ate something dodgy last night and has the worst diarrhoea. You should have smelt the bogs this morning.'

'Enough!' Father Young stared at Matthew, daring him to continue. 'We need to get on with work.'

As he was just about to start, the door flew open and Brother Thomas, whom he'd spotted patrolling the corridors earlier, stood in the doorway clutching the wrist of a terrified-looking Garr. As though a switch had been flicked, the boys sat upright and focused their attention on the front of the class.

'You!' He pointed at Father Young. 'See me when class is over.' Without another word, he turned and closed the door.

Once the sound of his footsteps receded, Father Young picked up a stick of chalk, but it slipped through his fingers and fell to the floor. Matthew rushed over, picked it up and handed it to him.

'Thank you,' he said.

With the chalk, he shakily wrote the words MUTUAL RESPECT on the board.

CHAPTER 7

MONDAY 6TH NOVEMBER 1995

Colin changed into a tracksuit in the gent's toilet, then made a call home from a pay phone in the school foyer. He didn't like leaving his mother on her own and wanted to check Jeanie had arrived as agreed, which of course she had.

'I made your mum a soft-boiled egg and chopped it up into a wee teacup,' she said. 'Wolfed down the lot, so she did.'

'That's good,' he replied. 'She didn't eat anything again last night.'

'Well, you just get on with your day, son, and don't worry about what we're up to.'

'No good, by all accounts.'

'Well, if you can't have a bit of mischief at our time of life, I don't know when you can.' She chuckled. 'Now run along and I'll hear all about your day when you get home.'

He returned to the sofa next to the reception desk. After his meeting with Charlie Murray, Sarah had asked him to wait, saying that she'd take him up to the playing fields in time for his first lesson, as it could be tricky to find. As he waited, he watched her tear around the school office: filing bits of paper, scribbling down reminders and politely answering the phone. He was amazed at her professionalism

A Prayer Before Killing

and efficiency, as pupils, staff and parents were all spoken to as if they were the most important person in the world.

Just after nine, she emerged from behind the desk wearing a long, black duffle coat buttoned up to the neck. It was strangely at odds with her otherwise chic style. 'We're heading that way.' She pointed to a gap in the trees, then handed him a football, but as they stepped from the side entrance she tutted loudly. 'Hold on a second.'

She marched out onto the main driveway where a group of elderly women, all wearing matching orange cagoules, were chatting and laughing with Brendan. As she drew close, the women saw her and quickly hurried down the hill towards the school gates. For the second time today, Brendan appeared to be getting a telling off.

Colin edged towards them.

'Why encourage them?' Sarah was asking, her tone both annoyed and disappointed.

'I didn't think,' he replied. 'But seriously, what harm can it do?'

Both turned as Colin approached. 'Sorry to interrupt,' he said, 'but I'd rather not be late for my first class.'

Sarah pulled away from Brendan, who was caressing her arm. 'Of course not. But you can blame my husband if you are.'

Brendan shook his head. 'As per usual, you're over-reacting.'

'That bangle is not some sideshow exhibit to be gawped at by a bunch of crazy Holy Joes,' she called back, before returning to Colin. 'This way.'

Without a word, she led him up a track and into the surrounding woodland. Soon, the school disappeared from view, and the trees were displaced by thick rhododendron bushes which crowded round the path. He wondered if the Polaroid he'd been given of Sister Oran had been taken close by.

As the path turned, a view of a waterlily-filled pond – like something out of a Monet painting – opened up to his left. And above that, half in shadow among a grove of Scot's pines, lay the ruins of a castle.

Feeling a need to fill the silence, he asked, 'Those women – do they think the bangle is some kind of miracle?'

'The whole thing's a pile of nonsense,' Sarah said, nudging a branch to the side of the path.

'Does everyone think that?'

'Not everyone. But I do.'

'Why's that?'

She stopped for a moment, took out a pack of cigarettes and lit one. 'Don't tell Brendan. He'd kill me.'

'Don't worry, your secret's safe.'

'Want one?'

Colin declined. 'You were saying.'

'Sister Oran's death was tragic, not something to be pored over and gossiped about and made into some kind of farce. Or is it just me who thinks that?' Sarah turned and carried on up the hill. After another few minutes' walk, she pointed towards an uneven patch of grass carved out of the hillside, with a net at either end. 'There you go.'

'Is this the only pitch?' The ground was marshy with bracken encroaching from all sides.

She nodded and glanced at her watch. 'Look, the boys will be here soon, and I need to get back. Sorry.'

'But I presume there are other facilities?' he asked.

'There's a small gym in the basement for when the weather's bad,' she said. 'But that's it, I'm afraid.' She avoided looking at him and moved towards the path. 'You'll soon realise, Mr Buxton, that despite the school's wealth, things such as accommodation, food and facilities are often poorly catered for. It's how the wealthy seem to like it – spend their well-earned cash on holiday homes and expensive clothes,

A Prayer Before Killing

then send their sons off to live in penury.' Without a goodbye, she disappeared down the track.

As Colin turned back towards the pitch, the wind picked up, agitating the golden-brown fronds of bracken. At this height, the trees were sparser, opening up views south to the silver estuary and the dark hills of Inverclyde beyond. There could be worse places in the world to have a kick about, he supposed. He tested the ground; while it was firm around the edges, the closer you got to the centre of the pitch, the more of a quagmire it became. He questioned how safe it was to expect students to play on this – they could easily twist an ankle. Had he known there was a gym, he'd have suggested they work out of there instead.

Best to start them with some aerobic exercise he decided. A few laps around the perimeter, followed by stretches, and maybe try them with some yoga positions – beginner ones he'd learned in India. And then what? A full match seemed risky. His only previous experience of football coaching was when he was fourteen, and he'd been given an under-10's parish team to look after. But with a class of teenagers, there would likely be more questions. He'd need to improvise, hope they wouldn't suss out how ill-equipped he was.

As he heard the rumble of boys approaching, his heart beat faster. How bad could it be? A little charm and a little chutzpah might be needed before he found his feet.

A dozen boys appeared through the bushes, dressed in matching sports kit in the school colours of maroon and gold. Aged about fifteen and sixteen, this was half the senior group. They appeared an incongruous bunch – the identical outfits only accentuating their differences. A strapping boy, well over six-foot, led the way, followed by an overweight boy eating a bag of crisps, then right at the back, two small, wiry boys, whispering to each other. One of the other boys even had his arm in a sling. Contact sport would not be an option today.

Gathering around him, their faces expectant, he began his

introductions. 'Hello. It's good to meet you.' He paused, hoping for a response, but none came. 'I'm Mr Buxton, your new sports coach.'

The two smaller boys caught each other's eye, but as he explained his role, how it was similar to the one Father Traynor had done a couple of years earlier, and what he planned for them today, their expressions changed from doubtful to something approaching eager.

'It's good to meet you too, sir.' The tallest boy approached and shook his hand, a little too firmly. 'I'm Matthew,' he said, stepping back to join the others.

'Nice to meet you, Matthew.'

Following that, a flurry of hands reached out and a slew of names were thrown at him. There was no way Colin was going to remember them all, though he did catch the name of the boy who'd been eating crisps, Luc, who had a thick French accent.

Without him having to say another word, Matthew instructed the boys to run around the circumference of the field; exactly as he'd wanted them to do. For fifteen minutes, the boys cajoled each other as they sprinted, pushing themselves physically.

'Come on Danny, don't stop!' they yelled at the boy with the sling. 'That's it, Johnny, forget about your asthma. You can do it!'

Red-faced and panting, they eventually came to a halt around Colin, asking his opinion on their performance and what sports he played. Their familiarity seemed too good to be true, as if he'd been teaching them for years. He needed to remember he was new – an unfamiliar face – that this openness might not last. But as they caught their breaths, bent over, coughing and spluttering, he saw himself at their age: innocent and unquestioning, unassailable in his convictions, there to uphold the morals of the Catholic Church.

Sweat dripping from his brow, Matthew stepped forward.

Out of them all, he'd pushed himself the hardest, easily outlapping everyone, but still shouting encouragement as he ran. 'You're a good sport, sir,' he exclaimed, patting Colin on the back. 'You'll fit in well.'

Then, once again, without him having to ask, Matthew instructed the other boys to drop to the ground and do fifty push-ups.

CHAPTER 8

Trying to cross Glasgow at rush hour was challenging at the best of times but add in gale-force winds and pelting rain, and Colin felt as if he'd put in a second shift.

As it happened, a large part of his day had been spent with Matthew, Garr, Luc and Johnny – or the Apostles as they were jokingly referred to by staff and boys. Whether the nickname was affectionate or not, Colin couldn't determine.

In a study class that afternoon, he'd taken the opportunity to examine their behaviour up close. Matthew appeared to be the ringleader, with Luc his right-hand man. Luc instantly backed up anything Matthew said. They bantered constantly, expressing their shared outlook through a private language of looks, gestures and in-jokes. The two small boys who had arrived last at the playing field that morning turned out to be Garr and Johnny. Polite and observant, they were as unlike the other two as you could get. Johnny was distracted and gentle, Garr focused and observant, keenly watching everything around him. He'd yet to hear either of them utter more than a couple of words, but he'd noticed that Matthew and Luc never spoke down to them like they did with the other boys.

Entering through the back door, Colin found the house in complete darkness. 'Mum?' he called. Even if she'd gone to bed early, Jeanie should still have been about. He crept upstairs to his mother's bedroom – the silence amplifying every creak of the floorboards – but it was empty.

He rushed downstairs, his mind going into overdrive. There was nothing in the kitchen or the living room to indicate where they were, however within seconds he noticed a scrawled note propped against the phone on the hall table:

Gone to A&E at the Victoria with your mum. Nothing to worry about, just being careful. Back soon, Jeanie xx P.S. There's a mince round and some mash in the fridge.

Ten minutes later, Colin screeched to a halt in the hospital carpark. Dodging evening traffic, he crossed the road and looked for signs to A&E. The hospital site was confusing, a hodgepodge of disparate structures, dating back over a hundred years with no apparent logic in how they connected. Taking the first door, a labyrinth of long corridors, dusty stairwells and confusing signs delivered him back to where he'd started. On his second attempt, he still failed to find A&E, however he did manage to locate a reception desk, where he was told his mother was in Ward 16.

In a waiting room next to the ward, he found his mother sitting in a wheelchair with her back to the door, her hands noticeably shaking. Father Traynor was on his knees talking to her.

Jeanie noticed Colin first. 'You're here, son,' she said. 'We weren't expecting you.'

His mother turned away from Father Traynor and sneered, 'About bloody time!' Although her tone sounded scathing, there was a tremor behind it.

'She's not herself, darling,' Jeanie interjected, her hand – the skin paper-thin, almost translucent – pressing his mother's shoulder. 'Took a tumble, didn't you? But there's nothing to worry about.'

'What happened?' Colin asked.

Ignoring his question, Moira gave Jeanie a scornful look and blurted out, 'Easy for you to say, Jeanette Walsh. When are you ever ill? You're like a damned cockroach.'

With a grimace, Father Traynor stood.

Unfazed, Jeanie nodded. 'It's true, I've been blessed.'

Father Traynor shook Colin's hand. 'Nice to see you. Everything's absolutely fine. The doctor would prefer if she stayed in overnight for observation as her blood pressure's a little high, but she says she's good to go. And who are we to argue otherwise?'

Dynamic and driven, Father Traynor had more the air of a city broker who'd found God as an adult than someone with an early calling to the priesthood. Revered by his mother, Colin knew all the important details about him: born in Dundee, the youngest of seven siblings, he'd an Irish father who was an engineer, and a Scots mother who was a librarian. Also, he'd turned down an invitation to study further in Rome, preferring to stay and serve in Scotland.

Colin remembered him from years before. As a trainee priest, he'd come to his school to talk to boys interested in joining the priesthood. He'd cut a dashing figure with his dog-collar, dark, slicked black hair and high cheekbones. He'd spoken with passion too and had made a huge impression on everyone. But this had been before Colin became disillusioned with the church, when he'd still had his own calling.

'Right, let's get out of this dump.' Moira's hands grabbed her wheels, but were too weak to grip them firmly.

'Not so fast.' Father Traynor put the brake on her wheelchair. 'The doctor's still to bring over your painkillers. Remember?' He turned to Colin. 'She's had a shock.'

'It's that blasted carpet in the hallway. I told Annemarie to

A Prayer Before Killing

fix it. But did she? No, she did not! By God, she'll be red-faced with shame when she hears.'

Colin glanced at Jeanie, questioning whether this was the whole truth.

'It wasn't the hall carpet, she was rushing to answer the door to the catalogue woman. You're not as firm on your feet as you were, Moira,' Jeanie said, her words falling on deaf ears.

'It's not fair to blame Annemarie, Mum. You need to take more care, not go hell for leather like you're used to.'

'I don't know what you're all talking about,' Moira huffed.

Father Traynor caught his eye, suggesting he'd like a word. 'Why don't Colin and I get some tea for everyone while we're waiting? Would you like that?'

'But I'm still going home, Father?' Moira asked, her expression pitiful.

'Of course,' he replied. 'And don't you fret, we'll be back in no time.' He gave her hand a squeeze and in return received the broadest, most unconditional smile Colin had ever witnessed.

'SHE'S IN DENIAL.' Father Traynor tried unsuccessfully to figure out the vending-machine. 'That's why she's lashing out.'

'Here, press this.' Colin reached over and pushed a button, feeding coins into the slot. The machine sprang into life, delivering a scalding, murky brown liquid into a thin plastic cup.

Father Traynor picked the cup up and began to drink, wincing as he took a steaming sip.

'You do realise this is her on her best behaviour?' Colin snorted. 'All because you're here. She's normally worse – a hell of a lot worse. Did you come in with them?'

Father Traynor shook his head. 'I was here already,

visiting an elderly parishioner who had surgery this morning. I bumped into them in the lift. Moira was very teary.'

'Teary?' Colin fed the machine more money and a second cup began to fill. 'Now, that genuinely doesn't sound like my mother.'

'Jeanie's a godsend. What she's doing for your mum, she does for so many others.' He took another slurp of his tea and stared at it. 'This is foul.'

'If it wasn't for Jeanie, I'm not sure I could cope.' Colin sipped his own tea, scrunched up his face, and then dumped it in a nearby bin. 'Thanks for the reference by the way – I started at the school today.'

'Jeanie mentioned.' Father Traynor drained his cup and discarded it in the same bin. 'You know I boarded at the school till I was eighteen?'

Colin hadn't; even his mother had omitted this detail.

'Charlie Murray was my maths teacher,' Father Traynor continued, his eyes misting over. 'What an exceptional man. The best.'

Colin had forgotten most of his teachers – the only ones he seemed to remember were the strict ones, like Mr Ellis, the art teacher with the sudden mood swings and Mr McDonagh who taught woodwork and had reputedly broken a boy's wrist giving him the belt. 'Pity he's moved on. I'd have liked to have got to know him.'

Father Traynor looked shocked. 'What! Charlie's not said a thing.'

'The removal men were packing up his office when I arrived.'

'Did he say where he was going, who's replacing him?'

'One of the pupils suggested Brother Thomas, but I don't know if that's true.'

'Come with me.' Father Traynor led Colin down a side corridor with a soft tug. He steered him into a sunroom on

A Prayer Before Killing

the corner of the building with a vertiginous view of the street below. Out in the corridor, a nurse was preparing some meds, ticking each pill off on a clipboard. Father Traynor closed the door.

'Is something wrong?' Colin asked.

'Did he speak to you about his suspicions?'

'I guess. Kind of. It was all a bit rushed.'

Father Traynor waited as the nurse manoeuvred her trolley along the corridor and disappeared through a set of double doors. Stepping closer to Colin, he lowered his voice. 'Originally, he was going to call the police about the bangle,' he whispered. 'Suggest its appearance needed further investigation.'

'Why?'

'In the court case, it was heavily implied that Father Young had disposed of it. Charlie thought its reappearance provided an opportunity to look at the whole case again, hopefully find new evidence to exonerate Father Young.'

'But he didn't?'

'The board put their foot down, said they were concerned about negative publicity. That's when he had the idea of bringing someone more specialist in and I suggested you.'

'Why me?'

'Moira's mentioned some of the work you've done previously. And Charlie and I felt it was a more discrete way of dealing with the situation. Keep everything in the family, so to speak.' Father Traynor adjusted his collar. 'Father Young's a friend. Or rather a former colleague who I now consider a friend. I visit him in prison once a month. The more I listen to that man's story, the more I believe he's innocent. I'm keen for him to withdraw his confession. Did Charlie tell you that?'

'Not exactly,' Colin replied, 'but I got the gist. I hadn't realised you were so close to Father Young.'

Father Traynor looked over Colin's shoulder. The nurse

had returned, but only to grab a small bottle of pills. Again, he waited until she'd gone. 'Charlie had to fight tooth and nail to persuade the board – well the members of the archdiocese – to give you the job. Staked his professional reputation on it.'

'If they weren't happy with the situation, why not just cancel my contract? Why get rid of him the first day I started?'

Father Traynor shrugged. 'It makes no sense. But Bishop Trocchi always has the final word. Or at least whoever's bankrolling the school does.'

'And you're sure Charlie didn't drop any hints he was leaving?' Colin asked.

Father Traynor shook his head.

Colin caught sight of Jeanie pushing his mother's wheelchair towards them. 'At my interview, the bishop gave me a couple of files about Sister Oran's case, one of which Charlie had pulled together from court transcripts,' he said. 'I was banking on him still being around to quiz him about it. He said you'd have a number for him.'

'It depends what number – where have they sent him?'

'To the sister school in Aberdeen.'

'You're kidding? They sent him there?'

Jeanie popped her head round the door. 'What are you boys like? We didn't know where you'd got to.' She held up a blister pack. 'The doctor came with the painkillers for Moira but she needs her tea to take them.'

'Sorry,' Colin said, 'we got distracted. The machine's just down the corridor.'

'We passed it,' Jeanie replied. 'You wouldn't have any change?'

He handed her a pile of coins and watched her turn the wheelchair round, his mother fidgeting in the seat as she strained her neck, complaining to Jeanie about something new.

A Prayer Before Killing

'I could visit him once he's settled,' Colin said. 'It would be good to fill in the blanks.'

'That might prove difficult,' Father Traynor said. 'The sister school might well be in Aberdeen, but it's in Aberdeen, Maryland. They've sent him to the States.'

PART 2

CHAPTER 9

In the days following Charlie Murray's sudden departure, the boys quizzed Colin repeatedly about what he knew, which was basically nothing. Their questions suggested gossip was running rife within the school community. Pupils asked if Dr Murray had had a breakdown, whether it was true a special task force was being sent from Rome to sort everything out, and even if the school was about to close. Speculation ended at the weekly assembly, with the announcement of Brother Thomas's appointment; the spontaneous cheer which erupted afterwards indicated this was a popular choice with students.

So far, Colin had only seen Brother Thomas from a distance. He cut a severe, almost medieval, figure; tall and with a strident walk, he wore a brown hooded robe, tied at the waist with a simple cord. The couple of times they'd passed each other in the corridor, Brother Thomas hadn't acknowledged him. On Friday morning however, Colin was told by Sarah that he'd been summoned for a meeting. 'An informal chat,' she'd said.

Accessed from the atrium, his office was situated in the

warren of rooms behind the chapel, via a stair which followed the curve of the apse. At the assembly, it had also been confirmed that, in addition to rector, he would continue in his role as Head of Religious Studies and remain in his current office. According to Brendan this had traditionally been the rector's office but when Charlie Murray took on the role, it had somehow become Brother Thomas's. Well-heated and with commanding views over the gardens, Brendan said it was the grandest room on the whole estate.

Colin knocked on the wooden door.

Two seconds after he knocked, a deep voice bellowed, 'Wait!'

Colin exhaled and drew his fingertip across the rough concrete wall which retained the ghostly imprint of the timber shuttering used to cast it. Hidden within the forest and contained within its concrete shell, time at the school seemed to move slower than in the outside world. Though he had only been working there for a few days, it felt like weeks.

'Come!' Brother Thomas finally declared.

On entering, Colin realised Brendan had been downplaying just how impressive the decor was. It exuded luxury. Religious icons, paintings and sumptuous tapestries filled the walls, and narrow, stained-glass windows cast long shafts of sapphire and emerald light across the polished concrete floor. On one side a huge plate glass window framed a spectacular view of the gardens, looking down the hill and beyond to the Clyde.

The monk stood to greet him. In his late-forties and rake thin, Colin had heard from the boys that he regularly ran marathons to raise money for charity.

'Please. Sit.'

Colin took a seat facing Brother Thomas, who remained standing on the opposite side of his long marble desk.

'You're settling in?' he asked Colin, placing one hand on

A Prayer Before Killing

an enormous, ornately bound bible which occupied a corner of the desk.

'Yes. The boys are making it easy.'

'I'm glad to hear that. They've been through a lot – it's our mission as a school to support them and heal where necessary.'

'Of course.'

'It's come to my attention that you're a lapsed Catholic,' he said, locking his eyes on Colin.

'It has? Well, yes, I suppose technically that's true. But I still consider myself a spiritual person. I've recently returned from India, where I studied a range of religions: Hinduism, Jainism and Buddhism, as well as Christianity. But no, I no longer attend church or pray.'

Brother Thomas's face remained expressionless. 'You must appreciate the boys here require the correct spiritual guidance to keep them on their chosen path.'

'I do, but I'm mostly organising team sports and other physical activities,' Colin reminded him. 'Religious study barely comes into it.'

His final comment was met with a dismissive pout. 'It all counts, Mr Buxton.'

'Right. Sorry. Yes, I understand.'

The silence between them was marked by the slow ticking of a clock.

'We don't often get your kind here,' Brother Thomas said, opening a drawer.

'My kind?' Colin cast his eyes around the room at the pictures of half-naked saints, their flesh aglow with masculine vigour.

Brother Thomas placed a newspaper clipping on the desk. Colin instantly recognised the headline – *Bent Copper* – from the Lawrence Delaney case. 'Recently, we did have one, a geography teacher, a Mr Smith. He was spotted during the summer on a march in Edinburgh. Waving a rainbow flag, I believe. He left our employ shortly after.'

While the disapproval of his sexuality was not unexpected, Brother Thomas's bluntness was. 'Is there anything else?' Colin rose. 'The boys will be waiting.'

'Please. Sit. I've not finished.'

Colin considered leaving but did as instructed.

Brother Thomas held up the end of the knotted rope he wore around his waist. 'I'm a Franciscan monk. The three knots on my belt represent the three cornerstones of the Franciscan Order. Do you know what those are?'

'I don't.'

'Poverty, chastity and obedience. In my role as a shepherd of young minds, it's obedience I promote above all else.' He gripped the edge of the desk. 'The point I'm making is we all have to work together, within an agreed framework, for the good of the boys,' Brother Thomas continued. 'That framework is the Catholic Church and its teachings. Am I making myself clear?'

'Completely.'

'Our boys are the top academic achievers from their peer group – that's why they're here – but the flipside of that is they can be a sensitive bunch.' He let go his grip of the table. 'Nonetheless, they've taken to you quickly, which is unusual.'

'I appreciate that. I've been surprised by it myself.'

Nodding, Brother Thomas drained his glass of water. 'I gather you spoke with Dr Murray before he left?'

Was this the real purpose of the meeting? 'Yes, briefly. He explained he'd been promoted.'

Brother Thomas snorted. 'Forgive me for asking, but did he say anything to you which sounded … well, out of the ordinary?'

'Such as?'

'Anything regarding the messy business with Father Young? Or rather, Mr Young.'

A Prayer Before Killing

Had others been eavesdropping on his chat after all? 'Only the bare bones – to put the appearance of the bangle into context.'

An unexpected knock was followed by the door edging open and the appearance of Sarah, who remained in the doorway. 'Apologies for interrupting.' Her gaze fell on Colin and she smiled warmly. 'It's just that I've made a mistake, Brother Thomas. Your meeting with Bishop Trocchi is on Monday, not today.'

'Are you sure? You reminded me ten minutes ago that it was today.'

'It's my fault. I got the days wrong.'

Brother Thomas scribbled a few words on his notepad and without looking up, or dismissing her, Sarah sheepishly withdrew from the room and closed the door behind her.

'Twice I asked her. The girl's a complete waste of space – her head's too full of that husband of hers,' he spat. 'Now, where were we?'

'Dr Murray wished me luck, said he hoped I'd be as happy here as he'd been.'

'And that's all?'

'As far as I can remember.'

Brother Thomas grinned and for the first time a hint of warmth coloured his expression. 'As soon as you've solved this bangle nonsense,' he said, 'I don't imagine there'll be much need for you here. I hope you understand. Budgets are tight, and too much flab leads to sluggishness. And we can't have that, can we?'

Had his meeting with the bishop not taken place, Colin was convinced he would have been sacked there and then, but even someone as pompous as Brother Thomas had a paymaster. He stood. 'I really should get back to my class.'

Brother Thomas walked him to the door. 'What's planned for today?' he asked, sounding genuinely interested.

'The seniors want basketball in the gym hall, but, since the weather's brighter, they're getting a cross-country run.'

'Good. Healthy body, healthy mind.' He opened the door. 'If you need anything, however small, please Mr Buxton, let me know.'

Colin left, wondering if passive-aggressive behaviour had just found itself a new poster boy.

CHAPTER 10
TWO YEARS EARLIER

Father Young crouched and trailed his hand through the pond's dark water, obliterating his reflection. A brood of ducks hesitated before paddling closer, honking softly as if expecting some scraps of food. They were going to be disappointed. Scurrying through the undergrowth, a red squirrel paused and sat back on its haunches, fixing him with an eye as black as jet. He snapped his fingers. Startled, it leapt and scrambled up the nearest tree trunk with barely a sound.

Pulling a used handkerchief from a pocket, he blew his nose – his hay fever had started early this year, and it was all the fault of this damned garden, bursting with too much life. At least he could blame his bloodshot eyes on the pollen, rather than the tears of frustration he'd shed earlier.

He checked his watch – it was almost time to head back to the classroom. Though Dr Murray had reassured him he needed to be patient, that it would take time to gain the boys' trust, he still doubted he'd ever achieve it. And this afternoon would be yet another trial: a two-hour lesson on how to write and deliver sermons. Another of Brother Thomas's bright ideas about what ought to be taught in a drama class, and an exercise Father Young knew the boys would loathe.

Brother Thomas had cornered him in the staffroom first thing that morning. He could easily have asked him to step outside and spoken to him discretely, but Father Young had come to understand that the monk enjoyed making examples of people.

The clink of teaspoons against cups stopped, and one of the older members of staff – aged eighty at least, with no discernible role – moved a few steps closer, his attempt at eavesdropping comical in its blatancy.

'Can you sit down, Father Kilpatrick? I'm having a private conversation.' Brother Thomas's mouth twisted and turned, mangling the words, before his attention returned to Father Young. 'The boys are bored,' he stated loudly. 'You'll need to find other ways to motivate them.'

Father Young felt a frisson of excitement run through the room as his colleagues sensed blood. 'But they won't listen,' he'd muttered. 'I've tried lots of different things to try and inspire them, capture their imaginations – games, different plays, role-play – but they've made it clear they'd rather be outdoors doing sports.'

'You need to step up or step out,' Brother Thomas had retorted. 'It's simple enough. Your job is to educate young men considering the priesthood and its many demands, prepare them for their lives outside this ivory tower. If you're not up to the task, perhaps another conversation with the rector could be arranged. And if that still has no effect, then a letter to Bishop Trocchi might be required.'

The room fell silent.

'I've only been here a few weeks—' Father Young began, but Brother Thomas cut him off.

'You're far too sensitive, far too self-absorbed. It won't do,' he barked. 'I'll provide your lesson plans for today, and you'll follow them to the letter. Is that understood?' Not bothering to wait for a reply, the monk left the room, slamming the door shut with such force that a mug, perched on the side of a table, fell to the floor, and broke in two.

Father Young leant down to pick up the pieces and when he stood, no one would look him in the eye.

STARTING down the trail which led to the main building, Father Young once more went over the series of events which had brought him to this godforsaken place. How he'd messed up the interview to join the mission and how he'd been persuaded to consider teaching by his mentor, Father Mahon. Then he'd had a conversation with his dad who had strongly suggested teaching wouldn't suit his personality. He cringed now at his reply, his insistence that he was thrilled at the prospect of shaping young minds. What an idiot. And if he was capable of making such a mess of his own life, what hope was there for him to help others? Maybe it wasn't just teaching which was the wrong fit; maybe he wasn't cut out for the priesthood either.

But such negative thoughts only made things worse.

The jagged silhouette of the school emerged through the trees, and he felt an ache deep in the pit of his stomach. Could he feign sickness and avoid teaching that afternoon? As he was working out what could sound vaguely plausible, Sister Oran came bounding up the track towards him, waving at him with a drawing pad in her hand, her muddy habit sticking to her bare calves.

'Hey! Father Young!' she shouted, immediately shoving the drawing pad into her pocket before he could to see what was on it. 'So, this is where you're hiding. I've spent an age trying to find you.'

Sister Oran was prone to exaggeration – at most, he'd been away half an hour. 'I've not got my times wrong, have I?' he asked.

'Like last week?' she laughed. 'Where were you again? Away skiving in the big city?'

He didn't need to be reminded. A timetable change meant his usual day off had been swapped, but he'd forgotten. He'd only realised his mistake when he arrived back from Glasgow to be met by Brother Thomas. Another dressing-down had ensued – 'unprofessional' was the word he'd used. It still rankled.

Father Young prayed Sister Oran wasn't still talking about it with the rest of the staff. It wasn't that she was a gossip as such, it was more that she was completely unfiltered.

She laughed again. 'It's okay for some, wandering off when they feel like it.' She looked at him and paused. 'Are the boys still not settling?'

Suddenly self-conscious, he rubbed his eyes. Could she tell he'd been crying?

'They'll come round soon enough – you'll see.' Her tone had changed to one of genuine concern. Her trick of leaping from one emotion to the next was impressive, but also unsettling. As a consequence, he was never sure where he was with her. 'They were the same with me when I started.'

Did everyone now know how incompetent he was? That he couldn't cope? That the boys were running rings round him? 'I just needed a moment's peace before the next period. Time to gather my thoughts.'

'Tell me about it. I've been up since five and I've hardly had time to piddle.'

This was another trait he'd noticed in her: an immaturity in her language, a determination to push at the boundaries, to see what she could get away with. He made sure his expression didn't change; encouraging her in any way would be foolish.

Down at the school, the squeals of boys enjoying their lunch break could be heard. At this distance, it was easy to imagine them as innocent teenagers running around freely;

A Prayer Before Killing

however, up close was a different matter altogether: undermining him, cajoling each other to unsettle the mood of the classroom, trying their hardest to break his composure. 'I'm not sure teaching's for me.' He'd blurted the words out before considering whether confiding in Sister Oran was a good idea or not.

'Don't be an eejit. They just don't know you yet.'

'But what if they keep acting up?'

'You're overthinking it. Lure them in with some sweet stuff – a bit of fun – then as soon as you've reined them in, hit them with the hard stuff. They're frigging kids – they want to learn. Sometimes, they just don't know how.'

Maybe she was right. From day one, he'd been too serious, imagining this might gain their respect. But as the weeks passed, he'd begun to worry it was the wrong tactic and wasn't sure how to backtrack without making himself look even weaker.

'Want me to show you a secret?' Excited, she pulled at the cuff of his shirt. 'Do you?'

He desperately wanted to get back to class and go over Brother Thomas's lesson plans, but the expectant look on her face convinced him otherwise. 'Will it take long?'

She shook her head. 'Five minutes. Ten, tops.'

'You sure?'

'I swear! C'mon,' she said, heading up the slope towards the castle ruins. 'No dawdling!'

A path led to a stone bridge which crossed a narrow ravine through which a stream flowed in a series of cascades and pools. The noise of the water drowned out any residual sound from the school, making the castle feel like its own island. Ahead, above the main entrance, someone had spray-painted a giant purple penis onto the thick sandstone lintel.

'Don't look at me like that,' Sister Oran giggled. 'It wasn't me. It's been there since I arrived. Considering most of these boys are planning to become priests, they sure are sex mad.' She guided him through to the interior.

'So, what's this secret?' he asked, following her through a maze of ruined spaces open to the elements.

'You'll see,' she said, pointing further ahead.

While the outer edges were almost completely ruined, as they moved towards the centre, the spaces became smaller and darker but more complete, with thick walls rising ever higher. Protrusions from the stonework suggested that the original keep had been at least three storeys high.

'It was built in 1508,' Sister Oran explained. 'Or was it 1308? I can't actually remember – anyway, that's not the point. It was built by Lord Such-and-such to keep his lady friend hidden from his wife. But wouldn't you know it, once he had her installed, he never came to visit her. Can you believe that? What an arse! Mind, she was her own worst enemy. Twenty-one years she waited, insisting each morning that'd be the day he'd finally come, getting all dolled up for nothing. Poor woman.'

Grateful for the distraction, Father Young listened, amused by Sister Oran's storytelling. 'I take it he never did?'

'Isn't that the tragedy!' They entered an enclosed space without any windows. 'Here, hold this.' Out of thin air, Sister Oran had produced a candle which she proceeded to light. A small, square room with water oozing from mould-covered walls was revealed, giving it a slippery, underwater feel. 'So, on the first day of the twenty-second year, she was persuaded to go visit her auld mammy who she hadn't seen for such a long time. And wouldn't you know it – wasn't that the day Lord La-di-da finally decided to come for some rumpy-pumpy, riding up on one of those big fat horses they used to have.'

'A bit of a coincidence?'

In the candlelight, her face glowed conspiratorially. 'Or planned? By someone close to her, who was loyal to his wife.'

A Prayer Before Killing

'So, she didn't make it back in time?'

'As soon as Milady appeared back, she was told that the Lord had been and gone. Sick to her stomach, she swore revenge on the maid who'd advised her to leave. A week later, she crept into her room while she slept and pushed a poisonous toad down her throat, holding her mouth shut till she was dead.' She threw her head to one side and let her tongue loll. This was followed by an almost uncanny impersonation of a toad croaking, which had her doubled-up laughing.

'I need to go,' Father Young said.

She pulled him back. 'Now don't say a word about this to anyone. Not to the staff. Not to the boys. Promise?'

'What do you mean? If it's part of the history of the castle, doesn't everyone know it?'

She shook her head. 'Only I know it.'

'Why only you?'

'I told you, it's a secret. A secret I'm sharing with you and you alone.'

'In other words, you've just made up a big, fat fib?'

She let go of him with a flash of her eyes. 'I thought priests were supposed to believe in fantastic stories. Isn't the bible full of them?'

'Those are allegories, made up by storytellers long after Jesus lived.'

As he said this a draught blew out the candle and plunged them into darkness. 'Heathen,' she said, her teeth glinting as she relit the candle. 'Come on. There's one last thing I need to show you.'

'Are you deliberately trying to make me late?'

'Two seconds and then you can go.'

He reluctantly followed her through a narrow doorway and into an even tinier stone room. She pointed to the floor. 'Look closely.'

One of the stone slabs was darker than the others and

appeared to undulate. He wasn't sure if it was an optical illusion. 'What am I looking at?'

As she held the candle closer, he realised the dark surface was water.

'Come and see – it's teeming with tadpoles.'

He joined her and could just about make out the tiny creatures darting about in the gloomy water.

She smiled and whispered in his ear, 'Even in the darkest place there's life. They say the maid's bricked up behind one of these walls. And though this place has got that awful feeling of death about it, God still manages to offer hope. Isn't that grand?'

He'd no idea what bigger point she was trying to make but found himself nodding. Before he could properly question her story, however, someone outside yelled his name.

'That's Garr,' she said instantly. 'Follow me.' She led him back through the warren of rooms and out into the open air.

Garr was framed at the castle entrance and lowered his head when he saw them appear. Father Young immediately stood apart from Sister Oran. 'Brother Thomas is asking where you are,' he said.

'Damn!' he cried, racing ahead. 'I told you you'd make me late.'

'I didn't mean to.'

'Didn't you?' he cried back.

'Don't worry,' she hollered. 'Just tell him you were exploring the castle with me.'

He sprinted down the hill towards the school, kicking himself for being distracted by her ridiculous stories. He wouldn't make the same mistake again.

CHAPTER 11
TUESDAY 14TH NOVEMBER 1995

'Does Mum know you're planning to visit Glasgow?' Colin asked.

'No, and don't you dare tell her,' Annemarie warned, as only a big sister could. 'It'll be good for the two of us to catch up.'

'Is everything okay?' Late night calls from Annemarie weren't that unusual, but a 300-mile round-trip from Newcastle to Glasgow for coffee was. 'You sound stressed.'

'How was she today?'

'She had some pain in the afternoon, according to Jeanie, but not as bad as it's been. She took a sleeping tablet before bed, and I've not heard a peep from her since.'

Annemarie paused, which troubled Colin. If there was one thing he knew about his sister, she looked for problems. 'And you and Mum are getting on?'

'Some friction, but no major fallouts. Not yet anyway. Why'd you ask?'

'Hold on a minute.'

In the background he heard his nephew, Liam, asking a question, followed by Annemarie replying with an emphatic 'No.'

'Look, Colin, we'll have a proper chat tomorrow. But you're absolutely sure you can manage?'

'I told you. I get Wednesdays off.'

'Good.'

Liam interrupted again, asking Annemarie for money to go out with friends to a party.

Annemarie swore under her breath. 'Sorry Colin, I need to go. Queens Café at eleven okay?'

'Perfect.'

A SOUTHSIDE INSTITUTION situated on Victoria Road, the café was where Colin, Annemarie and their brother, Sean, were taken by their dad as a Saturday treat after swimming at Govanhill Baths. Following their dad's hospitalisation, Annemarie had done her best to maintain the family tradition for Colin. Regardless of the weather, his order had always been the same: a fried tattie scone on a buttered roll with heaps of brown sauce, and a ninety-nine cone. Heaven!

Parking 0n Dixon Avenue, he walked round to Victoria Road. It was just as he remembered it: flanked by shops with tenement flats above, its wide pavements were busy with pedestrians, and the street packed with double-decker buses. Ahead, the wrought-iron gates of Queen's Park framed an avenue of majestic trees, the grandeur of the surroundings belying the relative poverty of the nearby streets. The familiar sign of the Queens Café was unchanged too; its scarlet art-deco lettering and stained-glass sunbursts gloriously colourful on a grey autumn morning.

In the far corner, by the gas heater, Annemarie was seated at their favourite table. A half-drunk cup of coffee sat cooling as she stared into space.

'Hey,' he said, slipping into a chair.

She jumped, surprised to find him in front of her. 'Christ, Colin, you scared me to death.' She removed her clutch bag

A Prayer Before Killing

from the Formica tabletop and placed it on her lap. 'You're early.'

'Not really, you said eleven. It's five to. What time did you get here?'

'I dunno – the back of ten or something.'

'Ten? When did you leave Newcastle?'

She shrugged. 'I was awake early.'

He picked up a laminated menu and quickly scanned through it. 'You eating?'

'I might have another coffee.' She glanced around, trying to catch the waitress's attention. 'Excuse me.' The girl didn't hear and continued wiping down a table by the door. 'Excuse me!' she repeated loudly.

'Annemarie!' Colin scolded.

'What?' she sneered, a reminder *she* was in charge, not him.

The waitress tottered over; her thin notepad already open as she scrabbled to find a pencil.

'I'll have another milky coffee,' Annemarie said. 'Colin, are you having a roll and tattie scone?' They both smiled; the childhood reference all too familiar. 'A cone too?' She was now entering the territory of babying him, as she often liked to do.

'I can't say I'm not tempted.' Colin scanned the menu. 'I'll take two scoops of ice cream in a bowl please. Chocolate and pistachio.'

'Good to know some of us aren't watching the pounds.'

Colin handed back the menu, adding he'd take a milky coffee, too. 'It's a treat, isn't it?'

Annemarie drummed her nails on the table and checked her watch. 'We'll need to make this quick,' she said. 'I've a meeting in Edinburgh and I need to be home in time to take Liam to his footie training.'

He could see how wound up she was – like his mum, Annemarie's emotions could seesaw wildly and she wasn't one to suffer fools gladly. As an accountant, he wondered how she coped with clients; did she explode when they submitted the wrong receipt, or have a melt-down when someone missed a deadline?

'I take it you want to talk about Mum?' he asked.

The mere mention of their mother caused Annemarie's bottom lip to tremble and he thought she might burst into tears. But before he could say anything, she shrugged her shoulders, breathed deeply and focused her gaze on him. 'On reflection, it's all too ad hoc – the current arrangement – so I think we need a proper plan.'

'Like what?'

'She's far too ill to stay in that house on her own.'

'I'm there.' That's why he'd been asked back. What was Annemarie suggesting? That he was incapable of looking after her? 'She's being well looked after.'

'But you're at work all day.'

'I've Wednesdays off. And Jeanie's there the rest of the week during the day, give or take the odd couple of hours.'

'She's a godsend, but isn't she about eighty or something?'

'Not quite, but she's good with Mum. That's all that matters.'

'She looks like she's about to keel over herself.'

'What? Jeanie's fit as a fiddle – have you seen her whip round the house with a duster?'

The coffees arrived, filled to the brim, spilling into their saucers as the waitress did her best to place them delicately on the table.

'Can you bring a napkin?' Annemarie glowered. 'Jeanie will only cope with her for so long – Mum's bound to snap and drive her away. And there's no way you can handle her on your own,' she quipped. 'You never could. She walks all over you.'

'Thanks for the vote of confidence! You know she wants to

A Prayer Before Killing

stay in her own home for as long as possible. I don't think that's a bad idea.' He took a sip of his coffee. Bitter, too hot, it scalded his lips. 'What are you proposing as an alternative?' As the eldest in the family, and ten years older than him, Annemarie always expected her ideas to be implemented. It was a position that had caused problems before, and Colin wondered if she fully appreciated this. What might have worked when they were younger didn't necessarily still apply.

'I think she needs professional, twenty-four-hour care.' She delved into her bag and brought out a glossy brochure. *Family Care* was written on the front in a cheery lilac font. 'And don't worry, I've the money to pay for it.'

'You mean a nursing home?'

'Take a look.' She pushed it towards him.

He leafed through the pages, observing the rictus smiles of patients in hospital beds with adoring families by their sides. 'There's no way she's going to agree to this.'

'Then something similar,' she said, grabbing it back and slipping it into her bag. 'That's just one option.'

Smiling wanly, the waitress returned with Colin's ice cream and extra napkins.

'Thanks,' Colin said.

Annemarie snatched a napkin. 'What a mess,' she muttered as she mopped up the coffee spills.

'Oh my god, you should taste the pistachio.' He offered her the spoon, but Annemarie shook her head. 'Is this what the argument was about? You suggesting she go into a home?' She stirred her coffee over and over, avoiding any eye contact. 'You didn't show it to Mum, did you?'

The spoon was discarded onto the saucer. 'She wouldn't even look at it. Told me to leave, threw me out.'

'What did you expect? It's a red rag to a bull.'

Annemarie raised an eyebrow. 'I don't know. Some level of appreciation? Her exact words were – "Get out my house, you useless waste of space!" That's what she said, in front of Liam too.'

'That's awful,' Colin conceded, 'but you know it's all bluster.'

'Bluster or not, the woman's a monster!' She slammed her cup down. 'Months I was looking after her before you came back, endlessly driving up and down that bloody motorway, taking her to appointments, still working full time, bringing up a teenage son with practically no help from anybody.'

'I hear you, and I know she's difficult, but we need to cut her some slack.' Time and distance had softened his opinion of their mother. There was no doubt she was irrational and opinionated, seldom satisfied and never thankful, but Colin sensed a pain behind it, a frustration borne of her childhood in Derry. His grandmother and great grandmother stared out of family photos with the same angry look of dissatisfaction as Moira. He'd concluded his mother never wanted children, but with few options, she'd found herself with three. That, Colin surmised, must have been brutal.

'I'll have some now,' Annemarie said, nodding at the ice cream.

Colin handed her the spoon and they sat in silence, taking it in turns to eat until the bowl was cleaned.

'I prefer the chocolate,' Annemarie said.

'Look,' Colin started. 'I'm here for the foreseeable future. Why don't we continue as we are? If her condition worsens, we can re-evaluate.'

'If? She's dying!' Annemarie's raised voice carried across the café and Colin felt a hush fall as the attention of the other customers turned to them. 'Of course it's going to get fucking worse,' she whispered. Tears formed at the corners of her eyes, but she quickly pulled a tissue from her handbag and dried them. 'Have you heard the cough? Witnessed the hands shaking? Seen how much she's wasted away?'

'You don't think I can cope, do you?' To his sister, he was

A Prayer Before Killing

still a child, not someone who'd made important choices in life or held opinions of his own. To her, he was just wee Colin, who used to follow her around like she was his mother.

Annemarie zipped up her bag and straightened her jacket.

'You're not off already? We could have met earlier.'

She looked for the waitress. 'I'll get the bill.'

'Don't worry, I'll pay.'

'But you don't have much—'

'I do have money of my own, Annemarie. I *am* an adult.'

She stood and slipped out from the narrow table. 'You don't realise what you've taken on, that's all I'm saying.'

'I agree, Mum's no pussycat, but I can handle her,' he said. 'I didn't exactly want to come back, but now I'm here, well, you know, it's nice to be needed.'

She shook her head. 'It's not just Mum being ill. What you went through in Berlin, rushing back from India, this job at the school – now that you're here, I'm just worried you've taken on far too much.'

'I can cope. Honestly.'

'When Father Traynor proposed asking you, I asked him not to.'

'Why?'

She narrowed her eyes and whispered, 'You do realise what they're asking you to do?'

'So far, teach a group of boys how to kick a ball. And investigate the appearance of a bangle on a statue of the Virgin Mary.'

She smiled knowingly, satisfied she was the big sister again, possessed with superior knowledge. 'If you listen to certain people, the priest who was convicted isn't guilty. According to them, the church conspired to make it seem that way. Speak to Father Traynor, you'll see what I mean.'

'Who says that's what I'm investigating?'

'Smell the coffee – of course that's what you're doing. Want to know what I think?'

'Go on.'

'I think the priest did it. One hundred percent. I mean, all the evidence is there. But Father Traynor decided it reflects badly on him – they're old friends. That's why he wants him to retract his confession – to make himself look better. But you just have to see the guy – there's something about him that doesn't add up. All that child star nonsense, it ruins people.' She kissed him on the cheek. 'Anyway, I need to go. Remember. Not. A. Word. I was never here. Got it?'

Without waiting for him to respond, she darted out of the door, the bell rattling above as it sprung shut.

CHAPTER 12

After leaving Annemarie, Colin went to the library to check the newspaper archive, but found nothing additional about Sister Oran's murder. Having lost track of time, he rushed to the chemist to pick up his mum's prescription. He'd barely stepped in the door when the phone rang. A clearly stressed Sarah was asking whether he could cover duties that evening.

'It's a perfect storm,' she explained. 'With Brother Thomas away, you'll have to oversee dinner alongside Sister Helena. Our head chef, Davey, has called in sick for the umpteenth time.'

'Sounds doable.'

'Plus, you'll need to help the boys with their homework and ensure they're in bed by ten. 'Can you manage to get here for five?'

'I'll try my best.'

'And of course, you'll be reimbursed for the extra hours at your standard rate – unfortunately, they don't do double time, even if it is your day off.'

'I understand,' Colin replied. 'I'm happy to help if I can, I just need to make one call.'

83

Dialling Jeanie's number, he stuck his head into the living room to check on his mother. Though the TV was on, she was distracted – sitting, staring out of the window with a smile on her face, watching sparrows hop in and out of the concrete birdbath which occupied the centre of her immaculate front lawn.

Jeanie had answered immediately, agreeing to stay the night almost before he'd asked the question, and he could hear the sound of her key going into the front door lock as he phoned back and confirmed with Sarah that he would indeed be at the school before five.

'Did you sprint here?' he asked a breathless Jeanie.

'Enough of your nonsense. I'm only across the road. Now, you get going,' she replied, scurrying past him and into the living room. 'It's only me again, Moira,' he heard her cry. 'Your Colin's needed at the school. An emergency – the chef's gone AWOL.'

As he dashed upstairs, he heard his mother's low-voiced retort and the pair of them erupt with laughter, but he couldn't make out what she'd said.

Returning ten minutes later with his backpack strung over his shoulder, he found Jeanie at the kitchen sink filling a basin with hot, soapy water.

'And you're absolutely sure this is okay?' he asked. 'I'm not taking advantage?'

'As if! There's nothing worse than finding yourself at a loose end,' she replied. 'Now, Moira's going to take a wee nap just now, so I'll clean up in here and then wake her for Countdown. Do you watch it? That Richard Whiteley's such a funny man.'

He shook his head. 'I'll see you tomorrow then.'

'Bye, love.'

In the hallway he grabbed the car keys and gently pushed open the living room door. The curtains had been drawn and his mother was already asleep on the sofa with a blanket tucked around her, the thin whistle of her snore like a kettle just about to boil. She looked peaceful but her cheeks were sunken and her skin greyer than he'd seen before, though she swore blind she'd eaten a full sandwich earlier that day.

'Mum?' he said softly.

Her head twisted a little, but she didn't wake.

He leaned over and kissed her on the forehead, but she still didn't stir. Just as well, he thought; Moira didn't do affection.

CROSSING THE ERSKINE BRIDGE, the wind howled down the estuary like a crazed animal, buffeting the car. He gripped the steering wheel tighter, for fear he'd be blown off the edge.

Reflecting on his mother and how vulnerable she'd looked, he thought about his earlier conversation with Annemarie. Maybe she was right. Maybe the time had come to be considering a nursing home, or even a hospice. But he still doubted Moira could be persuaded to leave the comfort of her own home and if she were to agree, what would that mean? That she'd stopped fighting? That she knew the end was near? It didn't bear thinking about.

It was a relief to reach the far side of the bridge, and the shelter of the Clyde's north bank. Hopefully, housemaster duties would take his mind off things for a few hours and he'd get a decent night's sleep.

The kitchen was a disaster. Euphemia, the chef's mother who occasionally stepped in when needed, disappeared into a tiny office as soon as he arrived. Her daughter, Martha, barely out of school, stood staring into space, slowly opening a tin of carrots. Brandishing a ladle, only Sister Helena appeared to be taking any initiative. A fixture of the school since it opened twenty years before in its current location, by all accounts she'd been old then. Suspicious and taciturn, what few dealings he'd had with her to date suggested she wasn't that interested in engaging with staff.

Without looking up, she continued stirring what smelled like a cauldron of cabbage soup. 'Sarah told me you'd be here at three.'

'Well, she told me five, but I got here as quick as I could.' He gestured upstairs to the dining hall. 'Have they had anything to eat yet?'

'I've only one pair of hands.' She glanced at Martha, who didn't react to her slight.

'Is there a menu for tonight?'

She stared at him as if he were stupid. 'Soup.'

'Just soup? Is that enough?' He checked the fridge and found some margarine, mayonnaise, ham and cheddar cheese. 'I take it there's bread?'

Stepping away from her pot, she opened the pantry door to reveal several packets of sliced white bread. 'Left over from yesterday,' she said. 'Davey usually places an order in the morning, but as he's not here, nothing's been done.' On cue, Martha slipped out the back and lit a cigarette, whilst Euphemia put on her coat and scurried down the corridor.

'Is the soup ready?'

'Yes. I've just to add that tin of carrots. Pass it over, will you?'

Colin did so. 'If you want to organise bowls, why don't I transfer the pot to the dumb waiter, and we'll send it upstairs? While they eat that, maybe we can make some sandwiches? Or toasties might be a better option; the bread's a bit stale.'

Unconvinced, Sister Helena tottered over to a tall cupboard and began stacking bowls on the centre island, counting as she went.

'How many do we need to feed?' he asked.

'Sixty! We've sixty boarders,' she snapped. 'You've made me lose count. I'll have to start again.'

A Prayer Before Killing

Donning a pair of slightly soiled oven gloves, Colin grabbed the handles of the pot. A noxious smell enveloped him, and he held his breath as he gingerly slid the pot into the dumb waiter, taking care not to burn himself.

Gaunt faced in her food-spattered habit, Sister Helena watched as he then carried the bowls over to the dumb waiter. Closing the door, he pressed the green button and sprinted upstairs, arriving in the preparation kitchen at the same time as the first course.

Noise levels in the next-door dining hall were beginning to rise and he spotted Matthew and Luc sat together at the nearest table. 'Boys,' Colin said, 'can you come and give me a hand?'

Bright-eyed, Matthew appeared through the door, with Luc trailing behind. 'You've picked the short straw,' he giggled.

'Yeah, Sister Helena should have been put out to pasture years ago,' Luc added, but spotting Colin's raised eyebrow, he quickly pivoted. 'Though she's very devout; she sets a great example to us.'

Colin pointed to the pot. 'If one of you grabs the ladle and the other deals with the bowls, you can start dishing up. Do you want to ask a couple of boys to act as waiters?'

Matthew turned to Luc. 'Go get Garr and Johnny.'

Luc leaned over the pot, his top lip curled in disgust. 'What the hell is this pig swill? It smells foul.'

Matthew elbowed him. 'Zip it – go get the others.'

'I'll be downstairs sorting out the main course and a pudding too, I guess,' Colin said. 'Any problems, come get me.'

'Don't worry, sir,' Matthew replied. 'We've got this covered.'

Back in the basement, there was no sign of Sister Helena other than a wooden spoon she'd left perched perilously close to a naked flame. 'Jeez!' Colin cried, turning off the gas ring and running the charred spoon under cold water.

In the pantry, he found some pickle to tart up the toasties, plus several malt loaves and two huge, catering tins of custard which would do for dessert.

After turning on the grill, he wiped down the island and laid out slices of bread, first spreading them with marge and then methodically assembling the sandwiches. As he started to toast them, the dumb waiter sprang into life and a minute later Matthew and Luc appeared.

'That's the first course dealt with,' Matthew said, 'and the verdict is, it wasn't as bad as it smelled.'

Behind them, Luc was peering under the grill. 'Croque Monsieur. My favourite.'

'Not quite,' Colin informed him, 'but it should taste good.'

'What do you need us to do next, sir?' Matthew asked.

'If one of you can start sending the toasties upstairs and the other get the custard on that would be great,' Colin replied. 'The malt loaf needs to be cut, too.'

The rest of the dinner service ran like clockwork. It definitely wasn't the most imaginative food Colin had ever created, but it did the trick and he and the boys made a great team. Matthew and Luc were surprisingly resourceful, and Colin wondered if being sent away to boarding school at a young age had forced them to become more self-reliant than most teenagers.

After dinner, Sister Helena reappeared with no explanation as to where she'd been. Shooing Colin away from the industrial dishwasher, she grabbed a pile of dirty plates from his hands insisting, 'Let me do it. If you stack it wrong, it'll all have to be done again.' She shouted at Martha, who'd been washing pots at the sink, to help her. Then, shortly after seven o'clock, she retired for the night to the 'convent' – in reality a flat-roofed outbuilding containing a pair of rooms which sat across a small courtyard from the

A Prayer Before Killing

kitchen. This left him to oversee the evening entirely on his own.

Upstairs in the library and common rooms, few boys needed help with their homework. A couple of fourth years asked his advice on essay structure and some second years were struggling with algebra. Mostly, boys just wanted to chat with him, to show him the books they were reading or explain the board games they were playing. At one point, he was called into the games room to adjudicate on a table-tennis disagreement, but that was the only incident of the evening. All in all, Colin enjoyed the interaction with the students; it was a much less formal role than teaching in class, almost parental, and he was encouraged by how cooperative the boys had been. After cocoa and biscuits, most students were in their rooms by ten.

'Goodnight, sir,' Matthew said, walking back from the bathroom in flip-flops and a towelling dressing gown.

'Goodnight, Matthew. And thanks for your help with dinner.'

'*No problemo*,' he said, closing the door of his room.

Colin made one final circuit of the dormitory level, dimming lights as he went. He paused outside the room he'd been allocated for the night and peered over the balustrade into the void below. Though the lower floors containing the library and classrooms stepped into this space, he could still see down to the ground floor dining hall with its neat rows of refectory tables and benches. Above him, the vaulted glass roof rattled as the wind continued to howl. Together with the ever-present hum of the air conditioning system, it made the building feel more like a ship than ever, with him as sole captain, responsible for the lives of his young charges.

Suddenly cold, he shivered and went into his room to find his jumper.

Sitting on the edge of his single bed, he was unsure what

to do with himself. It was too early to think about sleep and the boys had repeatedly complained about the lack of a TV room. In his rush to get there on time he'd forgotten to pack a book. Realising there was an opportunity, he waited half an hour.

Confident that the boys were asleep, he crept down a side stair and opened the heavy brass door to the church.

Since starting at the school, most of his time on site had been taken up with doing the job which was supposed to be his cover. Organising lessons and responding to queries from pupils and colleagues had left few chances to properly explore the building and grounds. To date, there'd been no opportunity to check the statue of the Virgin Mary on his own.

With the lights turned off, the church felt devoid of life – any sense of magic was completely absent. He lit a candle and was reminded of his time as an altar boy and that lonely sense of expectation, arriving in a cold, silent church to prepare for Mass before the arrival of the congregation.

Shielding the flame of the candle with his hand, he entered the side chapel.

Illuminated by candlelight, the statue looked more human – more present – than on his first day here with the rector. Colin touched her arm; it was cool and remarkably smooth, you could almost mistake the wood for real flesh.

He held the candle closer and scrutinised the gold bangle. Crouching down, he placed the candle on the statue's stone plinth and carefully examined the bangle with his fingers, the charms dangling from it gently glinting. It was definitely solid, with no fastenings or breaks. It was small too – like a child's – there was no way it could have been squeezed over the hand of the statue without seriously damaging the wood. Colin looked more closely at the left hand – though there were some woodworm holes and ancient traces of paint, there was no sign of recent damage.

A Prayer Before Killing

Moving the bangle away from the left wrist, Colin could see a faint line, a break in the wood, where the separately carved hand was joined to the wrist. He tried to turn the hand, to see if there was any give, but there was none. Examining the right hand, he found the same faint line. Exerting some gentle pressure, the right hand began to rotate and the line opened up to reveal a wooden dowel connecting the hand to the wrist. He rotated it back into position and lifted the candle to better view the left wrist. On the underside, where the hand connected to the wrist was a hard, shiny, white nodule. Colin ran his thumbnail over it. If he didn't know better, he'd swear it was a bead of plastic-wood glue.

One so-called miracle had been solved. Someone had removed the left hand and placed the bangle on the wrist, before gluing the two parts back together. However, that still left the question of who did it and why.

He heard a jangle of metal behind him. Looking round, Brendan was holding up a set of keys. 'I'm locking up now, but I can come back later.'

'No, I'm finished here.'

Brendan entered and began his security check of the doors.

From the floors above, Colin sensed movement. He checked his watch: 11.05. As he was teaching first thing, he thought it best to turn in. He'd keep the information about the bangle to himself for now. Annemarie's assertion that the school was full of liars, that Father Young was guilty, and that Father Traynor – and by implication Charlie Murray – were conspiring to get him freed, were enough to keep him interested.

Colin blew out the candle and placed it back on the votive stand. As he stepped back out into the atrium, a sudden extended scream from above was followed by the sound of doors opening and footsteps rushing along the upper gallery. All of a sudden, the atrium was filled with voices.

As a strange wailing echoed around the space, Colin rushed up the main staircase, taking two steps at a time, Brendan behind him. When they reached the dormitory level, Garr ran towards him, his dressing gown flapping. 'It's Johnny!'

'Is he okay?' Colin asked breathlessly, pushing past a large group of boys crowded around the door of Johnny's room.

Inside, he discovered Matthew perched on the side of Johnny's bed, holding him in his arms. Trance-like, Johnny looked over Matthew's shoulder, his eyes blank, his mouth loose as low moans emanated from his throat.

'Should I call an ambulance?' Brendan asked.

'No. He's had night terrors since he was a kid,' Matthew replied. 'He's not been like this for a while, but he should be okay in a minute or two.'

Colin turned to the boys standing in the corridor. 'Back to bed, please.' Immediately, they scurried back to their rooms.

As Matthew soothed Johnny, his moans gradually eased.

'Is there anything I can do?' Colin asked.

'No, he'll be fine. He won't even remember in the morning.'

Calm now, Matthew laid Johnny's head onto his pillow and pulled the sheets around him.

'Would it be okay if I sleep here tonight, sir? Just on the floor – in case he wakes up? It's what I've done in the past.'

'Sure,' Colin said. 'Why don't you go fetch your covers?' He turned to Brendan. 'Things are fine here. You carry on locking up.'

'If you're sure?'

Colin nodded and Brendan left.

While he waited for Matthew to return, Colin looked around Johnny's room. It was bare, with very few personal effects.

Johnny let out a low moan and turned on his side to face the wall.

A Prayer Before Killing

Colin noticed how thin his neck was – how prominent the vertebrae looked.

Clutching a pile of sheets and blankets, Matthew appeared back in the room.

'Any problems, come and knock on my door – whatever the time,' Colin instructed. 'You're a good friend, Matthew.'

'Thanks, sir.'

As Colin walked along the dormitory gallery to his room, he reflected on what might have happened in Johnny's life to cause such terrors. But also, how vulnerable he seemed physically and how much that reminded Colin of his own mother.

CHAPTER 13

TWO YEARS EARLIER

Tormented by insomnia, Father Young had taken to rising before everyone else; these days, it wasn't unusual for him to get up at 4 AM. He found some degree of solace in the quiet, a chance to think without distraction, to be by himself, free from the boys' unreasonable behaviour and Brother Thomas's caustic remarks. As far as he was concerned, if he didn't have to see or deal with any of them – even for five minutes – he was winning. Only Dr Murray and Father Traynor spoke kindly to him; as for the others, he was just a punchbag.

For the past two weeks, rather than sit alone in his room, he'd forced himself outside. The late spring weather had been warmer than usual, and he felt he ought to at least try and enjoy the surrounding countryside. What started out as short strolls had turned into longer walks of five, even six, miles. A few days earlier, he'd pushed himself to the limit and completed eight miles before breakfast. On his return, exhausted, he could barely lift the spoon to eat his porridge.

It was the mechanics of walking that he enjoyed; losing himself in the repetition, he was able to forget about the boys, the staff, the school. Himself. And while the destination

A Prayer Before Killing

didn't matter to him, the route did. Increasingly, he found himself heading out onto the barren moorland, to the hills above the school estate, or through the nearby commercial forests with their dark, sterile avenues of planted conifers.

His walk this morning had been relatively undisturbed. It wasn't until he returned to the school grounds at around 6.30, with the sun fully risen, that the sound of birdsong began to intrude, catapulting him back to reality. First period, he had his least favourite class. As ever, he was dreading it. Garr, his least favourite boy, had continued to appear five or ten minutes into almost every lesson, as if out of thin air. Each time, it reduced his classmates to fits of giggles, destroying whatever sense of order he'd managed to impose. It infuriated him and he still had no idea how Garr was doing it. He'd asked Father Traynor's advice and had even tried discussing it with Brother Thomas. Father Traynor hadn't grasped how humiliating it was, suggesting the boys were just testing him and that they'd soon get bored. Brother Thomas had simply looked at him as if he was insane.

He took a deep breath. A quick shower, he thought, attempting to pull himself together before joining the mob for breakfast and Mass. Then the real horrors would begin – another cycle of trials to endure as he watched the clock counting down the hours and minutes to the end of the day.

Following the path down from the playing field, he thought he heard singing coming from among the trees to his right. He paused. Distant sounds of laughter – a woman's voice – echoed up the slope. A gentle breeze, with a hint of warmth, rustled through the branches as he stepped from the path. Ahead of him, pink blossom fell from the trees, drifting through the air, like flakes of snow falling in slow motion before coming to rest on the dark soil. As he positioned himself behind the thick trunk of an oak tree, another wave of laughter rippled upwards and he squinted to see what was going on.

In the clearing below, in front of a large beech tree, Sister Oran was dancing with an enthralled Matthew, who had a white cross painted on his bare chest. Softly singing with her eyes closed, she looked completely lost in the moment – ecstatic almost – as she twirled him around. Hands outstretched, she floated from one tree to the next with him, touching each lightly, sending blossom cascading to the ground. But it wasn't just the two of them. Bathed in sunlight, at the centre of the space, the rest of the boys – Luc, Garr and Johnny – were sprawled on the grass, limbs intertwined and chests bare. Transfixed, their eyes followed her every move.

'Isn't God great?' Sister Oran, her eyes now wide open, smiled directly at him. 'Come and join us, Father Young. We won't bite.'

Shielding his eyes, he stepped out from the shadows and into the bright morning sunshine. Unconcerned by his presence, Matthew joined the other boys.

'Shouldn't the boys be getting ready for the morning prayer?' He held out his watch to show her the time.

'Father Young's right. Run along boys. If you're spotted out here, watching me dance around like an eejit, they'll have my guts for garters.'

The boys began to snigger.

'What's so funny?' she asked. 'Not because I said garters? Garters! Garters! Garters!' she repeated to squeals of laughter. 'You've got your minds in the gutter, so you do. Now skedaddle.'

The boys clambered to their feet, pulling on their discarded shirts. Like a mother hen with her brood, Sister Oran shooed them away towards the school. Finding the warmest spot in the clearing, she tilted her face to the sun.

Silence filled the air.

'What's going on?' he asked. His first thought was to turn around and report Sister Oran, but the idea of explaining what he'd seen to Brother Thomas filled him with dread.

A Prayer Before Killing

Smoothing down her habit, which he could now see was grubby – as if she'd been rolling around in the dirt – she placed a hand across her mouth to suppress a laugh. 'You should see the look on your face.'

He couldn't see the funny side. 'This is highly unusual.'

She dismissed his comment with a wave of her hand, turning her back on him to examine the leaf of a tree.

'You don't agree?' Her conduct was not just unusual, it was downright odd, wrong even. She must surely know what was expected of a nun: silence, duty, obedience. The idea of stumbling across Sister Helena – or any other nun for that matter – alone in a wood with a group of half-naked teenagers was inconceivable.

She placed her tiny forefinger against her lips and shushed him. 'Can you hear that?'

Bewildered, he shook his head.

Eyes sparkling, she placed her hand on his chest. 'Listen. Breathe slowly. Breathe deeply. It's the sound of nature. The sound of God.'

Caught off guard, he felt his eyelids droop and his heartbeat slow. For the first time in weeks, a sense of calm washed over him.

A minute or more passed before she removed her hand and he opened his eyes.

'But you're right,' she conceded. 'Dr Murray or Brother Thomas, or any of the others for that matter, wouldn't understand if they'd came across us.'

'You could get into serious trouble,' he said.

'It was such a magical morning,' Sister Oran replied. 'It would have been ungrateful not to enjoy it, to share the wonder of it with the boys. It was entirely innocent.'

'That's as may be, but it's not how it looked,' he stressed, 'and it's not how it would be received by a group of teenage boys. They have hormones … urges. Don't you get it?' Attempting to gauge her thoughts, he was taken aback to find she was smiling again. 'They've got classes all day, till eight this evening. They're going to be all worked up now. Totally distracted.'

'You're wrong – they're children. Innocents. We've communed with nature. Like Adam and Eve in Eden, before the Fall. There's only good in that.'

'Sorry, Sister, but I think you're being incredibly naïve.'

Her smile disappeared; he was rebuking her, and clearly didn't care for it. 'You don't know these boys like I do,' she said.

'That's true, but it could seriously compromise you.' He moved aside to let her pass.

'One morning, you should tag along,' she called back, making her way into the woodland. 'It's been a while since we last recruited someone.'

As she disappeared from view, he was left in no doubt: this hadn't been the boys' first morning with Sister Oran, communing with nature. It begged the question: what else was she up to with them?

CHAPTER 14
THURSDAY 16TH NOVEMBER 1995

Up early after a fitful night's sleep, Colin supervised breakfast, attended Mass, and delivered an outdoor PE session for one of the junior school classes in atrocious weather. Normally agreeable, today the boys had been uncooperative, constantly arguing amongst themselves. Drenched, and with a thumping headache, he was in no mood for further bad behaviour.

Now late for a senior study class on the second floor, he hurried along the gallery corridor to a classroom on the far side of the atrium. As he neared the closed door, a tumultuous roar erupted from within.

Throwing open the door, he was met with a scene familiar from his own schooldays. A circle of boys was gathered around one desk, arms and voices raised, their overlapping cries degenerating into a raw chant. *Hit him! That's it! Again!*

'What's going on?' Colin's yell cut through the cacophony, forcing the group apart. 'Take your seats.'

Avoiding eye contact, the majority of boys skulked back to their desks, trying their best to pretend nothing untoward had occurred. As they dispersed, it became clear that two boys – Matthew and Luc – were at the centre of the action. With their faces fiery and bodies pumped, they were torn between retreating with the rest of the class and trying to hide what was going on from Colin. A series of heavy sobs coming from behind put paid to that.

'Is anyone going to explain?' Colin demanded, stepping between Matthew and Luc to discover Johnny cowering beneath a desk.

'He got some bad news this morning,' a red-faced Danny volunteered, adjusting his glasses.

Ignoring what appeared to be a lie from an unpopular boy keen to curry favour, Colin turned to Matthew and Luc. 'Well?'

'It's true,' Luc said. 'His dog died or something, and he took it bad. Ask him – his gran called after breakfast.' He casually plonked himself on a chair, but not before Colin noticed a smear of blood across his knuckles.

Johnny continued to sob, his body trembling, his face hidden behind his hands.

'The dog was old, sir,' Matthew said, taking the chair next to Luc.

'And he can always get another.' Luc stared at the trembling boy. 'Can't you?'

Johnny gave a feeble nod.

'Come out from under there,' Colin said, offering him his hand. 'The rest of you, take out your workbooks.' The boys stared at each other, waiting for the first to react. 'Now!'

Reluctantly, the class pulled textbooks and pencils from their bags.

'Let's go somewhere quiet for a chat,' he whispered to Johnny as a dozen pair of eyes followed them out of the room. Colin pointed to a breakout area overlooking the atrium. 'Go and wait for me there. Take a breather. I'll join you in a minute.'

A Prayer Before Killing

Returning to the classroom he asked, 'Does anyone have a better explanation for what I just witnessed?'

Heads bowed and casting sideways glances, the boys remained silent.

'No?' Colin waited. 'Okay, if that's how you want to play it, I'll be informing Brother Thomas about your conduct, and there'll be no senior football practice after school tonight.'

The class groaned, their heads sinking even further.

'I'll be out on the atrium with Johnny. If I hear a peep from the rest of you, there'll be trouble. Understood?'

'Yes, sir,' Luc muttered through tightened lips.

Keeping the class door ajar, Colin took a seat opposite Johnny, noting his messed-up hair, a bloody scratch on his chin, and a large red mark on his forearm.

Conscious of Colin's eyes on him, Johnny pulled down his sleeve and stared at him defiantly.

'Are you going to tell me what happened?'

Johnny looked away.

'Has it got anything to do with last night?' Colin asked.

'No,' Johnny retorted. 'Can I go back to class?'

Typical boys. Defend each other till the last. He'd done it himself many times, got into fights with friends, refused to grass anyone up. Scratches and bruises healed, but a friendship could never recover from grassing to a teacher.

'Not until I know what happened,' said Colin firmly. 'I need to know you're okay.'

'I'm fine. It was all my fault,' Johnny said, going to stand.

Colin gestured for him to sit back down. 'How? You're going to have to explain.'

Johnny glowered, a dark-eyed look conveying a single message: *fuck off*.

The boys were a tighter-knit group than Colin had first imagined. Apostles, indeed. He was wasting his breath. There was no way Johnny was going to spill the beans.

'I was upset about my dog. I wasn't looking where I was going.' Though there were tears in his eyes, the boy's face was still defiant.

'You're sure? What about that cut?' Colin asked, pointing to his chin.

'It's nothing. The floor was slippery. I tripped and fell.'

The story was set in stone.

'Okay,' Colin relented. 'Well, I'm here if you need to talk.'

Johnny didn't react.

'You should get it cleaned at least,' Colin said. 'Head downstairs; Sister Helena will patch you up.'

Johnny's tiny frame hobbled over to the stairwell. He turned, a determined expression still etched across his face. 'Sir, it really was my fault.'

Not one of the boys glanced up as Colin returned to class. The room was still and silent, as if no one had dared to move a muscle since he'd left. Even when he instructed Garr to read a passage out loud, the others listened respectfully, apparently engrossed in the testimonial of a Scottish missionary who was intent on effecting change through the word of God.

At the end of the lesson however, after the pupils had left, Matthew and Luc remained seated, whilst Garr lingered at the door for a moment, finally turning and leaving. Ignoring the remaining two, Colin gathered his belongings, keen to let his irritation be known.

'Sir?' Luc sighed.

'Yes?' Colin stared at their faces: not yet men, but almost.

'Johnny was upset,' Matthew began. 'Then he slipped. He was embarrassed and crawled under the desk. Some of the boys were making fun of him. We were just trying to coax him out when you walked in.'

'That's not how it looked,' Colin stated. He could see blood on Matthew's hand.

Luc threw his arms to his side, sulking. 'I don't see why

A Prayer Before Killing

we need to explain ourselves. Everyone knows Johnny's a nutter. I mean, he—'

'Luc!' Matthew gave him a sideways glance.

'Well, he is. It's only me who has the guts to say it.'

Matthew shook his head. 'You're an idiot.'

'I need to go.' Luc stood. 'You coming?'

Tapping his foot rapidly on the floor, Matthew chewed his lip, refusing to move.

'Well, if no one has anything more constructive to say then I guess you'd better run along,' Colin suggested.

Reluctantly, Luc sat back down, adopting the same pose as Matthew, crossing his arms and staring straight ahead. Eventually, it was him who broke the silence. 'What I'm saying, it's true. Johnny's not right – in the head, I mean. You saw him last night. He was proper psycho.'

'And how does that end up with him scratched and bruised? Did he do that to himself?'

'That's not how it was.' Luc's childish, sing-song tone was failing to conceal his guilt.

'Luc's right,' Matthew added.

Colin turned to face him. 'Well then, what *is* the truth?' He kept his voice calm, his focus unflinching. 'I'm listening.'

Both boys remained staring at the floor, caught in a brotherhood of silence.

'This is supposed to be the part where you tell me what *did* happen,' Colin said.

Matthew glanced at Luc and shook his head almost imperceptibly.

Immediately, Luc rose again. 'So, will Brother Thomas be told?'

'Go to your class,' Colin sighed.

Luc grabbed his satchel and marched out of the room.

Colin waited while Matthew gathered his belongings, observing his relaxed manner. 'Would you like to tell me?' he asked.

Matthew slung his backpack across his shoulder and crossed the room. 'Sorry.'

'I *will* get to the bottom of this,' he said, as Matthew opened the door.

Matthew shrugged and left, his expression indifferent.

CHAPTER 15

On his return from work, Colin found his mother sitting motionless at the kitchen table, one hand gripping her fork, staring at a pork pie as though she'd spent hours considering whether to eat it or not.

'Sorry I'm late. Has Jeanie gone already?'

'Aye.'

'How have you been today?'

She shrugged.

'Not hungry?' Colin asked, throwing his backpack onto a chair.

'Past its sell-by-date.'

'You sure?' Colin opened the bin and found the crumpled wrapper. Sure enough, it was four days out-of-date. 'You can't eat that.'

As soon as he said it, she forced her fork through the pastry, wrestling off a large piece, which she then crammed into her mouth. 'Tastes fine to me,' she insisted.

He took the plate. 'Your immune system's low – you need to be careful. I'll fix you something fresh.'

Her eyes followed him as he swept the pork pie into the bin, then checked the fridge. 'What do you fancy?' he asked.

'A pork pie,' she replied.

Colin was in no mood for a fight – his day had been difficult enough already. At the end of the school day, after working on a lesson plan for his leadership class, Colin had hung around waiting to talk to Brother Thomas about the argument between the boys, but the monk's analysis that boys fight and it would soon be forgotten was unhelpful. By the time Colin left the school, it was after seven, and then there had been a delay on the motorway. It was now eight-thirty, and he was exhausted. 'I can make us omelettes.'

She turned her nose up at the suggestion, slowly gathered up her puzzle magazines along with her TV Quick, and shuffled through to the living room.

'You'll need to eat something,' he called out to her.

'I'll have a cup of tea and a slice of toast,' she shouted, 'and don't be stingy with the butter.' A blast of noise from the TV suggested she was settled for the evening.'

After fixing her tea and toast, and a cheese omelette for himself, he retreated upstairs to his bedroom and lay down. He gazed at the blank walls and ceiling, unsure how best to proceed with the investigation. Disturbed by the day's events, he closed his eyes, speculating about who might have had a motive to put the bangle on the statue and reflecting on his conversation with Luc and Matthew. Something was definitely going on between them, but what? Perhaps a call to Father Traynor might help.

'Who are you phoning?' his mother asked, her voice louder than the blare of the television.

He popped his head into the living room. 'Work stuff. Don't worry, I'll put money in the box.'

'But you've only just got back.' She picked up the remote control and, with her hands shaking, managed to turned down the volume. 'Who works at this time of night?'

A Prayer Before Killing

'It's just a quick call,' he said. 'What's on next? I'll come through and sit with you when I'm done.'

'*Crimewatch*.'

'How about I make us some cocoa and we can sit and watch it together?' This cheered her. 'Plus, there's an unopened packet of Jaffa cakes.'

She shook her head. 'That's Jeanie's idea of a treat. I'll not be touching them.'

Maybe Annemarie's prediction was about to come true; Moira had a long history of falling out with friends, family and basically anyone else she came into regular contact with. He thought it might be different with Jeanie; while Moira constantly berated her over the tiniest misdemeanour, Jeanie took it all in her stride. 'You two haven't had a fight, have you?'

'That woman's not to step one foot inside this house again. I'm telling you right now.'

'You don't really mean that, do you? What happened?'

Mouth clamped firmly shut, his mother turned the TV volume back up to full and focused her attention on the opening credits of *Crimewatch*.

It took several minutes for Father Traynor to come to the phone. Initially, his housekeeper had stalled, insisting he was too busy with parish work to take a call, before she finally agreed to check.

'Hey Colin, what can I do for you?' Rather than tending to the spiritual needs of his flock, Father Traynor's breathlessness suggested he'd been occupied in some vigorous exercise.

'Sorry, is this a bad time?'

'Not at all. I was just in my study, reading.'

Which definitely didn't sound like the truth.

'How's Moira?'

'Not too bad. More like her usual self today. But we take it one day at a time.'

'It's all you can do in the circumstances,' Father Traynor

said. 'And how's Annemarie? I was thinking about her earlier.'

Pulling the phone flex, Colin moved towards the stairwell to get out of earshot of his mother and lowered his voice. 'We met for coffee yesterday. She thinks we should be looking at a home – professional care.'

'She mentioned that to me too,' Father Traynor said. 'Asked if I might try and have a word.'

'She won't be persuaded.'

'I said I didn't think it was an area I should be interfering in. You as a family need to discuss it with Moira and her medical team, then reach a decision.' He paused. 'I did suggest however that she needs to sort out their differences before it's too late.' He paused again. 'That she might try seeing some things from Moira's perspective.'

'That's never going to happen. They're both as stubborn as each other,' Colin said. 'Anyway, that's not what I was calling about.'

'Okay. Hold on a second, I'm going to switch to the extension.'

Colin heard a muttered conversation, a door close and a click on the line.

'That's better,' Father Traynor said. 'I'm back in my favourite armchair. I'm all yours.'

'Can I ask why you specifically wanted me for this job?'

'Eh. Sure,' Father Traynor replied. 'As you know, part of it was to help you as a family, allow you to be with your mother. Besides that, you're well qualified professionally and you have a good understanding of how the church – the Glasgow archdiocese – functions. I guess we felt you were someone who could be trusted, who wouldn't be swayed from certain truths. But listen, Colin, if it's not for you, I'd understand.'

'No, no. I'm intrigued by the case – or rather the cases. Though I wasn't expecting to have to do so much actual

A Prayer Before Killing

teaching, plus Charlie's sudden departure has thrown me a bit. You know, not having that immediate support and guidance on hand?'

'Yes. I get that. I'm not sure what I can do to help on that front.'

'I don't know either. A sounding board maybe? I suppose I'm thinking I just need to take my own lead on it all.'

'That makes sense.'

'So, in that spirit, perhaps you could tell me what you know about a couple of things?'

'Sure.'

'First up, the bangle. What do you know about it?'

'Well, it originally belonged to Sister Oran's widowed aunt; I know that much. Sister Oran showed it to me once; each enamel charm celebrated one of her aunt's favourite saints. Her uncle – her aunt's husband – had commissioned it specially as a twenty-fifth anniversary gift. But there's more to it. When Sister Oran arrived in Scotland there was a bit of a buzz. In certain circles she was a bit of a celebrity – in certain religious circles that is. The story goes that this aunt had incurable cancer – they'd given up all hope, her body was riddled with it. But Sister Oran took it upon herself to pray for twenty-four hours a day, for six days solid. And do you know what happened?'

Colin grinned. 'I've a suspicion but go on.'

'A miracle. Or so they say. Without any more chemotherapy or radiation, the old dear's cancer was cured. Completely gone. And the bangle that was so precious to her was given to Sister Oran, not just as a thank you, but as a symbol of the power of prayer.'

'Do you really think that's true?'

'According to the press in the County of Tipperary.'

'Have you contact details for the aunt?'

'She passed away recently.'

Colin raised his eyebrow. 'Of cancer by any chance?'

'I don't actually know, but here's the thing,' Father Traynor said. 'That bangle, which Sister Oran never took off, somehow reappeared on the wrist of Our Lady four days after the aunt died. A solid bangle on the wrist of a statue,' he emphasised.

Colin decided not to mention his theory about how the bangle came to be placed there. 'Can I ask you about the boys?'

'Which ones?'

'Sorry – Matthew, Garr, Luc and Johnny specifically. I was given a file on each of them by Bishop Trocchi.'

'Right. I see. Well, of course, they were close to Sister Oran.'

So, their files had been included for a reason. 'Just those four? None of the other boys?'

'I was in and out of the school a lot during that time. Teaching a bit, running the cycling and athletics clubs, even helping with maintenance around the grounds. I didn't know Sister Oran well, but it was obvious she took an interest in the welfare of all the boys. I know from Simon – sorry, Father Young – that she was particularly close to Matthew, Garr, Luc and Johnny. It was she who christened them the Apostles.'

'At the time of Sister Oran's disappearance did suspicion fall on any of them?'

'Goodness no. Besides they were all away on the retreat.' In the background Colin heard a door bang and a whispered conversation. Father Traynor cleared his throat. 'Sorry Colin, just give me a moment.' He returned moments later. 'You don't get a moment's peace in this place. Mrs Beattie's asking me what I want for my breakfast, when I've had the same thing every day for the last two years.' He took a breath. 'I'm mystified as to why the boys' files would be given to you. What do they say?'

'Nothing very much, but there is a suggestion that they're not entirely innocent.'

A Prayer Before Killing

'Honestly, I'm surprised the bishop would allow that to be included. Garr's and Luc's in particular. Both families are very influential – their money practically bankrolls the school.'

'You don't happen to know who discovered the bangle on the statue?' Colin asked.

'Actually, that was Johnny,' Father Traynor replied. 'And he was the one who spoke to a journalist, much to everyone's horror.'

The night terrors, him being beaten up by the other boys… It fitted, but still didn't make sense, unless the boys were forcing him to keep quiet about how the bangle ended up there in the first place.

From the living room, his mother yelled that she needed another cushion. He placed his hand over the receiver and called to her, 'I'll be with you in a minute.'

'How have your dealings with Brother Thomas been?' asked Father Traynor.

'I don't think he's a fan.'

'Don't trust a thing he says or does. According to my sources, he was the one who engineered Charlie's removal. And if I've learned one thing about the guy, he always gets what he wants.'

Colin said his goodbyes and put down the receiver. He loudly dropped some coins into the box, knowing his mother would be listening for their clatter. This investigation was becoming more intriguing. Just as he was about to ponder Father Traynor's words, his mother screamed out that she needed her cushion right that minute.

CHAPTER 16

Unable to sleep, Colin left the house early to avoid the rush-hour traffic. Despite the relentless rain, for once he had time to enjoy the scenery: the wide expanse of the river Clyde, the small villages dotted along the route, the woodland which gradually thickened on the approach to the school, devouring the sky above. Maybe this could be his new routine – far better than sitting bumper-to-bumper on the M8.

His plan was to explore the school grounds in more detail. While he was familiar with the path up to the playing fields, there'd been few opportunities to investigate much beyond that. Leaving his car outside the main building, he zipped up the hood of his parka and headed for the duck pond. In the grey light of dawn, rain splashing on the water's surface made for a tranquil scene. However, as he drew closer to the water's edge, he noticed ducks sheltering amongst the reeds, eyeing him suspiciously.

Initially deciding to follow the track to the castle, he was distracted by a light shining from the slope below. Following a narrow path through the undergrowth back towards the school, a large wooden shed with a single lit window appeared, set within a small garden, and beyond that, a neat

A Prayer Before Killing

stone cottage cloaked in darkness. As he approached the shed, Colin heard the sound of whistling and could make out a figure moving within.

A gravel path led him to the front of the shed, the double doors of which had been thrown wide open. What Colin had assumed was a simple garden shed, was in fact a full workshop. Its walls lined with tools, the space was equipped with a workbench, bandsaw and lathe. Inside, dressed in a dusty pair of quilted overalls and with plane in hand, Brendan was working on a length of wood held in a vice.

'Up early?' Colin didn't want to startle him, so remained standing in the doorway.

Brendan looked up and smiled. 'Since five.' He checked his watch. 'But this is early for you. You weren't on dreaded house duties again, were you?'

'No. I wanted to avoid the traffic.'

'There's fresh coffee if you fancy,' Brendan said, nodding towards a stove in the far corner as he continued to plane the piece of wood.

'I'm okay,' Colin replied. 'By the way, thanks for your help the other night.'

'Not at all. Wee Johnny's a sensitive soul.' Brendan removed the piece of wood from the vice and rubbed his hand across its surface. 'One of the boy's beds needs mending,' he said, laying it on the bench. 'God knows how he managed to break it.'

Colin stepped further inside. The space was well looked after – every tool had its place, and the surfaces were spotless. 'This your hideout?' he asked.

'When I've time.' Brendan pulled a tobacco tin from his pocket. 'Which is never.'

'They keep you busy?'

Brendan rolled his eyes. 'Put it this way, I live for my holidays.' He produced a handmade cigarette from his tin and lit it. 'Don't tell Sarah,' he said with a wink. 'She thinks I've stopped.'

Colin laughed. 'Your secret's safe with me.'

'You want one?'

'I don't smoke,' he replied. 'That's what I wanted to ask you. The group of women the other day – had they come to see the bangle?' He decided not to mention that Sarah had already confirmed this.

'Oh yeah. The story's been spreading like wildfire. They were the fourth or fifth lot we've had since it first appeared.'

'And do you usually let people see it?'

'If it was up to me, I'd let them all in.'

'Why's that?' Colin noticed Brendan's expression change; his smile grew wider, his eyes more alive.

'It's a miracle, isn't it?'

'That's what you believe?'

'Yes. I guess so.' Brendan ran a hand through his hair. 'I'm not exactly the holiest guy around these parts, but it seems it's only me. Sister H thinks I'm an idiot.'

Colin hadn't heard anyone refer to Sister Helena in this way before. The pet name seemed incongruous when he hadn't seen her exhibit any sign of warmth towards anyone except the pupils. 'How come you believe when everyone else seems convinced it's a hoax? Sarah doesn't think it's true, does she?'

'No, she doesn't and she's at Mass every Sunday.' Brendan tapped his ash into an empty mug. 'If you'd asked me the question two months ago, I'd have laughed in your face.'

'So what changed?'

'It's simple. I check the church every night as part of my locking up routine – usually around 11, never later than midnight. And once in a while I'll have a word with Our Lady – have you seen the statue? I mean really looked at it?'

'I have. It's beautiful.'

'It's more than that. It's a masterpiece. Those guys in the

A Prayer Before Killing

Middle Ages knew what they were doing. Anyway, I remember standing in front of her that night. Like I said, I'm not particularly religious, but I'd said a wee prayer to her. So, when I locked up that night, I knew there was no bangle on her wrist, no shadow of a doubt. And when the church is locked, no one – none of the boys, no staff – can access the church. It's only me – I'm the keyholder.'

Colin could think of several explanations as to how someone could have gained access to the church – hidden themselves amongst the pews, borrowed the key and made a copy – but by the look on Brendan's face, he was convinced it was a miracle. Which seemed odd, given his relative lack of religious conviction. He glanced at Brendan and sensed a change in his focus. 'I should let you get on.'

Brendan held up the piece of wood. 'Once I've got this sorted, there's a toilet needs unblocking in the library. It's a glamorous life!'

As the caretaker followed him out of the shed, Colin noticed a beautifully carved crucifix on a shelf. 'Your handiwork?'

'God no. I can't claim to be that artistic. Go on, pick it up,' he said. 'It's solid oak. From a tree that came down in a storm.'

Colin held the cross in his hands. It had weight and on closer inspection, the design was even more impressive. 'Is it difficult to carve oak so intricately?'

'With these paws? Impossible!' Brendan held up a calloused hand, his thick fingers with their nails bitten down to the quick. 'That's actually one of Johnny's pieces. He made it when he first got here, maybe four years ago. For a while I ran a woodwork club for the younger boys. It took him weeks, but he came here after school every night and spent hours on it. Not bad for a young un, eh?'

'It's great.' Colin placed it back on the shelf. 'Why's it not displayed anywhere?'

'Dunno. He didn't want a song and dance made about it, I suppose.'

They exited and Brendan closed the doors, locking them and returning the key to a ring attached to his belt. 'Is Johnny one of yours then?'

'I have him for a few periods. He's one of the quieter boys, so I've not had a chance to get to know him that well.'

'It's worth taking the time. He's an old-fashioned boy – respectful, humble not like the others. There's a lot of them could do with a good slap if you ask me.' He caught sight of Colin's disapproving look. 'Sorry mate,' he winked. 'I'm a bit more old-school.'

It was true – Johnny was different from the other boys; quiet, self-contained and sensitive. So how was it that he seemed to attract so much of the boys' attention?

Brendan produced another bunch of keys. 'I need to collect a couple of things from the cottage.'

'No worries, I'll see you around,' Colin said and set off towards the main school building.

CHAPTER 17

Later that day, on one of Colin's free periods, Brother Thomas appeared in his classroom. Not only was this the first time he'd come to Colin's room, it was also the first time they'd spoken since their awkward exchange the previous week. His stiff demeanour had gone, replaced with something altogether more casual. It didn't suit him.

'The very man,' Brother Thomas announced loudly from the doorway, checking up and down the corridor. 'I need your help.'

'Sure. What can I do?'

Satisfied the coast was clear, Brother Thomas stepped into the room. 'Three of the senior boys – Daniel McKendrick, Johnny Doyle and Garr McGuigan – require assistance with their essays. They're writing statements to accompany their seminary applications.' He handed Colin three sets of photocopies. 'Nothing too complicated – grammar, phrasing – that sort of thing. They'll come here in turn, at the end of the day. Fifteen minutes for each should be enough; they've other commitments. Is that convenient?'

Judging by Brother Thomas's tone, whether it was convenient or not seemed irrelevant. 'Of course.'

Brother Thomas hesitated, as if expecting further questions. When Colin asked none, he took a step back. 'Much appreciated, Mr Buxton,' he said, forcing a smile before scurrying down the corridor.

It struck Colin as an odd request. If he were being cynical, he might assume it was a deliberate ploy, setting him up to fail, in order to get rid of him sooner. Or perhaps he was being paranoid, and it was simply that no one else was available. However, until proven otherwise, he decided to give Brother Thomas the benefit of the doubt.

At the end of the school day, Danny arrived promptly after the bell rang. He was nervous, a facial tic pulsing each time Colin asked him a question. However, apart from a few mistakes in his grammar and an ending that didn't fully sum up his reasoning, the essay was solid, and in places sparkled with sincerity and passion. Colin was impressed and said so.

As Danny left, Johnny entered.

The first thing Colin noticed was that he'd changed his hairstyle. The usual mess of knotted curls had gone; his hair was now neatly combed over to the side. And his uniform, for a change, was immaculate. There was no dirty shirt collar, no blazer with frayed cuffs and no scuffed shoes; instead, he wore a crisp white shirt with the tie knotted perfectly, a newly pressed blazer and his shoes were gleaming. Colin was about to compliment him, but as Johnny sat, he could see the discomfort in his eyes. Had he been forced to dress like this?

There was a contradiction between the sixteen-year-old sitting before Colin – pale, underdeveloped, fearful – and the boy described in Johnny's application form. That boy was sociable, a champion chess-player, an excellent debater – that boy would surely look him in the eye, not stare off to the side as he picked at the scab on his chin.

'You write superbly,' Colin said, handing it to him, 'but

A Prayer Before Killing

there are parts which don't quite hang together, where it's hard to understand what you're driving at. I've made some suggestions.'

Johnny scanned the detailed notes Colin had provided at the end.

Danny and Garr's applications had talked about how devout and spiritually enlightened they were, and how they had a deep-felt calling to enter the priesthood. Johnny, on the other hand, had written a piece that appeared to be part autobiography and part allegory. Telling the story of a child, 'Antony', taken in by his grandmother and finding solace in faith, streams of consciousness were punctuated by paragraphs which demonstrated insight and emotional maturity.

'You've clearly got talent,' Colin said, hoping the praise might make him connect more. It didn't. Rather than engage with him, Johnny seemed more interested in the posters which lined the walls of the classroom: images of sad-looking saints and proverbs plucked from the bible, promoting moral rectitude. 'I mean it. I never used to read fiction, but I've read a lot of novels over the past year and I think it's a skill you should develop.'

'It's all my own work,' Johnny asserted.

'I'm not suggesting it isn't.' The detail was too personal to be anything else.

'Don't I get a grade?' Johnny asked, turning the pages back and forth to check.

'Not for an application. The comments I made should be enough to help you redraft,' Colin said, before adding, 'but it's got the potential to be an A+ essay. Honestly.'

A satisfied smile crept across Johnny's face. He folded the photocopy in half and tucked it into his blazer pocket. 'Thanks.'

'When it's finished, you should show it to your gran. It might help cheer her up, if she's still sad about the dog.'

Johnny stood.

'Hold on,' said Colin. 'Can you spare two more minutes?'

'I'm late for bible class.' Johnny gripped the back of the chair and his gaze began to wander again. 'Brother Thomas is expecting me.'

'It's fine. I'll explain to him that we needed to chat.'

'Is it about the other day?'

Since the fight, Colin could see that relations between the boys had improved, that Brother Thomas had most likely been correct in his advice. He nodded. 'I'm happy to put it to bed, unless you want to tell me what went on.'

'It was nothing important.'

'Then let's draw a line under it,' Colin suggested.

Johnny hung onto the chair, as if unsure whether or not to leave. With a sigh, he sat back down. 'But I did tell a lie, sir, about my gran's dog. He didn't die. I'm sorry.'

Colin smiled. 'It's never a good idea to lie, but I appreciate you telling me. It's the right thing to have done and I accept your apology.'

Johnny met his eyes for the first time. He returned the smile, and his entire face changed; instead of suspicious and defensive, it was now open and attentive. 'It's too long anyway, bible class,' he said. 'Two hours after school every Friday – it's too much.'

'That's quite a commitment.'

Johnny was about to agree but stopped himself. His expression became more reticent again, as though a voice in his head had warned him not to continue. 'I'm serious about joining the priesthood. There's nothing I want more, so it's important I attend.'

Colin had once felt the same calling. Eager to satisfy whatever the church demanded, like Johnny he'd forsaken other teenage activities, dropped out of the school football team, missed school dances and repeatedly let down friends. By the age of sixteen, the church owned him. 'Missing a few minutes of one class won't do any harm.'

A Prayer Before Killing

'Matthew's giving a presentation,' he explained. 'I'm helping him with the slides.'

'I won't keep you longer than necessary,' Colin assured him. 'It concerns the bangle you found.'

Johnny's face went scarlet. Whereas before his avoidance was directed at the posters on the wall, he now stared at his feet.

'Johnny?'

He stood, the scrape of his chair across the floor creating a painful, high-pitched squeal. 'Can I go?' he asked, his voice returning to a whisper.

'One more minute,' Colin requested.

Reluctantly, Johnny sat down. 'Are the police coming back?' Eyes unfocused, he stared over Colin's shoulder. 'Brother Thomas promised they wouldn't. That the police were happy it was a practical joke played by one of the boys and wouldn't be asking any more questions.'

'In your essay you mention that as a child "Antony" told a lie and allowed another boy to take the blame. I think in your conclusion what you're trying to say is that people are defined by their choices, good and bad. That we need to be honest with ourselves and others about all aspects of our character. Now, I may be wrong here, but was it you who placed the bangle on the statue?'

Johnny crossed his arms, his nails digging into his flesh. 'No. That never happened. I found it, that's all.'

Colin walked around his desk to sit beside him, placing a hand lightly on his shoulder. 'You can tell me the truth.'

It was the wrong approach.

Kicking the chair from beneath himself, Johnny sprang to his feet. 'You think you can come in here and be our best friend, don't you? Listening to everything Matthew and Luc spout. Well, it doesn't work like that.' He strode purposefully to the door and wrenched it open, flooding the room with cold air. 'Yes, I found Sister Oran's bangle, but that's all. My big mistake was telling the newspapers. They saw it as a way to ridicule the Church. I should have aimed higher, gone straight to the Vatican. That's what Sister Oran would have wanted.'

'Why would she have wanted you to do that?'

His expression was one of disbelief, as if the bangle was the most meaningful thing imaginable. 'You don't get it. No one does.'

Footsteps could be heard coming along the corridor, quick, certain. They would arrive at any moment. 'Tell me what I don't get.'

As the footsteps drew closer, Johnny slammed the door shut. Luc's face peered in through the glass, searching. Johnny gripped the door, his puny body managing to stave off the force of Luc trying to enter. 'The bangle – it's a miracle,' he whispered, 'and Sister Oran's going to be a saint. Wait and see. It's not the first miracle and it won't be the last. We're going to make sure everyone knows. That's what I told Dr Murray. But he wouldn't listen, said I was talking nonsense. But where is he now? He's a nobody. A loser.'

As Johnny got to the end of his sentence, unable to hold the door any longer, Luc pushed through. 'What are you playing at? Matthew's about to start and Brother Thomas is going apeshit.' He turned to Colin. 'Excuse the language, but are you done with him?'

'Yes.'

Luc took Johnny's arm and led him outside. As their voices trailed down the corridor, Colin heard Luc asking, 'What's up? Did he upset you?' But they were soon out of earshot.

He wondered if he'd pushed Johnny too far, and how he could have approached the subject another way, but there were few opportunities to question the boys individually – especially with Matthew and Luc around – and in the class-

A Prayer Before Killing

room those boys seemed determined to set the agenda for their classmates.

He didn't have long to wait for Garr to arrive. Humming a tune, he appeared at the door and settled himself on a chair.

'Is my application any good?' he asked.

But Colin was too busy looking at him to answer. From head to toe, he was dressed exactly like Johnny: immaculate uniform; hair neatly combed to the side. Then he realised Luc's appearance had been precisely the same.

CHAPTER 18
TWO YEARS EARLIER

Sister Oran ambushed Father Young outside the library to propose an expedition early the following morning. Involving a three-mile hike through dense woodland, the destination would be a small cove, where they would eat breakfast before returning.

'I'm not sure. We'd need to be back here by 7.40. Anyway, won't Sister Helena wonder where you've gone?'

'She's too busy praying.'

He thought for a moment. 'I don't know.'

'It's our special place,' she enthused.

'Our?'

'Mine and the four boys.'

'They'll not want me tagging along.'

'You couldn't be more wrong.' She squeezed his arm. 'They're just as keen as I am to show you there's nothing weird about our little jaunts.'

Though he was suspicious of her connection with the boys, another part of him could see how the trip might bring them closer and go some way to repairing relations. It might even make school life more bearable.

A Prayer Before Killing

'Okay,' he said. 'You've convinced me.'

However, he was far from convinced about the innocence of their relationship. Since catching them together in the gardens the week before, he'd paid close attention to their interactions, and it had become clear that the bond Sister Oran shared with Matthew, Garr, Luc and Johnny was extremely close, bordering on odd.

Across several days, subtle signs and gestures became apparent. For example, each evening at dinner she would place her left hand on top of her right, but it was actually a cue. All four boys – first Matthew, followed by Luc, then Garr, and finally Johnny – would stand and excuse themselves, with Sister Oran departing shortly after. Where they all went for those ten minutes before making a staggered reappearance he'd yet to determine, but he was confident he would, because the more he watched, the more he learned.

He'd also noticed during morning Mass, how the four boys constantly looked to her rather than Brother Thomas. Whatever topic was being discussed, with tiny nods and shakes of the head, Sister Oran provided them with a subtle commentary, an indication of the points on which she agreed and disagreed. Quite why they were so fixated on her, and why she had chosen to position herself as the arbiter of what was right and what was wrong, he didn't yet understand.

'We'll have a great time, I promise,' she continued. 'Now the only favour I ask is that you don't mention any of this to Brother Thomas.'

'That's not likely,' Father Young stated. 'But do you think it's wise to be so secretive?'

'It's not a secret. I just don't think he'd be open-minded; not like you.' Drawing closer, she stood on her tiptoes to murmur in his ear. 'Don't forget: 4.30. Beside the duck pond. Don't be late.'

He watched her dash down the corridor, only to be

accosted at the top of the stairs by Sister Helena, who appeared angry as she steered her in the direction of the laundry. Regardless, Sister Oran continued to smile.

THE SKY WAS clear and dark when Father Young arrived at the duck pond. There was a chill in the air and the water's surface was dead calm. He waited, wondering whether he'd been stood up.

After ten minutes, as light began to bleed from the east, he heard movement below. A moment later, Sister Oran emerged at the top of the path with the boys trailing behind her, subdued and bleary-eyed.

'Thank God. You're still here,' she whispered. 'This one,' she pointed at Luc, who hung his head, 'didn't he only manage to wake Brother Thomas? Had to dive back into his bedroom while we hid round the corner and waited until he'd returned to his lair. I swear that man has a sixth sense.' Sister Oran crossed herself. 'Shall we go?' Without waiting for a reply, she continued ahead.

The route was new to Father Young. Usually, he'd head north towards the hills, where the paths through the commercial forests were straight and clear. But Sister Oran took them south-west, downhill along a steep, rocky track which followed the course of a burn as it snaked through older woodland. Given how challenging the terrain was, he expected complaints from the boys, but as the sun rose into the sky and warmth filtered through the trees, they appeared content. Where the way was densely overgrown with thorny bushes, Matthew took the lead, holding back the more lethal-looking branches to allow Sister Oran, then Father Young, to pass.

'Thanks, Matthew,' Father Young said. A blank expression met his words. Good relations might exist between the boys and Sister Oran, but despite what she insisted, this did not

A Prayer Before Killing

appear to extend to him. He wondered what he'd need to do to win them over. Disappear?

'Thanks, Matthew,' Luc mimicked, causing the other boys to snigger.

Sister Oran stopped and waited until they'd finished laughing. 'Are you done?' she asked. 'I won't tolerate this sort of behaviour. Just as I chose each of you, I've chosen Father Young. Now apologise.'

The boys eyed each other, before muttering in turn, 'Sorry, Father Young.'

'You can never forget; we were all sinners once, alone and in need of love.' She turned to Father Young. 'We could cut across farmland at this point but we're going to keep following this gully down to the sea. We're less likely to be seen and it's quicker, but it's very steep. You need to watch out for loose stones.' She raised her voice. 'Matthew, if you can help Johnny. And Luc, see to Garr.'

'I don't need looking after,' Garr cried, jumping onto Luc's back. Luc grabbed Garr's legs and spun around, both boys screaming wildly.

'Quiet!' Sister Oran shouted. 'Or we'll turn around right now.'

Luc let go of Garr and they stepped into line.

Father Young stayed at the back while Sister Oran began to descend. Every few seconds she'd call back, 'Watch your step here' but mostly she led by example, manoeuvring her way from rock to rock, avoiding any loose soil and treacherous roots. She reminded him of a deer he'd spotted a few days ago, nimbly springing through the forest as if about to take flight.

The sulphurous scent of the sea was soon followed by the sound of waves lapping as the view opened up to reveal the Clyde. Minutes later, they were down by the shore. Father Young checked his watch – it was 5.45. If he was to be back at the school on time, they could only stay for half an hour and not a second longer.

'Isn't it the most glorious spot?' Sister Oran beamed. 'Named after St Fillan.'

Father Young looked around. Though relatively low, the cliffs on all sides were sheer; he couldn't quite believe they'd made it down safely. But the gently curved beach was sandy, and in the soft, morning light, the water sparkled – glimmers of silver and gold dancing on its surface. It was calm too, protected on both sides by rocks which extended out to create a natural harbour. 'Yes. You're right. It's beautiful.'

The boys sprinted towards the shore, throwing off their shoes and socks. Kicking and splashing each other, they met the cold of the estuary with squeals of shock.

'Can we go for a swim?' Matthew asked, tearing off his T-shirt.

'Five minutes,' Sister Oran shouted back. 'No more.'

Perched on a rock, Father Young and Sister Oran watched as the boys stripped, and wearing only their underwear, began a race out towards a buoy anchored a few hundred feet offshore.

'Is it safe?' Father Young asked. 'Won't they freeze to death?'

'Don't worry,' she replied. 'They're made of strong stuff and I haven't lost one yet.'

They remained sitting on the rock, basking in the early morning sun. There were so many questions he wanted to ask her: how this arrangement with the boys began, whether anyone else besides him knew of their early morning adventures and what each of them got from it, but that was for another time. For the moment, being at one with the surroundings felt enough.

'It's magical,' she murmured, her eyes closed. 'Don't you think? A place to heal.'

A Prayer Before Killing

He exhaled and felt the tension leaving his neck and shoulders. Gazing out to sea, he whispered, 'Yes.'

'It's crazy to think this is where many of the early Christian missionaries arrived from Ireland.'

Father Young turned. 'Honestly?'

'This very spot.' Her face glowed as she gripped his hand. 'Can't you sense their presence? Their righteous sense of purpose?'

An excitement rose in his stomach, a flutter in his chest. He wanted to hold onto this moment, ask Sister Oran more questions, but before he could, the boys emerged from the sea, shouting and shivering as they dried themselves with their T-shirts. Throwing their clothes back on, they made their way back up the beach, assembling in a semi-circle before them.

'Shall we?' she suggested.

The boys knelt in the sand and bowed their heads.

'Aren't we going back to school?' Father Young asked, confused. The boys laughed, but it wasn't the mocking laughter he was used to – its tone was more personal, kinder. Matthew looked up, smiled and nodded towards Sister Oran.

'Father Young,' she said, 'can I introduce you to some special friends of ours?'

Assuming he'd been tricked, his first reaction was to look around, expecting to find the rector and Brother Thomas emerging from behind a rock, declaring it all an elaborate joke. Instead, Sister Oran pulled back the sleeve of her habit to reveal her slender wrist. The boys' eyes followed as she raised her arm and gold glinted in the sun's rays.

Father Young squinted at the six enamelled charms which hung from the bangle on her tiny wrist. The largest was dedicated to Our Lady, but he couldn't put a name to the others.

'Go ahead, Matthew,' she instructed.

Standing, Matthew held Sister Oran's hand and raised it to his mouth. Delicately taking each charm between his thumb and forefinger, he kissed them in turn. As he came to the last – to the Virgin Mary – he closed his eyes and pressed his lips against it as though he might never release it. Once complete, he sat, then Luc rose and followed suit, followed by Garr and lastly Johnny.

The hand was not extended to Father Young.

As Johnny sat, she pulled her sleeve down, the bangle hidden away like the Communion host locked within the tabernacle. 'Our little ritual,' she explained.

They sat in silence as a slow breeze swept over the water, picking up grains of sand which swirled around them like fairy-dust.

Father Young finally asked, 'Who are the saints?'

Sister Oran smiled broadly. 'Well, the first is Saint Oran, the first Christian to be buried on Iona. Then, Saint Francis is Matthew's lucky saint. He renounced all his wealth and vowed poverty, chastity and obedience.' She crossed to Matthew and leant to kiss him on the forehead, cheeks and mouth – the sign of the cross, her lips barely brushing his skin. 'Saint George is Luc's. He was brave and selfless: a warrior-saint and a martyr.' Again, Luc's upturned face received the blessing of her kisses. 'Saint Thomas Aquinas is Johnny's, chosen because of his great mind.' The ritual of kisses continued. 'And lastly, Saint Michael is for Garr, the strongest defender of the church, chief opponent of Satan, and the one who assists people at the moment of death.' The ritual ended with a kiss to Garr's lips. 'Come on, boys,' she yelled. 'Shoes and socks on, we need to get back.'

They ran back to the shoreline, leaving Father Young and Sister Oran alone again.

'Don't I get a saint?' Father Young asked.

'You were given one the first day we met. D'you not remember?'

He shook his head.

'I took you into the church and showed you the painting.'

A Prayer Before Killing

'Of Saint Oran?'

'My namesake. One of the most special – a handsome fella, he came from my home town,' she said and kissed him lightly on the forehead. 'You can share him with me.'

'Come on,' voices shouted. 'You'll get us into trouble.'

Following Sister Oran, Father Young ran along the sand behind her, the boys' raucous laughter heralding their way.

CHAPTER 19

SUNDAY 19TH NOVEMBER 1995

That Sunday, after weeks of pressure, Moira finally got her way and Colin accompanied her to Mass. 'It might be my last,' she'd proclaimed. While he resented the emotional blackmail, and had deployed every tactic he knew to resist, once he relented, the pleasure on his mother's face was clear. Deciding to go all in, he even dressed for the occasion – his 'Sunday best' – a hand-me-down polyester suit from the 80s which Sean had outgrown.

In her good grey coat, with matching shoes and handbag, his mother had joined him at the hall mirror, hanging onto his arm while they waited for Jeanie. She beamed at their reflection. 'Us Buxtons, we don't half scrub up well.'

'Yes,' Colin lied, struck by her skeletal appearance.

Though Father Traynor was a charismatic speaker, even he had struggled to make the subject of that week's sermon – the indissolubility of marriage – sparkle.

'He's usually a lot better,' his mother insisted.

'You're not wrong,' Jeanie concurred. 'I was thinking he looked a bit peely-wally.'

A Prayer Before Killing

Colin laughed. It had been a while since he'd heard that term.

'It's all that jogging,' Moira declared. 'It can't be good for him.'

'I was actually hoping to have a word,' Colin said. 'Are you okay to sit with Saint Jude for ten minutes?'

The painting of Saint Jude – the patron saint of hopeless causes, which hung in the side chapel – was his mother's absolute favourite. Before she became ill, she would pray to it several times a week.

With Jeanie's help, he settled her on the front pew. 'I'll be quick,' he promised.

'You'd better be,' his mother stressed, gripping her bible with one hand, and handbag with the other.

As he walked down the aisle towards the exit, the first few lines of *Ave Maria* floated shakily towards the rafters. Pausing, Colin turned; his mother and Jeanie were transfixed. Saint Jude smiled down on them benevolently, an image of Christ clutched to his chest as he received the Holy Spirit in the form of a single flickering flame. Whether it was the upward tilt of their chins, or the uncertainty of their quavering sopranos, Colin couldn't say, but there was something enviable in their shared devotion.

He knocked at the front door of the parish house. Long familiar with the layout of St Bridget's from his days as an altar boy, he could have approached via the short corridor which connected house, vestry and church, but that would have been presumptive. Father Traynor wasn't expecting him, so a formal approach was best.

Mrs Beattie, the housekeeper – who he hadn't met before, yet always sounded stern on the phone – opened the door to reveal a physically formidable woman with a penetrating stare. She had the air of a cardsharp or a sniper even; Colin had to resist the urge to apologise and turn around.

'Yes?' she asked, her tone clipped.

'I'm Colin Buxton. I'd like to speak with Father Traynor.' He felt like a kid again, chapping on a friend's door to ask if so and so could come out to play. 'I know he's just finished Mass, but would you be able to check if he's available?'

To his surprise, she stepped aside and ushered him in.

'Wait there,' she said, pointing to a wooden chair before marching down the dark, panelled hallway.

The interior was unchanged. From the ages of twelve to seventeen, he'd been in and out of the parish house on an almost daily basis, jumping to Father McIlvanney's orders, terrified of the repercussions should he be found wanting. But after Father McIlvanney attacked Michael, his fellow altar boy, he'd never returned.

Pinny now exchanged for a beige Mackintosh belted tightly at the waist, Mrs Beattie returned down the hall, adjusting her headscarf. 'He's waiting for you in his study,' she said, sweeping past. The windows shuddered as she pulled shut the front door behind her.

While the furniture in Father McIlvanney's old study remained the same, the desk had been repositioned away from the window to be less confrontational, more welcoming. Colin found Father Traynor perched on the edge of the leather sofa lacing up a pair of trainers. Out of his vestments, he looked ten years younger. Wearing grey Levi's and a fitted white T-shirt, it was clear that Moira and Jeanie's assessment of his health was wrong; from the way his tanned biceps flexed, all that jogging was keeping Father Traynor exceptionally fit. The shock of the transformation was akin to finding him naked.

'Sorry, I've interrupted your—' Colin stuttered.

'Come on in, sit,' he beckoned. 'I've a few errands to do in town, but they can wait.'

'Are you sure?'

'Of course,' he insisted. 'It was good to see you at Mass. Is this going to be a regular thing?'

A Prayer Before Killing

'If my mother has her way, yes. But I don't know. It's strange to be back.' Colin sat on the armchair facing the sofa. 'A lot of ghosts.'

'I'll not push it.' Father Traynor smiled and met his gaze.

'I've left Mum with Jeanie in the church, so I'll not take up too much of your time.'

'How is she?' he asked.

'Not great, but her GP finally agreed to up her pain relief.'

'She's a persuasive woman.'

'She knows her own mind, that's for sure.'

'And you?' Father Traynor leaned forward. 'Feeling more settled at the school?'

'I'm gradually finding my feet,' Colin replied. 'But I've come to say I've an idea who planted the bangle.'

'Already?' Father Traynor raised an eyebrow. 'Who?'

'I've not got definitive proof – it's more circumstantial – but I think it was most likely Johnny.'

'Acting alone?'

'That's what I'm less sure of.'

'You think another boy – one of the Apostles – put him up to it?' Father Traynor seemed eager to hear Colin's response.

'Perhaps. But I can't work Johnny out and I'm struggling to understand how he fits into the group. He strikes me as a loner, but despite all the tension with the others, when he had a nightmare the other night, Matthew was there for him.'

Father Traynor shifted in his seat. 'Matthew was?'

'Whenever something's going on, he's never far from the action.'

'Thinking back, I suppose Johnny always looked up to him – idolised him like a big brother,' said Father Traynor. 'He had a hard time when his mother remarried – she basically abandoned him with his gran, went off and started a new family – and it was Matthew who took him under his wing.'

'Maybe I've jumped to a conclusion about the bangle, but there's definitely something weird going on between the four boys and Johnny seems to be at the centre of it. On Friday, they were all dressed identical: shirt, trousers, socks, shoes, ties pulled up right to the collar. To cap it off, they're each styling their hair the same, with the top slicked over to the side. They look like Oswald Mosley's blackshirts.'

Father Traynor shook his head. 'What's Brother Thomas saying?'

'Doesn't see anything odd. I spoke to him before I left on Friday and as far as he's concerned it's a phase – attention seeking – and they'll soon tire of it.' He noticed Father Traynor roll his eyes. 'There's something else – it's really what I came to ask you about.'

'Go on.'

'Johnny mentioned Sister Oran, and his desire to have her recognised as a saint. It's the sort of thing you would dismiss as fanciful, but his insistence wasn't normal. It was as if his life depended on it. Did Charlie ever discuss this?'

Father Traynor nodded. 'He did. But it's not just Johnny who wants this, the other Apostles have been pushing for it too. Charlie had to have words with them a few months ago; he thought they were becoming obsessed with the idea. His theory was they weren't coping with their grief, and that it was beginning to express itself in strange ways. He thought some of their behaviour was becoming a bit cult-like.'

'Well that's what it looked like on Friday.'

'I was under the impression that it had been dealt with, but with Charlie out of the picture, perhaps it's been allowed to ramp up again.'

'Have you heard from him?'

'The school keeps telling me he's not arrived in Maryland yet.'

'If you do, let me know. Meanwhile, I'll keep digging at the school, no doubt rubbing people up the wrong way. See how long I last.' Colin rose to leave. 'I'd better go. There are

A Prayer Before Killing

only so many prayers to St Jude my mum and Jeanie can make.'

'Thanks for popping by. I'll try phoning the States later.'

'Are the Apostles close to Brother Thomas?' Colin asked as he opened the door. 'If another boy – or staff member for that matter – steps out of line, he's down on them like a ton of bricks, but not them.'

'Close the door a moment; there are ears everywhere.' Father Traynor retreated to the sofa, doubt gripping his face. 'I'm not sure I should be sharing this, but here goes.' He held Colin's gaze. 'This needs to remain between us.'

'Of course.' Sitting, Colin waited while Father Traynor gathered himself.

'When I was a pupil at Holy Trinity, Brother Thomas taught me History. But only for a short time, thank God. We were all terrified of him. He was sent to Rome, plucked from obscurity to be put on some kind of fast-track programme for up-and-coming priests. But in those days, he went by a different name: Father Dunlop.'

Colin was unsure where this was headed, but was intrigued. 'Go on.'

'I don't know how much of this is true, but as they say, no smoke without fire. There was a big financial scandal at the Vatican a few years after he got there – accusations of fraud. It didn't make the papers in the UK but it was a huge story in Italy and a key witness in the case – the *star* witness – was a Scottish priest.'

'Father Dunlop?'

'He was never publicly named, but that's what I've been told. The rumour is Brother Thomas was up to his ears in it but managed to negotiate a deal in exchange for his testimony.'

'Which enabled the authorities to nab the big fish?'

'Yes.'

'Wow! It's a classic Mafioso tale,' Colin said. 'But no one's suggesting he's in witness protection? I mean he wouldn't have returned here if that was the case.'

'No. I think changing his name was a way to distance himself from the case and draw a line under it. That was Charlie's theory, anyway. He was gobsmacked when Brother Thomas walked right back into a teaching role at Holy Trinity five years ago with the full support of the church, no questions asked. But when Charlie queried it with Bishop Trocchi, he was shut down and given a lecture on forgiveness instead.'

'It might explain why he seems so keen to get rid of me,' Colin said. 'Having an investigator sniffing around will rankle.'

'It might not always seem like it, but he still has the bishop's ear. Trocchi's a weak man, more concerned about what others think of him than modernising the church. And possibly for good reason. There's a lot of talk about him having his own skeletons.'

An insistent rap on the front door interrupted their discussion, but neither moved.

'Mum'll be spitting feathers,' Colin said. 'I should let you go. But Father Traynor—'

'Call me Patrick. There's no need for formalities.'

'Okay. Patrick—' Saying his Christian name sounded odd, but much better than referring to him as *Father*. 'If you're so sure Father Young's innocent—'

'He is. One hundred percent.'

'Then who do you think killed Sister Oran? One of the Apostles? All four of them? Brother Thomas? Bishop Trocchi?'

Patrick shrugged. 'They all need to be looked at. Everybody does.'

'What about Charlie?'

Patrick shook his head. 'Rest assured; you can trust him. But be careful, Colin, and watch who you speak to. Just like here at St Bridget's, the rooms at that school have ears.'

PART 3

CHAPTER 20

For the first week or so no one had bothered to tell Colin there was a staffroom. Sitting at ground level and facing east, its floor-to-ceiling windows jutted out into the garden, angled to catch the morning sun. When it was bright outside the space had a certain drama but on a grey day it felt oppressive, as if the entire weight of the building was bearing down on everyone. Today was one of those days. It didn't help that the décor was terrible. In contrast to the public spaces which were kitted out with built-in, bespoke pieces or modernist classics, the room's mismatched armchairs and stained coffee tables suggested someone had decided to offload a pile of battered furniture on the way to the dump.

Since discovering it, Colin had made a point of visiting regularly; always busy, it was proving a good place to observe the mechanics of the school. Teachers would pop in to collect mail from their pigeon-holes or more usually, lounge around correcting work whilst grabbing a coffee and a cigarette.

As the newbie, there had been zero interest in him. While his colleagues were polite, when it came to conversation, they preferred to stick to their usual cliques. As far as Colin could tell, those were divided largely along subject and faculty lines. There was a stifling uniformity too; the staff was overwhelmingly male, white, with an average age of at least fifty-five. And from what he'd overheard, it sounded as if they were former pupils almost to a man. The exceptions were Caroline Wilson, a Classics and History teacher in her mid-forties and Ms Griffin, who pupils claimed had come out of retirement to teach Art and who routinely fell asleep during lessons.

'What do you make of our little sect?' It was Caroline – one of the few who'd bothered to acknowledge him in the corridors. As usual, she was dressed in tweed. Colin couldn't decide if she was extremely fashionable or extremely conservative; the pearls she wore today suggested the latter, but the car she drove – a bright red Audi coupé – hinted at a more adventurous side. However, there was no doubt she was posh; sounding like a BBC continuity announcer from the 50s, she'd the plummiest accent he'd ever heard. Unlike many of the staff, she conveyed a professional confidence; Colin knew she was the first to arrive at school as her immaculate car was always parked in the best spot beside Brother Thomas's. Although she didn't come across as pious, she typically occupied the front row at morning prayers and Mass. If not exactly popular amongst the boys, she was seen as a force to be reckoned with.

'I take it you mean—' he began.

'The four Apostles,' she said, finishing his sentence. 'You're helping them with their seminary applications, I gather?'

'Done and dusted.'

She drew a cigarette from a packet of Silk Cut and lit it. 'Is their fascist attire serious? Or perhaps an attempt at some pitiful performance art?'

Colin had expected the staffroom to be full of whispers and theories regarding their adoption of identical looks, but comments had been thin on the ground. 'I think they're trying

A Prayer Before Killing

to make a statement, but there seems more to it than simple attention seeking.'

She touched his arm lightly and drew him aside. The staffroom had almost emptied – it was only five minutes before classes started – but Caroline seemed as if she'd all the time in the world. 'Of course, Garr's the brains behind the outfit,' she said, carefully observing his reaction. 'Everyone thinks Matthew's in charge, but I'll bet any money it was Garr's idea. He looks the type who'd stick a knife in your back. A little Brutus in the making if ever I saw one.'

Colin frowned. Singling out Garr seemed odd – his impression had been that both Matthew and Luc were very much the group's ringleaders. 'I don't know them that well,' he said diplomatically.

She raised an eyebrow and blew a plume of smoke from the side of her mouth. 'You can't be much older yourself.'

'I'm 28.'

'As much as that?' Her eyes wandered across his face, then up and down his body. 'Surely not?'

'Well—'

'You're not like us old fuddy-duddies,' she grinned. 'As far as the boys are concerned, we're ancient relics, dug up from our crypts. They're much more likely to speak to you. And it would be good to know what's behind it all, don't you think?'

He'd had all four boys for a Social Education class the day before and had tried to steer the conversation towards the topic of community and identity, but uncharacteristically, the Apostles had sat back and allowed others to contribute. In fact, they had mostly remained silent throughout.

By this time, Colin and Caroline were the only two left in the staffroom. 'I spoke briefly with Brother Thomas about them before I left on Friday,' he said.

Caroline sniggered. 'Him? You might as well speak to that bloody wall over there.'

He smiled in agreement. 'I didn't get very far,' he said. 'His assessment was basically "boys will be boys". It seems to be his answer to everything.'

'That's par for the course.' She took a final draw on her cigarette before grinding it into an ashtray. 'While he might come across as your classic despot, Brother Thomas works in mysterious ways. It was no different under Charlie. A lovely man, but lazy as hell. He delegated most of the day-to-day management to Brother Thomas.'

'How long have you taught here?' he asked, attempting to steer the conversation onto another subject. He could always return to the thorny issue of Brother Thomas later.

'Too long,' came her curt reply. 'I should have got out years ago. But when the average size of a class is ten, the idea of trying to wrangle thirty sullen teenagers in the state sector doesn't bear thinking about. Best sticking with what I know, don't you think?'

He thought the question rhetorical, so was surprised when her expression suggested a reply was expected. 'It's never too late to teach an old dog new tricks,' he said before realising his mistake. 'Sorry, I didn't mean to offend.'

She pursed her lips. 'Colin, isn't it?'

'Yes,' he nodded, awaiting the slap-down.

'I bet no one's shown you around. Properly I mean?'

He shook his head.

'In that case, I'm going to show you the ropes – let you see how things actually operate round these parts.' Adjusting her skirt, she yelped. 'Shit! Is that the time? I'm supposed to be introducing the seniors to the Iliad!' Patting him on the arm, she whispered, 'We need more like you round here. Youngsters, I mean. Have you tried having a conversation with any of those boring old farts? It's like pulling bloody teeth.'

Colin followed her out of the door. 'I'll walk you to your class. I'm not teaching until second period – Sex Education.'

A Prayer Before Killing

'Poor you. They persuaded me to do it two years ago – or was it three? Then they tried to get me to teach it again, but I told them in no uncertain terms, "No. Way." It's a thankless task.' She strode ahead. 'Anyway, do you think anything will be done?'

Colin was trying to keep up with her quick, staccato steps. 'What about?'

'The four Apostles.' She turned briefly to stare at him. 'You do know why families send their sons here?'

'For an education, no?'

Caroline smiled. 'Adorable – so innocent! This place is all show; the building might look spectacular but neither the facilities nor the teachers are the greatest. And that's a fact. Yes, boys get a bit of education, but primarily it's about buying exclusivity, respectability and influence. Unless your child's on a scholarship – and there aren't many of those – you need to be rich and connected to send your son to Holy Trinity. And you've got to realise, the boys that families send here are not their firstborn. God no! They don't waste them on the priesthood. We get the not quite runts of the litter – more the ones that need taken care of, or steered in a safe direction, if you get my meaning. And you know it's not the worst option for an oddball. Within Catholic society, there's still cachet in having a son who's a priest.'

'So that's why Brother Thomas does nothing? To maintain a façade of what? Normality?'

'That's definitely part of it.'

'And is that why the whole bangle incident is being downplayed?'

They arrived at her classroom. Opening the door, she gave her boisterous class a look and without a word they quietened and took out their books. She closed the door over. 'When Sister Oran died – God bless her soul – at the behest of the parents there was a whole damage limitation exercise implemented to protect those boys; to distance them from the scandal so to speak. But the truth is all four followed her around like puppy dogs.'

'I knew they were close.'

'Close?' Again, the raised eyebrow questioned his naivety. 'Colin, if she wasn't shagging at least one of them, then strike me down and call me the Virgin Mary.' She shrugged. 'Even if the rumours were true – and I'm not saying they were – that girl should never have been allowed anywhere near children. She was too familiar, too fanciful. The fact those boys' names remained out of the press is down to one thing, and one thing only.' She rubbed her fingers together. 'Hard cash.'

'Where does the rector fit into this?'

'Charlie Murray?'

'Are you suggesting he orchestrated it on behalf of the families – keeping the boys out of the press and away from the police enquiry too? Because that's not been my understanding.'

She sighed. 'Charlie fancied himself as a politician, someone who could play both sides. And we can see how successful he was at that now he's been removed to God knows where.'

'Your sister school in Maryland, I believe.'

She let out a laugh, but it was tinged with darkness. 'Maryland? Well, that's news to me. What a comedown!' She opened the classroom door. 'Jasper,' she shouted, 'get your feet off that bloody chair or I'll break both your ankles.'

'Patrick – I mean, Father Traynor – has been trying to contact him.'

'What? The closet case who worked here for about two minutes and who had Charlie's ear from the get-go, whilst the rest of us had to make an appointment two weeks in advance?'

Colin didn't know what to say; he hadn't considered Patrick's sexuality. He had assumed, perhaps naively, that he was straight – albeit celibate.

A Prayer Before Killing

'One of the Apostles put the bangle there for sure,' she confided. 'Which one is anybody's guess, but it's Garr who pulls the strings, believe me. And yes, everybody wants it buried; after all the reputational damage to the school nobody wants the whole sorry scandal dredged up again. Besides, Father Young is guilty, I've no doubt about that. He was weird – pervy – always ogling me. I mean, if you enforce a vow of celibacy on someone, it distorts them.'

'But is a murderous priest not a bad look for a Catholic school?'

'Priest or not, at the end of the day, round here, it's the staff who are disposable. Not the pupils.' She turned the door handle. 'Watch who you talk to,' she warned. 'There are alliances stretching back years.' She smiled. 'But there's no need to worry about me, because I don't give a fuck about any of them and their nasty little secrets. I do my job, take the money, and count the days till my next holiday comes around.' Disappearing inside, she turned and smiled. 'Coffee break tomorrow?'

He smiled back, the expression *keep your friends close, but your enemies closer* ringing in his ear.

CHAPTER 21

TWO YEARS EARLIER

Since their adventure to the cove, Father Young had noticed a change in the boys' behaviour. Gone was the attitude as they entered his class, replaced by a grudging acknowledgement that he actually existed. He knew it wasn't much, but it felt like progress, however fragile.

Last period on a Thursday had always been the worst lesson of the week – the one he dreaded most. Regardless of which drama exercise or script extract he gave them, they'd reject it outright, refuse to cooperate, snigger and continue discussing the upcoming weekend or how much they enjoyed so and so's class better. But the first Thursday after their early morning jaunt had been different; all the boys, including Garr, had turned up on time, and he'd managed to steer them through most of his lesson plan without it descending into chaos.

However, it soon became clear that the ceasefire had only been temporary.

'This is utter shite,' he heard one of them say as he turned to write on the blackboard.

'Who said that?' He knew it was Luc, but before he could reprimand him, a pile of text books toppled to the floor. 'I

A Prayer Before Killing

need you all to concentrate,' he insisted, as he stooped to pick them up, aware that what little authority he had was unravelling.

He'd been working with them on an excerpt from *Blood Brothers*, trying to persuade them to adopt Liverpudlian accents, but all complained it was impossible. No matter how much he explained or modelled it, the class stared at him dead-eyed, as if he'd landed from Mars.

'Can't we just do our own?' Matthew asked. He rolled his script up into a tube and bashed it rhythmically against his leg. 'Cos there's no way I'm going to get it.'

'Me neither,' Johnny whispered.

'We sound like complete tossers,' Garr added. 'Why won't you let us use our own accents? What difference does it make?'

'I've already told you. It's about getting into character, understanding the rhythm of the text, not being afraid to fail.' But his words quickly trailed off as pandemonium took hold.

Matthew was the instigator – poking Johnny with his rolled-up script – but soon Luc was rolling on the floor with Garr trying to pin him down, as the rest of the class roared them on.

'Boys, can you stop that?' Father Young begged. 'Please.'

'We're getting into character, sir. Just like you wanted.' Garr thumped Luc's back.

The classroom door flew open and the boys scrambled to their feet, retreating to their seats. Silence fell. 'Is everything alright, Father Young?' Sister Oran stood in the doorway, her sharp gaze scrutinising each face. 'Are the boys behaving themselves?'

Her instant authority contrasted with his complete impotence. 'We're getting there,' he lied. To demonstrate his command of the class, he strode over to Garr and Luc and took their scripts. 'Let's show Sister Oran your scene.'

'But Father—' Garr complained.

'No buts, Garr,' Sister Oran interrupted. 'I'd like to see what you've been rehearsing.' She placed a chair in front of the two boys and sat. 'You know I like a good story.'

'They play brothers, Edward and Mikey,' Father Young explained, 'but they don't know they're brothers – one of them was given away as a baby.'

'That's me,' Garr muttered. 'I play Mikey.'

'You'll have to project more if I'm to hear you,' Sister Oran suggested. 'And it's a musical?'

'We're doing the play version,' Father Young said.

'Pity. They have beautiful voices, don't you? Like little angels.' Her withering look reduced both boys to quivering wrecks, terrified she'd make them sing.

'Can we have the script?' Luc asked, his hand stretching towards Father Young. 'Please?'

'What?' Sister Oran shrieked. 'You don't know your lines? What about you, Garr?'

Both boys bowed their heads.

'How long have you been practising?'

'They started last week,' Father Young said, 'so not long.'

'Rubbish. That's plenty of time.' She settled into the chair and held out her hand. 'Tell you what, I'll prompt them.'

He handed her a script. 'Page twenty.'

'From the top,' she said, flicking to the correct page. 'That's what directors say, isn't it?'

Father Young smiled and nodded, wondering why, with all his experience, he couldn't achieve what she was doing so effortlessly.

The ten minutes which followed were excruciating. Each time the boys opened their mouths, Sister Oran would correct either the line or the pronunciation. The other boys sniggered as lines were mangled, and the boys' pleading stares to stop were met with repeated commands to 'Do it again!' and 'Speak louder!' and 'Start from the top!'

When the bell mercifully rang, both boys rushed to pick

A Prayer Before Killing

up their belongings, cowed by the experience, as shouts of mockery from the other boys – 'Prompt, please!' – chased them out of the door.

'Thank you,' Father Young said, gathering discarded scripts from the floor.

'Let me help you.' She took the pile of scripts from his hands and laid them neatly on his desk. She then stacked the chairs. 'Really, you should make the boys do this.'

'There's never any time,' he explained, placing the last of the chairs against the wall. 'No matter what I do, they run rings around me. And Garr constantly appearing halfway through almost every lesson is causing a major disruption, but I can never catch him coming through the door. He's like a magician.'

'Oh no!' Sister Oran held a hand to her mouth and laughed. 'You're not serious? Surely you know how he does it.'

'If I did, I'd have stopped him.'

She crossed to the furthest wall and pressed her hand on one of the wooden panels. It immediately sprang open. 'It's a hidden door to the service stair – it runs from the laundry room in the basement all the way to the top floor. Sister Helena and I use it all the time, though Garr has no right being there. He knows that. I'll have a word with him.'

Father Young stared down into the darkness, then pulled the panel over. 'I'm an idiot, aren't I?'

'I can't believe no one showed it to you.'

'It's my own fault – I've not mentioned the Garr thing to anyone else.'

'They're playing you like a fiddle, and you're letting them. All the boys need is some basic leadership; it isn't complicated.' She gazed at the posters he'd put on the walls, images of classical amphitheatres from around Europe: Verona, Arles, Nimes. 'Have you been to all these places?'

He nodded. 'A few times over the past few years. I always

try to time my visits to coincide with a concert or a play. Most of them put on summer programmes.'

She peered closer, inspecting the detail of each. 'The furthest I've been is Dublin, then here.'

'We should go sometime.' The words were out his mouth before he knew it. Unlike priests, nuns took a vow of poverty, and all their earnings went into the convent. There was no way Sister Oran could afford such an extravagance. 'Couldn't the school organise a trip?' This placed him on safer ground, but even then, he knew that nuns didn't take holidays, and that any spare time would be spent with their families. 'I mean, for the boys.'

'They wouldn't be interested in that sort of stuff,' she said. 'Now, if you threw in a football, that'd be another story.' She pulled a chair towards his desk and sat. Picking up a large, heavy stapler, she turned it around in her hand, as though it was the first time she'd seen one.

He took the seat behind his desk, keeping a clear distance between them. 'When did you come here?'

'Three years ago. Something like that. Maybe four.'

He wasn't sure if she was being deliberately vague. 'You like it though?'

'I enjoy it, for the most part. Working in the laundry can get a bit monotonous, but I love being around the boys, helping to shape all that potential.' She replaced the stapler on his desk and looked at him. 'It really pains me that you detest it. You do, don't you?'

A tear stung the corner of his eye. His throat dried, and suddenly he couldn't speak. Instead, he nodded quickly.

'Not to worry. Fate's brought you here for now, and it'll soon be over. You've only got another, what? Nine months? Something like that.'

'Just over a year,' he corrected. 'But I'll be thirty by then.'

'There you go. You'll be entering a new decade and a free man before you know it.' Kindness shining in her eyes, she

A Prayer Before Killing

stared at him. Her compassion made him nervous. Envious. How could this nun – a girl from the middle of nowhere – possess so many qualities he lacked? She and every member of the clergy possessed confidence, empathy and understanding in abundance. But not him.

'Tell me about your acting career,' she said.

Father Young squirmed in his chair, unused to be asked such personal questions. Was she toying with him, trying to get under his skin? He was overcome again by a fear that she and the boys were in collusion, determined to set him up for more humiliation, but he didn't want to believe it. He pushed the thought to the back of his mind. 'You can hardly call it a career – *Skooch* when I was wee, then a few walk-on parts in TV shows nobody watched; it was all over with so quickly. There's not much more to say about it.'

Sister Oran leaned back and crossed her arms – as she did so, he glimpsed the bangle on her wrist, hidden in the folds of her habit.

'What's your passion, Father Young?' she asked. 'I mean, if you'd to choose one thing to do, what would it be?'

'That's simple. To be a missionary and help those less fortunate than myself. I was rejected for the programme – that's why I'm here – but I'm determined to apply again next year.'

'So you know your purpose. That's something precious to hold onto.' She stood and crossed to the poster of Verona's amphitheatre, scrutinising a spectacularly lit night shot of a singer standing centre stage amongst a sea of people.

'*Carmen*.'

'What?' She seemed lost in the world of bright lights and extravagant colours.

'It's an opera by Bizet,' he explained. 'She dies in the end.'

'How come?

'Her lover, José, kills her in a flight of jealousy.'

'That's sad.' She gazed at it for a little longer. 'I love the architecture. It's so dramatic. You think I could come and draw it sometime?' With her finger she outlined its shape.

'Of course. Just let me know.'

'It's the only thing I've kept doing since I was a kid. I can lose myself for hours sketching.' Moving away from the wall, her sleeve rose up to reveal the honey-coloured bangle against the pale white of her skin. She caught him looking at it. 'The boys revere this, you know.'

'I saw.' He realised he'd thought of little else since witnessing them kiss it one by one.

'Would you like to?' She ran a finger across the charms, causing them to chime faintly against each other.

He stepped forward, the faces of the saints shimmering in soft daylight falling through the window. He fell to his knees and, taking her hand in his, delicately held the first charm between his thumb and forefinger.

'Go on, you can kiss them all.' She turned away as he took each charm and kissed it, before his lips returned again to the first charm and kissed them all again.

A weird sensation gripped his body – akin to the one and only time he'd had sex. That had been in his late teens with a girl who he thought was the most beautiful being he'd ever seen. Stripped naked, he'd hungrily explored her body, his mind overcome with a feeling of exaltation he'd never experienced before or since.

That was until now.

CHAPTER 22
WEDNESDAY 22ND NOVEMBER 1995

'I need to ask a favour,' Colin said, pressing the phone to his ear to block out the sound of *Family Fortunes*, one of Moira's favourite quiz shows.

'Sure,' Father Patrick replied. His voice always sounded eager, willing to help, whatever the situation.

'Can you show me where Sister Oran's body was found?' From the press reports, Colin knew she was discovered in the tunnels beneath the castle, but without precise details, he could be scrambling around for hours, or even days, trying to find the exact location.

'I've not been down there for a while, and I'm no expert.' Patrick's tone wasn't exactly enthusiastic, but as ever, was friendly.

'I mean, only if you've time. I don't want to take you away from—'

'No, no,' he interrupted. 'I do know how they connect together.' He took a long pause, and Colin wondered if he should say something to fill the gap, but before he could, Patrick continued, 'Of course I can help you,' he said. 'When do you want me?'

Colin had been nervous about drawing Patrick further

into the case – his preference would have been to work alone – but he needed to make progress. And while everyone – including his own sister – seemed adamant that no one could be trusted, he'd decided to follow his instincts and ask for help. Given Patrick's connection to the church and previous association with the school, Colin knew it was a risk, but he felt it worth taking if it allowed him a better understanding of the circumstances of Sister Oran's death.

'Would tomorrow after ten work for you?'

Again, there was a hesitation. 'In the evening you mean? What about the boys?'

'Don't worry. I'm covering Thursday night duties; I'll make sure they're in their rooms by then.'

'And what about Brother Thomas?'

'He has Thursday evenings off.' Caroline had mentioned that Brother Thomas went wild camping every week – regardless of the weather – and that he was never back before six on Friday mornings. 'I think it's a safe bet he'll not be on the school grounds.'

IN AN ATTEMPT TO wear the boys out, Colin had organised a mini-football tournament after classes. He then press-ganged them into helping prep for dinner on the pretext that Sister Helena deserved an evening off after covering for Davey – the absent chef he still hadn't met. In truth, he'd negotiated a deal with Sister Helena whereby in exchange for covering her evening shift, she'd cover the first hour or so of his night duties. With her out of the way, Colin was free to dictate the boys' timetable.

He hurried them through their homework, persuaded them to take part in another mini tournament – this time table tennis – and started to dim the lights just before nine. By 9.45 all but a couple of the boys were in their rooms and five minutes later the final stragglers were tucked up in bed.

A Prayer Before Killing

Before slipping out to meet Patrick, he'd knocked on Sister Helena's door to let her know he was leaving. 'I'll be back by 11.30 at the latest, but there won't be any trouble – the boys are dog-tired.'

'I should really ask what you're up to,' she said.

'Nothing untoward,' he assured her. 'Just some business I need to take care of.'

'I'm not sure I believe that.' She narrowed her eyes. 'But on you go.'

Returning to his room to collect his parka, he was congratulating himself on how smoothly everything had gone when Garr caught him heading back downstairs.

'Off somewhere, sir?' He stood at his bedroom door in pyjamas and a dressing gown, holding a dog-eared book. 'Aren't you supposed to stay in the building when you're on duty? Brother Thomas always does.'

Colin zipped up his coat. 'I need some fresh air. Sister Helena's on hand if there are any problems. Anyway, shouldn't you be in bed?'

'I was getting my book from Luc.' He held up a copy of *Lord of the Flies*.

'It's great.'

'I know. I've read it several times.'

'Then you already know how good it is.'

Garr eyed him suspiciously, though there was nothing unusual in that. While on first impressions Garr came across as quiet and unassuming, he was anything but. When Colin explained something in class, it was always Garr who cross-examined him, ensuring not only he, but everyone else, understood. He was also the first to put his hand up, the one whose work shone above everyone else's, and a savage debater should any boy dare to contradict him. His mind sparkled.

'You could open a window,' Garr said.

'Sorry?'

'To get some air.'

'I need to stretch my legs.'

'What? After you refereed the football earlier?'

Garr's attempts at dominance were laughable. In his loungewear and slicked-back hair, he appeared less Mafia don and more child extra from *Interview with the Vampire*. 'Garr, get to bed, or I'll put you in detention this Saturday.'

With a sniff, Garr stepped into his room, slamming the door behind him. Colin still doubted Caroline's assertion that he was the real leader of the Apostles but he could see what a mean enemy he'd make, if pushed.

Outside, winter was fast approaching. A wind blew through the trees, cold and relentless, carrying a haze of rain that froze as soon as it hit his face. He pulled his hat down around his ears and made his way uphill towards the castle.

Anxious at being noticed, he knew the terrain well enough to guide himself without a torch. It wasn't far, and the path was clear of branches. Passing the duck-pond – eerily silent, its mirror black surface momentarily disturbed by a fish rising to the surface – he yawned and realised how little sleep he'd had. His mother's health was deteriorating daily, and her new medication was causing insomnia. The previous night he'd sat up with her until well after midnight, holding her hand and reminiscing about happier times, but she eventually grew bored and restless. In desperation, he had suggested a prayer, but she'd refused, turned her head away and asked him to leave, complaining, 'I can't do this anymore. I want to be on my own.' Annemarie's suggestion of a nursing-home was beginning to feel like the next logical step.

As the track grew steeper, the surrounding trees thickened and the view of the castle ruin narrowed. Continuing up the slope, the sound of running water told him he was close to the bridge.

A Prayer Before Killing

'What took you so long?' Patrick appeared from behind a tree, shining a torch in his face.

'You can't sneeze without someone noticing in that place.' Colin gave Patrick the once-over; wearing black from head to toe, he looked like the Milk Tray man from the adverts. 'You've certainly dressed for the part,' he joked. 'All you need is a balaclava.'

From his pocket, Patrick produced one and slipped it over his head. 'Scary enough?'

'Terrifying.'

'And you're sure you've not been followed?' His voice sounded a little panicked.

'Absolutely. They're all tucked up in bed,' Colin reassured him. 'Okay, let's get this done.'

'Where's your torch?'

Colin explained his reason for not bringing one, but this was met with an unimpressed *hmph!*

He soon appreciated Patrick's reaction. Even with the light from one torch, entering the castle felt like a plunge into the abyss; and the further they went, the darker the shadows became.

'Is it safe?' Colin asked.

'Don't worry.' Patrick gently took hold of Colin's arm. 'Stick close to me and you'll be fine.' With him leading the way, they scrambled through a series of rooms, the ground beneath their feet slippery and uneven.

'You're sure you know where you're going?'

'This was the main banqueting hall of the medieval keep.' He waved his torch around the tall, roofless space, disturbing a pair of roosting pigeons. There was nothing to suggest its previous grandeur; water seeped down the rough stone walls, collecting in puddles at their feet, and the stench of fungi filled the air.

'It's as old as that?'

'Older. It all started with a shrine to some saint in the 11th or 12th century; he came ashore nearby and the school chapel is supposedly built over the site. I was obsessed with the story as a teenager because he was a bit of a bad boy!' Patrick tugged at Colin's arm. 'C'mon.'

'Bit of a rebel in your day, were you?'

'I had my moments. Me and my pals used to come here for a smoke,' he said. 'Mind your head.'

Colin ducked and smiled.

'And we were sneaky – in all my years here I never got caught once.' He nimbly entered a narrow passageway, pulling at Colin to follow. 'Somehow I always remained in the teachers' good books. It's one of the reasons they invited me back after I was ordained.'

Colin remembered Caroline's other comment about Patrick having Charlie Murray's ear despite not being at the school for long. 'How did you find the job?'

'Honestly? They made it up on a daily basis. I covered classes a fair bit, then on other days I'd help Brendan in his workshop or out in the grounds. The core part of the job though was promoting the priesthood, going out to schools and youth groups trying to drum up business.'

'A bit of a spiritual jack-of-all-trades?'

Patrick smiled. 'I was also involved in organising school social events – fundraisers really. They don't seem to do them so much these days. Now, those were an education; people with more money than sense being given tours of the place whilst sipping champagne and talking about their holiday villas in the South of France. Horrific.'

'And you first met Father Young here?'

'Not exactly. I knew who he was before he arrived – we've a couple of friends in common from the priesthood – but I don't think we'd ever spoken before.'

Colin tripped over a large stone and was only saved from falling by Patrick's quick actions.

'Careful. The ground here's treacherous.' Patrick shone his

A Prayer Before Killing

torch ahead, illuminating a long, descending corridor with dank walls and a low vaulted ceiling. The smell of damp had intensified. 'This way.'

'You became friends?'

'Sorry?'

'You and Father Young?'

'I wouldn't say that. I'm more friendly with him now. It was a shame really – the guy arrived with all this fanfare about him being off the telly and how he was going to make education fun for the boys. But nothing could have been further from the truth. The boys didn't take to him, and he couldn't turn it around. He never settled. Too devout. Too fixed in his ways. Too boring. That was Brother Thomas's analysis anyway. On reflection, with a bit more support, I think something could have been salvaged, but the experience broke him. And the way his breakdown got mixed up with Sister Oran's death – it's tragic.'

In the darkness, without his dog-collar, Patrick seemed able to open up. 'And what was she like?'

'To me, uncomplicated. A naïve Irish girl, you know? The idea that she had this hold over Father Young seems absurd; she hardly registered with me. I don't think we ever exchanged more than a nod. When she disappeared, I could barely put a face to the name.'

Colin wondered how, in such a small community, this could happen. Had the relationship between Sister Oran and Father Young been overstated in the press? 'And you've never doubted Father Young's innocence?'

'Never. And I attended the trial every day.'

'Really?'

'Well, someone had to.' Colin wanted to press him more about his insistence of Father Young's innocence, but before he could, Patrick pointed ahead. 'We're nearly there, but if you're at all claustrophobic, prepare yourself.' He aimed the torch towards a turning at the end of the corridor. A narrow opening led into a stone tunnel less than two foot wide and six foot high. 'Watch your head.' Patrick gestured to the low ceiling and followed the path of the tunnel. Minutes later, he stopped. 'Here we are,' he said, his face masked by shadows.

'This is where she was murdered?'

'Not quite.' Patrick led Colin through a stone archway and cast the torch about, lighting up a small, square room, its walls black with damp and moss. He focused the beam on the ground; in the centre of the floor was a square of metal, like a manhole cover. 'There's another network of tunnels below which connect the castle to the chapel. Nobody knows why they were built or when exactly – whether it was a private route for the laird or whether it was built as an escape route for priests around the time of the Reformation. Certainly they go back centuries,' he said. 'The tunnel that leads to the chapel is gated and locked at this end. And there's another shorter tunnel which ends outside at the duck pond. There's a locked gate at the foot of the waterfall, but it's mostly hidden by the bushes and easy to miss. When I first came to the school, we were warned not to go anywhere near the tunnels. We were told they were used by local poachers but I'm not sure that was true.' He shone the torch back towards the manhole cover. 'The old dungeon is below us. It's where the tunnels converge and that's where Sister Oran's body was found.'

CHAPTER 23

Patrick positioned the torch on a ledge, focusing its beam on the ground where they were crouched, struggling to lift the manhole.

'I think you need to get your fingers into the grooves,' Colin explained.

'Like this?' Patrick asked.

He nodded.

'Damn,' Patrick cried. 'I think the batteries are starting to go. And I didn't bring any extra.'

'Then we'll have to be quick,' Colin replied. Though the flickering light and the slipperiness made it challenging, they persevered. 'This isn't easy,' he said. 'My fingers are freezing.'

'When I was a pupil, it was bolted and padlocked – very much out of bounds – but it looks like someone's taken a hammer to it. See here? That's where the bolt used to be.'

'You've never been down on the lower level before?'

'Once. An archaeological dig in my final year, organised by the chaplaincy. That's the only time.'

With brute force and a lot of sweat, they gradually manoeuvred the manhole cover out of position.

Colin paused to catch his breath. 'And Father Young did this by himself?'

'Supposedly,' Patrick's disembodied voice replied. 'And he's just an average size guy. About the same height as me, I suppose.'

'It's impossible.'

Patrick picked up the torch and shone it at Colin. 'But in court, it was never properly addressed. The prosecution said it wasn't secured and could have been opened using a lever – there was a piece of metal railing found here. But the defence didn't really challenge that. The prosecutor even suggested Father Young forced Sister Oran to help him.'

'Wasn't she tiny?'

'Five feet nothing,' he said. 'If the two of us are struggling, you do the maths.'

With more effort, they dragged the cover to one side to reveal the opening.

Patrick flashed the torch beam into it. 'Good. At least the ladder's still there; though I don't know how safe it is. It was pretty rusty when I went down with the dig.'

'I'll go first.' Colin took the torch and put his foot on the first rung. 'Wish me luck.'

'It shouldn't be too far. About ten, fifteen feet is my memory.'

Careful not to slip, Colin gripped the torch between his teeth and held tightly onto the rungs. As he descended, a smell of sewage filled his nostrils, and an icy blackness enveloped his body. It felt as if he was being buried alive.

'You okay?' Patrick shouted from above.

'So far,' he cried back, carefully manoeuvring his way down until he finally reached the bottom safely. 'That's me,' he called up, glad to be standing on firm ground. 'Make your way down but take each rung one at a time. You'll feel the ladder moving but it's stable enough. No need to rush.'

'Okay.'

A Prayer Before Killing

Colin held the torch up to light Patrick's way as the ladder creaked disconcertingly.

'Shit!'

'You alright?'

'My foot just slipped.'

To lessen its movement, Colin wedged his foot against the bottom of it. 'Keep coming,' he called. 'You've not far to go.'

'Fucking hell,' he heard Patrick mutter, the words echoing around the tunnel.

'You slipped again?'

'It's these shoes.'

'Almost there.'

Finally, Patrick hopped off the bottom rung. 'Christ, I must be getting old. Last time, I remember zipping down the ladder.'

Colin shone the torch around a long, low rectangular stone space with three openings off. 'What was this space used for?'

'This was the medieval castle's dungeon. Later, the Victorians used it as an icehouse.'

'I can believe that.' Colin shivered. 'You wouldn't want to be down here on your own.' The beam shut off for a second, plunging them into darkness, but then almost immediately reappeared.

'It's not the batteries – I think it's got a loose connection.' Patrick held out his hand. 'There's a knack.' He took it, swivelled the bottom of the casing, then shook it violently and the beam reappeared. 'Come on, this way.' He led Colin through the nearest opening into a stone tunnel even smaller than the one above them. 'Hold onto the walls, it's icy underfoot – and watch your head.'

Colin ducked and pressed his hands against the sides of the tunnel – water seemed to ooze from them. As they descended, cold air blew persistently, and the sound of running water could be heard in the distance. 'What's that ahead?' He squeezed past Patrick and found himself at the end of the tunnel where the sound of water was much louder. 'Can you hold up the torch?' he asked, raising his voice against the loud gush of water.

'Sure.'

A heavy metal gate, locked with an ancient, rusted padlock filled the mouth of the tunnel. Colin inspected the lock and pulled at the gate, but there was no give. 'And you're saying we're at the foot of the waterfall?'

Patrick shone the torch beyond the gate, lighting up a muddy patch of ground and some shadowy undergrowth. 'You can't see it, but it's a couple of yards to our left and the duck pond's straight ahead.'

'And that awful smell – is that from the ducks?'

'Maybe. I guess they might nest out there.'

'You mentioned another tunnel?'

'Yes. If we go back to the dungeon.'

Colin followed Patrick back along the tunnel. 'And this one leads to the school chapel?'

'Underneath it, yes – or that's what I've been told – I've never actually been in it.'

'So the only way someone could get into the dungeon would either be by one of the tunnels or via the manhole?'

'As far as I know.'

It was disturbing to imagine Sister Oran here on her own as the life of the school carried on above ground with prayers and lessons, and the relentless buzz of pupils. Down here was like a crypt.

'There's not much more to see,' Patrick said as they arrived back in the dungeon. He crossed the space and shone the torch into a shallow alcove. 'This is the start of the chapel tunnel.'

Colin stepped past him. Another heavy gate filled the chapel tunnel's entrance. On the other side of it, the tunnel proceeded for a few feet before descending into a stairway. The padlock to the tunnel's entrance was brand new, its silver

A Prayer Before Killing

casing glistening amidst the darkness. Colin tugged at it but there was no give.

'That looks recent,' Patrick said.

Colin looked more closely at the gate; as with the one at the duck pond, the bars were solid and tightly spaced, offering no opportunity to slide through. To access the dungeon from either tunnel, you would need a key. 'This tunnel must be some length – you say it goes all the way down to the chapel?'

'Yes, it's a serious piece of engineering.'

'Who has the keys to the gates?'

'I don't know. Brendan?' Patrick suggested, moving on. 'Okay. Last stop. And I warn you, this is going to be grim.'

The light from the torch dimmed as he took them through the final opening at the furthest end of the dungeon. Patrick shook it like before. 'The batteries are definitely starting to go now.'

'Then let's make it quick.'

A short passage led into a small, cell-like space with a low, vaulted ceiling which immediately felt colder and more claustrophobic than any of the other spaces.

Colin shook his head. 'This is where she was kept?'

'Not quite. It's up ahead.' Patrick approached the far wall; it was brick-built but had partially collapsed on the left-hand side. He shone along a ragged edge of loose bricks.

Colin joined him. Behind the brick wall was a further space, no more than three-foot square and five foot high.

Patrick stood in front of it. 'Father Young was accused of holding Sister Oran here. The prosecution said he bricked her up in this space, fled, then returned three weeks later and bludgeoned her to death.'

Three weeks spent here, cold and without food, would have been enough to kill her. So why hadn't Father Young killed her immediately? 'It was with an unidentified blunt object, wasn't it?'

'That was the accusation. Though they never found the murder weapon.'

'It's more than an accusation. That's what Father Young confessed to.'

'He did, but he wasn't in his right mind. The confession was coerced and that's why he's going to be seeking a retrial.'

'It's definitely happening?'

'Well, I'm encouraging him to.'

'I'd read a detail about a half-empty packet of crisps and an empty bottle of water being found with Sister Oran.'

'Yes, she'd eaten on the day she died.'

'But why would Father Young bring her food if he was planning to kill her?'

'The prosecution painted a picture of him as a sadist – that it was all part of his game, that he wanted her to suffer as much as possible. Raise her hopes before dashing them.'

'How long was she down here for?'

'She was missing for six weeks, but when they eventually found her, she'd been dead for almost three.'

Colin flinched at how much she must have suffered. 'So, she was definitely alive during the first few weeks of the search?'

Patrick nodded. 'The police searched the whole estate several times immediately after she went missing – that included the duck pond, the castle and the tunnels. They were out with divers, sniffer dogs and teams of volunteers but no one found any trace of her.'

'How could that happen? Even with her bricked up behind a wall, surely they would have heard her crying out for help?'

'I know, but they didn't.'

Colin squeezed through the break in the wall and crouched in the space behind. The cold and damp penetrated his body. In absolute darkness, how frightened and lonely must Sister Oran have felt? The horror of what she endured

A Prayer Before Killing

was overwhelming, and yet, nobody heard any cries for help; not even the police. 'Let's get out of here.'

Patrick helped Colin through the gap. 'We'd better hurry, my torch won't last much longer.'

They soon emerged from the lower levels of the castle and replaced the manhole to how they'd found it; it felt like resurfacing from a deep dive into treacherous waters. Thankfully once outside, the clouds from earlier had cleared. Colin exhaled and looked up at the starlit sky. It was a relief to breathe fresh air again. He checked his watch; in total, it had taken them twelve minutes to retrace their steps. 'I'll walk you back to your car,' he said.

Just as they were about to set off, a sound rose from below, howling and inhuman.

'What in God's name is that?' Colin asked.

'Believe it or not, it's the wind,' Patrick said. 'When it blows from the north it can make that noise. It used to terrify us as school kids.'

'I'm not surprised; it sounds like the dead rising.' Colin shook his head. 'I think that's our cue to leave.'

PATRICK HAD PARKED in a lay-by outside the school grounds, further on from the entrance gates. Huddled in the steamed-up car, they could still make out the top storey of the main building, its jagged profile rising darkly above the treetops.

'Can you go over what happened the week of her disappearance?' Colin asked. 'The bishop gave me the bare bones of the case, but it would be good to hear from someone who was at the trial.'

'On the Monday, the entire school had left to go on retreat to Grange Lodges.'

'And where's that exactly?' Colin wished he'd brought a notepad.

'In the middle of a forest in the Trossachs, less than an

hour's drive northeast. The school goes there every year. It's at the end of a treacherous B-road but the views of Ben A'an are stunning.'

'And everyone stays there together?'

'Absolutely, though it's as much a week-long team-building exercise as a spiritual retreat. The boys love it. They all stay in the lodges – well they're dorms really – which sleep four or five. Each day starts and ends in silent prayer but the rest of the time there's canoeing, orienteering, abseiling – fun, outdoorsy stuff. So, when Sister Oran went missing, the boys and the teaching staff were all away and accounted for. In fact, she waved them off.'

'And you didn't go?'

'No. Originally I was meant to, but I'd left the school by then.'

'So, who was left behind?'

'Besides Sister Oran, only Sarah, Brendan, Sister Helena, and Father Young. The last anyone saw of her was at 8 PM on the Monday but it wasn't until later in the week that she was actually reported missing.'

'Why was that?'

'Early on the Monday evening, Sister Helena saw her in the church praying and had a few words with her about not having stripped the bedding. But it was Sarah who said she saw her after that, heading off into the woods with someone she later identified as Father Young. He now says he left the school grounds on the Monday afternoon, well before Sister Oran was last seen alive.'

'To go camping?'

'Yes, though more like his forty days in the wilderness. On the Tuesday, Sister Helena woke up to find a note pushed under her door. It was from Sister Oran saying that she'd had to rush back to Ireland to care for her aunt. This had happened before, so Sister Helena didn't think anything of it. It wasn't until the Friday, when the aunt rang asking to speak

A Prayer Before Killing

to Sister Oran, that all hell broke loose. As soon as it became clear that the aunt was well and that Sister Oran had never made it to Ireland, Charlie reported her missing to the police and brought everyone back from the retreat. By the time they arrived at the school, the police had found Sister Oran's empty suitcase stored underneath her bed, clothes still in the wardrobe and toiletries in the bathroom, and had already faxed a copy of the note to the aunt who said it wasn't in her handwriting. Things really ramped up then: the police scoured the place, grilled the staff and then proposed questioning the boys. Believe me; that caused a hullabaloo.'

'The parents?'

'Got it in one. The term was about to end, and there was no way they could stop them going off, not with all the pressure from the families. But all the boys had alibis. Then, out of the blue, Father Young arrived back late July, saying he'd been camping in the hills close by. He was in a state of distress – exhausted, starving. Initially, he claimed that he knew nothing about Sister Oran's disappearance – which I believe is the truth. He happened to mention to the police a place she once showed him below the castle. They decided to search the tunnels again and that's when her body was found.'

'But there was evidence linking him to her?'

Patrick lowered his eyes. 'Yes, once Sarah decided it was definitely Father Young she'd seen walking Sister Oran into the forest, a semen stain found on her clothing was identified a few weeks later as a strong match to him. He confessed soon after but by that point he'd completely unravelled.'

On one hand it was pretty conclusive: a crucial witness, forensic evidence tying Father Young to the murder victim, and a confession. Little surprise then that he was convicted. But Colin had questions. If Father Young was the killer, why would he volunteer the location of her body? And why was the prosecution's assertion that he moved the manhole cover himself, or – just as implausibly – with Sister Oran's help, not queried? It also struck him as strange that it had taken Sarah weeks to identify Father Young as a figure she saw going into the woods with Sister Oran. Something didn't add up; even if Father Young was guilty, Colin sensed that the whole truth about the circumstances of Sister Oran's murder wasn't being told.

'There's one more thing,' Patrick said.

Colin leaned closer. 'What's that?'

'One detail didn't make it into the press, but everyone at the archdiocese knew before the trial. You see, during Sister Oran's post-mortem, it had been discovered she was two months pregnant.'

Colin couldn't believe he hadn't heard about this. 'Was it Father Young's?'

'According to him, forensic tests couldn't say for certain.'

'How come this wasn't reported?'

'That part of the case was heard in closed court.'

'That's highly unusual.'

'The Church pulled in every favour – I mean, every favour – to protect Sister Oran's reputation.'

'You mean *their* reputation?'

'Well, yes. By the way, Father Young maintains that there's no way he could be the father, and Charlie also suggested—' He stared ahead at the blackness of the forest.

'Go on.'

'Well, he thought one of the boys could have been.'

From what Colin had heard so far, this could well be a possibility. 'I'd like to see him,' Colin said. 'Father Young.'

Patrick smiled. 'I hoped you'd say that.'

'There's a lot that doesn't hang together.'

'That's what Charlie and I have been saying for months – years – now. With you on the case and Simon on the verge of retracting his confession, I think there's a real opportunity. I'll look into requesting a visit, but be warned, it can take up to two weeks.'

Colin let himself out of the car and waved Patrick off. As he watched the taillights disappear down the road and fade into darkness, he knew in his gut there were too many gaps in the week of Sister Oran's disappearance for there not to be something seriously amiss.

CHAPTER 24

Colin gazed out of the window as black clouds gathered in the distance. Typical. Soon, they'd be hovering above the school, and he'd organised his next few lessons outside. Though the boys wouldn't mind; rain, wind or hail, there was no stopping them. Anything that got them out of the classroom was considered a bonus.

He wrestled a box of bibs from the sports cupboard and placed it in the centre of the changing room. Buried within the lower ground floor of the main building, the space had seen better days; the stench of sweat had seeped into the wooden benches, ensuring no one spent more time there than necessary.

'So, this is where you're hiding.' Ever since their chat in the staffroom, Caroline had taken to bringing him a coffee in the morning break. She plonked herself on the nearest bench, her nose crinkling at the offending smell.

'Decades of teenage boys,' he said.

She slurped her coffee. 'You'd think I'd be immune to it by now.'

He took a drink of his own. Black, no sugar – just as he

A Prayer Before Killing

liked it. It was even the right temperature. 'You always get it spot on.'

'I'm trained to,' she explained. 'I worked as a waitress my whole time at Oxford.' She paused before blurting out, 'I hope you don't think I'm doing this because I fancy you?'

'Because you bring me coffee?' His expression of *What the hell, Caroline?* was met with a howl of laughter.

'I have this effect,' she teased. 'Men find me irresistible. But you don't, do you?'

He shook his head in disbelief, then realised from her widening grin that she'd caught him out again. 'When did you realise?'

She took a sip of coffee before answering. 'Call it woman's intuition.'

'Rubbish!'

'Okay. I'm used to men – and boys – looking at me. I know instantly.' She clicked her fingers. 'When you look me in the eye as opposed to these.' Feigning modesty, she adjusted her silk blouse. 'Either you're straight and actually interested in what I have to say – and, let me tell you, that rarely happens – or you're gay.'

Colin roared with laughter. 'How did they ever let you into the teaching profession?'

She drained her coffee. 'I turned up at the door one day and asked for a job.' She winked. 'You think I'm joking? Most of the teachers here aren't qualified. Though I'm glad to say, I'm one of the few who is.'

'I'm not qualified.' The words left his mouth before he'd time to think of their implication. They'd employed him for other reasons; reasons that couldn't be shared. Not even with Caroline, whom he liked and hoped to trust. 'But then again, I'm only showing a bunch of teenage boys how to kick a football around a field. It's not rocket science.' He hoped his self-deprecating remark might be enough to move the conversation on.

'Don't let the Grim Reaper hear you say that,' she said. 'Football's like a second religion to him.'

Colin coughed in warning as Brother Thomas's sudden appearance caught them both off guard.

Caroline stood as if standing to attention, spilling coffee down her front in the process. 'Shit!'

'Miss Wilson, I believe Sarah's looking for you. There's been a parental complaint.'

Blotting her blouse with a handkerchief, she moved towards the door, smiling demurely. 'I'll go see her,' she said, before turning and mouthing to Colin, 'Catch you at lunchtime.'

Brother Thomas waited as she left and the sound of her footsteps had faded. He then closed the door but remained standing. 'We need to talk, Mr Buxton,' he said. Whenever he appeared, it was typically straight to business – there were rarely any niceties.

Colin looked at the wall clock. It was 11.05. 'Right now?' He'd still to lay out the kits, and the boys would be arriving in ten minutes. The last thing he needed was a pep talk from the Grim Reaper – his new nickname from now on. 'I've not got long.'

Brother Thomas inspected the posters of some of the current Scottish football team which Colin had pinned on the wall – Ally McCoist, Paul McStay, a few others – their grins brightening up the dark room. 'This place needs a good spring clean,' he said, wiping his hands on the sides of his robes before lowering himself onto a bench.

Colin finished his coffee and set it aside. 'How can I help you?' he asked as he started to lay out bibs.

'This is quite delicate.' His tone had changed. Not friendly as such – that would be overstating it – but Colin hadn't heard him sound quite so human before.

He stopped what he was doing and gave Brother Thomas his full attention. 'Is something wrong?' His first thought was

A Prayer Before Killing

that the bishop had agreed to end his contract. After all, Brother Thomas clearly didn't want him sniffing about – perhaps, if Patrick was to be believed, as much out of self-interest as anything else.

'One of the boys came to me this morning,' he began. 'Rather upset if I'm being honest.'

Colin didn't like where this was headed. 'Who?'

'I'm not at liberty to say.' The veneer of friendliness had evaporated, replaced with a more characteristic sneer.

'Is there a pastoral concern? Or does this involve something I said or did?'

'You invited a man onto the school premises last night. Is that correct?'

So, this was how he was going to get him. 'Yes. I had a visitor.'

Brother Thomas appeared puzzled, as though he'd expected him to lie. Perhaps that's what he was used to.

'A friend popped by,' Colin continued. 'To say hello. He wasn't here for long and he didn't enter the school building.'

'Regardless, I'm afraid it's still against school policy,' Brother Thomas stated. 'If you read your contract, it prohibits any personal visitors whilst on night duties.'

'I apologise.' Colin crossed to the door and opened it. 'If that's all, the boys are about to arrive.'

Brother Thomas remained seated. 'Please close the door, Mr Buxton. I'm not sure you want anyone overhearing the rest.'

Colin gripped the door handle. The corridor was still empty, but there were rumblings at the top of the stairs. In a few minutes, the boys would appear.

He took a few seconds to find his words, as though rehearsed; Colin could see the machinations.

'As I mentioned, the boy who came to see me was very upset. In fact, I had to stop him from phoning home. Had he done so, we'd be having a very different conversation.'

Colin closed the door, its thud reverberating around the room. 'What's he told you?'

'That he saw you sitting with your "friend" in a car. That he saw you talking together. And that he saw you kiss. Each other.'

Colin remained with his back against the door. By now, a small group of boys had gathered outside, their faces peeking in through the long rectangular pane of glass.

Brother Thomas stood and lowered his voice. 'Such an occurrence, Mr Buxton, is grounds for immediate dismissal.'

'It's a lie. Yes we sat chatting in his car but the suggestion we kissed is ridiculous.'

'But the boy saw it with his own eyes.'

'And you're going to take his word over mine?'

Danny slammed against the door and flew into the room. As he picked himself up off the floor, Brother Thomas thundered, 'Out!'

Stepping over the threshold, Matthew grabbed Danny's arm and dragged him back into the corridor, pulling the door shut.

'I'll ensure no other friends visit in future. But to ease your mind about any kiss, the visitor was my parish priest, Father Traynor.' Colin held Brother Thomas's gaze. 'I really don't care what this boy says he did or didn't see me do, but surely you wouldn't want a priest's reputation to be tarnished by what I can assure you is a malicious accusation? I mean, after everything else that's gone on here.'

Brother Thomas's face turned ashen. 'No. Quite.'

'Was it Garr by any chance?'

'I've already told you, I'm not at liberty to say.'

'But we both know it was. Right?'

'It was *not* Garr.' Brother Thomas glanced at the door, searching for a chance to escape. 'I'll deal with it.'

'And before you go.'

Brother Thomas glowered at him.

A Prayer Before Killing

'Can you tell me when the new padlock was put on the gate of the tunnel which connects the chapel to the castle?'

Brother Thomas scowled. 'Is this to do with your investigation?'

'It's why I'm here, isn't it?'

'Speak to the caretaker. He'll know.'

Colin opened the door and was met by a sea of faces eager to know what was going on, but too terrified to ask.

'Morning boys,' Brother Thomas said, moving briskly along the corridor. 'Mr Buxton's ready for you now.'

Colin watched him hurry upstairs, off to ruin someone else's day.

CHAPTER 25
TWO YEARS EARLIER

Soaked in sweat, Father Young lay on his narrow bed staring at the ceiling. All around was silent. He glanced at his watch: 3 AM. With temperatures soaring, he hadn't slept a wink, and in a few hours he would be forced to get up and start the whole hideous school routine again.

He turned on his side, determined to snatch the smallest amount of sleep, but it was hopeless. An image of Sister Oran kept invading his thoughts. The same one he'd been dogged by for days – her breasts straining against the cloth of her tunic, her lips upturned, urging him to kiss her. But each time the image appeared, he made a ball with his fists, digging his nails deep into his palms. Usually the pain worked, however tonight it refused to go.

Rather than have a cold shower, he switched on his bedside lamp, picked up his bible and turned to a random page. Matthew, Chapter 5, verse 28: *But I say to you that everyone who looks at a woman with lustful thoughts has already committed adultery with her in his heart.*

He tossed the bible aside and threw back his covers.

Thrusting his head under the sink tap, the shock of ice-cold water brought him back to some kind of sanity. He rescued his bible from the floor and sat at his desk. *For everything in the world – the lust of the flesh, the lust of the eyes, and the pride of life – comes not from the Father but from the world.* John, Chapter 2, verse 16. Overcome by frustration, he clutched the pages to his chest.

His calling had come early. At sixteen, he was already an avid churchgoer: obsessed with his parish priest, Father Mahon, fascinated by the respect he commanded and by how much people listened to him. He seemed to occupy a different realm – a better one. And he became transfixed by the rituals Father Mahon performed. The calm authority with which he conducted himself was in stark contrast to his own chaotic life: the pressures of filming as a child actor, the demands of school, and his parents' neediness.

Having discussed it with no one, he went to Father Mahon and told him his plans.

'Are you certain?' the priest asked repeatedly. Still in his twenties, he had a confidence and control Simon found inspiring. 'Do you truly understand what you'd be giving up?

Immediately, an image of Jane Fonda exploded in his mind. Lips parted, staring into the camera, she lay on a bed of fur, wearing a black see-through outfit. In her hand she gripped a pistol, pointed upright into the air. He'd seen *Barbarella* twice and she figured prominently in his private rituals beneath the covers.

'Why not wait a few years?' Father Mahon's insistence suggested he wasn't quite ready, and so he reluctantly complied. It would take him another four years before he began his training.

But despite his unwavering commitment to the church over the years, deep down, his desires remained. Worse, they grew, morphing into all kinds of new cravings. Some he understood and allowed himself to indulge, others he refused to tolerate outright, wiping them from his mind, smothering them whenever they resurfaced.

Defeated, Father Young crept along the gallery barefoot. Moonlight lit his way, filtering down from the windows above, illuminating the edge of the atrium. Passing the boys' bedrooms, their soft snores sounded peaceful and innocent. Why couldn't they stay that way? Soon, morning would bring a cacophony of noise and the usual avalanche of abuse. It was all life had to offer him these days.

At the top of the stairs, he paused and tried to calm the shaking which engulfed him; the darkness below seemed threatening, an unknowable void of shadows. Using the handrail to steady himself, he made his way down to the drama studio. Truth be told, this had been his intention since Sister Oran told him about the secret panel; tonight, he would finally act upon it.

Though he knew each step took him further from the solitude of his room and closer to something forbidden, he kept moving forward. As hard as he'd tried to pull the blankets over, clamp his eyes shut and banish the invasive thoughts, they'd become too much to contain. They pressed him on towards Sister Oran's room; two floors below and across the little courtyard.

It was 3.30 AM.

Motionless, he stood in the drama studio, in front of the false panel. It wasn't too late to turn around. He could go back to his room and pray. In a few hours' time, people would begin to stir and there would be no possibility of going through with his plan. He'd rise as normal, have a shower, go for a walk before breakfast, then return to start the day. No one would ever know. He had no doubt this was the right thing to do.

But another urge took over. With both hands, he pressed on the panel and it swung open, inviting him to enter.

The shaking stopped.

Like a cut in the fabric of the building, a narrow window

A Prayer Before Killing

ran the height of the service stair. It allowed in just enough moonlight for him to find his way to the basement.

Stepping from the stairwell, he remembered the laundry room was to his left and the kitchens to his right. He'd been here once before when Sister Helena had appeared in a panic and asked him to help unload groceries. It wasn't the usual delivery man, and the groceries had been dumped in the loading bay. Father Young had said of course he'd be happy to do it. No problem.

It was the first time she'd smiled at him.

'Through here,' she'd said, guiding him into the kitchen. 'This is where the magic happens.' She'd rummaged through boxes, ticking off the order on a checklist stuck to the wall.

For the first time since arriving, he'd felt useful. Following her instructions, he'd stacked tins into cupboards, dairy, fish and meat into allocated fridges and sorted all the fruit and vegetables into their correct baskets.

'You can be my go-to man from now on,' she'd said as he made his way out. 'It used to be Brendan, but all he seems to think about these days is that wife of his.'

Remembering that conversation now, Father Young made his way through the kitchens and opened the door to the courtyard. Outside, the air was hot and humid, and the smell of rotting vegetables strong. Positioned outside the kitchen door, rubbish bins were overflowing in the dank courtyard, and as he crept forward, he stepped on something cold and soft. Juice oozed between his toes and he regretted not wearing shoes. On a rough area of concrete, he scraped his sole clean.

In front of him were the living quarters of Sister Helena and Sister Oran, a plain, single-storey structure. It was strictly out of bounds to staff and boys alike – not that anyone had told him – it was simply understood.

With a sense of relief, it occurred to him that the door to the nuns' quarters would be locked. Of course it would. He would be saved from this madness. So he took it as a sign to discover it ajar – possibly to let in some cool night air.

With the faintest of squeaks, the door swung open onto a modest space with a tiled floor – part hallway, part living room. In a corner niche, a votive candle burned at the feet of a small statue of the Virgin Mary. To either side of a square window sat two upright armchairs, and in the centre of the space, two dining chairs were tucked beneath a table. Ahead, the far wall was punctuated by three evenly spaced doors.

The middle one lay open and Father Young could see it was a shower room. He approached the door on the right and listened intently. The nasal snoring on the other side suggested an elderly person; it had to be Sister Helena's room. Which meant one thing; the door on the left was Sister Oran's.

With the lightest of touches, Father Young knocked. Though his aim was to waken her, he wanted to make it seem as if something had accidentally brushed against the door. As if he wasn't really there. If she didn't hear, he could return to his room, safe in the knowledge he'd tried. But a second after he knocked, a light turned on. There was no turning back now.

He held his breath.

A faint rustling was followed by the soft pad of bare feet on tiles. He was seconds away from having to explain why he was here, at her door, at this ungodly hour. Would she scream? Report him?

The door opened to reveal Sister Oran in a pink, quilted dressing gown, her hair neatly plaited. It was the first time he'd seen her hair, and his first instinct was to look away. But she appeared unbothered, smiled and his fears were replaced by relief. 'Father Young,' she whispered.

Overwhelmed by her lack of surprise, to him the words sounded like a welcome. But rather than step inside her bedroom, his legs failed and he found himself collapsing into her chest, tears flowing down his face, his hands gripping her shoulders.

She put her arms around him.

'I'm sorry,' he repeated over and over again, until she ushered him inside.

'We should pray,' she murmured in his ear, closing the door.

CHAPTER 26
SATURDAY 25TH NOVEMBER 1995

Colin turned off the portable TV which he'd positioned on top of the dressing table in his mum's bedroom. Having spent the morning in bed, too weak to get up, Moira had insisted she was well enough to go downstairs to the living room for her usual Saturday afternoon viewing, but as soon as she'd attempted to stand, she took a turn and he helped her back to bed. Bringing the portable upstairs from the kitchen had been his idea but she'd immediately complained that the picture wasn't colour, the reception dreadful and that she might as well listen to the "bloody radio". Drained by her outburst, she tried to watch a David Attenborough documentary about plants, however five minutes later she was dozing. He stayed by her bedside for another ten minutes in case she woke again, before switching off her bedside lamp and heading downstairs.

Dragging the telephone into the kitchen, he closed the door over and dialled. If Moira heard him on the phone, she'd wake and shout down, demanding to know who he was speaking to. He'd also started to sense that she wasn't altogether happy about him spending time with Father Traynor.

A Prayer Before Killing

For once Patrick picked up the phone, so Colin imagined Saturday must be Mrs Beattie's day off.

'It's good to hear from you,' he said. 'A nice distraction from the stack of parish paperwork sitting on my desk.'

'It's not exactly a social call.' At first, Colin had wondered whether to tell him about the accusation, but after weighing it up, he thought it best to be upfront.

He filled Patrick in on his conversation with Brother Thomas.

'What? You said it was me?'

Patrick was clearly rattled.

'Sorry. Only to appease him. But honestly, I wouldn't read too much into it,' Colin said. 'It's just boys making mischief. It's not exactly a secret that I'm gay, so if a boy sees that as a weakness, it's not surprising he'd try to exploit it.'

'Which boy was it?'

'Brother Thomas wouldn't say, but I suspect it was one of the Apostles.'

'Which one?'

'It's not Garr. I'm thinking Johnny. Maybe.'

'So, not Matthew?'

'Why'd you say that?'

'Well—' His voice sounded shaky. 'I don't know really, but he's the most observant, isn't he?'

'Certainly the most controlling.'

'And the one most willing to spin a story to save his own skin.' Patrick cleared his throat. 'A dangerous combination.'

'At the end of the day, it could be any one of them, or not even an Apostle,' Colin said. 'But don't stress – this particular accusation's going nowhere.'

'How can you be sure?'

'Because I reminded Brother Thomas that the last thing the school needs is another scandal involving a priest. That shut him up.'

'And you're absolutely positive?'

'You've absolutely nothing to worry about.'

'Then, good, I'll have to take your word.' Patrick sounded only partially relieved. Colin understood why; gossip tended to travel quickly across the parishes, and the last thing an ambitious young priest needed was their name associated with something salacious.

Colin turned as a knock at the back door was followed by a distressed-looking Jeanie hurrying inside, headscarf knotted tightly at her chin, overcoat buttoned to the top. 'That wind is something else – it near lifted me off my feet,' she cried, dumping her handbag on the worktop. 'Sorry, love,' she gasped, realising Colin was on the phone. 'Fifty feet from my house to here and I'm exhausted.'

'Make yourself a cup of tea. I'll just be two minutes,' he whispered. 'Sorry, Father Traynor, I'll need to run – Jeanie's just arrived.'

'Give her my blessings,' Patrick said, 'and thanks for calling. It's good to have a heads-up.'

'One thing before you go, is there any news on my visit with Father Young?'

Jeanie stopped what she was doing and pretended to look for something in a drawer. Colin could tell the name had aroused her suspicions.

'He's agreed to meet you, but a date's not been confirmed. I'll keep you posted.'

And with that, the line went dead.

'Why would you – why would anyone – want to visit that man?' Jeanie took off her scarf and threw her coat over a chair. 'You know the former rector tried to protect him? Suggested it was a bunch of boys who'd held that wee nun captive before cracking open her head. Imagine.'

Colin stared at her. 'How do you know this?'

'I know the woman who cleans for one of the families. The McGuigans – very well to do. What their poor boy went

A Prayer Before Killing

through was terrible.' She turned the cold tap on to fill the kettle. 'I don't know what the world's coming to; what with priests murdering nuns and others molesting boys. Is it any wonder congregations are leaving in their droves?'

At least Jeanie's point of view differed from his mother's, who continued to defend the church even when it was clearly indefensible.

'Garr was actually accused?'

She wasn't listening. Banging two mugs down on the counter, she continued, 'Though I suppose it's best to leave no stone unturned. In the end the police were having none of it. But the notion that a child could have committed such a crime – it's unthinkable.'

From the agitated way Jeanie's fingers drummed against the metal caddy, Colin decided not to press the matter. 'Mum's having a rest. I take it that's who you've come to see?'

'Tea?' she asked, but it was more of a command.

'Sure.' He poured milk into a jug and brought the sugar bowl across from the table. 'Is everything okay?' With her back turned to him, she nodded and plucked a couple of tea bags from the caddy. 'Jeanie?'

When she faced him, he could tell she'd been crying.

'Is there something wrong?' he asked. 'You've not fallen out again?'

'Don't mind me,' she said, pulling a hankie from her sleeve and blowing her nose. 'I'm just being daft.'

The kettle clicked off, and before she could reach out to pour the hot water, he took over. 'Go sit in the living room and I'll sort out a tray,' he said. 'I'll even see if we have any biscuits.'

She retrieved a packet of custard creams from her coat pocket and handed them to him. 'Your mum's only got Wagon Wheels left, and chocolate's not agreeing with me at the moment.'

Emptying the biscuits onto a plate, he carried the tray

through to the living room. There, he found Jeanie perched on the edge of the sofa, dabbing her eyes with the crumpled hankie.

'It's not like you to be upset,' he said, setting the tray on a small table beside her and turning the heat up on the fire. 'Tell me, is it Moira?'

She shook her head and bit her lip.

'You know you can talk to me?' He sat next to her and squeezed her hand. 'Take your time,' he said. 'Sugar?'

'Two,' she whispered, 'and lots of milk.'

She watched Colin pour, giving him a nod when he'd added enough milk.

'If it's not Mum, then what is it?' he asked. 'Is it something I've said? Or Annemarie?'

'Oh no,' she gasped, 'nothing like that.' She placed her half-empty mug on the tray, her eyes filling with tears. 'It's the anniversary of my Alec's passing and I just needed someone to chat with.'

Childless, Jeanie and her husband were known on the street for their close bond, despite their differences; she was kind and gentle, whereas he had a temper. He had died the year before from cancer, but it had been a long illness, and she'd nursed him the entire time. His mother said his death had devastated Jeanie at first, but miraculously she'd pulled herself together within weeks. Ever since, she'd devoted herself to caring for others. Not a day passed when she wasn't visiting someone: chatting, doing their shopping, keeping them company. It was the one topic on which Colin and his mother agreed. Jeanie really was a saint.

'He was seventy-nine when he died. Last month he'd have been eighty.' She picked up her mug and gazed pitifully at the milky liquid, lost in her thoughts.

'I'm so sorry, Jeanie.' It was the only words he could find to say. Perhaps she didn't need him to say anything, which was fine. He was happy to sit with her.

A Prayer Before Killing

'I shouldn't take up any more of your time.' She stood abruptly as if she'd realised she wasn't actually in her own front room. 'Ignore me, I'm being maudlin and there's no excuse.'

'Don't worry. Let me get you some more tea.'

But there was no stopping her. She was already headed back into the kitchen

before he could pick up the teapot, so he followed her through.

'I can go and check if Mum's awake.'

'Don't risk it, son. I just popped in for a chat on the off chance.' She collected her scarf and bag. 'After all, your mum knows what it's like to lose a man.'

'But my dad's still alive,' Colin said, helping her on with her coat.

Jeanie looked at him sideways. 'You know what I mean.'

He didn't and wondered if that's how his mother regarded his father, as if he'd already died. 'I'll tell her you popped by.'

Shuffling towards the back door, she turned to face him. 'I wasn't going to say, but it's better I do.' As if about to pray, her eyes dropped. 'Father Traynor's a good man,' she said, 'but he places too much trust in Dr Murray, if you ask me, especially when it comes to that wee nun and—' She couldn't finish her sentence. 'Your mum thinks the world of him. He's like a second son.' She patted his arm. 'Though now you're back, she's more settled, and it's good that she doesn't need him as much.'

'I'm not going to be awarded Son of the Year anytime soon.'

She gave him a tired smile. 'But you're a good boy. Not like that brother of yours, who barely picks up the phone to call her.'

'Why do you say Father Traynor trusts Dr Murray too much?'

'Because he led him astray. Persuaded him to step in and support that awful man – against all advice, even after all that terrible evidence in court. I've a lot of time for Father Traynor but on this I'll never agree – it reflects badly on him and it reflects badly on us, his parishioners.' She spat out the last words, her face agitated, the creases tighter.

The phone rang.

'You'd better get that,' Jeanie said, 'before it wakes your mum. I'll let myself out.'

The loneliness was etched on her face – a lifetime of it. 'Stay. I'd like to chat more,' he said, lifting the receiver. 'Hello?'

'Colin? It's Caroline.' Her voice was sombre, hesitant.

'What's wrong? How did you—?'

'I knew roughly which area you lived in and there aren't many Buxtons in the Glasgow phone book.' She fell silent.

'Caroline, has something happened?'

'I thought you should know,' she said. 'One of the boys has been involved in an accident. He's in a coma.'

'What? Who?'

'Johnny.'

His mind racing, Colin barely heard the rest of what she said – something about the police refusing to say whether it was suspicious or not – and Brother Thomas withholding further details.

'I need to go,' she continued. 'I'm on house duties later tonight.'

'Should I come in?'

'No, no – you've enough to deal with. Sister H and I have got it covered. The boys are okay – a bit subdued, though. Speak soon.'

He hung up.

'It's bad news, isn't it?' Jeanie said.

'Give me a second.' He dialled Patrick's number,

wondering what he'd make of this latest development, and was told to come round straight away.

'No need to explain, son.' Jeanie undid her coat. 'Go do what you need to do. I'll stay with your mum.'

CHAPTER 27

When Colin arrived at the parish house, darkness was falling. However, as he made his way down the path an outside light sprung on, illuminating the heavy oak door and surrounding shrubs. He knocked and an anxious-looking Patrick answered.

'Come on inside,' he said, shepherding him along the corridor and into his study. 'Have they said what his chances are?'

'I got the impression it was touch and go,' Colin replied.

Patrick crossed to a cabinet and opened it to reveal several bottles of spirits. 'I'm going to have a whisky – can I get you anything?'

'If that's a bottle of Ardbeg, I'll join you.'

Nodding, Patrick poured them both a drink. 'How did you find out?'

'Caroline rang to say.'

Patrick had to think for a moment. 'Is she the elderly teacher?'

'No, the posh, middle-aged one.'

Patrick grimaced. 'I know exactly who you mean. She really didn't like me.' He pointed to the sofa. 'Let's sit.'

A Prayer Before Killing

As Colin made himself comfortable, the phone rang. 'Get it if you need to,' he said.

Patrick lay his glass aside and answered. 'St Bridget's, hello?' Turning his back from Colin, he stared out of the window; a bright 'Hi!' was followed by a chuckled 'He's here' and a few minutes later by, 'Not a lot by the sounds of it.' Finally, Patrick said, 'I'll pass you over.'

Colin took the receiver from him, asking, 'Who is it?'

'Charlie Murray. He wants to speak with you. He has information about Johnny you should hear.'

Was this the first time Patrick and Charlie had spoken since he left the school? If so, the conversation between the two sounded very relaxed. 'Hi,' Colin said.

'Good to speak with you,' Charlie shouted above the noise of busy traffic. 'And a stroke of luck that you're at Paddy's.'

'Are you calling from the States?'

'No. No. Long story. But I'll have to be quick. I'm speaking from a payphone.'

'Okay. Patrick says you've information about Johnny. I take it you've heard the news?'

'Yes. Dreadful business. Let's hope he pulls through.' In the background, a car horn blared and another honked back, making it impossible to hear what he was saying.

'Can you repeat that last bit?' Colin yelled as Patrick hovered at his side.

'This morning, Johnny attempted to drown himself in the Clyde but was pulled out by a couple walking their dog. They called an ambulance and stayed with him. Saved his life. Apparently, Brother Thomas discovered a suicide note, addressed to him, in Johnny's room.'

'How do you know all this?' The line crackled, and it took all of Colin's concentration to catch the reply.

'Through a friend. A contact of Luc's family,' Charlie said. 'But I'm convinced this is connected to Sister Oran's death – that one of the four Apostles was the father of her child.'

'And you think that's been the motive for her killing? Even though they were away on the retreat with you?'

'Call it gut instinct. After years of teaching, you develop a sense of when people are lying and when they're telling the truth. I honestly believe Father Young's innocent.' Charlie paused. 'Damn, that's my money about to go.'

'Is there a number I can contact you on?'

'Sorry, but I can only be contacted at specific times.' The pips began to sound. 'I'll let Paddy know,' Charlie said as the connection was cut.

Patrick took the receiver from Colin and placed it back on its cradle. 'Did Charlie tell you about the note?' he asked, sipping his drink.

'Yes,' Colin replied, wondering how Patrick knew about it.

'Had you spotted any signs something was wrong?'

Colin reflected on Johnny's night terrors and his subsequent run-in with the other boys. 'Not really,' he shrugged. For now, he wanted to keep certain information to himself. 'I suppose I'll have to wait until Monday to see what's being said at school.' He looked at his watch and gulped down his whisky. 'I need to scoot – I've left Jeanie with my mum.'

'No worries. You actually saved me a call. I was planning to get in touch to let you know Charlie had phoned.'

'So, you'd spoken to him already?'

'Yes – he called me just before you did. But that was the first I've heard from him since he left.' Patrick swept his hand through his hair, tucking a stray hair behind his ear. 'You know he's not in America.'

'He mentioned. So where is he?'

'In Paris, staying with Hayley Falco.'

'I don't recognise the name. Should I?'

Patrick poured himself another drink. 'She works for Luc's family. Some kind of high-level advisor. Ensures that the family's reputation is never brought into disrepute.'

A Prayer Before Killing

'That's an odd pairing if Charlie thinks the Apostles know more about Sister Oran's death than they're letting on?'

'I think he just wants to get to the truth. He's cut ties with the school, so any loyalty he had to the church and the archdiocese has gone. He's not a priest after all.'

'And what's his relationship to Hayley Falco?'

'They met at a school fundraiser I organised a few years ago. I knew they had a professional relationship, but until today I'd no idea they were friends. Seemingly, it was Hayley who persuaded him to go to Paris rather than the US.'

'Does that not point to some sort of conflict of interest?' Colin stared at Patrick. 'For both of them?'

Patrick's expression clouded. 'Yes, I guess it does.'

CHAPTER 28

A grey shaft of light illuminated the altar as the entire school knelt, their heads bowed in suffocating silence. All except Matthew, Luc and Garr. They remained seated, staring straight ahead, their glacial expressions giving nothing away.

Since Colin's arrival at the school early that morning, no one – not a single boy or teacher – had said anything meaningful to him about Johnny. There had been no conjecture, not even any gossip. And when the special Mass with Bishop Trocchi was announced over the Tannoy, staff and pupils had made their way to the church and obediently filed into the pews.

To best monitor everyone's demeanour, Colin made sure to position himself on one of the side rows, close to the front. So far, there'd been only one, split-second break in the united front the Apostles presented; as Luc turned to Matthew and opened his mouth to speak, Matthew had flashed an admonishing stare and Luc, thinking better of it, had immediately resumed his fixed gaze.

Colin reflected on his recent visit to the parish house and

A Prayer Before Killing

what his conversations with Patrick and Charlie had revealed: Charlie's conviction that one of the boys was the father of Sister Oran's unborn child, that all four boys were on the retreat when she disappeared, but more importantly, Charlie's attachment to a woman who worked for Luc's family, a family who'd been instrumental in keeping the boys' names out of the press and the murder investigation away from them.

But the collusion between church and family to maintain appearances was nothing new – it was very much part of the culture. Since yesterday morning he'd been arguing with his own mother about that very thing. Tired and angry, she'd been on the attack as soon as he'd popped his head into her bedroom to ask if she wanted a cup of tea.

'What's this about you visiting Father Traynor again – and on a Saturday evening?' she'd demanded to know. Obviously, Jeanie had gossiped about the phone call she'd overheard. According to Moira, Patrick was overworked and should be saving his time for his parishioners, not a heathen and a sinner like Colin. The real giveaway however had been her final accusation, 'What will people think?'

Colin could understand her being jealous of his friendship with Patrick, but the subtext of her argument – that as a gay man Colin was somehow going to ruin Patrick's reputation by spending time with him – hurt.

Relations had still been tense that morning and he'd left for work slamming the door, saying he wasn't sure when he'd be back. As he stormed down the path, he'd instantly regretted it and almost turned back to apologise, but he didn't.

Looking flustered, Caroline appeared through the side door and sat on the same pew. Seeing him, she edged her way along, clasped his hand and smiled. This small act of intimacy felt like the first he'd experienced in weeks, like a hug from an old friend. He'd missed it. She seemed to read his mind and squeezed tighter.

'It'll be okay,' she whispered, before kneeling and bowing her head in prayer. 'He'll pull through, I'm sure.'

Colin glanced at her reciting prayers under her breath. She was such a contradiction; for all her bravado, she always seemed to toe the line when duty or deference called.

Heads bowed, Brother Thomas and Sister Helena sat behind the altar, awaiting Bishop Trocchi's arrival. Before taking his place, Brother Thomas had made a beeline for Colin, instructing him to stay after the service but offering no opportunity to ask why. Clearly, Brother Thomas knew more than he was saying, but given how antagonistic he'd been, Colin was struggling to see how he could ever be brought into his confidence. Sister Helena, on the other hand, though spiky, was an easier proposition.

Sarah and Brendan sat opposite on the far side of the church, their hands firmly clasped together; obviously, their relationship had its ups as well as its downs. Sarah was as immaculate as ever but Brendan, clean shaven, with his hair slicked back and wearing a suit and tie, could have been mistaken for a different person.

Sarah glanced up, caught Colin's eye and smiled, before leaning her head against her husband's shoulder. Both had been at the school on the evening of Sister Oran's disappearance, so he'd need to question them separately.

While Colin believed Johnny had placed Sister Oran's bangle on the statue of the Virgin Mary, he still lacked definitive evidence. Following his visit to the castle tunnels with Patrick, his theory was that Johnny must have somehow accessed the church from there, using a key. Therefore, Brendan might be able to explain how this could have come about.

Ten minutes late, Bishop Trocchi entered in a flurry of robes and took his place, centre stage, at the altar. In unison,

A Prayer Before Killing

the congregation stood, waiting until he gestured for them to sit. After the weight of silence, the harsh sound of school shoes scraping against the rough, concrete floor came as a relief. And, as everyone sat, the exhalation of breath around the church demonstrated they were human; maybe Sister Oran's killer was not here with them after all.

Without uttering a word, Bishop Trocchi retreated to the back of the altar, where he sat like an exiled king on a gold brocade presider's chair. Brother Thomas rose and stared out at the half-bowed heads before him, his new role of rector befitting him perfectly. 'This will be brief,' he began.

Caroline rolled her eyes muttering, 'Then get on with it.' But her voice carried, and a few of the boys turned to sneak a peek at the offender. Caught red-handed, her eyes darted towards Brother Thomas, but he didn't appear to have heard.

'As you'll be aware, we received terrible news on Saturday that one of our senior pupils, Johnny Doyle, was involved in an accident.' No gasps, no turning of heads followed. Instead, a silence of several seconds gripped the air. 'As a valued member of our scholastic family, we hope he'll make a full recovery. To that end, Bishop Trocchi has kindly joined us this morning to lead us in prayer.'

For thirty minutes, pupils followed Bishop Trocchi's sing-song delivery, repeating prayer after prayer; a chorus of hushed words filling the church and soothing their concerns. Matthew, Luc and Garr maintained their composure throughout, their identical attire and hairstyle strangely monastic.

Having concluded the extended Mass with a blessing, Bishop Trocchi returned to his throne, and Brother Thomas took centre stage again. 'Go directly to your period two classes,' he announced. Subdued, pupils followed his order and left the church in single file.

'I should dash. I'm teaching Italian fascism,' Caroline said, an ironic smile playing on her lips.

'Catch you at lunchtime?' Colin asked.

'Perfect,' she replied, before hurrying after the boys.

Colin remained seated. At the altar, Bishop Trocchi stood talking to Brother Thomas. This was unusual; whenever the bishop said Mass – which was seldom – he'd normally be out of the door and in his limousine back to Glasgow before the boys could reply 'Thanks be to God.' Though Colin couldn't see Bishop Trocchi's face, from the staccato movement of his hands and Brother Thomas's cowed expression, it was clear a reprimand was being meted out.

The bishop's rant over, Brother Thomas proceeded to bow and grovel, a pained scowl on his face. With a dismissive wave of his hand, the bishop disappeared through the door to the vestry.

Attempting to regain his composure, Brother Thomas turned to Colin. 'Mr Buxton, Bishop Trocchi would like a word with you. Now.'

'In the sacristy?'

'Indeed.'

'Is everything okay?'

'He simply wishes an update,' Brother Thomas said through gritted teeth.

'Of course,' Colin said. 'Can I ask, is there any news on Johnny's condition?'

'That's confidential,' Brother Thomas replied. 'His family – well, his grandmother – is at his bedside, praying. It's all we can do,' he added, stepping from the altar and heading down the aisle.

'Was it Johnny?' Colin asked, his voice echoing around the empty space.

'Was what Johnny?'

'Was it Johnny who reported seeing me in the car with Father Traynor?'

His lip curling, Brother Thomas stared at Colin. 'First Garr, now Johnny? Is this the calibre of investigator Dr Murray has foisted on us? One who thinks the world revolves around him and who makes random accusations?'

'Was it?' Colin asked again. 'Because if so, it might have a bearing on this so-called accident.'

'There's nothing so-called about it,' Brother Thomas said, his voice rising. 'Now, if you'll excuse me, I've a school to run.'

CHAPTER 29

Colin exited the main church to find Bishop Trocchi at prayer in a small side room staff referred to as the Rector's Chapel. Head bowed before a wrought-iron crucifix and murmuring softly to himself, the gold embroidery of his robes glinted in the soft candlelight. Unsure whether to disturb him, Colin waited.

'Mr Buxton? This way please.'

Colin turned. To his surprise, beckoning him from across the hallway stood the woman he'd seen leaving Bishop Trocchi's office on the day of his interview.

'Hayley Falco,' she said, offering him her hand, a heavy gold bracelet rattling at her wrist. 'Executive Assistant to the Colbert family.'

Her accent was difficult to pinpoint – French mingled with perfectly clipped English tones and a hint of American. 'Luc's parents?' he asked.

'And an acquaintance of Dr Murray's,' she replied, her emphasis on the word *acquaintance*, 'but then you know that already.'

'Pleased to meet you,' Colin said, puzzled by her presence.

Behind him, the bishop coughed.

Hayley's expression, which until that point had been serious, broke into a smile. 'Why don't we leave Bishop Trocchi to his devotions?' She pointed to a seating area. 'Shall we sit and chat?'

Following the heady trail of her perfume, Colin took a seat on a leather sofa.

Hayley sat opposite on a wide armchair, beneath a painting of the dying Christ, with Mary Magdalene and the Virgin Mary weeping at his feet. She crossed her legs. Everything about her appearance and attitude spoke of wealth and privilege: the bespoke suit, the flawless make-up, the unwavering assurance of someone who knows they're in charge.

'I take it you know why Johnny tried to take his own life?' Colin asked.

Hayley smiled. 'I think you're getting a little ahead of yourself, no?' She nodded towards the Rector's Chapel. 'But if you're asking do I have the confidence of Bishop Trocchi, then yes. And whether you and I can talk candidly, then again, the answer is yes.'

Given that she'd potentially interfered in the original investigation and then spirited Charlie Murray out of the country, instinct told Colin that her aim was to try to manipulate him. But was Hayley really the power behind the bishop's throne? If so, perhaps she was the missing piece of the puzzle. One theory suggested the case might be exactly as it appeared: that Father Young had abducted and killed Sister Oran to hide the fact he'd fathered a child, and the Apostles were simply a bunch of attention-seeking teenagers. However, Johnny's attempted suicide followed by this sudden intervention implied that some sort of cover-up may have taken place after all. 'So, what do you wish to discuss?'

She grabbed her handbag – Prada, Colin noticed. From it, she brought out a mirror and made a slight adjustment to her hair. 'You already know quite a lot.'

'Who told you that?' he asked.

'*He* did.' She nodded towards the bishop. Snapping her bag shut, she put it aside. 'Both here and in Europe, the Colbert family do business with the Catholic Church but they are also good friends.'

'You mean they give money?'

'I think a more fitting description would be benefactors. Yet, for all their generosity, there are those who criticise, implying that they have undue influence over church matters.' She leaned forward. 'As a representative of the family, I can assure you such criticisms are unwarranted – the family's motivations are purely philanthropic. Given the nature of their business, reputation is everything. And under no circumstances can their good name be compromised.'

Colin was tempted to question this contradiction, but stopped. He needed to hear more.

'Sister Oran's death was unfortunate. Therefore, when questions were asked about Luc, they acted swiftly.'

'You mean her murder?' Colin interrupted.

Hayley raised an eyebrow. 'Since the outset, the family have been keen to keep Luc's name as far from the case as possible, hence why they solicited Bishop Trocchi for his support. Which parent wouldn't?'

'The solicitation, what form did that take?' Colin asked. 'If we're speaking candidly?'

'A simple conversation between friends, a request for discretion.'

'And if I were to inquire about what donations were received around that time, there would be none from the family?'

Hayley's features tightened. 'As I've said, Mr Buxton, the Colberts are very generous. That summer there was, I believe, a substantial donation made by the family to help with a programme of restoration work; however, the timing is purely coincidental.'

'I appreciate why a parent would want to protect their

A Prayer Before Killing

child, but the interest Luc and his friends took in Sister Oran was unusual. You do concede that?'

Hayley glanced towards the bishop. His head had drooped to one side and he was snoring softly. 'A number of boys – Luc included – were close to Sister Oran. There's no doubt about that. But I don't think that's particularly odd in a male-dominated institution,' she explained. 'From what Luc has said, she was more like a surrogate mother to them all.'

'There's a theory that one of the boys – rather than Father Young – was the father of her unborn child.'

Hayley shrugged. 'Well, it can't be Luc. Sadly he was born with Klinefelter syndrome and is therefore infertile.' She briefly looked at her watch then settled her gaze on him. 'Mr Buxton, let me quickly tell you why I'm here. The Colbert family has changed their position on how they want the investigation to proceed.'

'But I'm not working for the Colbert family.'

She smiled. 'Recent events have reinforced the need to protect Luc at all costs.' Hayley sat upright. 'I'm thinking how best to put this, particularly in the context of Johnny's suicide attempt. Should an alternative narrative arise, we – the Colbert family – won't stand in its way. However Johnny's recovery plays out, it is now our belief that Matthew or Garr were somehow involved in Sister Oran's death. Murder,' she corrected herself. She stood and smoothed the creases from her suit. 'Which is why the family will be withdrawing Luc from the school today.'

'If I've got this right, what you're telling me is Johnny's suicide note points the finger at either Matthew or Garr?'

Hayley remained blank-faced.

Colin sighed. 'Can I interview Luc before he goes?'

'I'm afraid he's far too distressed to speak with anyone right this moment, and there's administration to sort out. Of course, we're all praying Johnny pulls through, but until we fully know his prospects, Luc will be saying nothing. I hope you understand?'

The bishop began to stir.

'Have you seen Johnny's suicide note?'

'With a little persuasion, I managed to obtain a copy.'

'And is there anything you can tell me about it?'

Hayley opened her bag and took out an envelope. 'Here.'

'What's this?'

'A photocopy of the note.'

He stared at it as she handed it over.

'What, did you think I'd keep it from you?'

It wouldn't have surprised Colin if Hayley Falco could produce anything he wanted from her handbag, though whether the note proved to be genuine or not was another matter. 'I appreciate the help but as far as I'm concerned, protecting the Colbert's good name has not been and will never be part of my remit.'

She held his gaze. 'You can assume that Bishop Trocchi … that *everyone* is now happy for the scope of your investigation to be widened. Brother Thomas is aware of this, too.' She handed him her card. 'Isn't that so?' Her words were directed at Bishop Trocchi whose ample frame now filled the doorway of the Rector's Chapel. He didn't respond.

'Phone me anytime,' she said. 'Now, I really should get going. I need to ensure Luc's departure goes to plan. It's been a pleasure.'

CHAPTER 30

Colin didn't have a class until after the mid-morning break and was determined to catch Sister Helena and, if possible, Sarah too. Both were at the school when Sister Oran went missing, and he needed to understand what they believed happened on the day she disappeared.

Colin retreated to an alcove, away from the din of the school refectory. Pulling the photocopy from the envelope Hayley had given him, he unfolded it again and scrutinised every detail. Scrawled on a lined piece of paper with a faint margin, it appeared to have been ripped from a jotter. He recognised Johnny's handwriting and it didn't look as if the content had been doctored in any way. The message was so short, so succinct, there was precious little to interfere with:

Dear Gran,

Please forgive me. I can't live with the guilt any longer. I'm sorry.

Love,
Johnny

Its simplicity was stark. As he re-read it, Colin tried to imagine Johnny writing these final words and picture his state of mind. While Johnny was a quiet boy – introverted – in the time Colin had known him, he'd exhibited a steeliness which seemed at odds with a suicide attempt. Considering this was a boy with ambitions to become a priest and who believed in miracles, what could have driven him to break such a Catholic taboo? The only explanation Colin could come up with was that the guilt he referred to must have been caused by something terrible: the worst sin imaginable. Murder. Was this the same conclusion Hayley had come to?

Colin refolded the photocopy, put it back in the envelope and placed it in his pocket. He prayed that Johnny would pull through – that he'd have the opportunity to speak with him again – to persuade him that forgiveness and redemption were possible in this life.

COLIN FOUND Euphemia sitting outside on the step, staring into the courtyard, smoking a roll-up. 'You haven't seen Sister Helena by any chance?' he asked.

'Oh yes,' Euphemia replied. 'She's commandeered the walk-in pantry.'

'Thanks.'

'I've told her we don't need any of her bloody soup,' she shouted after him, 'but it's like talking to a brick wall.'

Sister Helena was chopping carrots by the pantry window when he entered. The radio was playing, and she was humming along to an aria, but switched it off as he approached.

'No need to do that on my account.'

'The boys have asked for my special lentil soup for dinner tonight,' she snapped.

'Well, I can help, if you like.' Colin picked up a knife and began to chop an onion.

A Prayer Before Killing

She eyed him suspiciously but continued what she was doing.

'The boys are very subdued,' he said.

'Our Johnny's adored by them all.'

Her rosy take on the boys' relationships might bring her solace, but Colin wasn't convinced. 'No one seems to have any idea why he did what he did.'

She grabbed a leek, split it in two, and began to expertly shred it. 'He wasn't himself first thing on Saturday morning. He told me he felt sick and I made him some hot milk with sugar. He sat right there drinking it.' She pointed to a stool in the corner, now occupied by a large bag of potatoes.

'How long was he here for?'

She shrugged and grabbed another leek. 'Half an hour. Maybe less.'

'And did he say anything else? Anything out of the ordinary?'

'Johnny's not a big talker. Not like some of them,' she replied. 'There's some you can't get to shut up, but not my Johnny. He's such a gentle child.' She paused and lay down her knife. 'After a while he seemed to perk up. He said he felt fine and I told him he should get some fresh air. That he should go up to the pitch and watch the football; the junior team had a match against St Augustine's. But apparently, he didn't. Instead, he went straight to the cove. That's where he was found.'

'Whereabouts is that?'

'St Fillan's. It's a few miles along the coast.' Sister Helena collected the onions he'd chopped and placed them in a large saucepan along with the shredded leeks. 'I need to get this on the heat, if it's to be ready on time.'

'Did he walk there?'

'I imagine so. Apparently, it's where Sister Oran used to take him. And the others too, of course – Matthew, Luc and Garr.' Her dismissive look told him everything he needed to know; she disapproved. 'Their little jaunts were done in secret, and I only found out about them during the court case. If I'd known...' Sister Helena lowered her head and Colin wondered if part of her blamed herself for what happened.

'And Johnny was found at the same spot?'

'Bring the carrots,' she said, nodding.

Colin followed her through to the main kitchen where she poured oil into the pot and placed it on the gas hob.

'Can you fetch my lentils?' she said. 'They're soaking in the bowl over there.'

'No problem. Here you go.'

'Why he'd do something like that to himself is beyond me.' She made a sign of the cross and kissed the rosary beads attached to her belt. 'He's the sweetest of them all. An innocent.'

'What he did – do you think it had anything to do with Sister Oran's death?'

She shrugged as she tipped the lentils into a colander and rinsed them through. 'Maybe. Maybe not. It's not something we ever talked about.'

'They were close though?'

'I suppose. I know that he did look up to her, even though she was just a slip of a girl herself. Pass me that wooden spoon.'

'You were here the day Sister Oran went missing, weren't you?'

'I wasn't the only one,' she replied, snatching the spoon from him.

'Don't worry, I'm not accusing you of anything.'

She gave the pot a stir, then with a sigh, placed both hands on her hips and gave him a long, hard stare. 'Good. Because if you were, Brother Thomas would be keen to know. You're not one of his favourites.'

Colin smiled. 'Tell me something I don't know.' He waited for her response and was surprised when she giggled.

A Prayer Before Killing

'He's particular about who he likes and who he doesn't. It's all very arbitrary. Some might even say contrary.' She stepped towards him and whispered, 'He couldn't stand Dr Murray, for instance. Now fill that kettle and put it on.'

Perhaps there was more to Sister Helena than met the eye. He hadn't put her down as a gossip, but here she was ready to spill the beans without much provocation.

'What do you remember about that day?' he asked. 'You don't mind me asking?'

Sister Helena dragged the bag of potatoes from the stool onto the worktop and began to peel. 'The bus left for the retreat at 9 AM on the dot – me, Sister Oran, Brendan and Euphemia Baird waved them goodbye.'

'Father Young wasn't there? Or Sarah?'

'Sarah had a dentist's appointment in the village and got back around 10. As for Father Young, I assume he was in his room.'

'What about the other teachers? Had they all gone on the retreat?'

'Yes. Well, no. A couple were excused. Mr Oakley had left the day before to go down south; his father was ill. And Miss Wilson, she'd been having health troubles herself, so Dr Murray had given her the week off. Though she did pop up from the village around lunchtime and must have left mid-afternoon. I remember hearing the roar of her sports car speeding off – she's always on the go, that one. But all the other teaching staff were on the retreat. It's expected. Anyway, after the boys left, we all went inside to help the Bairds clean up the kitchen, to let them get away early. Apart from Davey, their eldest son, they were heading off to the retreat, too. Then I did my book-keeping, which I do every Monday morning. Around one o'clock, I came out of the office and spoke with Sarah – she was still in quite a bit of pain with her tooth – and we had a brief chat. She told me that the bus had arrived safely.'

'Would the bus have stopped off anywhere along the route?'

'For a toilet break, nothing more.'

'And Sister Oran?'

The kettle boiled and Sister Helena poured boiling water into the pot. 'Could you do me a favour and fill that again and put it on?' The smell of cooking filled the kitchen. 'Sister Oran had laundry duties the rest of the morning and would have been in her room most of the afternoon, studying scripture. She'd become much more diligent in the weeks before she died. I spoke to her briefly about 7 to remind her of her duties, but the last time anyone saw her was when Sarah spotted her heading up the hill with Father Young. That was around 8.'

'And when did you last see Father Young?'

'I made him a sandwich at about 1.30 – ham and cheese with some Branston pickle – but he just stood staring out of the window.' She stirred the pot. 'He took one bite of it, threw it back on the plate, then left without even so much as a thank you.'

Sister Helena's account fitted perfectly with the timeline outlined in the file given to him by Bishop Trocchi. 'I'll get out from under your feet,' he said. 'But tell me, you said you do the books?'

'Every week for the last twenty years. I studied accountancy at university.'

'Does that mean you have an overview of all the day-to-day expenditure?'

'I do, but I'm not the only one. I report to the rector. Why are you asking?'

'There's a new padlock on one of the gates up at the castle. I was wondering when it was replaced.'

'I wouldn't have the details on something like that. A padlock would come from the maintenance budget and Brendan has his own petty cash for that sort of thing. Or

A Prayer Before Killing

rather, Sarah would have done it for him and dealt with the receipt. He's not the brightest spark, our Brendan.'

She continued to stir the soup and Colin left, making a mental note to ask Brendan about it.

SARAH, he'd come to realise, had the aura of someone older who'd worked at the school for years. As far as he could gather however, she was about the same age as him and had only been at the school since she and Brendan married, six years earlier.

He placed a KitKat – taken from the staffroom – onto her desk. A neat bundle of folders obscured the offering, but she pushed these aside, picked up the biscuit and placed it in a drawer beneath the reception desk.

'Not got a chocolate tooth?'

'I wish! The complete opposite. Chocolate's my Achilles heel so I have to manage it. I'll keep it for my tea break.' She cast her eye back over the document she was working on, then realising Colin was going nowhere, looked directly at him. 'Sorry. Is there something else? It's just I'm a bit snowed under.'

'Five minutes of your time?' Before she could answer, he reached for a chair and dragged it closer to her desk.

She pushed her glasses further up her nose and swivelled round to face him. 'You can have two, otherwise I'll never finish typing up these reports. Actually, Brother Thomas had mentioned you might come to see me. It's an open secret you're a police officer.'

'From the age of eighteen to twenty-six. But not anymore.'

'I can see you in a uniform.' A light flashed on the telephone and she pressed a button to stop it.

'Please, don't on my account.'

'It's fine.' She looked at her watch, a designer brand he'd seen advertised on posters around the city. 'One second,' she said, jumping up from her seat and crossing to a filing cabinet. 'Before I forget, I need to file something.' As she opened and closed drawers, switching folders about, he noticed her hands were shaking.

'Can I ask about the sequence of events the day Sister Oran disappeared?'

She crossed behind him and returned with another pile of folders. 'Why does it matter what did or didn't happen that day? Father Young was convicted.'

'But not everyone believes that.'

A file slipped to the floor, its contents scattering. 'Let sleeping dogs lie, I say.' She crouched to gather the escaped pages, placing them neatly back inside the folder.

Outside the glass entrance, he could see Brother Thomas and Bishop Trocchi talking – it seemed the latter was leaving. There was no sign of Hayley. 'How sure are you that you saw Father Young with Sister Oran that evening?'

She wiped her hands against her skirt, glancing towards Bishop Trocchi and Brother Thomas. 'As certain as I can be.' She peered outside again, as if to reassure herself neither man was about to enter. With no more filing to do, she returned to her seat but swivelled back to face her typewriter.

'You told the police you spotted Sister Oran going into the forest at about 8 that night and that you were positive you saw Father Young walking with her. What made you so sure? As you know, Father Young insists he left the school hours before.'

'His height,' she said. It's what she'd told the police, and having read through the court transcripts, this hadn't been challenged by Father Young's defence team.

'What height is he?' Colin asked.

'Roughly six foot I'd say.'

'He's actually five eight,' Colin informed her.

She shrugged. 'They were on an incline. And Sister Oran was much smaller.'

A Prayer Before Killing

'Five feet in her stocking feet.'

She turned her chair to face him again as Brother Thomas's voice grew louder; it sounded like he was saying goodbye to Bishop Trocchi. 'The contrast must have made him appear taller.'

'For four months you saw Father Young every day. And in all that time, you couldn't distinguish whether he was six foot tall or five eight?'

Her attention was distracted by Bishop Trocchi's chauffeur-driven car drawing up. 'Well, I never took much notice of him, if truth be told.'

'Yet you staked a man's freedom by insisting that you knew for certain it was Father Young.'

'It *was* Father Young.'

Brother Thomas's voice was now declaring that he'd work to do in his office, but the car hadn't driven off yet, so Colin had a little more time. 'Can I ask why it took several weeks for you to come forward with this information?'

'I didn't put two and two together at first.' Her eyes were focused on Brother Thomas's movements. 'I didn't want to believe a priest could be capable of such a thing.'

'What was your impression of the relationship between Father Young and Sister Oran?'

'I didn't really have one. Colleagues, that's all. I wouldn't have put them together. He was a bit off-hand, if you want my honest opinion. As if he thought he was too good for the school. She was very young, a little eccentric; a bit of a country bumpkin. She wasn't a woman's woman, if you know what I mean?' The corner of her mouth twitched as if she was about to smile, but she stopped herself.

'You didn't see any glances between them, or touches, to make you think they might have been closer?'

Outside a car door slammed and she pushed back her chair. 'You don't need me to remind you, but Father Young was prosecuted in a court of law and rightfully convicted.

What he did – the shame he brought on this school – it doesn't bear thinking about. Now, if you'll excuse me, I really do need to get on.' She smiled. 'But thank you for the biscuit.'

The sound of footsteps crunching on the gravel outside increased as Brother Thomas approached.

'One last thing,' said Colin. 'It's a bit trivial, but you wouldn't happen to know if petty cash has been used recently to buy a new padlock?'

This caught her off-guard and she stared at him, confused. 'Sorry?'

'You look after petty cash for maintenance, don't you?'

'No, but I do occasionally help Brendan with it.' She thought for a moment. 'I seem to remember him talking about buying a new one, but I'd have to check the receipts.'

The entrance door was pushed open, and Brother Thomas entered. Without making eye contact with either of them he strode up to the reception desk, speaking over their heads. 'Sarah, can you ensure Brendan's packed Luc's belongings? Ms Falco's leaving with him shortly.'

Without hesitation, she jumped to attention and scurried towards the main stairs leading up to the dormitory level.

Brother Thomas turned to Colin. 'Haven't you any work to do?'

'My next class starts after the break.'

Colin waited for a barbed retort but instead Brother Thomas let out a sigh, 'I'm away the rest of today. Last period, cover for my class is still required, and from the timetable, Mr Buxton, I see you're free.'

'That's not a problem,' Colin said. 'I just need to make a phone call.'

'YOU'RE POSITIVE YOU CAN STAY?' Colin asked Jeanie, grimacing as the sound of his mother yelling in the background reverberated down the line. 'I know I'm always asking.'

'It's no trouble, though I don't know what's got into her today. She's like a dog with a bone,' Jeanie said. 'She's got it into her head that I'm going to forget to pick up her prescriptions. As if!' The sound became muffled as Jeanie placed her hand over the receiver and shouted down the hallway. 'Moira! It's just Colin. He's not going to be back till later.'

'If it helps, I can go to the chemist on my way back?'

'No, it's fine. I was planning to pop out anyway when Dr Hendry comes – get some fresh air. But I have to be away by 6. It's bingo night at the community centre.'

'Don't worry, I'll be back in plenty of time,' he said. 'Thanks Jeanie. You've been amazing these last few weeks.'

Her voice softened, became almost girlish. 'It's a privilege.'

As he hung up the receiver, the sound of raised voices filtered down into the atrium; above him, on the second floor, Brendan was wrestling with a trolley stacked with boxes, while Sarah gestured in front of him. As Brendan attempted to turn it, the boxes swayed and would have fallen had Sarah not stepped forward to steady them. Laughter filtered down through the atrium as they made their way towards the service lift.

Seconds later, Luc emerged from his room, followed by Hayley. Dragging his feet and with his head bowed, he was ushered down the main stairs. Still smartly dressed like the other Apostles, he cut a sorry figure. As they passed Colin, heading for the main entrance, Hayley gave him a sharp nod.

Colin checked his watch; there were still some time before break started, and with attention focused on Luc, he took the opportunity to go upstairs.

As Colin opened the door to Johnny's room, a gust of cold air hit him; opposite, the window sat wide open and curtains flapped wildly in the breeze. A puddle of rainwater had collected on the carpet too, making the spartan decor look even more pathetic.

As he closed the window, he caught sight of Luc and Hayley below, speaking with Sarah. Close by, Brendan was placing cardboard boxes into the boot of a maroon Bentley.

Working clockwise, Colin examined the room's contents. It didn't take long. A small stuffed bear sat on the bed, but there was nothing under the bedframe or the mattress. Johnny's wardrobe contained a few clothes and an empty suitcase. Jotters, folders and school text books were stacked on the desk but the drawers were bare, save for a few pens and pencils, and a jar of loose change.

He glanced out of the window again, to see the Bentley make a three-point turn and disappear down the driveway. Luc had left, along with any chance to interview him.

A long shelf above Johnny's desk offered the only hint at his personality; besides a well-thumbed bible, which used a photo of Johnny with an older woman as a bookmark (Colin presumed this was his gran) there were some comics and several sci-fi novels. A chipped ceramic piggy bank with its pink tongue hanging out was being used as a bookend, and Colin picked it up and shook it. The sound of something metal clinking against the inside definitely wasn't a coin. He frowned. Peeking through the coin slot, he saw a large greyish key nestled at the bottom. As he looked for a way to break it open and get at it, the door swung open.

Matthew filled the doorway, a frown on his face. He turned his head away from Colin and said something in a low voice. Seconds later, Brother Thomas appeared at Matthew's side.

'I can explain.'

'Mr Buxton – at this moment I've no interest in your pitiful explanations,' he snarled. 'We can talk about this violation of Johnny's privacy tomorrow.'

CHAPTER 31
TWO YEARS EARLIER – SUNDAY 13TH JUNE 1993

Father Young stepped outside into the warmth of the early June night. The sky was a kaleidoscope of colour: soft purples, deep oranges and countless shades of red. Glorious. He breathed in the summer smells of nature and made his way towards the castle ruins, guided by the full moon rising above the horizon.

Earlier that day, he'd discovered a note from Sister Oran pushed under his door, inviting him to meet her by the castle entrance at 11 PM. It was signed with several kisses. He'd gripped the letter in his clammy hands as he re-read it. Folding the note over, he'd placed it in a drawer beneath his socks; no one would think to look there.

His growing sense of anticipation had made today's humiliations almost bearable. It was the day of the annual football match – staff versus pupils – and he'd been dreading it for weeks, ever since Brother Thomas had press-ganged him into participating. The ninety minutes of play had been agonising, but while the boys ran rings around him, for once he wasn't the worst. Father Cochrane had managed to score two own goals and Mr Baines had had to be stretchered off with an asthma attack.

'Can't we admit defeat?' he'd asked Brother Thomas who, of course, was refereeing.

'Certainly not,' came his tart reply.

Father Young had struggled on. Younger than the others, the ball was passed to him repeatedly, despite his obvious lack of skill. And each time, before he'd even had the chance to think what to do with it, one of the boys – usually Matthew or Garr – would swoop in and snatch it from under his feet, scraping their studs against his shins. Yet when he protested, Brother Thomas waved for them to play on, telling him to 'man up'.

Sister Oran had watched the entire match from the sidelines, cheering them on. He'd tried to catch her eye several times, but she always seemed to be looking elsewhere. Had it not been for the note, his paranoia would have gone into overdrive. Over the past few days – in fact, since he'd appeared outside her room – whenever he tried to speak with her, she'd offered a feeble excuse and rushed off, or simply ignored him. He'd begun to worry she didn't like him anymore, that perhaps she regretted their friendship. But the note was confirmation they were on the same page, that his feelings were reciprocated, and that tonight – surely – she would fully commit to him.

He picked up his pace as the duck pond came into view – its still surface a perfect mirror in the moonlight. Reaching for a stone, he threw it and watched, waiting as the ripples spread out in concentric circles before calm returned.

He'd not been back to the castle ruins since Sister Oran brought him there that first day he'd arrived. With its smell of damp stonework and rotting vegetation, it was not his idea of a romantic meeting place, but he understood her choice: far enough away from the school to evade, yet close enough to dart back if their names were called.

Save for the chattering flow of the water, all was quiet as he crossed the bridge.

A Prayer Before Killing

The giant penis graffitied above the main entrance glowed in the moonlight. However crude, this time it made him smile – a reminder of Sister Oran's irreverent spirit and the depth of his own feelings. Tempted to pick up a stone and scratch their initials on the wall, he hesitated. The boys would notice immediately.

Father Young checked his watch and rubbed his arms against the growing chill. It was now closer to 11.30, and Sister Oran still hadn't appeared. He listened carefully, but there was no sound of anyone approaching. He wondered if she'd forgotten, or worse, had got cold feet. But why? After all, it was her suggestion to meet. Perhaps Sister Helena had caught Sister Oran slipping out of her quarters and was forcing a confession.

'Father Young?' Sister Oran's whisper rose from inside the castle, followed by footsteps which seemed to head deeper into the ruins.

She'd arrived before him.

He entered and struck a match, lighting up a cavernous space; a hollowed-out husk of stone, with half a roof, held together with creeping shrubbery. As he stood in the centre, trying to get his bearings, the match flickered and went out. Around him in the darkness, water dripped, not from rain but the constant dampness which seemed to pervade the place. He struck another match and slowly spun around. On the other side of a low doorway, he heard giggling and more footsteps, this time running away.

Ducking through the opening, he set off in pursuit, but the flame immediately went out, plunging him into darkness. He stopped and struck another, but it wouldn't light. Taking a couple more from the matchbox, he struck again and they flared into life. At the far end of the corridor a torchlight bobbed and he caught a glimpse of Sister Oran's habit disappearing round a corner. Holding the match up high, he hurried towards her, careful not to topple on the uneven floor.

That evening days before, when he'd knocked on her door and she'd opened it, he wasn't sure what he had wanted.

'I'm sorry…' he'd stuttered. 'I'm sorry…'

Sister Oran had placed a finger to his lips, repeating 'We should pray.'

Tears blinded him as he and Sister Oran knelt face-to-face on the soft fibres of the carpet. Her cool hand cupped his chin, as she encouraged him to raise his head. Wiping the tears from his eyes, all he could see was the bangle glinting at her wrist. In the lamplight, the charms turned and twisted, mesmerising him. Gently, the charm he now knew to be Saint Oran's, grazed against his cheek. He parted his lips, and took it between his teeth, drawing the charm deeper into his mouth, letting it rest on the tip of his tongue, as though receiving the communion host. In that moment he knew he'd finally found true meaning. He'd found a place to call home.

Arriving at the corner, he struck another match; the corridor continued ahead. Once again, he could just about discern the light from Sister Oran's torch fading around another corner. Why was she teasing him like this?

Hurrying to the end, Father Young called her name. From deep within the depths of the castle basement, a whisper replied, 'I'm here, Simon.' Striking match after match, he carefully made his way towards the source. Drawing closer, he emerged into a small stone room. She was nowhere to be seen, but for a second, light glowed from below. Shuffling closer, it became apparent there was a hole in the floor, with a steel ladder plunging into the abyss.

He put his foot on the first rung of the ladder and began his descent into absolute darkness. *This is madness*, he told himself. He counted twenty rungs, each more slippery than the last, before his feet stepped onto solid floor. Relief. In the musty, damp space he lit another match, and there in the corner, Sister Oran stood, her back turned to him.

'Sister Oran?' he whispered, but there was no reply, no

movement. He approached her and wrapped his arms around her tiny waist. Pulling her close to him, he leaned down to smell her neck, and she giggled.

At that moment, a series of torch beams lit up the entire space, blinding him. He backed away, almost stumbling over. It was the laughter he heard first, then as his eyes adjusted, he saw Johnny in front of him, ripping off the nun's habit. Matthew, Luc and Garr surrounded him.

'Man, he was totally going to shag you,' Matthew yelled, struggling to get all his words out without laughing. 'Look, he's even got a boner.'

'That's not true!' Father Young cried.

'What a paedo,' Luc said.

'We should have brought a camera,' Garr added.

Only Johnny, standing in shorts and a T-shirt, remained silent, his head bowed. But as he was closest, and because he'd been the one to fool him, Father Young shoved him aside, making him fall to the ground with a heavy thud.

'Fuck's sake, can't you take a joke?' he heard Matthew shout, as he turned and clambered back up the ladder, sick to his stomach with the knowledge that Sister Oran must have been party to this wicked prank.

CHAPTER 32

MONDAY 27TH NOVEMBER 1995

Colin returned home early evening to find his mother fast asleep on the sofa with the TV on mute. He crossed towards her, thinking she might wake, but she didn't. Up close, her cheekbones were sharp against her thinning skin, and both hands, rested one on top, twitched ever so often.

In the kitchen, a note from Jeanie sat next to the kettle, explaining that Dr Hendry had been late. It went on to say she'd been forced to leave early to get to the chemist's before it closed, but she planned to return the next morning with Moira's prescription. In shaky handwriting, the note ended by pointing out there were enough painkillers to see her comfortably through the night, whatever his mother tried to tell him.

Unsure what to cook for dinner, Colin opened and closed the fridge and a couple of cupboard doors. He was still thinking about being caught red-handed in Johnny's room by Matthew and Brother Thomas. It was clear he'd overstepped a mark and that, most likely, it was the opportunity Brother Thomas had been looking for to persuade the bishop to get rid of him. So be it, he'd continue his investigation regardless.

He wondered whether Patrick might be home and if he

could drop by and discuss the latest developments with him. Just as he was debating whether to give him a call or not, his mother appeared in the doorway looking woozy and with her dressing gown buttoned wrongly.

'I'd almost forgotten what you looked like,' she mumbled, her emaciated body shuffling past him. 'Have you put the kettle on?'

'Not yet, Mum. Do you want a tea?'

'No, I'll take a black coffee with three sugars.'

'Sure?'

'Haven't I just said?'

'You don't want some milk in it? So's not to upset your stomach?'

'Christ, am I going to have to make it myself?' She stared out of the kitchen window, into the darkness of the back garden and shook her head, muttering, 'Tea's for bloody invalids.'

Whenever she was in this melancholy mood, he'd usually leave her for half an hour, then return to see if she'd brightened, but there was something about her frailty that made him stop. 'Penny for your thoughts, Mum?'

'You wouldn't understand,' she sighed.

'Try me.'

She dragged herself over to the table and sat down. Even this small action left her panting. 'It's this life, son. It's done with me.'

'Don't say that.'

She shrugged, her eyes glazed and watery from the medication. 'I'm entitled to my opinion.'

He added three sugars to the instant coffee and stirred in boiling water before handing her the mug, ensuring both her hands were gripping it tightly. She took one sip before placing it on the table and pushing it away. 'Nothing tastes the same nowadays. I'm going to bed. Help me up.'

He took her arm and slowly guided her into the hallway

and then painstakingly upstairs to the bedroom, where she sat on the edge of the bed, catching her breath. 'Your brother Sean's not called in a fortnight. And Annemarie hates me.'

'Hate's a strong word, Mum.'

'Well, they don't like me, that's for sure.'

She wasn't wrong, but what did she expect? Her default position was to push people – including her children – away. 'You know they're busy, Mum.'

'Too busy to speak to their dying mother? And your father's no better.'

'But—'

Before he could chide her, she'd covered her face with her hands. His father had been in a home for over ten years, and they hadn't lived as husband and wife for as long as he could remember. His mental illness, then his recent diagnosis of dementia put paid to that. 'I'm sorry, son,' she whispered. 'I shouldn't have said that. Your daddy can't help himself. I'll say a prayer for him.'

After helping her off with her dressing gown, Colin settled his mother back on the pillows and folded the duvet around her. He then sat with her until she fell asleep, which wasn't long. As he turned off the light, he wondered if she'd remember any of this the following morning.

COLIN NO LONGER NEEDED AN ALARM. It was 6 AM and he was wide awake. He got up, did yoga for an hour, then took a shower. Regardless of what Brother Thomas thought, he intended to return to Johnny's room first thing and check what was in that piggy bank. If it was a key, he needed to find out what it was for.

There was no time for breakfast if he wanted to beat the traffic. Just as he was about to go upstairs to check on his mother, Jeanie appeared at the back door, brandishing an M&S plastic bag.

A Prayer Before Killing

'You're early,' he said. The fact that she stayed across from them on the cul-de-sac meant an easy commute to see his mother as early as she could.

'I'm always up with the lark, and I saw your lights were on. Did she have another bad night?'

'She didn't look great last night, but I think she's still asleep. It's me – I need to be in work sharpish.' Colin gestured to the bag. 'Is that my mum's pills?'

'Aye. I knew she'd be fretting about running out,' Jeanie muttered, placing the bag on the table behind the teapot. 'Have you had your breakfast?'

'No time. I'll grab a bite once I'm at school.'

'Why don't you run along?'

'You sure? I can wait another—' He looked at his watch. It was 7.30, later than he'd thought. 'On second thoughts, I'd better get going.'

Collecting his jacket and backpack from the hallway, he heard Moira moving about upstairs. 'That's me away, Mum. I'll see you later,' he shouted. But there was no response. He rushed upstairs and was about to enter her bedroom when she replied.

'Bye, son,' she said.

CHAPTER 33

The boys were going into Mass when Colin arrived at the school. Once again, there'd been an accident on the ramp to the Erskine Bridge, and he'd had to wait twenty minutes before it was cleared. There was just enough time to go upstairs and check Johnny's room again.

This time he ensured no one else was about.

The door was still open, so he stepped inside and closed it over. Picking up the piggy bank from Johnny's desk, he could immediately tell it was now empty. Had Brother Thomas or Matthew taken the key? Of course, neither would admit it. Why hadn't he stood his ground the day before? By backing down he'd lost the chance to prove once and for all that Johnny had had a key to the tunnel padlock in his possession.

Returning to the ground floor, Colin ran into Brendan who was carrying a step ladder. 'Just the man – can I have a word?'

'Sure. If you don't mind walking with me? I've a bulb to change out front.'

Colin nodded. 'Perfect.'

Brendan set the ladder up outside the main entrance as it

A Prayer Before Killing

started to rain. 'Not again! This has to be the worst weather for years,' he said. 'I swear it's rained solidly for two months.'

Colin agreed. Having got used to the warmth of India, adjusting to a harsh Scottish autumn was proving tougher than expected. 'I've been away for so long, I'd forgotten how grim it can be.'

'Nearly December though. Perhaps we'll get some of the white stuff.' Brendan's eyes twinkled at the thought. 'Do me a favour – can you steady this while I climb up?'

'Of course.'

'What is it you're after?' Brendan asked as he unscrewed a light fitting.

'Who holds onto the keys for the school?'

'Well, teachers have their own classroom keys, and I hold spares for those.' He fiddled about in his pocket and brought out a large key ring attached to his belt with a keychain. 'For pretty much everything else, that'll be me.'

'And that include keys for the castle ruin and the tunnels?'

'Uh-huh.'

'They're the only copies?'

'No, I keep duplicates of most locked in a cupboard in my workshop.'

'But it's only you who has access to the tunnels?'

He smiled. 'Can you imagine if the boys ever got hold of them? There'd be mayhem.'

'You're sure they haven't?'

'Look.' Brendan demonstrated how difficult it would be to unhook the key chain from his belt. 'This is with me every hour of every day. If they got a chance, sure, they'd take it. But no one would dare.' Again, the twinkle returned. 'Keeping them out of there is part of my job; it's dangerous down there, like a maze. And then after everything that happened…' His voice trailed off. 'Too many ghosts.'

'You recently changed the padlock on the gate to the church tunnel?'

He could see this register with Brendan. 'I replaced an old padlock with a new one during the summer. But like I said, the key's safely with me.'

'Why was that?'

'When the police were looking for Sister Oran, they understandably borrowed my keys, but unfortunately, I didn't get all of them back. I only noticed a couple of months ago that they hadn't returned that one.'

'So, you never had a duplicate copy of that key?'

'No, the old padlock was ancient and I only had the one key. I had to hacksaw it off, hence the new padlock.'

'Can I borrow it?' After everything Brendan had said, it was a risk to ask. But he needed to check for himself the various ways in and out of the school building.

Brendan drew closer. 'So it's true then?'

'What?'

'My wife's theory that you're not a teacher at all, that you're here to carry out some sort of investigation?'

Colin smiled. 'I couldn't possibly say.'

Brendan shrugged, then unhooked the key from the ring and handed it to him. 'Mind, I'll need it back.'

Emerging from the office, Colin noticed Sarah rushing towards them. Something in her concerned expression and hurried movements alarmed him.

'Sarah?' Brendan said, descending the ladder.

'Is everything okay?' Colin asked as she stopped in front of him.

'We've just received a phone call.' She glanced at Brendan. 'A Mrs Walsh has been in touch.'

'Jeanie?' His mind raced. 'Why?'

'Your mother's—' Sarah took his hand. 'I'm sorry, I don't know how to say this.'

'Sarah?'

'She's dead, Colin.'

A Prayer Before Killing

'But I—' He'd only left the house a couple of hours ago. 'You're sure?'

Sarah nodded. 'You need to go home immediately.'

CHAPTER 34

Driving up to his mother's house, Colin saw Jeanie standing on the front doorstep. As soon as she spotted his car, she put a hand to her mouth and rushed inside, returning seconds later with Dr Hendry.

He stepped out the car.

'I'm so sorry, son.' Jeanie wept.

'My condolences,' Dr Hendry said. 'With your mother's condition it happens – people can be taken quickly. She died peacefully, that's all you need to know.'

The reality of the situation began to sink in. 'I want to see her. Where is she?' he asked.

'Upstairs,' Jeanie whispered, 'in her bed.'

'The medical certificate's on the kitchen table,' Dr Hendry said. 'I'm afraid I have to go now, but here's my card. I've written my home number on the back. If you've any questions, you can call me later.'

The sky darkened and rain began to fall in large drops, spattering the front path. And as Colin watched Dr Hendry drive off, the entire scene played out in slow motion as the words 'died peacefully' echoed in his head. It wasn't possible;

only a few hours earlier, he'd heard his mother whisper goodbye.

'Come here, son. Let's get you inside and out of the cold.'

Wrapping her arms around him, Jeanie drew Colin into the hallway and closed the front door. His head was pulled to her chest, and suddenly he was like a child again, being comforted after falling from his bike.

'You're sure you want to see her?' Jeanie asked, wiping her eyes.

'Yes,' Colin replied.

She led him up to the landing and opened his mother's bedroom door, releasing a strong smell of disinfectant. 'Your mum's finally at peace,' she said. 'Do you want me to stay with you?'

'No, I'll be fine.'

As Jeanie went downstairs, he crossed to the foot of the bed and stared, dry-eyed, at his mother's body. Though he'd seen dead bodies before, this was different. Of course it was. This was his mother. Lying with her eyes closed and hands resting at her sides, it was easy to imagine she was asleep, like yesterday when he arrived home and found her dozing on the sofa. The idea that less than twenty-four hours earlier she was bickering with him in the kitchen made no sense.

A sheet had been pulled off the bed and lay on the carpet, crumpled at his feet. The mess reminded him of washdays when he was growing up, the beds in the house stripped bare as his mother set about washing and drying all of the bedclothes in one day. As a child, the task had appeared both thankless and herculean to him, and his mother a miracle worker at getting it all done.

Colin sat on the edge of the bed and took his mother's hand. For a moment he imagined it still warm, but when he pressed his lips against her palm it was stone cold. However, her smell, so distinctive – a sweet, vanilla concoction derived from perfume and creams – lingered. He closed his eyes and breathed deeply, vowing never to forget.

When he re-opened them, the objects in the room appeared more real than ever, as if they'd been superimposed. The ornaments his mother kept dotted about – sentimental knickknacks that she polished each day – stood out colourfully against the dull, magnolia walls. There were framed photos too, of him, and Sean, and Annemarie as children. Like religious icons, they'd been placed carefully on the dresser to one side of his mother's jewellery box. To the other side, pictures of her grandchildren stood in front of his favourite photo: his parents together at the beach, young and in love, just before they got married, their whole lives ahead of them. For someone who had constantly railed against her family, it was comforting to see they featured so heavily in her most private space.

The screech of a car coming to a halt outside was followed seconds later by an ungodly wailing. Footsteps bounded up the stairs and the door flew open. Annemarie flung herself at him, hugging him close. They clutched each other, her sobs beating against his chest.

'I can't believe she's gone,' she sobbed.

'I know. I know.'

'Were you with her?'

'No, I was at work. Jeanie was here, I think.' Colin glanced over Annemarie's shoulder. 'You were, weren't you?'

Jeanie, stood in the doorway, made the sign of the cross. 'I was.'

'At least she wasn't alone,' Annemarie said.

'How did you manage to get here so quickly?' Colin asked.

'I was at our Carlisle office when Jeanie was put through.' She stared down at her mother's body and her eyes began to well up again.

As Colin had done minutes before, Annemarie took their

mother's hand and held it. 'Have you told Sean?' she asked, wiping away a tear.

'I've not had a chance,' he said. 'He'll still be in Tenerife, won't he? Do you have a number for him?'

'Yes, I asked him for one before he left, but it's at home.'

'Can you get hold of it?' he asked. 'I don't mind telling him.'

Holding back more tears, Annemarie nodded and bit her lip. He could see her going through a to-do list in her head; it was her way of coping.

'We'll need to contact an undertaker, and tell Dad,' she said. 'My God, I'm going to have to tell Dad, aren't I?'

'Hello?' a voice called gently from the bottom of the stairs.

'That sounds like Patrick. I mean, Father Traynor,' he corrected himself. 'He'll want to bless the body.' Colin went to the top of the stairs. 'Come on up.'

He re-entered the bedroom and took Annemarie's hand as they waited for Patrick to appear. As soon as he entered, they bowed their heads and clasped their hands together in prayer. *Mum would have been proud*, Colin told himself.

The blessing only took a minute. Afterwards, Annemarie and Jeanie thanked Patrick, but to Colin it felt inadequate, too small a gesture for the force that had been Moira Buxton.

'I'll make some tea,' Jeanie said.

They followed her downstairs and sat at the kitchen table.

'I only spoke to her yesterday and she was in great form,' Patrick said. Jeanie offered him a plate of biscuits and he selected three.

'You should take a seat, Jeanie.' Annemarie pulled up a chair. 'You've had a shock too and I can get the tea.'

'No, no, I'd rather keep busy and tidy up,' she replied, picking up a cloth and wiping down some surfaces.

'I need to call Liam's school and tell him,' Annemarie said. 'He'll have to stay at his dad's tonight, but he can go home first and find the number for Sean's hotel. I think it's by my bed. Excuse me, Father.' She got up and left the room.

'Your mother was one tough lady, but never forget she gave you a good life and she loved each and every one of you,' said Patrick. 'I know there were issues, but that's behind you now. It's best to remember the loving moments.'

'Thanks,' Colin said.

'I take it you were at school when you heard the news?'

'I'd just arrived.' Colin watched Jeanie go outside with some rubbish, open and close the bin twice before sitting on the garden wall to the side. 'I think it's hit Jeanie the hardest.'

'They've become very close this past year,' Patrick said. 'Like sisters. It's been a wonderful thing to witness.'

They sat in silence for a moment, listening to a tearful Annemarie babble into the phone. The words were disjointed, so unlike her, but soon she found her stride and began to make sense.

'Before I forget, Hayley Falco gave me this,' Colin said, determined to change the subject. He handed over Johnny's suicide note.

'What is it?'

'Take a read.'

Patrick unfolded the piece of paper and read through it. Once he'd done so, he looked up. 'What do you think he felt guilty about? The bangle?'

'Maybe. Who knows? But Hayley made it clear Luc was not involved and was happy to throw Garr and Matthew under the bus. What's more, Luc's family have removed him from the school, with immediate effect.'

'You realise Luc's family basically runs the church across half of Europe? Centuries ago they started out making the Pope's vestments and now they've got their fingers in every pie. Name any business the church is involved in and they're receiving a cut. Luc's father's just a cousin, but even he's ridiculously wealthy.'

Annemarie stepped back into the room, dragging the telephone flex behind her. 'I've still not spoken to Liam,' she said. 'The switchboard has put me on hold even though I've stressed how urgent it is.'

Jeanie returned from outside and sat at the table. Taking a hankie from the cuff of her cardigan, she wiped her eyes and cleared her throat. 'I've things I need to give you both – and Sean,' she said, 'but I haven't got them here. They're at home. Things your mum wanted you to have.'

Colin looked at Annemarie, who was still holding the receiver up to her ear. She rolled her eyes. 'Can you say what they are?'

'Letters,' Jeanie said. 'One for each of you. To be opened once you've put her to rest and not a moment before.'

'What kind of letters?'

Jeanie shrugged. 'Your mum gave them to me last year. She made me swear not to tell you until she'd passed.'

'At last,' Annemarie cried. 'Liam, darling, I've some bad news…' Her voice trailed off into the living room.

'I should get going,' Jeanie said.

'You're welcome to stay.' Colin was half listening to Annemarie crying, explaining to Liam that his grandmother had gone.

'No, this is a time for family.' She picked up her bag, squeezing past Annemarie and out in the hallway.

Patrick placed his hand over Colin's. 'I can stay for a bit.'

PART 4

CHAPTER 35
TWO DAYS LATER – THURSDAY 30TH NOVEMBER 1995

At four AM, unable to sleep because of the freezing cold, Colin rose and pulled on some clothes, then, crossing the room, he wiped condensation from the window and peered outside. Through the pitch dark, a fresh coating of frost glistened below. His mother had loved this time of day – her favourite – when the world was still asleep, and there were no noises, no intrusions. *God's time*, she used to say.

Downstairs, he switched on the central heating and filled the kettle. With his mother's body now at the undertakers, all he needed to do that day was to register the death.

Picking up the medical certificate, he scanned it for the first time and frowned, unable to believe what he was reading. In addition to lung cancer, scribbled underneath was a mention of early onset Parkinson's. Had anyone else known about this? His sister? Annemarie had dealt with a lot of his mother's medical issues before he'd arrived home from India; surely she would have known? But she was in Newcastle dealing with urgent business and wouldn't be back for a couple of days.

He opened the back door and was met by a nip of cold far harsher than he'd expected. Reflecting back the sodium glow of the streetlights, thick clouds filled the sky and it looked like there could be snow on the way. A change of landscape would be welcome, he thought.

Hungrier than he realised, he closed the back door and opened the fridge. On a shelf sat the chicken pie Jeanie had made several days before. The smell made him feel sick, so he took it outside and scraped the contents into the bin. He paused as the first few snowflakes began to fall, and for the first time since his mother had died, he choked up. Why had love been such a battle for her? Why had she never conceded, not even once?

He stared back at the house he'd been brought up in since the age of five. His mother's presence was all pervasive, as if her personality was built into the fabric and had become part of the fixtures and fittings. Even with her gone, it still felt like that. Being there, especially alone, felt like he was being haunted.

Returning inside, he picked up his car keys and left.

'WHAT THE HELL are you doing here?' Caroline asked, her mouth full, brushing crumbs from her cardigan. 'You should be at home.'

He poured himself a coffee and took a sip. 'Wow. That has to be the most bitter drink I've ever tasted. Why aren't you in class?'

'I've a free period first thing,' she said, taking the mug from his hand. 'There's a fresh jug right there. Let me sort it for you.'

She busied herself as he checked his pigeon-hole: the weekly school newsletter, a memo about reporting deadlines, and his payslip.

'Here.' Caroline handed him a steaming black coffee.

He blew on it. 'You're a life saver.'

'C'mon, let's take a seat while it's quiet.'

A Prayer Before Killing

They sat in a bay window overlooking the gardens, gazing at the snow falling.

'I'm so sorry about your mother,' she said.

Colin laughed. 'You might not have been, if you'd ever met her.'

'Still, you must be hurting.'

Mr Oakley walked in, spotted them, then abruptly left.

'But I know the feeling,' she continued. 'My own mother died a few years back, and we didn't have the easiest relationship. Whatever the circumstances, it's very soon to be back at work, don't you think?'

'I don't know; I needed to busy myself.'

'And this madhouse was your best option?'

'It's all I could come up with. A bit of structure, use my brain, and avoid having to think about how I'm feeling.' He took a sip of his coffee. 'So, what's been happening?'

'Lots.' She leaned forward. 'The big news is that yesterday morning, Johnny's St Christopher turned up in the chapel.'

'Is that so unusual? The boys are always losing things.'

'Oh no, it wasn't lost, this was deliberately placed.'

Colin's pulse raced. 'Let me guess – the statue of Our Lady?'

She nodded. 'Around her neck.'

'You're kidding?'

'And, same as last time, Brendan swears the church was locked. Go take a look for yourself before classes start.'

As instructed by Caroline, he entered the side chapel, where the expression on the Virgin Mary's face appeared more hopeless than previously.

Just as Caroline had described, in addition to the bangle on her wrist, a silver St Christopher medal now sat around the Virgin Mary's neck. However, this was far less of a mystery than the bangle; the chain the medal hung from had

245

a catch, so had been easy to attach. Nonetheless, someone other than Johnny was keen to attract attention. But who – and why?

He remained in the quiet of the chapel, waiting for the school bell to ring. Lighting a candle, he sat appreciating the peace before saying a short prayer for his mother.

Thankfully, he had a full day of lessons timetabled, mostly outside. As flurries continued throughout the morning, by lunchtime a layer of snow had collected across the playing field. At the first years' request, rather than a game of football, he let them have a snowball fight instead, on condition none were thrown at him. Seeing the boys having such unadulterated fun brightened his spirits. However, by the end of the afternoon his head was spinning.

Passing Caroline's classroom, on the way to his final lesson, she dived out. 'You look terrible.'

'Honestly, I'm fine.'

She looked him up and down. 'You've a study class next, haven't you?'

'A double.'

'I'll cover for you. I only have four in my class, so I'll put them together and they can all catch up on their homework.'

'Are you sure?'

'Of course. Go home. Get some rest. No one expected you here today. Take advantage of it.'

'Thank you,' he said.

'Colin, we're all here for you. Or at least I am. Take it from one who knows, grief can affect you in strange ways. You need to look after yourself.'

On the way to his car, he began to regret taking Caroline up on her offer. What was he going to do all evening on his own? Opening the car boot, he grabbed a torch and headed uphill. There were a few things he needed to explore, and this was as good a time as any.

A Prayer Before Killing

. . .

BY THE TIME the castle ruin came into view, it was beginning to get dark and snow was falling steadily. He switched on his torch and started climbing the track to the bridge. As he made his way up, the snow became heavier and the surrounding landscape fell silent. Crossing the bridge into the ruin, with only the sound of his own breath for company, he felt cocooned from the rest of the world. He took one final breath before entering.

Inside the castle, the labyrinth of crumbling rooms and corridors was familiar at first, but after five minutes he had no idea whether or not he was heading in the right direction. Trusting his instincts, he continued deeper into the structure, taking care with his footing on the slippery stones underfoot. After all, if he fell or hurt himself, no one would think to come and look for him here.

Finally, he recognised the small stone room where he and Patrick had lifted the manhole cover to access the lower level where Sister Oran died. Try as he might, he couldn't get any purchase. A scrap of wood he attempted to use as a lever snapped, and a length of metal rod he found quickly bent; there was no way he could shift it by himself.

Retracing his steps, he trudged through a thick layer of snow, down the slope towards the duck pond. Though it had stopped for now, the heavy clouds suggested there would be further snowfalls that evening.

Where the stream met the pond, he scrabbled around in the mud and the slush, searching for the gated entrance to the tunnel in the undergrowth. Finding it hidden behind a tight grouping of reeds and saplings, he knew right away that the key he had wouldn't fit. The gate was locked with a large, rusted padlock, the type that required a huge key. He inspected the bars of the gate, but they were spaced so closely together he doubted even someone as small as Johnny or

Sister Oran could squeeze through.

He was about to call it a day when the bar he was holding moved slightly. He checked the others, but they were all secure. He pushed and pulled at the loose bar, but there was only a little give back and forth. Standing back, he shone the torch at the top of it. Directly above, there appeared to be a deep hole in the stonework. Similarly, directly below the bar the stonework dipped. Grasping it firmly, he rotated the bar, while pushing it up at the same time. Bit by bit, like a screw unthreading from its socket, the bar began to rise, until a gap barely wide enough for him to squeeze through appeared at the bottom of the gate.

Brushing mud from the front of his jacket and trousers, Colin scrabbled to his feet and gagged. The air inside the tunnel smelt putrid. He pulled his scarf up around his nose and followed the route of the tunnel upwards. He'd assumed from his previous visit that there was a direct path to the lower level of the castle, but this turned out to be anything but. After several wrong turns and dead ends, he finally arrived in the stone room below the manhole cover.

He approached the gate to the chapel tunnel. Gripping the torch between his teeth, he held the padlock in one hand and slid the key into it. With a satisfying click, the padlock sprang open.

He began to descend the short flight of stairs, then stopped. The torch beam illuminated a crude stone passage. Lower and much narrower than the others, it curved downhill, forcing him to crouch. Beneath his feet, the ground was wet with sticky mud, and he dropped to his knees, focusing the beam in front of him. Where the ground was less wet, a fresh set of footsteps had been captured in the mud. The imprint was distinctive and he recognised the logo. Someone wearing Air Jordan trainers, a similar size to his own, had passed this way recently.

Navigating the full length of the tunnel took some time.

A Prayer Before Killing

However, unlike the rest of the castle ruin, there were no passages off to the left or right, just a steady descent in the direction of the school.

After about twenty minutes, the tunnel began to widen and the mud floor was replaced by stone. Ahead, Colin could make out a faint source of light. The passageway ended in a low, drum-shaped chamber topped with a square wooden grille, locked from the inside with a simple barrel bolt. Releasing the latch, he carefully opened it and pulled himself up into a room he immediately recognised as the Rector's Chapel. The sound of a bible class leaked through from the main church, Brother Thomas's distinctive voice droning on and on.

It was clear that with a bit of determination, anyone with a key to the padlock could access the church whenever they wanted. The question remained: who?

CHAPTER 36

It was dark when Colin arrived home. Here in the suburbs, a light snowfall had coated his mother's and the neighbours' gardens making them appear orderly and uniform. As he pushed open the front door, he spotted a letter from the Scottish Prison Service lying on the carpet. Ripping it open, he saw his request had been granted; he was to report at ten the following morning for his visit with Simon Young.

Placing the letter on the telephone table, he threw off his coat and looked around him. Everything was as he'd left it; the light was still on in the hallway, the living room remained in shadow and the fridge hummed in the kitchen. The ordinariness of it all was unsettling. Despite his mother's death, it would be easy to pretend nothing had changed.

The phone rang, making him jump. He was tempted not to answer, but the insistence of its ring meant it was probably his sister.

'Hello.'

'You're home, then.' It *was* his sister, her voice as sharp as ever. Did she realise how like their mother she sounded?

'I went into work.'

A Prayer Before Killing

She said nothing, which suggested only one thing: she'd done the same. When she spoke, her voice was hoarse, as though she'd been crying. 'Sean's arriving home tomorrow mid-afternoon, so maybe we can get together? I'm coming up for a few days with Liam but I've booked a hotel. There's no way I'm sleeping there. I don't know how you can do it.'

He started to explain how strange it had been, but she interrupted. 'Sean's insisting on doing a reading at the funeral.'

'Wow. Okay. I wasn't expecting that.'

'Have you registered the death yet?' she asked.

'Not yet. There's something I wanted to discuss first.' He dragged the flex through to the kitchen and picked up the medical certificate. 'Did you know Mum had early onset of Parkinson's as well as lung cancer?'

There was a moment's silence before Annemarie said, 'She mentioned it about six months ago but asked me not to say – she didn't want people knowing her business.'

Colin pushed the certificate away. 'Not even me?'

'You knew about the cancer.'

'That's not the point.'

'It hardly matters now, does it? It's typical Mum, trying to sow division from beyond the grave.'

'You're right,' he said. 'Sorry, my head's all over the place.'

Annemarie's voice softened. 'Same here.'

'I'll register the death tomorrow. I promise.' He read through the rest of the certificate and something caught his eye. 'Hold on, this is wrong.'

'What is?'

'It says here that the time of death was eight-fifteen.'

'How's that wrong?' Annemarie asked. 'That's when Jeanie rang my work.'

'Then why didn't she call the school until after nine?'

'That's odd, but you'll have to ask Jeanie, she told me she

was going to call you as soon as she hung up. But, you know, she had a lot to deal with on her own. Mum. Calling Dr Hendry. She was pretty upset, poor love.'

'It's been a shock to us all, I guess,' he said. 'You know Mum was awake when I was leaving? She even said cheerio.'

Her voice cracked. 'Did you see her?'

'No, she just called to me. But we'd had a nice chat the night before.'

A knock on the back door took Colin by surprise. It was closely followed by a second knock. 'I'll need to go.' On the third knock, Colin trailed the phone wire to the back door, expecting to see Jeanie. Instead, Patrick stood on the step, dressed in running shorts and vest, sweat dripping off him. He held a Pyrex dish covered in tinfoil.

'Call me in the morning,' Annemarie said.

Colin set the handset down. 'This is unexpected.'

'Sorry, I was passing, and I saw the light on.' His hands were outstretched, holding the dish as he did at Communion.

'Were you running with it?'

Patrick looked down at the dish. 'This? No,' he laughed. 'I found it on the back step. But I've been meaning to drop off Charlie's number.' He placed the dish on the kitchen table and took a slip of paper from his pocket.

'I bet it's from Jeanie,' Colin said, lifting a corner of foil. 'Looks like her famous shepherd's pie.'

'What a woman. She's been at the church all day praying for your mother.'

Before Colin knew what was happening, he was being clasped in a bear hug. As he pulled away, Patrick held on, tightening his grip, his cheek on Colin's neck. He felt Patrick's lips brush against his skin and rest there. Was that a kiss?

Colin stepped back to release himself, searching Patrick's face. That had definitely been a kiss, but there was no reaction, no acknowledgement of it. If anything, he seemed unwilling, or unable, to look Colin in the eye.

A Prayer Before Killing

'How are you?' Patrick finally asked.

'I'm not sure,' Colin replied. After what had just happened, this was the truth. Plus, he now had a whole host of questions to ask. *Are you gay? Have you acted on it? How does this affect your position as a priest?* This wasn't the time to go there, though. 'Thanks for organising the visit to Father Young, by the way. I just got confirmation.'

'He's just plain old Mr Young now.'

Colin pointed to the shepherd's pie. 'Would you like to stay and eat? I'll never manage it all and I'm sure Mum's got a bottle of red somewhere.'

'No. Sorry, I should go. I've another five miles to run. I'm in training for a fundraising marathon in the New Year. It's for the archdiocese; in fact, it's been organised by Luc's family. You do know he's still in the country? He's staying till the end of the week apparently, in the hope that Johnny comes out of the coma, so there's still a chance you could speak with him. Why don't you try Hayley again? Ask her.'

'I'll think about it.'

Patrick stepped towards the back door.

'You know there's been another miracle?' Colin asked.

Patrick's eyes narrowed. 'At the school?'

'Well, not that the first one was, and this one definitely isn't. A chain belonging to Johnny was discovered around the neck of the Virgin Mary, but it's easily explained. Matthew or Garr must have put it there, I'm sure.'

There was an awkward pause as Patrick opened the door and seemed to think about hugging Colin again but thought better of it. Instead, he stepped outside and called back, 'Catch you later,' before running off into the snow.

Colin closed the door and retreated to the living room, where he collapsed onto the sofa and sat staring into space. Why had Patrick tried to kiss him? Had he given off the wrong signals? He didn't think so. Sure, Patrick was attractive, but the thought of getting involved with him romantically was absurd.

Digging into his pocket, he brought out Hayley's business card. To hell with it, he thought, I may as well. He got up and dialled her number.

CHAPTER 37
TWO YEARS EARLIER – MONDAY 14TH JUNE 1993

'And you've thought this through?' Charlie Murray asked, clearly concerned. 'Surely there's another option?'

'Such as?' This was a waste of his time, Father Young thought. He'd made a decision and wouldn't be talked out of it. After being humiliated, the idea of being in the same room as the Apostles, let alone teach them, was unbearable. 'My mind's made up. I'm not cut out for life here at the school and prolonging it won't do anyone any good.'

As Charlie rose and came round to his side of the desk, Father Young noticed how good he smelled. At the seminary, to promote humility, they'd been discouraged from using anything with a marked fragrance. While he'd followed this advice, Father Young worried that he smelt bad, and that as a consequence he carried about the musty stench of the church: its burned out candles, the sickly smell of incense. But he daren't admit to any of this, or that leaving the priesthood was foremost in his mind. To do so would raise too many difficult questions, and he wasn't equipped to deal with those right now. He feared if he began to speak he wouldn't be able to stop, and that he'd let slip his true feelings for Sister Oran. Then the whole house of cards really would come tumbling down.

'Honestly, there's no need for you to come on the retreat,' said Charlie. 'We've more than enough staff to supervise the pupils. All I ask is that while we're away you stay here; relax, take time for yourself to reflect and pray. Trust me, things will seem a whole lot better in a week.'

In the floors above, Father Young could hear the excited chatter of boys packing; an oppressive noise that made him want to scream. 'Okay,' he lied. He'd absolutely no intention of staying at the school, but Dr Murray was kind, and he didn't want to disappoint him any more than necessary. 'A week of prayer might help me focus.'

Charlie grabbed both his shoulders and brought his face closer. His aftershave was subtle, expensive. In that moment, it smelt of freedom. 'Good man. We'll chat again when I'm back. And as I've said before, if any of the boys are making life hard for you, just let me know and we'll sort it out. There's no problem that can't be solved with a bit of kindness and understanding.'

Father Young gazed at his possessions scattered on the bed. Besides his priest's attire, which was uniformly black, he owned three frayed T-shirts, a pair of jeans he'd had since he was eighteen, and a striped shirt that once belonged to his father. Apart from his clothes and a small bag of toiletries, there was only the handful of books he'd arrived with. The fact that everything fitted easily into one tiny suitcase made him want to weep; it didn't speak of a life well lived.

But that was all about to change; a plan was beginning to take shape. Using money he'd inherited from his grandmother, he would get as far away from the school as possible. An overnight bus from Glasgow would take him to London,

A Prayer Before Killing

and from there he could fly absolutely anywhere. Perhaps Istanbul? He'd always wanted to go to Turkey; he could easily get lost in a country that vast. And there were classical theatres he'd been longing to visit, ones he'd been reading about since he was a boy: Aspendos, one of the best-preserved ancient theatres of the Roman era; Hierapolis with its marble reliefs of mythological stories; and Pergamon, situated on a steeply sloping site with magnificent views of the city of Bergama. Living would be cheap and he could pick up casual work to get by. Anything to get out of this rut.

Outside, the bus driver revved his engine, drowning out the morning birdsong and the rising cacophony of the boys' screeching and howling as they boarded the coach. Father Young willed the driver to press his pedal to the floor and keep it there, so he never had to hear the noise of the birds or those damned boys ever again. He hated them all and the sooner he escaped from this hell, the better. The only place he'd found any solace in his entire time here had been on the barren uplands. And, of course, in Sister Oran's arms, but last night's events had cast a shadow over that.

He picked up his bible and tossed it into the suitcase, pressing it deep into the folds of his clothes until he could barely see it. Then, after second thoughts, he grabbed it and threw it across the room. It hit the wall with a slap, its spine tearing as it dropped to the floor, but he no longer cared. He locked his case and placed it by the door. In a few hours, the school would be a distant memory. There'd be no more sleepless nights tormenting himself, trying to figure out how best to teach the boys or encourage them to engage with his lessons, and no more lusting after Sister Oran. Suddenly, a tremendous sense of relief swept over him.

He crossed to the window and peered out: one last look at what he was leaving behind. Brother Thomas – as officious as ever – was corralling pupils onto the coach. Euphemia Baird was by his side, ticking off a register as they boarded. Sister

Oran stood alone to one side, but as the remaining boys filed onto the bus, she beckoned Matthew over. Drawing him close, she stood on her tiptoes and whispered in his ear. He laughed before hugging her tightly. Garr was the next to receive the same treatment, then Luc, then Johnny, all hugging and laughing in turn.

What was so funny? It could only be one thing; she'd been party to his humiliation. The orchestrator of it, even. But why? He needed to know.

As the bus moved off, Sister Oran stood on the driveway, grinning and waving energetically until the boys were out of sight. He tried to read her expression, searching for signs of guilt or regret.

As if aware of his scrutiny, she looked up at his room and he instinctively jumped backwards, retreating into the shadows. But why, when he had so much to say? Instead, he should stand his ground, shout her name from above, call her out. He took a deep breath and stepped back up to the window, but she was gone.

He lay down on his bare mattress and closed his eyes, praying for strength, to find the courage to confront her. If she was innocent, he would be able to tell. But if she wasn't, and she'd planned the trap in the tunnel, then he wasn't sure what he'd do.

When Father Young woke, he felt refreshed, as if he'd been asleep for days. He checked his watch; he'd only dozed for twenty minutes at most.

He stood and, for the first time since arriving at the school, he raised himself to his full height. No more stooped shoulders, he told himself, no more staring at the ground to avoid eye contact. He took another breath and opened the door. The atrium was empty, devoid of its usual racket. Walking along the gallery felt odd, as if he had entered a parallel world. Was

A Prayer Before Killing

his mind playing tricks? Was he still asleep? Was all of this a dream?

Only the sound of Sister Oran's voice, humming an annoying tune he'd heard played on the radio endlessly over the past week, told him it wasn't.

CHAPTER 38

FRIDAY 1ST DECEMBER 1995

Caroline had been right to insist Colin take some time off from school, but a visit to Scotland's largest prison was probably not what she'd had in mind.

He gazed up at the grim Victorian block: Barlinnie, or 'The Big Hoose', as some preferred to call it. Infamous for holding the most hardened criminals, many of them gang members, it wasn't a place anyone wanted to end up, least of all a sensitive young priest who'd been accused of killing a pregnant nun.

After showing his identification at the front desk, Colin was frisked and directed to a waiting area. Ten minutes later, his name was called. A heavy metal gate swung open and a prison officer beckoned him inside. 'You've twenty minutes,' he said, kind eyes belying an aggressive tone.

'I thought I had thirty?'

The officer shook his head. 'Not anymore, pal. He's got an appointment.'

'And will we be alone?'

'Why d'you ask that?' He looked Colin up and down, as though deciding whether to answer. In the end, he nodded.

A Prayer Before Killing

'He's being kept away from the other inmates at the moment, so yes.'

Something in his tone suggested he didn't agree with this arrangement, but Colin couldn't tell if he blamed Father Young for the situation or not. 'Any particular reason?'

'Unbelievable,' muttered the officer. 'For his own protection, of course. That's as much as you need to know. This way.'

Colin was led through two more metal doors, each one unlocked by a different key. The deeper they delved, the more fetid the air became. Colin held a hand to his nose; it was as if they were making their way to the building's rotten core.

'You get used to it,' the officer said, noticing his disgust. A smile twitched at the corners of his mouth. 'No amount of scrubbing washes it away.' A final door was unlocked and Colin was shown to a plastic chair. 'Sit there.'

The officer crossed through a side door into a room with a small, rectangular window. There, he spoke with another guard, who was sitting in front of two black-and-white monitors. Each was split into four grainy images, showing rotating views of corridors and rooms; in Barlinnie, there was nowhere to hide. Colin sat back and waited for the officers to complete their checks.

He wasn't sure what to expect from Father Young. Would he be wracked with guilt? Or, like everyone else in this investigation, would he struggle to tell the truth? If Patrick was to be believed, Father Young had absorbed the crime, confessed to a murder he didn't commit; but what had propelled him to such a futile act? The church? A vulnerable person could lose themselves in its rituals. Catholicism asked you to believe strange things: invited you to eat the body of Christ, drink his blood. And it viewed the world in absolutes: good and evil, virtue and sin.

The officer returned. He beckoned Colin to follow, and yet

another door swung open. This brought them into a wide corridor lined with strip lights that made the white walls glow.

'How far now?' Colin asked.

'This wing's a warren,' the officer replied.

'You ever get lost?'

The question was ignored as they came to the end of the corridor and the officer opened a final door. 'This is it,' he said, nodding Colin through.

In the centre of a windowless room, Father Young sat behind a scruffy, metal table, his fingers drumming on its surface. The first thing Colin noticed was a scar across the right-hand side of his face. It was a fresh wound, the skin red and swollen. It looked painful. 'Hello, I'm—'

Before he could finish, Father Young interrupted. 'I know who you are. Patrick's told me all about you.'

Their eyes met. He was markedly older than in the photo the papers had used during the trial, where he had still appeared boyish.

'Thanks for seeing me, Father Young.'

'It's just Simon,' he said, gesturing to his prison clothes, the yellow vest an indicator of his crime. 'The church wasted no time in defrocking me.'

The guard reminded Colin he'd twenty minutes and no more, and he'd be outside if needed.

'Thanks,' Colin replied.

There was a short silence while each assessed the other: similar age, build, background. Yet one of them was free, and the other was doing life in a hellhole.

'Why are you here?' Simon finally asked. He was soft-spoken with only a trace of a Glaswegian accent. Colin wondered if he'd taken elocution lessons.

'I'm reinvestigating the case, looking for new evidence with the hope of clearing your name.'

A Prayer Before Killing

Simon sat back in his chair and looked up at the ceiling, as though he was willing it to collapse and crush him.

'Patrick told me you're planning to withdraw your confession.'

Simon's focus returned to Colin, but his expression had darkened. What little light there had been in his eyes was gone and his skin was grey. 'Patrick says a lot of things.' He tilted his head. 'He said you were being groomed for the priesthood as a boy. Why didn't you follow through?'

The question was off topic and they had little time, but perhaps answering would help build a connection. Both had undoubtedly been damaged by the church, its hierarchies and hypocrisies.

'It didn't suit,' said Colin. 'I felt there was a lack of honesty.'

'He said you were one of the best candidates he'd ever met.'

'Really?' Colin struggled to remember if that was ever the case, but then recalled a period in his teens when he'd been diligent: always the first to arrive at church, never missing a charity event or an opportunity to help with the elderly, the disabled, the needy. He'd done it without thinking for so many years, that when he'd broken with the church, those deeds felt as though they belonged to someone else. 'We all make our own choices, don't we?'

'You had a lucky escape, I reckon.'

'Well, I…' It was something he often said to his mother, usually as they were arguing about his chosen career path as a police officer; she'd dismiss it as being no more than a glorified vigilante and without a moral purpose. Her actual words. He found himself smiling at the memory. 'Can I ask what happened to your face?'

Simon instinctively went to touch it but stopped himself and returned his hand to the table. 'I wasn't looking.'

'You didn't get into a fight?'

He gave Colin an expression of *What do you think?* 'In prison people do things, there are consequences, the world moves on. It's logged as an accident: I slipped on wet tiles.'

'How do you cope?'

Simon shifted in his chair and glanced over Colin's shoulder. 'I'm not sure I do. I killed a nun. That's what the world believes, whether it's true or not.'

Colin studied his face, hoping to find signs of passion or vengeance, but Simon's expression remained blank. 'And did you?'

The question was met with an uninterested shrug. It appeared as if he was counting the seconds until Colin left.

'You confessed to a crime you didn't commit. Why?'

Simon sat up straight. 'I'm still trying to work that out.'

'Patrick doesn't think you're guilty. And there are others who think so, too.'

'What, like Charlie Murray?' Simon clenched his fist. 'You think anyone listens to that bozo? The guy might look the part, but he's useless.' He leaned forward, and Colin smelt the staleness of his breath. 'His main interest is working out which of the new boys' mothers he can shag.' His voice rose. 'So, if all these people believe I'm innocent, why am I being left here to rot?'

The guard knocked on the door. 'Everything okay?'

'We're good,' Colin replied. He turned back to Simon. 'Bishop Trocchi and the Colbert family are now happy for me to widen the scope of the investigation. I've a meeting with the Colberts after this.'

Simon stared at Colin. 'Why would they agree to that? What's happened?'

'Johnny Doyle tried to kill himself earlier this week. He's still in a coma.'

Simon shook his head.

'He wrote a note saying how guilty he felt.'

'About what?'

'That's what I want to work out.' A jarring call came through the door that they'd five minutes left. 'Okay,' Colin shouted back, before returning his attention to Simon. 'Can I focus on Sister Oran? Who do *you* think killed her?'

'At first I thought it could be one of the boys, but they've all got alibis for the day she disappeared.'

'You saw her that day though? Later, after everyone left for the retreat?'

Simon nodded and lowered his gaze.

'In what state did you leave her?'

There was a pause before Simon spoke. 'I can't go over all this again. What does it matter?'

'If you've any chance of getting out of this hellhole, I need – everyone needs – to understand your version of events.'

'But she's gone.' A tear trickled down his face. 'That's the only real truth.'

'Catching who did it matters, too,' said Colin, gently. 'Sister Oran knew a lot of people at the school – she was popular, right?'

Simon raised an eyebrow. 'She'd talk to anyone about anything, but I wouldn't say she was popular. With the boys, definitely. Maybe with Charlie Murray, too. With me, so-so. But others not so much. Brother Thomas and Sister Helena tried to give her a hard time, but it was like water off a duck's back. And I don't reckon there was a single woman in the school who had much time for her – not the Bairds, not Caroline, nor Sarah. I was the closest thing she had to an actual friend.'

The door was thrown open. 'That's time up.'

'Can I have two more minutes?' Colin pleaded. They'd had fifteen minutes at most.

'You'll have to arrange another visit,' the guard said. 'Come on, let's go.'

'One minute. It's all I'm asking.'

Without agreeing, the guard left and slammed the door shut.

'What time did you leave the school grounds on the day Sister Oran disappeared?'

Simon gazed at the grey metal surface of the table. 'I think you should go,' he muttered. 'I've been through all this before and it's got me nowhere.'

'Simon,' Colin said, moving his hands towards his – not to touch – but to remind him he was on his side. 'I know a lot of the background stuff, but what I need to hear is your memories of that day. Can we focus on that?' Simon stared at him, then nodded. 'So, when did you finally leave?'

'I spoke with Sister Oran at about three.'

'What was said?'

'This and that. It's fair to say we had a difference of opinion. I can't actually remember all the details – my head was everywhere – but some time later I grabbed a tent, took some food, and headed into the hills.'

'You had an argument?'

Simon didn't respond, but his face turned red, either with fury or embarrassment, it was difficult to tell.

'What time did you leave?'

'I don't know. Four, five maybe?'

'Did anyone see you leave?'

'I don't know. If they did, they haven't come forward.'

'So, you didn't speak to anyone?'

Simon hesitated before shaking his head. 'It was pouring with rain. I didn't see anyone. I was wearing my cagoule, with the hood pulled up. I didn't want to speak to anyone.'

'The whole time you were away – all those days – you didn't go into a café, a pub, buy a stick of chewing-gum?'

'I headed straight into the hills and stayed there. I didn't see a soul. I couldn't even tell you where I went. It was a dark time. I wasn't myself.'

No wonder the police couldn't verify his alibi; it was as if he'd literally fallen off the face of the earth. And the fact that Simon was so vague about details himself and – by his own admission – was not in his right mind, didn't help his case. 'I need something else. I mean, is there anything that you've not shared?'

Simon remained silent.

'Tell me something, anything, that will help you get out of here,' urged Colin. 'The last thing you think of before you go to sleep and the first thing you think of when you wake up.'

Simon smiled. 'That's easy.'

'What?'

'Sarah, the school secretary, deliberately lied. She told the police she saw me walking into the forest with Sister Oran at eight that evening. That is impossible.'

'Why would she lie?'

'You'll have to ask her.'

'I will.'

'Ask her why she was working late that evening – she never usually did. And ask her why she tried to get Sister Oran removed from her role. See how she answers.'

Colin could hear the door behind him being unlocked. He'd one last question. 'You knew Sister Oran was pregnant when she died?'

Simon hung his head.

'Were you the father?'

'Time's up,' interrupted the guard. 'Young – the doctor's waiting for you.'

'We never had sex,' Simon said as he stood.

'And yet there was a semen stain belonging to you found on her clothes. How did it get there?'

Simon wouldn't look him in the eye.

'Why won't you tell me?'

'Young, you're coming with me.' The guard turned to Colin. 'My colleague will take you back to the entrance.'

As Simon was led away, Colin shouted, 'Can I visit you again?'

'What's the point?'

Colin watched him walk down the corridor. There was nothing in their conversation to convince him of his innocence. Nor of his guilt, for that matter. Colin's main impression was of a ghost of a man, resigned to his fate.

CHAPTER 39

Colin drove across the frozen city to Park Terrace in the West End, where he'd arranged to meet Hayley. The phone call he'd made the previous night, at Patrick's suggestion, had paid off, and she'd been receptive to meeting him with Luc. Her only proviso was that she needed to be present throughout the meeting and if the boy didn't wish to answer a question there'd be no comeback. It wasn't ideal, but as it was the only offer on the table, he'd agreed.

A five storey Victorian townhouse, the Colbert home overlooked the leafless trees of Kelvingrove Park. What Colin assumed to be the family crest was emblazoned in gold leaf on the fanlight above the entrance. No expense spared, then. Arriving at an impossibly glossy black front door, Colin rang the bell, which was immediately answered by a housekeeper. He was led into a vast marble hallway with a carved mahogany staircase, which hinted at the grandeur of the floors above. On the walls, contemporary artworks alternated with religious paintings; to the rear a narrow, stained-glass window let in soft shafts of coloured light, giving the interior a church-like serenity. It was clear that someone with great taste and a massive budget had worked on the design.

The housekeeper, a sprightly older woman, led him upstairs to a room at the front of the building. 'They're expecting you,' she said, as she opened the door.

His first sight was of Luc sipping through a straw from a bottle of Coca Cola. He was seated on a sofa between Hayley and another elegant woman of a similar age. Dressed in a neon-yellow T-shirt, red baseball cap, light-blue jeans and oversized trainers, his appearance in a room full of antiques, designer chairs and *objets d'art* was incongruous. He looked like a very large toddler.

Both women rose as Colin entered, and the unknown woman stepped forward to greet him with a firm handshake. Slim, in a tailored grey suit, she had a glossy pink smile painted on her lips.

'I'm Luc's mother, Fiona Colbert,' she said, meeting Colin's eye whilst holding onto his hand a little too long. Unexpectedly, her accent was Scottish, most likely from the islands. 'My deepest condolences on your mother's passing. We said a prayer for her this morning. I hope you don't mind?'

'No. Thank you.' He tried to gauge the sincerity of her words, but the sheer luxury of the room was distracting. Out the corner of his eye he spotted a small Gauguin, and to the left of Hayley a series of Picasso prints. Elegant contemporary furniture sat next to traditional pieces, with everything tastefully considered and perfectly placed to show off the proportions of the room; five floor-to-ceiling windows framed a panoramic view of the city beyond.

'Shall we get down to business?' Fiona asked. 'After all, we don't want to waste your time, do we?'

Hayley, who'd been searching for something in her handbag, tucked it securely into the corner of the sofa. 'You'd like me to stay?'

'For now,' Fiona said.

Luc finished his Coke and handed the bottle to Hayley.

A Prayer Before Killing

'Are you ready?' Fiona asked her son.

'I'm ready,' Luc replied.

Surprised by Hayley's lowly position in the pecking order, Colin sank into the soft leather of an armchair and took out his notebook. 'Luc, let me first say how sorry I was to hear about Johnny.'

Luc glanced at his mother, who nodded that he could respond. 'Thank you, Mr Buxton. He's a special person, and I hope he pulls through soon.' Obviously rehearsed, but there was at least an attempt to sound genuine.

Fiona clasped her hands on her lap. 'You need to tell Mr Buxton everything you told me, Luc.'

'I will,' he said.

His mother sat forward, her smile becoming strained. 'Luc has recently confided in us some delicate information.'

'I know what happened with the bangle,' Luc mumbled, picking at the hem of his T-shirt. 'If that's the kind of stuff you want to know.'

Colin couldn't tell if the childishness was an act or if Luc was even more immature than he'd imagined. 'Please. Go ahead.' Outside, a gust of wind agitated the treetops and rattled the windows. 'In your own time.'

'Johnny found it,' he began. He bit his bottom lip and rolled it between his teeth. 'It had been hidden somewhere.'

'Do you know where and by who?'

Luc shook his head. 'Garr seemed to know, but I didn't. He was furious with Johnny.'

'So, Johnny took the bangle and put it onto the statue of the Virgin Mary? Is that what you're saying?'

Luc nodded.

Fiona took her son's hand. 'Darling, you're not in any trouble.' She looked at Colin. 'He's a shy boy and is finding all of this very difficult. I'm sure you understand.'

'Of course. We can take a break, or I could return another time.'

'We're returning to Paris first thing tomorrow.' Her words were emphatic; this was his one and only chance.

'I think Johnny was fed up with waiting for Sister Oran to perform a miracle, so he did one himself.' Luc sat back on the sofa and crossed his arms. 'That's the truth.'

'A miracle?' his mother asked. She stared at him. 'Are you sure that's the word you want to use?'

'It wasn't much of one.' He shrugged. 'All he had to do was make a copy of Brendan's key and let himself into the church. Brendan's such a dumbass he didn't notice.'

'If we can keep the language civilised, please,' Fiona interjected.

Luc rolled his eyes. 'And the statue's just bits of wood slotted together. Johnny pulled off one of the hands, shoved the bangle on and glued it back together. It's a lot of fuss over nothing.'

'So, when you were fighting in the classroom, what was that about?' Colin asked.

Luc was in full flow now. He leaned forward and waved his arms around. This was the boy Colin was used to seeing. 'We didn't know he was planning to do it, but once he'd done it, we'd no choice but to go along with him. And that's what the fight was about. That he'd done it in the first place and brought all this attention onto us.'

'From me?'

'From everyone. And then all the religious nuts started turning up to see it. I mean, all credit to Johnny, it kind of did what he wanted it to do.' Luc stared down at his oversized trainers: a pair of clown shoes that teenage life forced him to wear. It dawned on Colin that his entire outfit today had been chosen to make him appear ordinary.

'And who placed Johnny's St Christopher around the statue's neck?' he asked.

Luc snorted. 'I dunno. Those two probably. As it's all gone on, they've got hooked on the attention.'

A Prayer Before Killing

'Matthew and Garr?'

'You saw how they made us dress? I didn't want any part of it.'

'And what about Johnny?'

'He started having doubts. They took over the whole show and were trying to manipulate him. It's their fault he did what he did. And it's their fault I'm having to leave. Wankers,' he muttered.

His mother glowered at him. 'What did I say?'

As Colin scribbled down notes, Hayley began searching through her bag again. 'Are you going to be much longer?' she asked. 'I'm hoping to grab a cigarette break before my next meeting.'

'You can go if you like,' Fiona said.

'No, it's fine. I'll stay.'

'I've only a couple more questions,' Colin said, which seemed to appease Hayley. 'Now Luc, this is the most difficult question I'm going to ask, and you need to answer truthfully. Do you think you can do that?'

'That rather depends on what the question is,' Hayley interrupted, but was discreetly silenced by Fiona.

Colin held Luc's gaze. 'Do you know who killed Sister Oran?'

Luc shook his head, then mumbled, 'Father Young, I suppose.'

'Good boy,' his mother said. 'Now, is that us done?'

'And do you know who fathered Sister Oran's child?'

He sensed Fiona's body stiffen and Hayley, noticing it too, leaned forward. 'I think we're done here,' Hayley said.

'Matthew had sex with her,' Luc blurted out. His cheeks turned scarlet, matching his baseball cap. 'So, it must have been his.'

'That can't be true, Luc,' Fiona said. She turned to Colin. 'I apologise for my son's slip of the tongue. This is news to me.'

But no rebuke – even from his mother – could stop him. 'He used to say how many times he made her come.'

'Luc!' Fiona cried.

He grinned at her horrified expression.

'So, he boasted about it?' Colin asked.

Fiona murmured something to Hayley, who nodded in agreement.

'You've seen what he's like at sports,' Luc went on. It was true. Running, scoring goals, tackling; Matthew had to win and let everyone know about it. 'I thought you'd have guessed it was him,' he added, shrinking back into the sofa.

Hayley pointed at her expensive gold watch. 'Mr Buxton, that's definitely time up.' Reaching over, she pressed a button on a side table. 'Mrs Ashford will take you downstairs.'

Colin stood. 'Is there anything else you'd like to tell me, Luc?'

'I think you've heard all that he has to say,' Hayley snapped.

'No. Let him speak,' his mother interrupted.

'There's just one thing.' Luc chewed his bottom lip before deciding to continue. 'The night Sister Oran disappeared, Matthew wasn't at the lodges. He pretended to have a migraine and left.'

'What?' Hayley gasped. 'He left the retreat?'

'For how long?' Colin asked.

'Till about midnight,' Luc said.

'And no one noticed? Not Dr Murray, for example?' Colin continued.

At the mention of Charlie's name, Fiona's mouth tightened; it was clear she wasn't a fan.

'Mrs Colbert, I think we should stop there.' Hayley scrambled to her feet.

'Charlie Murray was always busy. Usually on the phone.' Luc began to chuckle. 'Wasn't he, Hayley?'

A Prayer Before Killing

Hayley blanched, and stuttered, 'I don't know what you're implying.'

Colin watched as Luc's mother took in the full meaning of her son's remark – it was obvious she was unaware of the full extent of Hayley and Charlie's relationship. She fixed her gaze on Hayley, who had opened the door to reveal the housekeeper. Without looking at Colin she stated, 'Thank you for your time, Mr Buxton. Mrs Ashford will show you out.'

CHAPTER 40

After registering his mother's death at the local registrar's office, Colin drove home, and turned into the neat cul-de-sac of post-war council houses he'd known his entire life. For a moment, the weak winter sun appeared through the clouds, illuminating their grey facades. He wondered about all the family dramas that had taken place behind each front door: affairs, divorces, suicide, abuse. The list went on, but what of those dark goings-on which remained hidden, their secrets taken to the grave?

He dropped his rucksack by the telephone table and considered calling Barlinnie to request another visit but decided to sleep on it. Although Patrick had claimed Simon was close to retracting his confession – was even considering an appeal – this wasn't Colin's impression. However, perhaps Luc's revelations about Matthew could help persuade Simon to think again. If Matthew really had left the retreat on the night of Sister Oran's disappearance, if he was the father of her child, then it wasn't beyond the bounds of possibility he had returned to the school that night. Could he really have made the round trip so quickly? It pointed to a bigger question: could Luc be believed? In the short time Colin had known him, he'd found him to be petty, arrogant, and happy to twist the truth to suit his own ends. He needed to find evidence to corroborate Luc's accusations.

The fact Fiona Colbert hadn't known the true nature of Hayley and Charlie's relationship was surprising, too. It proved there was a covert aspect to their relationship.

Through in the kitchen he found Jeanie's shepherd's pie dish freshly washed and drying by the sink alongside a couple of plates and mugs. Annemarie must have popped by earlier and cleaned up. A scribbled note on the table confirmed this, saying that she and Sean had gone to the pub for lunch and a couple of drinks, and he was welcome to join them. That wouldn't happen; while Annemarie with a drink inside her was fun, the same couldn't be said for Sean.

In the living room, Colin peered out of the window. On the other side of the road, Jeanie's Christmas lights were flashing on and off, signalling she was home. Time to pay her a visit, he thought.

'COME on in out the cold, love,' Jeanie said, pushing aside a large suitcase. 'How are you doing? Can I get you a cup of tea?'

'Please. And thanks for this.' He handed her the dish. 'You off on holiday?'

'No,' she laughed. 'I wish. It's some stuff for the charity shop. Old clothes I never wear. They're sending someone round to collect them.'

He shuffled inside to be met by a tsunami of junk: cardboard boxes overflowing with a jumble of chipped crockery and newspapers were piled against the wall, with more boxes stacked up the staircase.

'I know, I know, it's a terrible mess. I'll get round to sorting it out one of these days,' she said, leading him through to the kitchen. 'I've just made a brew, so your timing's perfect.'

Unlike his mother's spotless kitchen where everything was scrubbed to within an inch of its life and neatly placed, Jeanie's kitchen was a tip. Tins of food lay open and uneaten, dishes were encrusted with leftovers, the floor was stained and littered with stacks of magazines, half empty plastic bottles, bags of rubbish, you name it. Dusty layers of grease coated every surface. It seemed Jeanie was so busy tending to others she didn't have time to look after her own home. Strangely, he'd not heard his mother mention this, but perhaps she'd never visited. If she had and she'd seen Jeanie's house in this state, she wouldn't have held back. Everyone would have been told.

'Did you enjoy it?'

'The shepherd's pie?' He watched her pick up two grubby mugs from the worktop, run them under some cold water before pouring tea into them. 'It was delicious.' Now he'd seen where it was prepared, he'd other ideas.

'Milk? Sugar?'

'Black's fine,' Colin replied.

With every chair stacked high with old newspapers and dirty clothes, Jeanie propped herself against the back door and sipped her tea. 'I'm sure I've a packet of digestives somewhere. Do you fancy one, son?'

Colin declined and placed his mug on the only free corner of the breakfast bar. 'It must have been a shock having to deal with Mum, us and Dr Hendry. All the phone calls.'

'I'm used to it, love. I was the first to find Mrs Dawson down the road, too, so I had a trial run, so to speak. And then there was my Alec, of course.' She crossed to a cupboard to retrieve the digestives and joined him at the breakfast bar. 'You sure I can't tempt you?'

Colin shook his head. 'What time did Mum die?'

'I'm not sure, love. She took a funny turn just after you

A Prayer Before Killing

left, and then I lost track of time to be honest.' She dunked a digestive into her tea and as she lifted it to her mouth, it fell back into the mug with a splash. 'Damn!'

'About eight? Or later?'

Jeanie fished the soggy biscuit from her tea with a spoon and slurped it down. 'That's right. Around about that time. Eight-ish. Or not long after.'

It didn't make sense. If that was correct, why had she taken so long to call him? 'Is it okay to go over the details with me?' He hesitated. 'I'm struggling to understand, Jeanie.'

From under the table, an overweight cat slinked towards him and curled its tail around his leg. As he bent down to stroke it, the doorbell rang.

'That'll be Deirdre here for my weekly payment. Do you know her? The catalogue lady? Littlewoods, not Kays.' She rummaged in her handbag which sat proudly at the centre of the breakfast bar. 'Don't let the cat out,' she said, as she left to answer the door, clasping her purse.

As he tipping his tea down the sink, the cat meowed and stared up at him. 'Are you hungry?' he asked, looking around the kitchen. In a corner by the sink an empty bowl sat on the floor on a filthy square of newspaper, and beside it a saucer of milk with what looked like a fat bluebottle floating dead on the surface.

Out in the hallway, Jeanie and Deirdre were cheerily exchanging stories. Maybe he should make his excuses and come back another time.

'She's a terrible gossip that one,' Jeanie said when she returned, placing her purse back in her bag. 'More tea?'

'Thanks, but I should be getting back. I think I'm having a chat with Annemarie and Sean about the funeral arrangements soon.'

'Your sister's been back and forth all day with Liam. He looked miserable as sin.'

'Teenage boys, eh?'

'Don't forget, you were one yourself once. But you were a good boy. Never in any trouble.' She pinched his arm. 'Not like that brother of yours.'

'And you're sure about the time of death?'

She looked irritated. 'It was Dr Hendry who pronounced her dead, not me. You're better off asking him.'

'It's just that I don't understand why you called me almost an hour after Annemarie.'

'Oh, love, is that what's bothering you?' She squeezed his hand. 'When Moira took her funny turn, I rang for an ambulance, but it wasn't needed – she slipped away within minutes. When I saw she was gone, I called Dr Hendry and then I called Annemarie because she had the longest way to come. After Dr Hendry saw your mum, I took some time to make everything nice in her room, to wash Moira and change the bedding. After that, I called the school – I didn't want you coming home and not seeing her at her best. I'm sorry, I didn't realise how much time had passed. I should have called you right away.'

'No, no. That's fine. You've nothing to apologise for. I needed to understand, that's all.' He hugged Jeanie, thankful that she'd been so thoughtful. 'You did so much for her.'

Jeanie wiped a tear from her eye. 'Please don't, son, you'll start me off.' The cat pushed between their legs and began to meow loudly. 'Now, I'd better get this greedy boy fed!'

Colin said his goodbyes and left.

SEAN'S CAR, a flash, metallic-blue Saab, was sitting outside the house, half on the pavement and half on the road. As soon as his mother heard the distinctive purr of its engine approach, she'd jump to the front door and stand watching him park. He'd be trying to manoeuvre it to make sure it didn't get scratched or scraped, while she'd be shouting that he wasn't leaving enough room for pedestrians to get by. 'What about a

A Prayer Before Killing

mother with a double buggy?' she'd scream but Sean always ignored her.

When he entered, Annemarie and Sean were sitting on the sofa, deep in conversation. They continued whispering, even after he sat on the armchair opposite them. 'How was the pub?' he asked.

Sean finished what he was saying before looking up. He narrowed his eyes. 'Where've you been?' Colin's brother reminded him of superintendents he used to work with in the police force, the same aggressive, accusatory tone used for everyone, suspects and officers alike.

'You should've come along to the pub.' Annemarie rubbed her face; he could tell from her smudged mascara she'd been crying.

'I was out and about earlier, seeing a couple of people, then I was over at Jeanie's.'

'You're working on a big case, aren't you?' Annemarie said.

Sean had put on weight since Colin last saw him, almost two years previously. A cousin had been getting married in Ireland and they'd gone over as a family for the weekend. Usually, spending so much time together would be a recipe for disaster, but Sean's twins had recently been born, and he'd been sociable, happier than usual. 'Oh yeah? Thought you'd left all that nonsense behind?' The extra pounds made him look lethargic as he stretched back on the sofa.

'I suppose you'd call it a private investigation.'

Sean laughed, the folds of his belly jiggling up and down. 'What, like Magnum?'

'God, remember those awful Hawaiian shirts?' Annemarie said, poking Sean's arm.

Colin had forgotten how tight his brother and sister were. Despite being so different, they'd always stuck together growing up, covering each other's back when one of them snuck out at night behind their mum's back. All his life, he'd felt on the outside of their connection.

Sean nodded at Colin. 'You going to make some tea, wee man, or what?'

'I'll get it,' Annemarie said. 'I need to sort my makeup anyway. I must look a right state.'

'No, I'll do it.' Any excuse, Colin thought, to get away from them. 'Is Liam not here?'

'I dropped him back at the hotel,' Annemarie called.

He stood in the kitchen, half-listening as Sean launched into an anecdote about his hotel in Tenerife, and how they'd been moved to the honeymoon suite after he'd kicked up a fuss about the original room. 'The balcony looked onto a quarry, I kid you not,' he shouted, as if he was still in the midst of making the complaint.

Colin made the tea, set out a tray, and carried it through to the living room. 'I spoke to Jeanie.'

'What about? Not the funeral arrangements?' Annemarie zipped up her makeup bag.

'No, about why she took so long to call me.'

'Why would she call you? She called Annemarie. Forget about that though. We need to talk about Mum's wishes,' Sean said, winking at Annemarie as he pulled a cigarette from his pocket. 'See they're followed to the letter.'

'Wondered when you were going to mention Mum,' said Colin.

A sneering look was thrown his way. 'There wasn't any point in trying to get an earlier flight. I'd have been home maybe a day sooner and for what? She was already dead.' Sean took out his lighter.

'You're not going to light that, are you?' Colin asked.

'Why?'

'Mum didn't like you smoking in the house.'

'Well, she's not here to stop me, is she?' He lit his cigarette.

A Prayer Before Killing

'Anyway, she was a fucking hypocrite – always sneaking a fly one herself, thinking we didn't know.'

'Have you been to see her yet?' Colin asked. 'At the funeral home?'

'Why don't you get off your high horse?' Sean stood up to his full six foot two and leaned into Colin's face, his breath stinking of beer. 'She was my mother, too, not just yours.' Despite being physically stronger and quicker with his fists, Sean hadn't squared up to Colin since he'd done his police training. Very different from when he was small, when Sean would slap him around the head at every opportunity. 'You're such a pain in the arse.' He burped. 'So, what did Jeanie do to piss you off?'

'Sit yourself down, Sean, before you fall down,' Annemarie quipped. As ever, big sister mode was her default position when things became tense.

As Sean fell back onto the sofa, Annemarie leaned forward and asked Colin, 'You asked her then?'

'Yes. She had an explanation for the delay.'

'What delay?' Sean asked.

'She phoned Annemarie to let her know Mum was dead, then waited almost an hour before she told me. I thought it was a bit weird, but she just wanted to make Mum nice and tidy up her room before I got back.'

'That's such a sweet thing to do,' Annemarie said.

'What did you think, Inspector Clouseau? That the old dear did Mum in?' From the side of the sofa, Sean produced a bottle of beer from which he took a huge gulp.

'No, but I did think it a bit odd, Mum dying so suddenly.'

'We talked about this,' Annemarie said. 'She'd lung cancer and the onset of Parkinson's; she'd been very weak for a long time.'

'With the discrepancy around timings, I just needed to ask.'

'Well, if she did do Moira in, good on her,' said Sean with a sneer. 'She's done us all a favour.'

Annemarie gripped Sean's arm in a way he'd seen her do many times with Liam. 'Wheesht a minute.'

'I'm going for a piss.' Sean stood and stumbled out the room.

Annemarie turned her focus back to Colin. 'I don't think he's coping,' she whispered. 'But you're happy with the explanation Jeanie gave you?'

'I suppose it makes sense.'

Sean returned and sat back on the sofa. 'All I know is I was the last to be told.'

Annemarie stared at him. 'Yes, because you were off on your second holiday in three months.'

'Don't blame me,' Sean said. 'Blame my high maintenance wife.'

'Did Jeanie say anything to you about Mum's wishes?' Annemarie asked. 'I got the details from her solicitor earlier – that's why Sean and I went to the pub. I needed a stiff drink.'

'I knew Mum had told her what she wanted but she hasn't gone into detail. Why, what's the problem?'

'It's a corker,' Sean said.

'What is it?' Colin asked. 'Does she want Bishop Trocchi to officiate? The pope?'

'God, if only,' Annemarie replied. She turned to Sean, seeking reassurance, then looked back to him. 'She wants to be cremated.'

'But she still wants a Mass?' Colin asked.

'That's just it.' Annemarie's shoulders sank. 'She doesn't.'

'What?' Colin said, incredulous. 'That doesn't make any sense.'

Sean raised his bottle of beer. 'To Moira Buxton – as crazy in death as she was in life.'

CHAPTER 41
TWO YEARS EARLIER – MONDAY 14TH JUNE 1993

Sweat rolling down his forehead, Father Young hid at the foot of the service staircase listening to Sister Helena clean the kitchen. If she stuck to her usual routine, she'd then go to the chapel and pray for an hour. He didn't have to wait long. Right on cue, she switched off the radio and closed the door. He waited as the sound of her footsteps receded up the main staircase.

The coast now clear, he made his way through the kitchens and crossed the inner courtyard towards the nuns' annexe, the summer sun casting deep shadows on the cobblestones. The last time he'd been here was over a week ago when he'd crept through the sleeping building, drawn to Sister Oran's room like a moth to a flame. That night she'd welcomed him warmly and whispered sweet words which had eased his mind. So, what had changed since then? He didn't understand. Even before last night and the cruel joke they'd played on him in the tunnel, he'd sensed her freezing him out, her attentions fully focused on the Apostles again. He was sure he wasn't imagining it. And this morning when she'd made such a show of hugging the boys, had that been for his benefit too? Had she known he was watching? The humiliation, the rejection, was like a stab to his chest. Tears stung his eyes. I cannot be treated like this anymore, he swore to himself, a mantra he continued to repeat beneath his breath as he gripped the door handle.

Entering the annexe's tiny living room, he immediately heard Sister Oran's voice, the softest murmur on the far side of her bedroom door. He assumed she was at prayer, however as he listened more closely, it became clear she was talking to someone. But he'd seen her wave the boys off, and apart from him, the only people left at the school were Sister Helena, Sarah and Brendan. It couldn't be Sister Helena as he'd just seen her head to the chapel, and Sarah had no time for Sister Oran, so there's no way she would be in her room. That only left Brendan. A jealous rage surged through Father Young's veins.

As he threw open the door, a kneeling Sister Oran shrieked and dropped her rosary beads. She jumped to her feet and started to back away. 'Father Young, what are you doing?'

He noticed how red and swollen her eyes were, as if she'd been crying, and his first instinct was to hold her, but the fear in her eyes stopped him. 'Who's here?' His voice sounded different from normal: assured, passionate, unyielding.

Sister Oran looked confused.

'I heard you talking to someone.'

'Only Jesus,' she replied, her voice shaky. 'I was praying, that's all. I swear.'

He stepped towards her and she took a step back. Was she scared of him? Glancing round the room it was obvious she was alone. A simple box room, it was sparser than he remembered, containing only a single bed, a narrow closet and a small chest of drawers. A copy of the bible sat on the window ledge alongside a few other paperbacks, a couple of religious posters were pinned to the walls, and that was it. There was nowhere to hide. 'I'm sorry,' he said. 'I...'

A Prayer Before Killing

She crouched to pick up her rosary beads. 'Father Young, I told you last time these quarters are private. You remember that, don't you?'

He took another step into the room, convinced she'd said no such thing. 'I saw you wave the boys off earlier.'

'I know. You jumped back when I looked up,' she said, stepping sideways.

His chest throbbed with a deep pain. 'Were you looking for me?'

She lowered her head and muttered some words under her breath which he couldn't catch. 'Father Young, please don't take this the wrong way, but I'd like you to leave. I need time alone.'

He reached for her hand, but she pulled away.

'No one knows I'm here,' he said. 'I promise.'

She edged further towards the door. 'I took vows – God is the only man I will ever care about. You understand what I'm saying?'

He didn't. From that first day, when he'd met her in the gardens, had it all been an act? When she took him to the cove, was she intent on leading him on – nothing more? And when she held him in her arms that night, was it merely a set up to make her final rejection of him all the more painful? He refused to believe it was all a lie.

'Please,' Sister Oran begged, 'go back to the main building and we'll pretend you were never here.'

'I'm leaving the school,' he blurted out. 'I've decided. I came here to tell you.' He'd imagined what her response might be – concern, disappointment, dismay – but hadn't expected her to look so perplexed.

She squinted at him. 'Why? Because you're finding it difficult to adjust to the boys?'

'Not just that.' He stumbled over his words. 'There are... Well, there are other factors, too.'

'Like what?'

It was now or never. If this place had taught him anything, it was that keeping his thoughts and words to himself would only lead to more misery. 'I hoped you might come with me.'

Colour drained from her cheeks. She sprang towards the door, saying, 'Sorry Father, I forgot, Sister Helena has asked me to pray with her.'

Before she could reach it, he stepped across her path, blocking her exit. 'It's the boys, isn't it? The Apostles?' he whispered. 'You're involved with one of them, aren't you? Or is it all of them?'

She lifted her head and held his gaze. A series of emotions crossed her face, none settling for more than a second: anger, hurt, guilt. He thought she might cry, but instead she took his hand. 'It's my fault. You seemed so lost when you got here and I felt the need to show you kindness when others didn't. To protect you, even. It's a failing I have. I'm sorry if you misread my intentions.'

Her words stung. Anger – immediate and searing – consumed any affection he'd once felt for her. He felt his hands coil up, his fists burning red at the knuckles, and he backed up against the door.

'If you've decided to leave and take a different journey, then that's what you should do,' she said. 'We all have our own paths to follow. Mine is with the church.' She tried to squeeze past him. 'Now, if you'll excuse me.' As she reached for the handle, he pressed his body hard against the door. She stared, her eyes chastising him. 'Excuse me.' Her voice was breathless. 'I said, excuse me.' Forcing him to move, she prised open the door and scurried out, darting into the courtyard, and disappearing into the main building.

Father Young had always imagined in a school like this there'd be silence: quiet contemplation, whispered words of solace and spiritual exchanges, but there'd been none of that. Since arriving here, there had been continuous noise. Every second of every day, the boys would be shouting or yelling or

A Prayer Before Killing

calling each other names. Even during Mass, their prayers were a racket and their singing discordant. The noise was unremitting and deafening. Now, in this longed-for silence, all he could hear was an empty nothingness.

Crossing the room, he opened the closet to reveal one of Sister Oran's habits hanging on its own. Removing the tunic from its hanger, he carefully spread it out on the bed, then lay face down on top of it. The smell was intoxicating, her natural odour, a scent that spoke to him of goodness and innocence. He closed his eyes and inhaled once more, slowly moving his body back and forth against the folds of fabric. Outside, he could hear the birds singing and the trees gently swaying. Resisting all thoughts of a life without her, he knew exactly what he needed to do.

CHAPTER 42

FRIDAY 1ST DECEMBER 1995

From the kitchen window, Colin watched his brother and sister sitting on the patio wall in the fading light, sharing a cigarette. With some gentle persuasion, Annemarie had managed to do what he couldn't and get Sean to smoke outside. They handed the cigarette back and forth, Sean taking long drags, too drunk to notice Annemarie was only pretending to inhale. Their animated expressions and lively conversation, however, suggested they were plotting. When he was a child, out of frustration at being constantly excluded, he'd taught himself to lip-read their words, but from this distance, their exchange was proving too difficult to decipher. Annemarie caught him looking and turned her head away.

He moved through to the hallway, picked up the phone and dialled the parish house. A lot had happened since yesterday and he wanted to let Patrick know how his meetings with Simon and Luc had gone. Still unsure whether to believe Luc or not, Colin was keen to get Patrick's take on the accusations against Matthew. He also wanted to quiz him about the nature of Charlie and Hayley's relationship, and

A Prayer Before Killing

whether he thought they might have conspired to hinder the original investigation into Sister Oran's death.

'Yes?' Mrs Beattie's calm, authoritative tone was reassuring amidst the recent chaos.

'Is Father Traynor available?' he asked. 'It's Colin.'

'I'm sorry, Mr Buxton. He's away on a trip.'

Patrick hadn't mentioned about going anywhere, though why should he? 'Can I ask when he's due back?'

'A couple of days, I think.'

'Okay. Could you let him know I called?'

'Wait a minute.' Her voice trailed off but returned almost instantly. 'There's a message for you. Let me find my glasses,' she said. 'Right, I'm sorted. Shall I read it?'

'Yes, please.'

She read it aloud:

'Colin, sorry, but I'll be unable to officiate at your mother's funeral. Instead, I've arranged for Canon O'Shaughnessy to step in. He knew your mother well. I know you'll understand. Father Traynor.'

'Is that it?'

There was a brief silence where he could hear Mrs Beattie breathing. 'Yes,' she replied. 'I don't see anything else. Do you need Canon O'Shaughnessy's number?'

'No. It's okay. I'm sure it's in my mother's address book.' Colin couldn't face trying to explain why his mother had decided she didn't want a Catholic funeral. 'Thank you.' He replaced the receiver and stood staring at the wall. A postcard of a painting of the Madonna and Child had been pinned to the little cork noticeboard which sat above the phone. He took it down; Father Traynor had sent it to his mum from Rome last year. Colin remembered her mentioning it and how flattered she'd been that he'd thought of her on a trip to the Vatican. He'd meant a great deal to his mother, and she'd have done anything for him. Colin couldn't think of a single reason why she wouldn't want a Mass, especially one led by Patrick, unless there'd been a falling out between them.

He re-entered the kitchen where Annemarie was pouring two glasses of red wine.

'Come and join us,' she said. 'It'll be fun.'

'I don't know how you can bear the cold.' He gestured outside. 'You know it's started to snow again?'

'Barely. Go and put a coat on and don't be such a wuss.' She held up the bottle. 'It's super expensive. Sean bought it in Duty Free.'

'Nah. I'm going to finish tidying up here then I've a bit of work to do.' He crossed to the pedal bin and lifted out the overflowing plastic bag. 'But don't let me stop the two of you.'

She took a gulp of wine. 'I need to ask you to do something.' She was avoiding looking at him, which always made him nervous.

'What is it?' He tied the plastic bag and placed it by the door.

'Will you go and see Dad? Try and explain what's happened to Mum? When Liam and I went the other day, it didn't register. There was barely a flicker.'

Their father had had a severe psychotic episode almost twenty years ago and had been in and out of psychiatric hospitals ever since. Unlike Annemarie and Sean, Colin had no memory of a time when he wasn't ill. And now, with his recent Alzheimer's diagnosis, any pretence that he was going to return home had been laid to rest. In truth, Colin barely knew him as a father. Despite visiting him as much as he could, he seldom recognised him, and on his last visit had called him Tommy, who was his father's youngest brother. 'Of course. Maybe I'll get him on one of his good days.'

'Are you okay?' she asked.

Sean shouted from outside, 'You poured that wine yet?'

A Prayer Before Killing

'Give me a minute,' she called back. 'You've got that lost look, Colin. Mum used to say it was like someone had taken over your body. It freaked her out.'

'It's this whole funeral situation. Had Father Traynor done anything to upset Mum?'

'Not that I know of; she thought the sun shines out his backside. Why?'

'I've just called the parish house. He didn't know Mum wasn't planning to have a Mass.'

'How did he take the news?'

'I didn't speak to him. He'd left a message saying he couldn't officiate at the funeral. That he'd asked Canon O'Shaughnessy to step in.'

'But Mum hates – hated – Canon O'Shaughnessy.'

Sean burst through the door. 'Forget the wine. I hadn't realised the time. Michelle's out with the girls tonight, and I'm supposed to be babysitting the twins.'

Annemarie frowned. 'I need to get to the bottom of this.' She hurried into the hallway. 'Bloody hell! It's the parish house answering machine.'

Sean looked at Colin. 'What's happened now?'

'I don't know why she's bothering,' he replied. 'Father Traynor can't do Mum's funeral.'

Sean shrugged and started to rummage through the kitchen cupboards. 'Let's see what we've got here.' He pulled out an unopened jar of coffee, almost dropping it as Annemarie returned.

'What in God's name are you doing?' she asked.

'Taking this. I brought it round the last time I visited.'

'No you didn't!' Annemarie grabbed it from him. 'You never brought her anything.'

As they squabbled over the jar of coffee, Colin sidestepped them, picked up the knotted bin bag and went outside. The air was refreshing, the falling snowflakes cool against his skin. There was another, more obvious explanation for

Patrick's decision not to officiate: the kiss. He needed to speak with him – he'd try phoning again on Monday.

'I'm off.' Sean stumbled out the back door and gave Colin a drunken hug.

'Should you be driving?' Colin asked.

'Do me a favour wee man, and zip it,' Sean replied with a fuzzy smile. 'Keep me in the loop about the arrangements. I don't think I want to say anything after all, but I'll need to arrange time off work.' He disappeared round the side of the house shouting, 'See ya.' Moments later the Saab revved into life before speeding off.

Through the window, he watched Annemarie head into the living room clutching the bottle of wine to her chest. He'd give her five minutes alone before braving the inevitable outburst against Patrick. He wondered what she'd say if he told her he'd made a pass at him.

Crossing to the bin, he removed the lid and was about to place the rubbish inside. As he did so, he caught sight of a plastic bag sitting underneath the pastry from the pie he'd thrown out yesterday. It was a distinctive bag – from M&S – the kind his mother always kept and would use until the bottom fell out. The same type that Jeanie had been holding when she appeared on the morning of his mother's death.

He reached in to pull it out and heard a familiar rattle of plastic. Searching inside, he discovered four empty pill bottles. Three were his mother's painkillers, dated the day before she died. But the other had the name Alec Walsh on it, Jeanie's husband.

CHAPTER 43
TWO YEARS EARLIER – LATE JUNE 1993

The first few days alone, out on the hills, had been cold and miserable. Rain had fallen in a steady drizzle and a low, suffocating mist clung to the moors. It wasn't until the third or fourth day, when the clouds broke and the sun shone bright, that Father Young began to feel alive again. How he had been so blind for so long to the wonders of the landscape, to the wildflowers, the birds, and the animals, he couldn't comprehend. They stirred something in the depths of his soul, a feeling that had been absent for a long, long time: contentment.

He decided to set up camp on the edge of a wooded area, not far from a fast-running stream. The trees offered shelter and the stream a supply of fresh drinking water, as well as the possibility of catching fish to eat. While impulse had propelled him onto the hills, and he could have planned better, he'd no intention of returning to civilisation any time soon. He was determined to make this work, to be self-reliant and – most important of all – to recharge spiritually.

Food was the main challenge. Though he rationed the contents, the various cans he'd taken from the school kitchen ran out after a week. While he improvised a fishing net from one of his T-shirts and tried to create traps using twigs and stones, his heart wasn't in it. He wanted this experience to be purer. He wanted to clear his mind, to have space to consider his next steps, to not make another mistake. If Turkey was his destination, a carefully thought-out plan was essential.

On the tenth day, he had a revelation: the existence he'd inadvertently chosen was that of the Christian hermits of old. This should be his own time in the wilderness – a time for prayer, and a time for penance. He committed to fast and pray for the next forty days; only then would he return.

With this renewed sense of purpose, each day brought new discoveries. His senses became heightened: the sounds, the changing light, the magic and mystery of nature which altered by the hour, the minute, the second, amazed him. He had no doubt this was the right decision. Forget the horrors of the school, the cruelties of Sister Oran, of Brother Thomas, and those boys full of hatred. There was an alternative, and he'd found it. His Eden.

He had begun to lose track of time when Our Lady came to him. It was night-time and he woke, startled by lights pulsing across the sloping sides of the tent. Blue and white rays shimmered, criss-crossing before his eyes, and a radiant white hand emerged, beckoning him. 'You need to ask,' she whispered.

'I'm not ready,' he replied, the coldness of his breath filling the air around him as her presence faded. In the morning, with the sun emerged above the horizon, he wept, fearful that she'd never return.

The days that followed passed in a haze of hunger and prayer. On his knees in the tent, head bowed, hands rigid, he prayed for hours on end, only stopping when sheer exhaustion forced him to sleep. With no time to fetch water or set a fire, he would crawl into his thin sleeping bag, his mouth dry, joints aching, and shiver through the freezing night.

He was dozing when she spoke to him again from outside

the tent. 'You need to ask,' she said. Too weak to stand, he crawled through the flap to find her suspended amongst the trees, her arms outstretched.

He buried his face in his hands. 'I'm sorry,' he cried. 'I don't know how.' Only when she touched his head and blessed him, did he feel able to look up. She was smiling down at him, and he knew her words were genuine.

'Sister Oran?' he asked, confused, suddenly thinking he was back in her room on the day he left.

She handed him a sandwich, the sandwich Sister Helena had prepared for him that same afternoon. 'Eat this,' she said. He took it, but as he brought it to his mouth it slid across his face, like water cascading through his fingers.

They sat for the longest time, Our Lady of the forest merging with Sister Oran in her room at the school, their different coloured vestments the only real difference. Their faces were the same: large and moonlike, kind and friendly, loving and compassionate. Their bellies, too: round and pregnant. How had he got her so wrong? How could he have acted so shamefully towards her? Only now did he get it; only now did he understand.

Head spinning and repeating his apologies, he stood and followed her to the stream, where it widened into a pool. Tearing off his filthy clothes, he placed one foot into the freezing water and then another. Nausea swept through him. The sun rose and he walked towards the centre, the peat-brown water consuming his naked body. He fell forwards, allowing himself to be fully submerged. Letting go, he floated back to the surface, and stared at the sun, arms outstretched, like Christ on the cross. Born again. The words came like a deluge, tripping from his tongue. *Our Father, Who art in heaven, Hallowed be thy name*. He'd a sense of the words' meanings like never before. *Thy Kingdom Come, Thy will be done, on Earth as it is in Heaven*.

All of a sudden, he had clarity. His own failures, his

vanity, had led him to this place and time. Everything, the entire calamity, could have been avoided had he not railed against the teaching position, had he simply accepted his fate – God's will – with humility and dignity. If he could remember this moment, hold on to it for ever, then he would be the priest he'd always wanted to be. Not a feeble man, blinded by anger and jealousy, but a man of wisdom, integrity and understanding.

How had he missed the signs? Even in the church, before he left that afternoon, he'd been given the opportunity to be that man and had failed yet again. When he took Sarah Kenny's confession, he had only thought of himself, only thought of the wrongs that had been visited upon him, only thought of revenge.

'Please forgive me,' he whispered to the bright sky, his voice hoarse with the certainty it was time to return.

CHAPTER 44
MONDAY 4TH DECEMBER 1995

A small group of oddballs – a mix of Holy Joes and eccentrics – were camping out in front of the gates when Colin arrived at the school. Seemingly oblivious to the freezing conditions, they held aloft placards with posters of Sister Oran plastered on them, and one even had a homemade sign with Johnny's name scrawled across it in thick felt-tip pen. Like the bangle, his suicide attempt appeared to have sparked renewed interest in Sister Oran's case. Colin drove past them, tooting his horn at a woman wearing a fancy-dress nun's outfit who deliberately stepped into his path. She gave him the finger, before letting him through.

'You gave me a fright, Mr Buxton.' Sarah was head-deep in a filing cabinet when Colin entered. 'We weren't expecting you back today.'

For yet another night, he'd barely slept. Any time he closed his eyes, images of his mother – angry or sad, sometimes in distress – came rushing into his head; then, it was game over. Had Annemarie not been returning to the house that morning he'd probably have stayed off school and tried to rest, but he couldn't face spending another day with her. She'd turned up first thing on Saturday morning, completely hyper, intent on getting the house in order. By that she meant sorting through all their mum's belongings and giving every room a deep clean. Colin thought it premature, even though he knew it was her way of coping.

He'd not broached the subject of the bag of empty pill bottles with Annemarie. On Friday night, after sending her back to her hotel in a taxi, he'd searched the house from top to bottom. Besides a few packets of paracetamol, there were no painkillers to be found anywhere. He'd resolved to speak directly with Jeanie as soon as possible, however there'd been no sign of her the entire weekend and her house had lain in complete darkness.

'How can I help you?' Sarah asked.

'We didn't get a chance to finish our chat,' Colin said.

She closed the filing cabinet and picked up her diary. 'We could schedule a time.'

'Would now suit?'

She stopped flicking through the diary. 'Sure. Do you want a coffee?'

'I'm fine,' he replied, taking a seat across from her. On her desk lay a to-do list for the day, with items highlighted in different colours: wages, meetings, phone calls, and administrative duties. 'This won't take long.'

'No worries; I've five minutes to spare.'

'I visited Father Young in prison on Friday.'

There was the slightest blink of her eye. 'How is he?' she asked.

'Not good mentally – or physically, for that matter,' Colin said, 'but we had an interesting chat.' He now had her full attention. 'He suggested you wanted Sister Oran removed from the school. That you requested it.'

Her eyelid flickered again. 'Surely you don't believe everything Mr Young says?'

A Prayer Before Killing

'I don't, but he seemed convinced, and I thought it only fair to ask.'

She picked up a ream of paper. 'Well, thanks for coming to tell me, but I can assure you it's absolutely not true. Once or twice, I might have raised an issue about her management of the laundry – timekeeping was not her forte – but that was all. At no time did I ask for her to be removed. What business was it of mine? And anyway, who would have paid any attention to me? I'm just the school secretary.' She divided the stack of paper in two, placing one half in a drawer. 'It's very sad that he feels the need to make these baseless accusations, but I should point out that *he's* sitting in a prison cell, no one else.'

'You're right.' Colin rose and went to leave.

'Before you go—'

Colin turned, hoping she might have more to add; he'd always found her open and honest, but he could tell his questions had irritated her.

'Brother Thomas is taking Matthew and Garr to the hospital today to see Johnny,' she said.

'Has there been any improvement?'

'No, he's still in a coma, but the boys want to sit with him. Brother Thomas let everyone know at Mass this morning that they'd be out of class. I don't know if you have them on a Monday?'

'I do, yes. When are they due back?'

'Before school ends, Brother Thomas said, so late afternoon I imagine.'

'When they get back, can you ask them to come and see me in the drama studio?'

She made a note and stood. 'I'm glad we had this chat.'

'One more thing—'

'Yes?'

'What time do you usually finish work?'

'Well, that depends.'

'Normally.'

'During term time around six, and the holidays, probably closer to five, I suppose. Why do you ask?'

'Never later?'

'Very rarely.' She picked up another stack of paper. 'I like to have Brendan's dinner on the table at seven.'

'In court, you said you saw Father Young entering the woods with Sister Oran at eight PM. That you were walking back to your cottage from the school office.'

'That's right, but as I explained to the police, I'd stayed on late that evening as I'd time to make up: I'd had a dentist's appointment in the morning. Who knows if he'd ever have been caught had I not happened to be there?'

'Thanks,' he said, leaving her to load paper into the photocopier machine.

It was just before nine-fifteen and registration was about to end before morning classes began. Colin was scheduled to take a class of juniors for a double period of athletics.

The muted sounds of teachers' voices could be heard as he walked through the atrium. Outside, Brother Thomas was escorting Matthew and Garr towards a car. Both still sported the same hairstyle and crisply ironed uniforms. As ever, in front of Brother Thomas, they were model pupils. Colin wished he could peer into their minds, discover what made them tick. After weeks of trying to get to know the Apostles, his relationship with Matthew and Garr still operated on a superficial level. He needed to find a way in, to repeat the breakthrough he'd had with Luc. Perhaps if he pressed them hard on Sister Oran? But that would have to wait. First, he had to work out what to do with the class of thirteen-year-olds who were eagerly waiting for his instructions.

'A cross-country run,' he announced, handing out bibs. 'Six miles in total. All the way along the forest path to the

A Prayer Before Killing

edge of the village, then up the hill to the castle and back down to the school. Do not take the shortcut along the main road.' Their disgruntled faces perked up when he told them that when they returned, they could take an early break.

With the class out the way, Colin returned to the PE department. At the end of the basement corridor, a set of double doors led to the senior boys' sports lockers. Grey and battered, these lined the walls of an area next to a side stair which led back up to the atrium; the space was rarely used by anyone except the senior boys. Matthew and Garr's lockers were next to one another, each secured with a lock. He'd come prepared. During his police training, Colin had taken part in a workshop where a locksmith had demonstrated different techniques for picking locks. He and another student had been the only two in the class who had managed to pick a padlock using a couple of paperclips.

However, after ten minutes of fiddling with the first lock, Colin realised it wasn't going to work. Though the locks looked simple, he couldn't unpick them. He went back down the corridor and into the PE store, scanning the shelves for something to use instead. Finding a broken golf iron, he returned to the lockers. If skill wasn't going to open them, then brute force would have to do.

Jamming the broken end of the golf club between the door of Matthew's locker and its surround, he used it as a lever. The door flew open with a loud crack. Colin listened to see if anyone had heard before rifling through the contents. There was nothing of interest inside, just some dirty kit, and a couple of well-thumbed copies of *Playboy*.

It took less force to lever open Garr's locker. A pair of muddy trainers – Air Jordans – sat at the bottom. He checked the soles; the heel of each included the outline of a figure jumping with a basketball. The shape was similar to the letter Y; it was a potential match for the print he'd found in the tunnel. He grabbed a plastic bag from Matthew's locker and put one of Garr's trainers in it. He had hoped to find the padlock key which he was convinced had been in Johnny's piggy bank, but this was the next best thing.

He then checked his watch; he still had time before the fastest of the cross-country runners got back to go and find Sister Helena.

'I'M TOO OLD FOR THIS,' she said, as he entered the laundry.

'Let me give you a hand,' Colin said, putting down the plastic bag and helping her pull a tangle of wet sheets from an industrial washing machine. 'Don't you have any help?'

'The youngest Baird girl sometimes takes pity, but only if her mother's looking the other way.'

'Surely this isn't part of your normal duties?'

Sister Helena nodded. 'Ever since Sister Oran's death, laundering the boys' bedding and towels has fallen to me.'

'That's a huge job.'

'It could be worse. At least their clothes get laundered by an outside company now.'

'What? You had to do their clothes too?'

'Only for a couple of days, but it nearly killed me.' Sister Helena opened the door of a huge tumble dryer. 'The archdiocese has been promising to send another nun here for well over two years now, but what girl in her right mind wants this life?'

'Take a seat and I'll put these in the dryer.'

Sister Helena collapsed onto a wooden chair beneath a narrow clerestory window. 'Thank you,' she said, mopping her forehead with a handkerchief.

'It's Sister Oran I wanted to ask you about,' Colin said. 'Or rather, I want to ask you a favour.'

Sister Helena narrowed her eyes. 'Go ahead.'

'Would you mind if I took a look at her room?'

'Now?'

A Prayer Before Killing

'If that's okay?'

He had thought she might refuse, but she immediately tucked her hankie into a pocket and stood. 'Come with me.'

'You're sure?'

'I don't mind,' she replied. 'Though I don't know what you think you'll find. The room was cleared after her funeral. It's been sitting empty ever since.'

Colin followed Sister Helena through the kitchens where the Baird women studiously ignored her. There was a man working there too – good-looking, in his thirties – who Colin hadn't seen before.

'That's Davey,' whispered Sister Helena. 'The chef who's never here.' Ushering Colin across the courtyard, she paused outside the nuns' annexe. 'Now, ordinarily, men aren't allowed in here,' she said, 'but I won't tell Brother Thomas if you don't.'

Colin smiled. 'Understood.'

She opened the door and he stepped into the tiny living space.

'That's Sister Oran's room on the left – the door's open.'

Sure enough, the room had been stripped bare; a single bed with a small bedside cabinet, a chest of drawers with the drawers pulled open, and a narrow wooden closet were almost all that remained.

Sister Helena joined him, standing in the centre to survey the space. 'It's such a sad end.' She retrieved her handkerchief and dabbed her nose. 'I can't lie, Sister Oran drove me to distraction but when I look back now, I realise that in those last few weeks before she went missing, she'd really lost her sparkle. When she first arrived here, she told me how she'd been blessed with a miracle – that she'd cured her aunt's cancer. She said she'd prayed to the saints for a week, and the cancer had gone.'

'Did you believe her?'

A deep sigh suggested Sister Helena was as sceptical as he

was. 'I've met nuns like Sister Oran before. Young girls who believe – who have a sincere faith – but whose heads are full of nonsense.' She sat on the edge of the bed and rubbed her neck. 'Was it a miracle? Who knows. Certainly, the aunt went into remission and that recovery lasted long enough for Sister Oran to gain a reputation of sorts as a healer; she was even featured on the local TV news. According to her, folk travelled from every part of Ireland to be healed. But, reading between the lines, when the results were – shall we say – unremarkable, she quickly decanted here, rechristening herself Sister Oran in the process. A born storyteller, I used to say.'

'Do you think Father Young killed her?' asked Colin. The question was deliberately direct to assess her reaction.

She looked startled. 'I don't, Mr Buxton. I honestly don't. He seemed sad – extremely sad, to me – but I never sensed any malice in him.' She stood. 'But what do I know? I'm just a silly old nun.' Crossing to the door, she took one last look around the room. 'I'll be in the laundry if you need me.'

Despite being tucked away from the main building, through its single window the room had a good view of the forest and the pathway leading up to the castle. If Sister Oran had been conducting a clandestine relationship with Father Young, or Matthew, or someone else, she could easily have come and gone through this window without being noticed.

Colin set about searching the room methodically.

Checking the mattress first, he was disappointed to find the fabric intact; there were no tears or signs of sewing to conceal a repair. Pressing with his hands from both sides at once, he felt across the entire surface, looking for any hidden objects or changes in texture, but again he found nothing.

He checked the bedframe and the rest of the furniture, pulling out drawers and searching for false panels. There were no hiding places within, behind or below the furnish-

A Prayer Before Killing

ings. Lastly, he felt around the edges of the carpet and across its surface, but again he drew a blank.

Most personal belongings had been removed a long time ago; a few religious images were dotted across the walls, and a couple of books remained on the windowsill.

He picked at the corner of a picture of the Virgin Mary; brittle and faded by the sun, it came away from the wall easily. Taken from a magazine, on its reverse side was part of an article about the daily routines of seminarians in Rome. He plucked another image from the wall. He didn't recognise the saint, but on the other side was an interview with the Vatican's press officer discussing an upcoming visit to Ireland. Taking each picture off, the backs were all the same: random bits of articles pertaining to religious matters. Nothing to suggest any hidden meanings in the images Sister Oran had chosen.

Moving to the windowsill, a line of dead flies indicated no one had cleaned the room in a while. A hardback book about sacred art by Sister Wendy Beckett sat in the corner. Inside was a handwritten dedication to Sister Oran from her aunt Catherine, dated May 1993. Next to that was a thin paperback, with a brightly coloured saint on the front, light spreading in a halo all around her. It contained stories about famous saints throughout the ages. Leafing through it, he found a page where the corner had been turned down: a chapter about Saint Oran. He began to read, but the prose was childlike and contained nothing that seemed noteworthy. The last book was the bible – a thick hardback, of a type he recognised only too well, as identical copies were placed in every single room across the school. He held it in his hands and flicked through it. Various pages had been marked in pencil, with key passages underlined, but nothing stood out as significant. As he placed it back on the windowsill, the dust jacket slipped from the bible's cover. Lifting it up to tuck back on, Colin discovered someone had taken a great deal of care to draw an intricate pencil diagram on the inside of it. Removing it from the bible, he spread the jacket out on the bed. A cross divided a heavily textured background. At its centre, a circle had been drawn, then on each of the arms, equidistant from the centre, a letter sat. There were four letters in total: M, G, L and J. It didn't take a genius to work out who the letters referred to.

Matthew, Garr, Luc and Johnny.

Colin carefully rolled up the dust jacket and placed it with Garr's trainer in the plastic bag, then left the room, shutting the door quietly behind him.

CHAPTER 45

At the last minute, Sarah asked Colin to cover Brother Thomas' mid-afternoon Latin class. 'He called me from the hospital to say they should be leaving shortly,' she explained. 'He says to get the boys to read Chapter 14 from their textbook and answer the questions at the end. I've written it all down.' She handed him a note.

The boys dutifully followed instructions and completed the work in plenty of time. There was an odd tension in the air, not exhibited in their behaviour or what they said, but in their troubled expressions. Johnny's attempted suicide had taken its toll on them, yet as far as Colin could see the school had done nothing to acknowledge, let alone lessen, the shock.

'Should we start reading the next chapter, sir?' a boy on the front row asked.

'No, why don't we treat the rest of the period as free study?' he suggested.

Another boy raised his hand. 'I don't have any homework to do.'

'You can read what you want, if you're all caught up on homework,' Colin said. Slowly, the class delved into their schoolbags and brought out an assortment of comics, paperbacks and textbooks for other classes. He saw their lack of enthusiasm, and said, 'Or we can take some time to relax and chat, if you like?'

The boys looked at each other, perplexed by his offer. He made a few attempts to strike up conversations but was met with monosyllabic replies. It seemed they preferred to get on with their reading. As he watched the clock tick down to the end of the lesson, Colin wondered what the boys were taking from their seemingly privileged education. With its focus on classics, theology and history, the school didn't appear to have any interest in creating rounded individuals. There was little joy and scant care in the boys' learning, minimal time for reflection. Excelling at exams was the priority and yet Colin thought they weren't being equipped for life in the real world, that they were being set up to fail in any career outside the priesthood, in relationships, in finding their true vocation.

When the bell finally rang to signal the afternoon break, he dismissed them and they trundled out, dragging their schoolbags behind them.

With enough time to make a couple of calls, Colin headed to the staff room where there was a payphone located in a small nook, with a sliding door for privacy. He'd tried calling the parish house several times over the weekend but only got the answer machine. If Patrick still hadn't returned, then perhaps Mrs Beattie would have a number where he could contact him. Just as before, the phone rang out four times and clicked through to the answer machine. He hung up and tried a second time but still no one answered.

The more Colin thought about it, the more convinced he'd become that Patrick's sudden departure was triggered by his clumsy pass. Colin felt if they could chat then he could reassure Patrick, let him know it was nothing to be embarrassed about. They'd become close over the last few weeks, and he didn't want to lose their friendship. Colin knew first-hand how the Catholic Church drilled the concept of shame into

A Prayer Before Killing

you from an early age. If you didn't fit into what was considered normal then exhibiting your true feelings, the real you, was never on the cards. It wasn't surprising therefore that Patrick's feelings had been revealed in such an awkward way. Colin decided he'd call round to the parish house that evening, see if he'd returned. Apart from anything else, he was keen to know whether Patrick had any inkling that his mother had decided against a funeral Mass.

Checking his phonecard for credit, he called Charlie Murray on the Paris number that Patrick had passed to him. With Luc's suggestion that Matthew left the retreat on the night Sister Oran disappeared, he wondered whether Charlie had suspected this. The first couple of times he tried, the line was engaged, but on the third attempt, a weary-sounding Charlie answered.

'Hello.'

'Charlie, it's Colin Buxton.'

'One moment.' There was a change of atmosphere on the line, as if Charlie was moving through to another room. Finally, a door clicked shut. 'I can't talk to you, Colin. Sorry.'

'When's a good time?'

'I mean, ever. Following your meeting with Luc, the Colberts have decided they won't be cooperating with your wider investigation.'

Colin had feared this might happen – just as quickly as they'd decided to cooperate, the Colberts had reversed their decision and pulled the plug. Worse still, it appeared Charlie was more aligned with – or controlled by – the family than he'd imagined. Hayley's reluctance to allow Luc to meet with him on his own told its own story, but when Luc diverted from what were clearly scripted answers, Colin had known it spelt trouble. The fact Fiona Colbert hadn't known about Charlie and Hayley's relationship was the final nail in the coffin.

'One minute of your time,' Colin said.

'I can't. You've no idea the problems your meeting with Luc has caused Hayley. In order for her to keep her job, I've had to sign a contract saying I won't have anything more to do with you.'

'Does Patrick know this?'

'What?' He sounded genuinely surprised by the question.

'Never mind,' Colin said.

'I'm sorry, but it's for the best.'

'One minute of your time. What harm can that do?'

'Wait.' Charlie answered a question in French about lunch, and Colin wondered who else might be there with him, and whether this might be hampering his ability to be candid. 'Okay,' he whispered. 'You've thirty seconds.'

'You only have to say yes or no.'

Charlie took an intake of breath. 'I won't commit to that.'

What could make someone pivot like this? Hayley was more than capable of manipulating Charlie, but it had been he who'd engineered Colin to come on board. Was the relationship more serious than Patrick implied or was something else going on? Whatever, he needed to make these questions count, as it could be his last chance.

'Is it possible Matthew left the retreat the evening Sister Oran disappeared, travelled back to the school, then returned?'

A pause signalled Charlie might be thinking, which could mean he had doubts, or conversely, was thinking up a story to withhold information. 'Hand on heart, I can say that didn't happen.'

'Why are you so sure?'

'It's true that Matthew went to bed early complaining of a headache, but when I checked on him at midnight, he was sound asleep in bed. He even came to my room about fifteen minutes later asking for some paracetamol.'

'Could he have made the journey and arrived back at the lodges by then?'

A Prayer Before Killing

'He can't drive and the retreat's in the middle of nowhere – there's no public transport. Theoretically, if someone else drove him there and back then perhaps, but I've no idea who that might be. Besides, my bedroom at the lodges was by the entrance and I'm a very light sleeper. I would have noticed any comings and goings.'

'Why do you think Luc made the accusation?'

'I hate to say it about one of my boys, but you need to take anything Luc says with a pinch of salt. He's always been prone to – how can I put this – exaggeration.'

A voice in the background – possibly Hayley's – was calling in English to say that a car was about to arrive.

'One more question.'

Colin heard him stand up.

'I can't. I need to go.'

'Please? You only have to confirm or deny.'

'Step away from this, Colin.' Charlie sounded more strained. 'There's no point in pursuing this investigation any further; the boys are untouchable. Plus, it'll save you and a lot of other people from a whole lot of grief.'

'A young boy's lying in a coma, and an innocent man is serving a life sentence in jail. Sorry, but stepping back is no longer an option until I get some answers.'

The voice – definitely Hayley's – called again in French, this time more insistently.

'Okay. One last question – if I can, I'll answer.'

'Did Sarah Kenny ask you to have Sister Oran removed from the school?'

Hayley's voice was now beside Charlie. 'Darling, the car's here,' she said. 'We need to go.'

'I'll be one minute,' Charlie replied. He paused for a few seconds as the staccato click of high heels could be heard retreating. 'Immediately before we left for the lodges, Sarah raised the subject of Sister Oran with me, informally. She suggested that Sister Oran was being over familiar with some of the boys and questioned whether our school was the best place for her. When I asked her for examples of inappropriate behaviour, she didn't seem to have any other than her being too affectionate. I said I'd keep an eye on things but I wasn't overly concerned. Some of the younger boarders can get homesick and there's a role – a motherly or sisterly one – which really only the nuns can fulfil. Events, as you know, took over so we never spoke about it again. I'm sorry, I need to go. Don't call again.'

CHAPTER 46

A dumping ground for redundant equipment, the former drama studio overlooked a dense area of woodland which spread up the incline towards the castle. At the brow of the hill, Colin could make out the dark silhouette of the building. A lone fragment of turret rose above the snow-flecked canopy of trees, a narrow opening at the top resembling the window from which Rapunzel uncoiled her hair in the Ladybird book he'd read and loved as a child.

He'd deliberately chosen this location to make the boys ill at ease. Having not been in use since Father Young's time, he hoped it would unsettle them and give him an advantage, however slight. Regardless of whether Luc was telling the truth, his instinct was that, when put under pressure, they'd work together. With his back to the window, Colin settled into a chair and waited for their arrival.

A few minutes later the door was knocked, and without waiting for a reply, both Matthew and Garr entered.

'You wanted to see us, sir?' Matthew, gregarious as ever, strode forward, Garr following behind at a slower pace.

'I'm pleased you could both make it.' Colin stretched out his hand. Matthew accepted immediately, with Garr offering the most tentative of shakes a few seconds later. 'How's Johnny?'

The boys exchanged a look before Matthew replied, 'Still in a coma but he's not got any worse since being admitted.'

'That's something. Hopefully, there will be signs of improvement soon,' Colin said.

Garr pushed his spectacles up his nose, a physical tic Colin had witnessed before, and exchanged a second look with Matthew.

Physically, they made an odd pairing, which was highlighted further by their decision to continue to dress and style their hair the same. However, where Matthew radiated a straightforward alpha-male energy, Garr offered something more nuanced. There was a definite edge to him. What Colin had initially taken as reticence was nothing of the sort; Garr was constantly observing and assessing. Whereas Colin could reliably predict what other boys might say or do, Garr remained an enigma. One minute he was the provocateur, the next the class joker, then his head would be buried in a textbook, the embodiment of concentration. Luc's assertion that Garr was as much of a leader as Matthew could not be ignored.

'Please, take a seat,' Colin said.

'I'll take the broken one, shall I?' Garr shook the chair to highlight the loose frame but sat without any fuss.

'How are you both doing?'

Matthew pulled his chair closer to Colin as he sat, his athletic frame shifting as the chair creaked beneath him. He stretched his legs across the floor, filling the space between them. 'It was sad seeing Johnny like that.' He crossed his arms. 'They still don't know if he has brain damage.'

'And what about you, Garr?'

'Do you mind if we pray?' Garr clasped his hands. 'Please, if you could both join me.'

'I don't think now's the time or place for that,' Colin interrupted. 'Perhaps you and Matthew might want to take a moment for private prayer in the chapel, after we've spoken?' He had seen Garr try to take charge like this before, by way of diversion, and was not about to entertain it.

Matthew straightened himself in his chair and gave Garr a quick prod.

Garr unbowed his head and smiled. 'You've made quite an impression since coming here, sir,' he said. The words aimed to flatter but carried no substance.

'Why do you say that?' Colin had never known Garr to go down the personal route with him. That was left to Matthew and some of the other boys, who would ask him about girlfriends or which team he supported.

'You're everyone's friend round here,' Garr continued. 'Even Sister Helena likes you, which is no small feat.'

'It's nice to be liked,' Colin said. 'Don't you think?'

Garr shrugged.

Matthew pointed to a poster on the wall depicting a burning landscape with Jesus and his apostles floating in the sky above; the foreground populated by naked figures. 'Father Young put that up when he was here. Kind of kinky, isn't it?'

'I'm your teacher, Matthew, not one of your pals out in the schoolyard.'

Matthew glared at Colin, his face reddening. 'Sorry, sir.' In that split second, as he attempted to regain his composure, the child showed through the adult facade. He might be sixteen and as strong as any man but lurking beneath was an impatience. Pushed far enough, he would lash out and stamp his feet.

Garr placed a hand over his mouth and yawned. 'Sorry. Will this take long?'

Again, the provocateur. 'I wanted to check in with you both,' Colin said, 'make sure you were okay.'

'Is that all?' Matthew asked, still distracted by the poster.

'I've a couple of other questions. If that's alright?'

'Fine by me,' Garr replied, suddenly alert.

'Fire away,' Matthew echoed, his attention returning to Colin.

From his pocket, Colin produced the padlock key and held it up. 'Garr, can you explain this?' Though neither boy flinched, Colin sensed their focus tighten on him. 'I know Johnny accessed the chapel from the underground passage and placed Sister Oran's bangle on the statue of the Virgin Mary.'

'And that's why you think he tried to kill himself?' Garr asked with a scowl.

'You used the same key to place Johnny's St Christopher medal around the neck of the statue, didn't you?' Colin took the trainer out the plastic bag. 'A footprint matching this was found in the tunnel.'

A flicker of fear crossed Garr's face. 'Who gave you permission to enter my room?'

Matthew leaned over and thumped Garr's arm. 'You've just given yourself up, dummy. That could be any old key,' he chuckled, 'and you put those trainers back in your locker the other day. I watched you.'

'Matthew's right, I've not been anywhere near your room,' Colin said. 'It is a key to the padlock though – but it's Brendan's original – and yes, I found the trainers in your locker.'

Garr took a second to react. Caught out, he was considering what to say and how best to say it, but just like in class, he needed time to ruminate. 'I'm not doing this,' he stuttered. 'And I don't know who you think you are anyway.' He stumbled to the door and slammed it as he left.

'Uh-oh!' Matthew raised his eyebrows. 'I think you've pushed a button. If there's one thing Garr doesn't like, it's someone showing him up.' He crossed to the poster. 'What have a bunch of nudists got to do with angels?'

'Look closer.' Colin had noticed the image when first

entering. Superficially, it appeared innocuous; only on further inspection was it clear that the naked figures were enduring an array of tortures and gruesome deaths at the hands of devils and horned demons.

Matthew stood staring at it, the end of his nose almost touching the poster.

'It's The Last Judgement.'

'Christ! So it is. That's horrific.' Matthew pulled away, a look of disgust on his face, and sat back down. 'I wouldn't have noticed if you hadn't said.' A smile crept across his face. 'The whole Virgin Mary thing was a bit of a farce. Johnny shouldn't have done what he did and then, with him in the hospital, Garr thought it would take the heat off him if something else appeared, that maybe people would think it was a miracle after all.'

Colin referred to his notes. 'Does the retreat happen every year?'

Matthew crossed his arms. 'It used to. It was Dr Murray's big idea, but it hasn't happened since he left.'

'Can you go over the journey to the lodges on the day of Sister Oran's disappearance?'

'What? Everything?'

Colin nodded.

Reluctantly and in a deadpan voice, Matthew recounted how Sister Oran had waved them off, that he'd sat at the back of the bus with others, how they'd played cards at the start, then he'd eaten a sausage roll he'd bought from the village newsagent's the day before. For the last half hour, he'd pulled his coat over his face and slept. He'd seen little else of what went on, he explained, and hadn't got off the bus at a local pub when some of the boys needed to pee.

'Did everyone get back on the bus?'

Matthew gave him an incredulous stare, then as if someone had jabbed him in the side to prompt him, he said, 'I was asleep, wasn't I?' He shrugged. 'But everyone was there when we got to the lodges.' He leaned over and tried to see what Colin was writing down.

Colin turned to a new page. 'How many lodges are there?'

'Fifteen, sixteen? I don't know exactly. Enough for everyone. All dorms. Four to a room.'

'And you shared with…?'

'Garr, Luc and Johnny. Like we always did.' On saying Johnny's name, he looked down at his feet. His school shoes had been buffed to a mirror-like sheen. He fidgeted, one foot rubbing at the other, as if he'd found a blemish which he needed to erase. With his face downturned, he resembled one of the angels floating at the shoulder of Jesus, high above the devastated landscape.

'Luc said you returned to school the night Sister Oran disappeared. Is that true?'

'Luc said that?' Matthew's lip curled. 'Unbelievable! That guy's a born liar. So privileged and up his own arse. He's a total shit.' He glanced up. 'Sorry sir, but he doesn't know the value of loyalty or friendship or kindness. It's all about him and what he can get.'

'So, you deny it?'

'Of course. I had a headache – a migraine – so I went to bed early and got up the next morning just like everyone else. Ask Garr, he was there, or ask any of the boys. Dr Murray even saw me when I asked for some pills.' His matter-of-factness was convincing, or was it well-rehearsed? After all, he'd had plenty of time to work on an alibi.

'Tell me about Sister Oran.'

He shrugged his shoulders. 'Nice. A bit out there, I guess. Said she could perform miracles. Healed her dying aunt, brought a half-dead dog back to life, that sort of thing.'

'But you were close, weren't you?'

Matthew's eyes burned. 'Sister Oran listened. She was kind. Unlike the other freaks around here.'

'Luc said you had sex with her.'

A Prayer Before Killing

Matthew laughed. 'Again, not true.'

'Why would he say it?'

'Because once, during a game of Truth or Dare I said I had, but I was lying. It was either make something up or shove my cock into someone's face.' He blushed. 'Sorry, sir.'

'But she was pregnant when she died.'

'So I'm told.'

'Were you the father?'

'No.' He drew his long limbs up around himself. 'Of course not.'

'Then who was? Garr? Luc? Johnny?'

'Seriously? You think one of them knocked her up? Johnny had barely developed pubes, Garr has zero interest in sex, and I'm pretty sure Luc bats for the other team.'

'Which leaves you.' Colin paused. 'Unless there's someone else?'

'Father Young's your man.' Matthew spat out his name. 'You know, the loser who's actually doing life for her murder? He was sniffing about her from the moment he got here. Ask anyone.' He rose from the chair and crossed to the window. 'Sister Oran was close to all four of us. I mean, she was different from any other nun I've ever met. At times she'd be a bit flirty, but mostly she was more like a big sister. We all liked her, but not in a dirty way. Or mostly not. I remember Johnny told me he dreamt about her, that she tied him up and had sex with him. But Johnny's weird like that.'

'And did she?'

Instead of looking shocked, Matthew smirked. 'You know what, maybe she did. I dunno anymore. We'll never know. But like I said, Father Young was the one trailing after her. God knows why she gave that saddo the time of day.' He stood, pulling himself up to his full height – six-three easily – and stared down at Colin. 'Father Young's the one doing time and he deserves everything he's got.' He gave Colin a snarling smile. 'Now, I've bible class to get to.' As he crossed the room, the door suddenly burst open and Brother Thomas entered. Garr stood outside in the corridor, peering from behind.

'Matthew!' Brother Thomas snapped. 'Out! Now! I need a moment with Mr Buxton.'

Matthew immediately left the studio and was led along the corridor by Garr, but as they were about to turn a corner, Colin saw Matthew deliver a sharp slap to the side of Garr's head.

Colin stood. 'I can guess what you're about to say.'

'Then I'll keep it short. You're sacked. Pack your things and leave. Bishop Trocchi's been informed and he's in agreement.' He pointed to the door. 'Now, if you could follow me.'

He'd got too close to the truth: to the Colbert family, the boys, Father Young, Hayley, Charlie Murray, Sarah – even to Sister Helena and Patrick. He'd known his days were numbered.

Retrieving his backpack from the staffroom, he followed Brother Thomas downstairs and past the office, where Sarah sat typing. She averted her gaze; it was obvious she'd been made aware of what was about to happen.

'I'd like a moment with Sarah before I go,' Colin said.

'I don't think so,' Brother Thomas replied, grabbing his arm and pulling him towards the main door.

It was his strength which surprised Colin the most. For someone so grey and sickly-looking, he had an iron grip. In the commotion, Colin stumbled and smacked his face against the open door. Blood oozed from his nose. He wrenched his arm away from Brother Thomas. 'Ask Sarah why she lied to me,' he said.

Sarah looked up, her eyes widening.

'Mr Buxton, you've caused enough trouble for one day.' Brother Thomas pulled a tissue from his pocket and passed it to him. 'Now, if you don't leave immediately, I'll have no choice but to call the police.'

A Prayer Before Killing

'Were you aware Sarah tried to have Sister Oran removed from the school? I've had it confirmed by a reliable source, so why would she deny it?'

Colin was marched outside and the door slammed in his face. Outside, it was freezing, and he realised he'd forgotten his coat. He turned, debating whether to go back inside or not, and was met by Caroline, emerging flushed and breathless from the building.

'What's going on?' she asked. 'My class saw Brother Thomas manhandling you downstairs.' She noticed his bloody nose. 'That bastard didn't hit you, did he?'

Colin shook his head.

'Let's get you cleaned up,' she said, taking his arm.

'No, I'll be fine. I think it's best if I go. I've been sacked, but I may need to call on your help. I'll understand if you—'

'Call me anytime,' she said. 'If I can help with your investigation, I will.'

CHAPTER 47

Colin arrived home to find Liam slumped on the sofa, flicking between the channels. 'Why's it so hot in here?' he asked.

'Mum's had the heating on full blast all day; she's decided there's damp in the walls.' Despite having been born and brought up in Newcastle, Colin was always surprised by his nephew's Geordie accent – it sounded put on.

'How's she been?'

Liam rolled his eyes. 'Manic. She's not stopped since this morning. There's a pile of stuff in the kitchen she says needs to go to the dump.'

'Where is she?' Colin asked.

Liam yawned. 'Upstairs.'

'You hungry?'

'Starving, but Mum's on a diet.'

Colin delved into his pocket and brought out a tenner. 'Go get three fish suppers,' he said. 'From the place on the High Street. You know the one I mean?'

'Yep!'

'And wrap up. It's freezing out there.'

A Prayer Before Killing

'Thanks, Uncle Colin,' Liam said, grabbing his coat and vanishing out of the front door.

Thuds from above suggested Annemarie was moving furniture, which he'd explicitly asked her not to do. 'Typical,' he muttered to himself as he climbed the stairs.

Opening the door to his mother's room, he discovered his sister on her hands and knees, vacuuming dust from the area of carpet where the bed usually sat. The bed itself had been dragged to one side and was piled with clothes she'd emptied from the wardrobe.

Colin switched the vacuum off at the mains.

'Why'd you do that?' Annemarie asked, sweat dripping from her forehead. 'This place hasn't been properly cleaned in months.'

He stared at her.

'What?' Annemarie said. 'You couldn't have picked up a duster?'

'It's not exactly been a priority, what with Mum being terminally ill.'

Annemarie's lip began to tremble and he immediately regretted his words. With a sniffle, she wiped her nose and pulled herself onto the corner of the bed.

'Sorry,' Colin said, sitting beside her and putting an arm around her shoulder. 'Why don't you leave this? I can do it any time. There's no hurry.'

'I know, but I just thought since I was here…'

'You look knackered.'

'I am. I've not slept.' She cupped his chin and scrutinised his face. 'You look like you've been in the wars.'

He put a hand to his nose. 'I walked into a door.'

'Seriously?'

'While I was being escorted off the school premises.' He grinned. 'I got sacked.'

'Is this not becoming a bit of a habit? Rubbing people up the wrong way?'

'Like mother, like son?'

'You said it.' She stood, brushing fluff from her jeans. 'Did I hear Liam go out?'

'I sent him to the chippie. He looked bored out of his mind.'

Taking a tissue from their mother's dressing table, she dabbed at her eyes. 'I told him to go to the pictures. Or – God forbid – make himself useful, but all he wants to do is mope around with his face tripping him.'

'He's fifteen, and he's been away from his friends for days. It's a desert around these parts.' He picked up a pile of magazines from the floor. 'Find anything incriminating?' he joked. 'No *Playgirls*?'

'It's all *Catholic Chronicles* and the *Radio Times*.' She grabbed a black plastic bag and opened it. 'Shove them in here.'

'Sums Mum up, eh?'

They both gazed around at the room.

'There were a couple of calls for you. Did Liam say?'

'No.'

'Some posh lady called Caroline – you've to ring her back as soon as you can. Her number's on the table.'

'When was this?'

'Maybe twenty minutes ago.'

'And the other one?'

'This morning – from Barlinnie – inviting you to visit Father Young at three tomorrow afternoon.'

'No way. I thought he'd had enough of me; he must have had a change of heart.' Colin lay back on the bed and stared up at the ceiling. 'I can go and see Dad first thing, since I don't have a job anymore.'

'He'll enjoy that.'

'What'll I say to him?'

'You'll know when you see him. You're much better at that sort of thing than me or Sean.'

A Prayer Before Killing

'True.'

Annemarie gave him a shove. 'Go set some plates out in the kitchen while I finish hoovering. To hell with the diet.'

Colin stood and stretched his back.

'And Jeanie was here this morning, acting weird,' Annemarie said.

'Did she say where she's been for the past few days?'

'I didn't speak to her. Liam saw her out the back, sitting on the wall staring into space.'

'Was she okay?'

'I don't know. She scarpered before he could get the back door open. He reckons she was in her dressing gown and slippers. Is she going a bit doolally?'

'I don't know.' He shrugged. 'I need to check in with her.'

Downstairs, he picked up the piece of paper on which Caroline's home number had been scribbled, and dialled, wondering what could be so important. It wasn't that long since they'd spoken; perhaps she just wanted to check he was okay. The bloody nose and sacking probably merited it.

'Hello?' Her voice, usually upbeat, sounded subdued.

'Everything alright?' As soon as the words left his mouth, he reminded himself that nothing at that school was ever alright.

'Someone wants to meet with you.'

'Who?'

'They'd prefer for me not to say, nor what it's about, in case they change their mind.'

So far, the secrecy was right on brand. 'Is this to do with my sacking or the investigation?'

'A bit of both.' She paused. 'Look, do you know the little café beside the post office in the village?'

'Manhattan Café?' The irony of its village location never failed to amuse him. 'Green door? Chintzy decorations?'

'That's the one,' she replied. 'Can you be there about midday tomorrow?'

He paused while he thought through the journey times. 'Sure, and you can't give me any clue?'

'Sorry,' Caroline said. 'I need to go.'

As he set the kitchen table, he went through a list of who might want to meet with him: Sarah? Brother Thomas? Patrick?

With no sign of Liam returning, he shouted to Annemarie that he was going to pop over to Jeanie's, that he wouldn't be long. If she was home, he wanted to quiz her about the bag of empty pill bottles.

DAYS OF FREEZING temperatures had made the streets slippery with ice, even more so in the cul-de-sac where the gritting lorry never bothered to come. Avoiding a huge patch of black ice, Colin carefully crossed the road to Jeanie's. Again, the house was in complete darkness, the unlit Christmas tree sitting forlornly in her bay window. She was probably out, perhaps ministering to the next parishioner in need, or maybe the bingo. He knocked on the door anyway but was met by silence.

'Jeanie,' he called through the letterbox, listening hard. In the distance, he could hear the sound of the cat meowing. He peered in through the window, but there was no sign of movement. Having not seen her for three days, Colin was starting to think she was avoiding him.

The route up to the parish house was wetter and Colin's feet were soon like blocks of ice, his battered old trainers offering little protection against the slush. On the far side of the road, taking a short cut through the little park that connected the estate to the High Street, he saw Liam returning with the fish suppers wrapped up in newspaper. Colin shouted, but Liam was listening to his Walkman and carried on, oblivious to his presence.

Colin's stomach was grumbling and he thought about

A Prayer Before Killing

turning round, but he'd only have to come out again later. If Patrick was at home, he'd give Annemarie a call to tell her he wouldn't be long. And if not, it would only be a ten-minute walk back and the chips would still be warm.

The lights in the parish house were off. And just like at Jeanie's, the Christmas tree which sat outside at this time of year, usually glistening with baubles, was in darkness. Someone had obviously forgotten to switch them on. An idea struck him. When he was an altar boy, the key to the parish house would often be left under a plant pot by the front door. He lifted one up, but only a dark disc of soil was revealed, contrasting with the gleam of white snow. Glancing about, he could see other plant pots scattered around; one by one, he lifted them, but there was no key. Useless, he thought. He was about to leave when he spotted a final pot which had recently been edged aside; he could see that the snow had been compacted around it. As he crouched to explore, a voice emerged from the darkness.

'Mr Buxton?'

He turned to see a familiar figure marching up the path.

Mrs Beattie, headscarf knotted tightly at her chin, repeated, 'Mr Buxton? Can I help you?'

CHAPTER 48

'Hello,' Colin said, rising from his crouched position. 'I was looking for a key. I was going to pop inside and turn on the Christmas lights. I thought someone had forgotten to do it.' Mrs Beattie glared at him. 'It was one of my jobs when I was an altar boy—'

'Mr Buxton,' she interrupted, 'you realise this all looks very suspicious?' Unlocking the front door, she entered and switched on the hall light before turning to him. 'Are you coming in or not?'

Colin followed her inside.

'The lights?'

'You want me to...? Okay,' he stuttered. 'Are they still plugged in down here? 'Yes.'

Colin flipped a switch and the tree sprang into life, pulsing with strands of multi-coloured lights.

Mrs Beattie removed her scarf and coat. 'You can close the door now. I think we're in for a heavy snowfall tonight.'

'So, Patrick, I mean Father Traynor... I take it he hasn't returned yet?'

She hung her coat on a hook by the stair. 'It doesn't look like it.'

A Prayer Before Killing

'He's been away for days.'

'He has.' Mrs Beattie moved further down the hallway and switched on a pair of table lamps. 'Can you turn off the main light for me?'

Colin did as he was told.

'That's better,' she said. 'Right, let's get you a cup of tea. You look frozen stiff.' Turning towards the kitchen, she called back, 'Take off your shoes and put them under the radiator. It's what Father Traynor always does after a long run.'

Padding through to the kitchen in his stocking feet, he found her filling the kettle. As efficient as ever, she'd already set out a teapot and cups on the counter. 'I wouldn't ordinarily invite loiterers in for tea, but I'll make an exception this once.'

'Sorry about outside, I wasn't thinking. I've had a bit of strange day.'

'I was actually going to call you.' Mrs Beattie spotted a random thread on her cardigan and picked it off.

'You were?'

'I'm worried about Father Traynor.'

'You've not heard from him at all?'

She shook her head. 'Not since last Thursday evening when he said he was going to visit his family in Dundee.' Mrs Beattie hesitated. 'This won't go any further?'

'Of course not.'

'When I think about it, he didn't expressly say that's where he was off to, rather, he allowed me to assume that's where he was going.'

'You don't think he's there?'

'He's not. His mother rang today asking to speak to him. I had to tell a white lie – I said he was busy with plans for Advent. I didn't want to worry her.'

'Where else might he have gone?'

'I don't know.' Again, a slight hesitation before she continued. 'He seemed upset before he left. I didn't pry – it's none of my business, he can get stressed – but I don't think I've ever seen him quite so out of sorts.'

Colin wondered again if he was the cause of Patrick's departure. Why couldn't Patrick have just spoken to him? Dozens of scenarios started to go through his head. Did Patrick think he would report him? That it might ruin their friendship? Nothing could be further from the truth. Though it had been unexpected, Colin saw it as an opportunity to get to know him better, for them to be more honest with one another. He felt sure Patrick would see it like that too, but then again, he was a priest who'd made a pass at a parishioner.

'There have been occasions in the past where he took a couple of days off for himself,' Mrs Beattie said, filling the teapot with hot water, 'but he was always back in time for Sunday Mass. Canon O'Shaughnessy had to step in yesterday; he'd told the archdiocese he was going away but they'd expected him back for Mass.'

'And he took his car?'

'Yes.' She smoothed down a wrinkle on her blouse.

There was genuine concern on her face. He'd previously thought her overly protective, but now he saw she genuinely cared. He got it. Patrick was an exceptional priest and it wouldn't have only been Moira's demands he was responding to within the parish. At any given time, he must have been ministering to dozens of Moiras. Working day in day out with that sort of pressure would be hard for anyone, but as a priest, especially lonely.

Mrs Beattie poured the tea. As always, the best china was employed, with cups and saucers, milk in a matching jug and sugar cubes in a bowl with a tiny set of tongs. She pushed a plate of digestives towards him. 'Help yourself.'

'What were Canon O'Shaughnessy's thoughts?'

'Much like mine. We were hoping he'd return yesterday or today with that big cheery smile of his, back to his usual self.'

A Prayer Before Killing

She plucked a biscuit from the plate and held it above her cup as if about to dunk it. 'If there's no sign of him by breakfast tomorrow, I've to call the archdiocese and they'll contact his family. But as soon as they get a hint of anything untoward, they'll be down here in a flash swarming all over the place, and that's the last thing Father Traynor would want. As close as he is to his family, he's very private.'

'Does Patrick have many friendships outside his work?' It was perhaps too loaded a question, but he felt it would be remiss not to ask.

There was a silence before Mrs Beattie spoke. 'I know how fond he is of you.' With that simple acknowledgement, she managed to sum up the contradictions of the Catholic Church. Here was a woman of faith, who cared for a parish priest, who understood his flaws, and was prepared to tell the occasional untruth to make sure any "failings" remained hidden. 'I know he once had a special friend, Finn – a sweet boy. They'd been at the seminary together, but he left before ordination. He lives in Canada now and still writes occasionally. And when Father Traynor started here at St Bridget's, a young man called David used to ring, but I never met him. All I know is they were close. They'd be on the phone for hours, and then they weren't. He was definitely not a parishioner; I got the impression they worked together over at the school. One of the times Father Traynor went away, I did wonder if David was the reason.'

Colin noticed the sparkle in her eye. She obviously enjoyed being privy to this aspect of Father Traynor's life. 'Would it be alright for me to take a look about?'

'You mean, around Father Traynor's rooms?'

'There might be clues as to where he's gone.'

'I'm not sure—'

'I think it might be wise.'

Her expression pensive, Mrs Beattie placed a hand to her mouth. 'You think something's wrong too, don't you?'

'It's possible. Father Traynor visited me on Thursday, while he was out on his run.'

'He didn't say.'

'Something happened between us – a misunderstanding, something trivial – but after what you've said, I honestly don't think it's enough to have made him want to run away. But there might be something else.'

'Go on.' Mrs Beattie leaned forward.

'He's been helping me with work.'

'Father Traynor mentioned that you're coaching sports at Holy Trinity College.'

'I am, or I was. The teaching role was a front – a cover.'

Curious, Mrs Beattie put down her cup.

'I've been looking into the death of Sister Oran, the nun who was murdered in the school grounds, and Father Traynor's been helping me.'

'He has?' Her expression became even more interested.

'I think the real killer may still be walking free.'

She nodded. 'Come with me.'

Colin stuffed another biscuit into his mouth and followed her out into the hall.

'If Father Traynor turns up tomorrow, he can never know I've allowed you to do this. You can check his study here on the ground floor – you know where that is – but not his bedroom upstairs. Even I don't go in there. Understood?'

'Absolutely.'

'Now, I've got the Christmas silver to polish in the church,' she said. 'So, when you've finished, you can let yourself out. Remember, no access to his bedroom at the top of the stairs.' She pointed above. 'Is that clear?'

'Yes.' Was she, in fact, telling him to go upstairs? He waited as Mrs Beattie exited to the church and remained motionless until he heard the sound of the connecting door being closed.

Colin knew the layout of the parish house well. As an altar

A Prayer Before Killing

boy, he'd spent many hours wandering through the rooms, peeking into cupboards and drawers he'd no business opening. As he climbed the stairs, a thrill went through him, remembering the times he and his fellow altar boy, Michael, had played hide and seek. Once, Colin had ended up on the top of a wardrobe in Father McIlvanney's bedroom, only for the priest to enter and lay down on his bed. Thankfully, he was asleep and snoring within minutes, his drunkenness very much part of the reason they could run riot. On the first floor at the back, Father McIlvanney's old bedroom was now Patrick's.

Colin opened the door and switched on the light. A narrow sash and case window, draped with old fashioned curtains, looked onto the snow-covered roof of the church. In front of this, a small bed with a satin eiderdown had been neatly made up. To one side, a row of shoes, including Patrick's running shoes, were evenly spaced. Colin doubted if Patrick would go anywhere for any length of time without them. Checking a wardrobe and chest of drawers, which both had carefully organised clothes within, it was impossible to determine if Patrick had taken any with him when he left. A bottle of aftershave sat on top of a dresser. On the wall around it were framed photographs of family members, group photos from what looked like the seminary, and some from Patrick's time at Holy Trinity College. One image stood out; it was of Brother Thomas refereeing a football match at the school, a staff and pupils' game. In the picture, Matthew was about to tackle Father Young. Although he must only have been about fourteen, Matthew looked like a man; he was already twice as broad as the priest, and half a foot taller. Any notion that Sarah could have unwittingly mistaken Matthew for Father Young was absurd.

Returning downstairs, Colin turned on a lamp in the study. The top drawer of Patrick's desk contained a bible and a set of rosary beads. The one down from it a spy thriller and various invoices. On the other side, the top drawer contained stationery, however the bottom drawer was locked. Colin tried to force it open, but the desk was too solid and it wouldn't budge.

He opened a box that sat on the desk and checked for a key but it only contained more stationery, plus a couple of personal letters from several years before. One was from Patrick's mother and the other from a sister called Bernadette. Stacked to one side of a typewriter were papers relating to parish business. He sifted through them but nothing of interest stood out. Similarly, there was nothing of obvious interest on the bookcases which lined two of the walls.

He returned to the locked drawer and tried to unpick it with a couple of paper clips, but for the third time that day his breaking and entering skills failed him. Remembering that a box of tools had always been kept in the hall cupboard, he went to investigate. However, when he opened the door, he was faced with shelves of old parish papers. On reflection, it occurred to him that taking a hammer and chisel to Patrick's desk might not be the best course of action. There was only one thing for it: he needed to find the key.

Colin worked through the obvious places – taped under the desk, the seat, hidden within the pages of a bible – but no luck. Flummoxed, he sat back at the desk and stared out of the window into darkness. Sitting on the windowsill was a small silver-coloured trophy. Colin picked it up. Patrick's name was engraved on the side in copperplate as the winner of a marathon in 1980 at some kind of international sports event for seminarians. As Colin placed it back on the sill, something rattled in the trophy's plastic base. He tilted it and a little key fell out into the palm of his hand.

Colin smiled. Only Patrick would hide a key there, he thought. He slotted the key into the lock and turned it.

The base of the bottom drawer was hollow and obviously fake. Using a letter opener, he removed the makeshift panel; it

A Prayer Before Killing

was no surprise to find a selection of porn mags – all very vanilla – hidden underneath. Colin smiled as he recognised a copy of *Blueboy*, the same edition he himself had at home. So that was it, Patrick's big secret, a stash of gay porn. Carefully replacing the magazines and the false bottom, he locked the drawer and placed the key back in the trophy.

Colin turned his attention to the phone pad. It was thick with Patrick's overlapping doodles and notes, which appeared to be written in his own shorthand. He tried his best to decipher the acronyms and abbreviations: "SB" was probably St Bridget's, "BT" possibly Bishop Trocchi or maybe Patrick's sister Bernadette. On the second page, the letters "HT" were circled in blue biro and an arrow pointed to "11 PM". Could "HT" be Holy Trinity? There was no way of knowing with any certainty. As for the others, he hadn't a clue where to start.

Beside the telephone, the answerphone was flashing. He listened to the messages: a good number were from Mrs Beattie, asking Patrick to please let her know if he was back yet, a couple were from himself, there was one from Canon O'Shaughnessy, and the rest were from parishioners. But again, there was nothing of note.

Finally, he hit the redial button on the phone, and almost immediately a young boy answered.

'Hiya.'

'Can I speak to Father Traynor?' Colin asked. 'Is he there?'

The boy giggled. 'Father Traynor hasn't worked here for a couple of years. I've no idea where he is. I could ask Brother Thomas—'

Colin put down the receiver. The last place Patrick had called was Holy Trinity College.

CHAPTER 49

FOUR DAYS EARLIER – THURSDAY 30TH NOVEMBER 1995

Cursing himself, Patrick kicked off his running shoes and stripped out of his vest and shorts. Half-naked, he stood staring out his bedroom window and into the night, where snowflakes were gathering on the steep slopes of the church roof, softening its harsh angles. Winter had barely started, but already he wanted it to be over. He longed for the warmth of sun on his shoulders and the endless days of a Scottish summer. Simple desires, he knew, but they made all the difference. Winter was too dark, the parish house too cold, and apart from Mrs Beattie, devoid of company. Was that why he'd made such a fool of himself with Colin?

When he became ordained, the sense of duty, however overwhelming, gave him a profound sense of purpose. From as far back as he could remember, the chance to preach and guide people with Christian values had filled him with drive and determination, but lately he'd found himself faltering. The congregation was the best part; it always had been. Despite their idiosyncrasies and demands – mostly reasonable, at times less so – he felt a kinship with his parishioners. The church's hierarchy, its rules and its petty politics, was another matter; it had begun to grind him down. On certain matters, at best there was no consistency and at worst a dubious morality. Why, as a priest, did he have to renounce having a partner? With the support of a soulmate, was it not obvious he could do an even better job than he already did?

The loneliness was becoming unbearable. Yes, he could pick up the phone and chat to his family every day of the week – morning, noon and night. He could visit them, play a part in the lives of his nieces and nephews, all fourteen of them, but the void he felt at the centre of his being was growing by the second. The annual arc of church life no longer consumed him, nor the daily Masses. What he lacked – and he'd thought long and hard about this as he ran through the streets and parks of Glasgow's southside – was genuine love and affection, someone he could share his delights with and tell his troubles to without fear of judgement. A person he could plan a future with. There had been days where he'd kept running, though his muscles screamed with pain, for fear he would fall to the ground and weep over the life being denied him.

Bad enough that a priest should desire a soulmate above his devotion to God, but far worse, in the eyes of the Catholic Church, was his wish to share his life with a man. To him, it didn't seem that unacceptable or outlandish. He'd known since he was a child that he preferred boys, and he sensed in his early teens that his family – at least, his parents and siblings – had guessed too. It seemed natural to sit with his sister, Bernadette, and flick through her copy of *Jackie*, asking each other which pop star they fancied the most. They'd giggle and pinch each other when they chose the same one, such as David Essex, but Patrick always felt a sense of satisfaction when he chose someone different, like Marc Bolan from T-Rex or David Bowie. The list, as he got older, became longer and longer. It would seem that there wasn't a man who'd ever appeared on the TV or in a film who was safe from his desires.

But his parents had had their own plans for him. His three older brothers had each been sent off to the seminary at various ages, but one by one they'd chosen a different path. Or, as he'd been told, God had decided the priesthood was not for them. None had received the calling, therefore the family's last chance was him. Little Patrick, who was brighter than all of them, would fulfil the family obligation to God and the Catholic Church, and his sacrifice would be far outweighed by the prestige this would bring.

And so, at the age of fourteen, he found himself far from home, at Holy Trinity College, on a scholarship funded by his local parish. His devotion was never questioned, any doubts he had were never expressed; instead, a process was set in motion which inevitably led to the seminary and his ordination as a priest.

The decision had never been his to make.

Now, looking back on that day of ritual, when he lay prostrate, accepting the death of himself and his rebirth into priestly service, he wondered if that was when the rot had started.

A shiver ran down Patrick's spine and brought him back to his bedroom, to the here and now. He lifted his dirty sports gear from the carpet and placed it in the laundry basket. Picking up his running shoes, he arranged them neatly against the wall. In the bathroom, he turned on the shower and stood under its flow, until the lukewarm water made his shoulders numb.

There was no avoiding what he'd done. He would have to speak to Colin: apologise, explain himself, come clean.

HAVING DRESSED, Patrick went downstairs to his study, picked up the phone and dialled. The line was engaged, so he hung up and called the archdiocese instead, and spoke briefly to Canon O'Shaughnessy. Taking a deep breath, he redialled the first number. This time the call was answered by the housemaster, a teacher whose voice he didn't recognise. It was a small mercy, but he was grateful, nonetheless.

'Can I speak to Matthew Penrose?' Patrick asked.

The sound of the boys' voices echoed in the background. At this time, they would be getting ready for supper. He was reminded of his own time as a pupil, and the smell of milky cocoa and chocolate biscuits. To this day, it was his favourite treat.

'Can I ask who's calling?' the housemaster asked.

'It's his uncle.' Patrick held his breath and waited for the lie to be challenged, but there was no follow up.

'Just a moment.'

Patrick imagined him leaving the little office in the housemaster's suite, where boarders could take personal calls each evening, walking out into the atrium and following the gallery corridor to Matthew's door. He pictured his surprise at being told there was a call from his uncle. Patrick was reasonably sure he had an uncle, but didn't know for certain.

There were muffled sounds as the receiver was picked up again. 'Uncle Ollie?'

'Matthew, it's Father Traynor,' Patrick said.

There was a short pause before Matthew answered. 'That's weird, Mr Cameron thought you were my uncle.' Another pause, then he continued, his voice much calmer after his initial surprise. 'How long's it been, Father?'

'A couple of years.'

'That long?'

Patrick coughed. 'We need to talk.'

'We do?'

'I think you know we do.'

'I really don't.' Matthew laughed.

'It's about what happened in 1993, on the retreat.' A bell rang to announce supper, and a rush of excited squeals echoed down the line as the boys made their way to the refectory. A passing voice asked Matthew how long he'd be, and should they keep a seat for him.

'Two minutes,' he replied. As the background noises faded, Matthew's slow, heavy breathing told Patrick that he was thinking long and hard about his next move. 'What do you want?'

'I'd like to meet. Tonight.'

'Seriously? Tonight? That might be difficult.'

'I'm sure you'll find a way.'

Another voice interrupted their conversation – Garr's – his middle-class accent dropping into Glaswegian slang. 'Fuckin' get a move on, Matty,' he cried. It was how the boys spoke when they were together, different from when they were around teachers and the clergy. Like they were two different people.

Matthew placed his hand over the mouthpiece, but not well enough to mute his response. 'Piss off! I'm talking to someone.' A muttered 'Sorry,' brought him back to the call. 'Later tonight. Sure. Why not?'

'By the duck pond?' Patrick proposed. 'At eleven? Or perhaps later?'

'Eleven's fine.'

'Okay. I'll see you then.' Patrick put the receiver down, his head spinning. He paced up and down the room. What was he doing? It was all too much. First, he'd provoked the situation with Colin, next he was abandoning his duties and now he'd opened a can of worms with Matthew. What the hell was wrong with him? He should phone Canon O'Shaughnessy back and tell him he was staying, then call Matthew again to cancel their meeting. But what good would that do? It would just be delaying the inevitable.

'Father Traynor?' It was Mrs Beattie.

'Christ! Sorry, Mrs Beattie, you gave me a fright. I thought you'd left.'

'I told you I was staying late tonight to do some batch

A Prayer Before Killing

cooking for the Christmas holidays. For the days I'm not here. We can't have you starving, not at your busiest time.' She looked him up and down. 'Are you alright? You look like you've seen a ghost.'

'I'm fine,' he blurted, 'maybe a bit tired. Actually, I spoke to Canon O'Shaughnessy a few minutes ago and asked him to cover for me.'

She looked surprised. 'You did?'

'I need to get away for a day or two,' he said.

'Has something happened?'

'No, no,' he insisted.

'You work far too hard.' She smiled. 'Some family time will do you good.'

He nodded. 'Did you need something?'

'Only to say goodnight. That's me finished; everything's labelled and in the freezer.'

'Great. I'll walk you out.' Patrick accompanied her to the front door. 'I'm going to write a note for the Buxtons. Can you pass it on, if Mr Buxton calls?'

'Of course.' Mrs Beattie buttoned up her coat. 'And you're definitely alright?'

'Never better.' Patrick smiled as he held the door open for her. As soon as she'd gone, he rushed upstairs and packed an overnight bag. After meeting Matthew, he'd drive a little further north. There was a hotel by the sea where he'd stayed before. One night away, maybe two, would do him the power of good, give him time to clear his head and work out exactly what he needed to tell Colin.

PART 5

CHAPTER 50
TUESDAY 5TH DECEMBER 1995

Colin woke, his room lit by a strange ethereal glow. Craning his neck, he peered outside. The whole neighbourhood was cloaked in a layer of snow, reflecting the amber light of the streetlamps onto his bedroom ceiling. He wrapped the covers back around himself and tried to sleep, but it was no good, a deep feeling of gloom refused to leave him. Eyes half closed, he felt for the alarm clock. Six AM. Defeated, he switched on his bedside light. Keen for a distraction, he picked up the dust jacket he'd taken from Sister Oran's old room.

He studied it more carefully. What he had thought was simply a pencil drawing was more complex. Over the base layer of graphite, ink details had been added to enhance and emphasise the Apostles' initials. What had appeared purely abstract, actually contained some naturalistic elements: there was a little tree, and possibly an animal, a small cat of some description. Someone, presumably Sister Oran, had taken a great deal of time and care over its creation, but what it meant, Colin couldn't fathom. Was it just an elaborate doodle?

He held the dust jacket up to the lamp, to check if any

messages or marks were hidden within, but there was nothing to see. The fact it was a dust jacket from a bible could hold significance for Sister Oran – there was, after all, a cross shape contained within the design – however, within its walls, the school must have dozens, if not hundreds of copies of the same publication. Putting it aside, he forced himself out of bed.

On the landing, he paused and was about to open his mother's door to check how she was when he remembered.

Downstairs, he stepped over the bin bags Annemarie had filled with Moira's belongings to switch on the central heating. Grabbing the dirty dishes from the table, he placed them in the kitchen sink.

By the time he had returned home the previous night, Annemarie and Liam were long gone, leaving only a plate of cold chips and half a battered fish on the counter. A note beside said *Enjoy!* but by then he'd lost his appetite and had scraped everything into the bin. Underneath, Annemarie had added, *Good luck with Dad. Let me know how it goes. A xxx*

Colin wandered through to the living room and opened the curtains. Not since he was a small child had he seen snow like this in Glasgow; the entire cul-de-sac was draped in soft quilts of pristine white. He remembered a photo from that winter in the 1970s, of him and his mother in the back garden having a snowball fight, caught in a moment of pure joy. Growing up, he would look at that image, perplexed, struggling to recognise the carefree woman in it as Moira Buxton. This morning, he wondered who had taken the picture – could it have been his dad?

Lifting the coffee table to one side, he stood in the centre of the room and stretched his back. As he gently began to move from one yoga pose to the next, he felt a warmth return to his body, his mind begin to relax and the gloom start to recede a little. Closing his eyes, he felt himself momentarily unburdened from the heaviness surrounding him.

A Prayer Before Killing

. . .

COLIN HAD VISITED his father twice since his return from India. Each time had been the same; his father had seemed unbearably far away and there was little conversation between them. On both occasions he had held his hand and they'd sat side by side in silence.

The room at the nursing home was small and clean but impersonal, with the dominant feature being a hospital bed and some nondescript landscapes on the wall that could have been anywhere. Dressed in brown slacks and a beige jumper – which was the same colour as the linoleum covering the floor – his father sat in a cheap vinyl armchair, staring out the window. Though the immediate view was of the carpark, beyond were trees, and beyond that, in the distance, the snow-covered Campsie Hills.

'Hi Dad,' Colin said, but there was no response. He dragged a plastic chair across and sat beside him. 'How are you doing today?'

One of the care assistants, Amanda, popped her head round the door. 'Everything okay?' she asked.

'Fine,' Colin replied, not sure whether it was or not. 'How's he been since my sister visited with her son last week?'

'You've been quieter than usual, haven't you?' She took a blanket from the cupboard and placed it over his father's knees.

Colin noticed a slight brightening in his father's expression, the beginnings of a smile.

'We need to make sure you keep warm,' she continued. 'Isn't that right, Ray?'

Moira always referred to him as Raymond, so Colin had seldom heard his shortened name used.

Amanda pulled at the curtains to let some more light into the room. 'On sunny days, in the late afternoon this room gets the full benefit. You love the sun, don't you, Ray?'

Again, a tiny response, as his dad's hand trembled. Colin reached over and squeezed it.

Amanda turned to Colin and whispered, 'Have you set a date for the funeral?'

He shook his head. 'Not yet. Next week probably.'

'I'll pop in on you a little later, Ray. We can put some music on. You love your jazz, don't you?'

His father muttered something to Amanda as she left which Colin thought might have been, 'Great.'

Even though Colin still gripped it, his father's hand remained freezing. 'Why don't we warm these up,' Colin said, tucking the bony fingers under the blanket. He shuffled his chair further round to better face his father and took a deep breath. 'Do you remember what Annemarie told you when she was here the other day?'

His father didn't respond. Colin sighed, unsure what words to use and whether any of it mattered. Of course it does, he reprimanded himself. Regardless of how much his father understood, he'd a right to know his wife had died and that a funeral would be held. It might make no difference to him at this moment in time, but who knew what memories might be sparked?

'Annemarie told you that Mum's passed away. Do you remember?'

His father looked past him and stared blankly out the window. Two years earlier, he could have engaged in a conversation to some degree. It might have shot off in random directions but there would be a definite sense of connection. Now, it felt there was little, if any, response. 'You remember how ill Mum had been? That's why she'd not been coming to see you.' His dad's hand slipped from his. Colin was unsure if this was a reaction to what he was saying or not.

A Prayer Before Killing

Though he made several more attempts to get through to him, there was no sign that the news of Moira's death was registering. As with his previous trips, they ended up sitting in silence together. No more words were said until Amanda returned forty minutes later, by which time both he and his father had nodded off.

'I didn't mean to wake you,' she said.

'Sorry.' Colin was a little disorientated and had to remind himself where he was. Outside, the grey sky had turned darker, with slate-black clouds gathering on the horizon.

'Don't apologise,' she said. 'It's a stressful time.'

As promised, Amanda put a tape into the cassette deck and turned it on. The voice of Ella Fitzgerald sparkled through its tinny speaker, bringing a smile to his father's face.

Colin kissed him on the forehead and stood to go. 'Bye, Dad. I'll see you soon.'

'Tommy?' His father's voice, once broad, Glaswegian and resolutely working-class, was now gentle, pleading.

'It's me, Dad. Colin.'

'Who's Colin?' he asked, turning towards Amanda.

'He's your son, Ray,' she replied.

'But I've only got one son – Sean. Haven't we, Moira? Sean's our son.'

Colin stepped out the door, and Amanda followed.

She touched his arm lightly. 'A final decision's not been made, but I think it's going to be recommended that your father doesn't attend the funeral. He's very frail, and the doctor thinks it may be too much for him. Too disorientating.'

Colin nodded, unsure if he was agreeing to this arrangement or not. 'I'll be in touch.'

Making his way to the exit through the labyrinth of corridors, the words *'But we've only got one son'* kept going round and round in his head.

CHAPTER 51

The journey out to the village next to the school was treacherous in places. While the motorway and the main roads had been gritted, as soon as Colin turned onto a side road, his car began to slip and slide. He slowed down and dropped back from the car in front.

On the radio, more heavy snow was being forecast for that evening; people were being warned to stay indoors, and to only travel if essential. Hinting at what was to come, a sudden flurry of snow fell as he entered the village and parked close to the café.

The main street was deserted and an eerie silence filled the air, broken only by the crunch of snow underfoot. It felt as if time had stopped. Colin stared at the garish neon sign – *Manhattan Café* – flashing in the window. It seemed an oddity in such a picturesque village.

Inside, there had been little attempt to follow through on the New York theme; the café abounded with the usual Scottish décor of tartan cushions and stuffed pheasants. In fact, the closer he looked, the more he noticed pictures and old photographs of the school grounds, from long before the school building was constructed, when it was still a private

A Prayer Before Killing

estate owned by the local laird. The only nod to Manhattan appeared to be a framed painting of the Brooklyn Bridge beside the toilets.

He glanced around the tables, expecting to see Caroline, but apart from a waiter in his early twenties standing behind the counter drying coffee cups, there was nobody.

'Table for one?' the waiter asked.

'I'm meeting someone—' As soon as he spoke, Caroline rose from a poorly lit booth at the very rear of the café. 'It's fine, they're already here.'

'I'll be over to take your order in a minute.'

'Thanks,' Colin replied, distracted by Caroline's appearance. Wearing a yellow beret and a large pair of dark glasses, she had clearly gone to town on the idea that this was a secret rendezvous.

'Too much?' she asked, spotting his expression.

'I think the glasses make you more conspicuous.'

She raised them above her eyes. 'Really?'

Colin nodded. It was only then he spotted who he was here to meet. Garr, in his neatly pressed school uniform, his hair combed severely to one side, sat staring at the table. 'Hello Garr.'

He didn't look up.

Caroline grabbed what looked suspiciously like a real fur coat from the booth and pulled it on. 'I'm stepping outside for a ciggie,' she said. 'I need to be back at school with him in ten minutes. Oh, and I've brought a jacket you left at the school.'

'Thanks, and that's no problem. I've a meeting in Glasgow after this.'

'Good luck with the roads,' she said gesturing out the window. She dropped her voice and leaned towards him. 'Garr says he needs to talk.' Lowering her glasses again, she scurried out the café.

Garr held up a key. 'It's for the padlock in the tunnel.'

Despite his austere clothing, there was a gentler expression to his face. A hint of contrition, perhaps?

Colin joined him in the booth. 'Thank you.'

'Please don't tell anyone the St Christopher was down to me. I thought it would take the heat off Johnny. I needed to do something to help him.' Garr glanced at Colin. 'I can't have my chances of entering the priesthood ruined. It's all I've ever wanted to be.'

'I can't promise that,' Colin said, 'but if I can, I'll ensure it stays between us two.'

Garr avoided making eye contact. 'Thank you.'

'Ready to order?' The waiter's cheery expression was met with two blank stares. 'I can come back.'

'No, wait. I'll have an espresso.' He checked Garr. 'You?'

Garr hesitated. 'I'll have the same.'

'Great,' the waiter said. 'Give me two minutes.'

As Garr focused on his hands and began picking at his skin, Colin broke the silence. 'Tell me about Sister Oran.'

Garr shrugged and looked towards the door, perhaps hoping that Caroline might reappear and whisk him back to school.

'You invited me here,' Colin said. 'So, what's it to be? Are you going to speak to me or not?'

'Sister Oran promised us miracles. The bangle and the St Christopher were all to do with that. Because, since she died, nothing had happened. Johnny got tired of waiting, I suppose.'

'What kind of miracles?'

'I don't know. Stupid ones. I went along with it, but I never believed – not like Johnny and the others. But there was never anything bad behind it. Sister Oran was a good person. She was kind. She had faith in us.'

The waiter returned with the coffees. 'Anything else I can get you?'

Colin shook his head. 'We're fine.'

Another customer entered with a Labrador puppy and the waiter turned to chat with her. The background noise seemed to help Garr relax a little.

'Luc told me that Matthew returned to the school the evening Sister Oran disappeared. Is that true?'

Garr took a sip of his espresso and grimaced. 'Not that I know of.'

'Try it with some sugar,' Colin suggested.

Garr took a cube of sugar and stirred it into his coffee. 'The four of us were sharing a room, so I would have noticed.'

'So, Luc's lying?'

Garr shrugged his shoulders. 'It wouldn't be the first time.'

Colin sipped his coffee and tried to ignore the inane chat behind him about how much snow was due and whether the café might need to close early. 'Were Matthew and Sister Oran having a relationship?'

Garr pushed his coffee aside. 'Matty said they had sex.' He glanced up. 'That is what you're meaning?'

Colin nodded.

'Sure, he was always her favourite and they had secrets, but she was like a mother to us all. She would never have betrayed the rest of us like that.' He held Colin's gaze. 'Never.' Garr shifted in his seat, then glanced up at the door. 'When will Miss Wilson be back?'

'Soon.'

'It's just I've got double English and I can't be late.'

'But there's something else you came here to tell me, isn't there?'

Garr edged the coffee cup back towards him and stared into the dense black liquid.

'Now's your chance, Garr. You know, sometimes we know things and are too afraid to say. But a man is in jail for a crime I don't think he committed, and if you know anything you should tell me.'

'Only that I had nothing to do with Sister Oran's death. Nothing. You've got to believe me.' Once more, he looked beyond Colin to the front of the café.

There was a commotion as Caroline entered and began oohing and aahing over the puppy, proclaiming how she used to have a Labradoodle.

'I can ask Miss Wilson to wait another few minutes.'

'No!' Garr began putting on his coat. 'I've said all I wanted.'

Before Colin was able to press him further, Caroline appeared at the booth.

'Ready?' she asked.

Garr slid along the seat and stood. 'Thank you, Mr Buxton, for agreeing to meet with me.' He strode towards the door, but stopped to pat the puppy.

'I'm sorry I couldn't give you more time with him,' Caroline said. 'It's just that what with the weather, and you not being there, the timetable's up in the air and I've to cover housemaster duties.' She kissed his cheek. 'Let's stay in touch.'

After they left, Colin remained seated in the booth, certain that Garr knew more than he was letting on. Once more, relations between the boys remained opaque.

At the counter, the waiter was still busy chatting with the woman whose puppy was receiving all the attention. As Colin waited at the till, his eye was drawn to a framed map on the wall.

'That'll be three pounds, please.' The waiter had suddenly appeared at the till.

Colin handed over a fiver and felt the puppy's snout snuggle against his leg. As he bent down to pat it, his eye was drawn back to the map. Something about it struck him as familiar.

The waiter handed him two pound notes in change, and Colin went to leave the café, but as he got to the door he turned back and returned to the counter. 'Excuse me,' he said. 'Can I take a closer look at the map behind you?'

'Sure.' With great pride, the waiter stood in front of it and began a rehearsed spiel. 'It's the oldest known map of the castle grounds,' he said. 'Here's the castle and this is the site of the old chapel which the modern school is built upon.'

He beckoned him round to take a better look, but Colin didn't need to hear or see anymore – he had already made the connection. The four points on the cross of Sister Oran's drawing corresponded exactly to locations on the school grounds.

CHAPTER 52

On the journey across the city to Barlinnie, snow began to fall in earnest – a haze of fine flakes, restricting visibility. Parking outside the prison, Colin trudged across grey watery slush to the entrance gate. A bitter wind blew from the north, making the entire building feel even bleaker than on his last visit.

A different guard led him through the labyrinth of corridors and locked doors to the same cold room where, once again, Simon was waiting. Keeping his jacket on, Colin sat down opposite.

The guard gave him a stern look. 'I'll be outside,' he grunted, slamming the door shut.

'Thanks for asking me back,' Colin said.

Simon blinked and pushed the hair back from his forehead. 'I didn't tell you the whole truth before,' he said.

'If it makes any difference, regardless of what you did or didn't say, I think you're innocent.'

Simon continued as if Colin hadn't said anything. 'But I omitted certain things for a reason.'

'I'm listening.'

A Prayer Before Killing

Simon turned his face awa and rubbed his hand against his eyes. 'None of this is what you think.'

'I'm not making any assumptions. What is it you need me to know?' Colin was determined to get to the truth this time; he couldn't risk Simon withholding again.

'I'm not sure where to begin.'

'Why don't you start by telling me about the time leading up to Sister Oran's disappearance?'

Simon touched the scar on his face. 'When I last saw her that Monday—'

'This was around three?'

He nodded. 'We'd had the disagreement in her room and she left.'

'And what was that about?'

'I was out of line. I accused her of sleeping with the boys – the Apostles – then I asked her to run away with me.' He held his head in his hands. 'I thought she'd played a trick on me, tried to humiliate me.'

'In what way?'

'I was completely wrong; she wasn't involved. It was the boys, I think they wanted her to themselves. They lied, led me to believe I was meeting her in the castle ruins, but it was a set-up, she was never going to be there, she didn't know anything about it. In my head, at the time, I wanted it to be true. I had these feelings I couldn't explain or control, feelings for her. That day, in her room, it all came out wrong. It was a total car crash. If I'm honest, I think I really scared her. I was obsessed.'

'And she left?'

'That was the last time I saw her.' He wiped his eyes with his sleeve. 'However, I did something in her room, after she left, which I'm ashamed of. Which I've never told anyone.' He bowed his head.

'I can help you,' Colin said, 'but only if you tell me everything. Don't you want to discover who really murdered Sister

Oran? Ensure they're put away? Don't you want to escape this hellhole?'

Simon nodded. Forcing himself to sit upright, he cleared his throat and said quickly, 'When she left, I took her habit from a drawer and I masturbated over it.'

'That's why your semen stains were on her clothing?'

Simon's face was scarlet.

While this offered an explanation for one of the most damning pieces of evidence against Simon, Colin knew it wasn't grounds for an appeal. There was no way of corroborating it. If anything, by changing his story, it painted Simon as an even more unreliable witness than the prosecution had already suggested. 'It's not enough to prove your innocence.'

'There's more.'

Colin grabbed his pen. 'Go on.'

'Afterwards, I felt so ashamed that I went to the chapel to pray. That's when I saw her.'

'Sister Oran? But I thought—'

'No. Sarah, the school secretary.'

'What? Why haven't you mentioned this before?' Colin asked. 'Why hasn't she? Why wasn't it covered in court?'

'I never said anything because I felt it would be wrong to breach her trust.' Simon closed his eyes. 'I took her confession. Not an official one, but I did offer her absolution, and it was the last occasion I ministered as a priest.'

Colin sat back and scrutinised his face. There was no suggestion Simon was lying or trying to concoct a story to serve his own end. 'And, of course, you're duty bound not to reveal what she said to you?'

'I'm now willing to break that confidence.'

Colin looked him in the eye. 'Honestly?'

'To you and only you. If you ever try to use it officially, I'll deny we ever had this conversation. But hopefully it'll fill in some blanks, help you find Sister Oran's killer.'

'Tell me everything,' Colin said.

A Prayer Before Killing

Simon wetted his lips and took a deep breath. 'Sarah was in a state of complete distress when I found her in the church. Someone working at the school had accused her of stealing money.'

'And had she?'

'Yes.'

'Did she say who had confronted her?'

'No, and I was in such a state myself, I didn't push her. But she referred to "he" and "him", so it was a man. I remember she kept trying to justify it, saying she'd needed to help her family, that she was always planning to repay it before anyone noticed.' He sat back and breathed a sigh of relief.

'It makes sense that she wouldn't volunteer this,' Colin said, 'but it's weird that the theft has never come to light. Don't you think?'

'I don't know. It could be the church, a case of one scandal too many.'

'I believe Sarah saw Matthew walking into the forest with Sister Oran that night,' said Colin. 'Luc claims he left the retreat to meet her, though for some reason Garr won't back this up.'

'Why wouldn't Sarah just say that it was Matthew she saw? It doesn't make sense.' He thought for a moment. 'Unless he was the one who had accused her. Maybe he was blackmailing her?'

'There might be something in that, but in those circumstances, would Sarah not have more grounds to blackmail him? Did she say anything else?'

'One thing.' Simon shifted in his seat. 'It's what pushed me over the edge.'

'Are you able to speak about it?'

Simon's bottom lip trembled and he began to stutter. 'Sarah said she was struggling with another secret.'

'And did she tell you what that secret was?'

He nodded. 'She told me Sister Oran was pregnant. That's how I found out.'

'Sister Oran had confided in her?'

'I suppose so. Though I don't know how that would have come about; they weren't friends.' Simon drew his arms around himself and gripped his chest. 'What I do know,' he whispered, 'is that was the moment my world fell apart. Nothing's made sense since then.'

Seeing his fragile state, Colin decided to pursue a different line of enquiry. 'Was Sister Oran artistic?' he asked.

'Very,' Simon replied. 'She was always dancing and singing. Once I caught her dancing with Matthew in the gardens, whilst the other boys watched, entranced. It was the first time I realised there was something really odd about their relationship.'

'But did you ever see her draw maps, for example, or plans of the school grounds?'

'Yes. Why do you ask?'

'I found a map hidden in a bible in her old room – hand-drawn and very detailed.'

'It could be hers,' Simon said. 'She had a theory, well, more than a theory – a belief – that the landscape around the school was sacred. She was fascinated by its connection to the early Irish missionaries. It's why she was always outside, exploring.'

'The map includes the initials of the boys. The Apostles. Do you have any idea what that might be about? They seem to be connected to particular locations.'

'I'm not sure. Sister Oran was always looking for signs; divine patterns she called them. I think it's part of the reason she was so taken with Matthew, Garr, Luc and Johnny – she saw the resemblance of their names to the Four Evangelists as a sign from God.'

'Is there anything in the grounds that relates to the Evangelists?'

A Prayer Before Killing

'Not that I can think of, but where I found her dancing, there's a huge beech tree with a bench around it, reputedly blessed as a sapling by St Francis and brought back from Italy. That was one of Sister Oran's favourite places. There's also St Thomas' Well.' As he warmed to the subject, Simon became more animated than Colin had ever seen him. 'But there are other features associated with religion. The tunnels that run under the estate are all to do with the Jacobites and having escape routes and hiding places for persecuted Catholics, not unlike the priest holes you had in Tudor England.'

'So, she wasn't wrong about it being a sacred landscape?'

'I guess not.' Simon smiled. 'Her faith was so much purer than my own. I envied that.'

CHAPTER 53

In the dusk, the city sparkled with frosted windows and Christmas lights as Colin drove home. The roads were busy with people leaving work early before the snowstorm set in. He, however, had other plans.

As he opened the front door, there was no sign of Annemarie. He rang her hotel, but she wasn't there either. The receptionist said she'd gone out with her son earlier. Maybe Liam had finally persuaded her to take some time to relax.

Now that Colin knew Sister Oran's drawing was of the school grounds, he was determined to check them out as soon as possible. And that was best done at night, when there was little chance of being spotted. If he was quick, he'd have a couple of hours to explore before the snow began.

He ran upstairs and collected the map, slipping it into a plastic sleeve for protection. In the kitchen, he found fresh batteries for his torch and, hunting through the display unit in the living room, he found his grandad's old compass in a velvet pouch at the back of a drawer.

Before leaving, he called the parish house, but it went straight to the answerphone. Had Patrick returned, he felt

A Prayer Before Killing

sure Mrs Beattie would have let him know. Patrick's disappearance was concerning, not least because the school was the last place he'd called.

COLIN TOOK a route through the village which avoided the entrance to the school. Though the main street was just as quiet as before, a mosaic of lit windows suggested it was populated after all. Turning onto a small road which followed the western edge of the school estate, his car made it to the top of the hill without too much bother. He parked his car in a lay-by.

Stepping outside, he was hit by a wall of ice-cold air. For now, the sky was clear, with an almost full moon, but he could see clouds moving in from the west. A second car sat at the far end of the lay-by, covered in snow. He changed into his walking boots, switched on his torch, and approached. Sweeping the registration plate clear, he instantly recognised it: Patrick's silver Ford Escort. Judging by the depth of snow on the roof and bonnet, it was feasible it had been parked there since last Thursday. He wiped the side windows and peered inside, but there was no sign of Patrick.

This was proof that Patrick had come to the school. But why? And why park here? And, most pressing of all, why had he never returned?

A narrow gap in the undergrowth revealed a path which led away from the lay-by towards the school, through a dense conifer wood. Underneath the canopy of trees, though there was little snow on the ground, it was bitterly cold. Emerging from the woods, he came to a steep field, beyond which he could see the high stone wall which marked the western boundary of the school estate. As snow had drifted in places, it proved tricky to cross, and took him longer than anticipated. Arriving at the wall, he realised it was too high for him to scale, so followed it north, hoping to find an opening. After ten minutes, he still hadn't found one. Anxious that he was running out of time, he decided his best option was to climb a large tree which overhung the wall. Swinging out on one of its branches, he was able to throw his leg across the top of the wall, grip on to the coping stone and scramble down the other side.

The garden was wilder here, thick with bracken and wild roses that ripped at his clothes. Using the compass to check his bearings, he headed in the general direction of the school, forcing his way through the undergrowth. Eventually, he came to an animal track. After following it for five minutes, the view opened and he glimpsed the lights of the main school building further down the hill. This meant he was close to Brendan and Sarah's cottage, and in turn, the castle ruin.

Turning northwest, Colin took an uphill path he recognised which was edged by an old deer fence in a state of disrepair. As he climbed, the wind picked up and the first soft flurries of snow began to fall. He pulled up his hood but kept an eye out for a gap in the fence he'd spotted before. In the snowy landscape it was hard to see, but he finally found it. Though it took him through dense woodland, it offered a shortcut to the castle.

He looked at his watch: ten to nine.

Within the wood, while the trees gave shelter from the wind, the moonlight didn't penetrate. In the darkness there no longer seemed to be an obvious route through. He had to check his compass repeatedly and began to question whether he would have been quicker sticking to the main path. When he emerged from the trees, clouds were covering the face of the moon and large snowflakes were beginning to fall.

While he was relieved to see the duckpond below him and the distinctive silhouette of the castle above, he realised he was not where he had expected to be; a steep slope separated

A Prayer Before Killing

him from the castle entrance. With more thick undergrowth ahead, he had no choice but to clamber up the rocky hill.

Cold and exhausted, he dragged himself up the last few metres and stumbled to the castle entrance. Pausing for breath, he looked up to the sky; the clouds had closed in overhead and the falling snow was threatening to turn into a blizzard.

He moved further into the ruin, where it was more sheltered, and took out Sister Oran's drawing. Focusing the torch beam on it, he wiped away droplets of icy water which fell in a steady stream from the stones above. Now that he was here, it was obvious the castle ruin occupied the centre of the map. Placing it on the ground, he crouched and rotated it until the outlines of the castle walls in the drawing were aligned with the real walls. Referencing his compass, he marked the north point.

Colin now knew exactly where the four points Sister Oran had attributed to the Apostles were located.

As he studied the map further, trying to work out which area to explore first, something scurried across his hand and he instinctively lashed out. With a high-pitched squeal, a rat, sleek and sinuous, scuttled back into the shadows.

Outside, the wind had softened and the snow tumbled around him in huge rotating swirls. He decided to cross the bridge and head southeast past the duckpond. Taking as straight a line as the landscape allowed, he came to a small clearing in the garden, represented in Sister Oran's map by the letter "J". Colin cast the torch beam about, looking for any distinctive features which might be associated with Johnny. Ahead, a small stone structure, only a few courses high, was built into the slope. Brushing the snow aside, he discovered it was a spring; water trickled from a tiny copper spout, pooling into a frozen puddle on a base stone which formed a shallow basin. Letters were carved around the edge of it. Colin traced each one with his finger: *SACRIS SOLEMNIIS*. From his days as an altar boy, he remembered it as a hymn written by St Thomas Aquinas for the feast of Corpus Christi, which all suggested this was considered some sort of holy spring. How this related to Johnny, he wasn't sure.

The second point took him west to the far side of the duck pond. As he approached the area denoted by the letter "L," a metal sculpture came into view. This had to be the little animal in Sister Oran's drawing. On closer inspection, he realised it was a reptile, or a mythical beast; sitting on its back haunches, it held an upright triangular piece of metal in its outstretched claw. Colin brushed away the gathered snow to reveal a circle with numbers set around it. This wasn't just a sculpture, it was a sundial. He circled around it and discovered webbed wings at the creature's shoulders. It was a dragon; if Sister Oran's reference was religious again, perhaps it was the dragon that St George fought?

As Colin tracked back around the edge of the duck pond and headed northeast up the hill to the area marked by the letter "M", there was a shift in atmosphere. The wind pivoted, driving in from the north with sudden force and bringing blizzard conditions. Struggling in the reduced visibility, Colin doubted he'd be able to find St Francis's tree, the one Simon suggested Sister Oran might have marked on her map.

He continued forward, wondering whether he'd overshot the location. Simon had described it as a large beech tree standing on its own with a bench at its base. Ordinarily, it would be impossible to miss, but in this near whiteout it could be inches from him and he wouldn't know.

Colin took a moment to check the map and his compass bearing. Deciding to turn around and walk southwest in the direction of the castle, he kept his head lowered and slowed his pace right down. After a couple of minutes, a large shape loomed from within the whiteness. A tall tree with a thick trunk stood before him. Removing his gloves, as he reached out to touch the bark, his shins hit a hard edge. Crouching

A Prayer Before Killing

down, he could see that the trunk was encircled by a structure – a bench.

The storm continued to howl around him, the bare branches above whipped by the wind. Taking shelter on the leeward side of the tree, he cast his torch beam about, looking for any markings, but there were none.

He knelt and looked below the bench. Underneath, gnarled and knotted roots created a series of cavities. Digging out the snow and then the rotten leaves that had gathered, he felt deeper towards the hollow of the trunk. After five minutes, he was on the verge of giving up when his fingers alighted upon a little, frayed object. Pulling it out, he shone the torch on it: it was a small figure with thin limbs, made of raffia or twine, akin to a corn dolly. He turned it over; on its chest, a tiny white cross had been painted. He lay down in the snow and felt deeper into the tree trunk; his fingers immediately landed on something crisp with a definite wedge shape. He pulled it out to reveal a clear, unopened sandwich packet. He gave it a shake – a hard, semi-frozen block of mould rattled around inside. He read the label: *Cheese & Tomato. Best Before: 14.06.93.* The day Sister Oran disappeared.

He placed the doll and the sandwich packet in his rucksack. These objects felt like vital pieces of evidence which had been overlooked, but what did they tell him? For the moment, he wasn't sure, but he was certain the police would be interested. He needed to alert them as soon as possible.

He stood and looked at the map. To get to the area marked with "G" it would be best to return to the ruin and walk northwest from there. Though the snow had eased, the forecast had been for further blizzards, so it would be the last thing he would do before heading back to his car.

As he was about to emerge into the open piece of ground which led to the duckpond, he noticed a flash of light moving below. Turning off his torch, he stepped back into the woods and waited. Someone else was quickly making their way uphill, through the snow, just as he had. Could it be Patrick?

The figure, wearing a hooded jacket, failed to notice Colin. Following in their footsteps, he pursued them at a safe distance. They didn't head up the track to the bridge but turned left towards the tunnel which led underground from the duck pond. A screech of rusted metal told him that they were removing the metal bar from the tunnel gate. This was someone who was familiar with the landscape. If only he could see who it was. There was only one thing to do. He needed to follow them down into the tunnel and discover what they were up to.

CHAPTER 54

Keeping the light from his torch shielded, Colin crept up to the tunnel entrance. The ground was frozen solid and whoever had just entered had not replaced the metal bar. He pulled himself through the gap and stood, listening for sounds of movement ahead. Besides the sigh of an icy breeze and the constant drip of water, all was strangely quiet.

He cast his torch beam about. There was no sign of anyone skulking in the shadows, waiting to pounce.

Carefully making his way up the tunnel, he sensed the temperature fall and the ground become icy underfoot. Placing a hand against the wall to steady himself, the moss was hard beneath his gloved hand – even that was beginning to freeze. As his breath billowed around him he paused, realising that the rank smell from days earlier was almost gone; the whole tunnel complex seemed to be in a state of suspended animation, frozen in time.

Continuing into the darkness, towards the heart of the ruin, a thought struck him. He stopped and looked at the map. He might be wrong, but was there a chance that the location where the arms of the cross intersected corresponded to where Sister Oran was incarcerated? Colin squinted. The pencil marks were most dense at the centre of her map and the light from his torch wasn't strong, but it was a possibility. In fact, the more he looked at the drawing, the more he began to see a letter "O" hidden at that point within the pattern.

He shivered. Standing still wasn't an option, the cold was too intense, too penetrating. Tucking the map away, he kept moving. Maybe this was a mistake. While he'd seen one figure enter, there could be more. What if he were overpowered, locked up within the priest hole just like Sister Oran? He considered turning back and going straight to the police. But just as he was about to, a groan – low and guttural – echoed down the tunnel, filling his ears. That was not the sound of the wind. It was human.

Switching off his torch, Colin stopped and stood as still as he could in the all-consuming darkness. Was it his imagination or could he hear voices? He closed his eyes and concentrated, using all the meditation skills he'd learnt in India to clear his mind and focus only on the present. Besides his own breathing, there was a distant sound of running water, but beneath that there was a voice or voices, talking urgently. He was sure of it. Keeping his torch switched off, he edged along the tunnel towards the sound. Inch by inch, the voices became louder, more distinct. There were two, both male, one agitated, the other calmer, but he couldn't work out what they were saying.

The route was one he'd taken before; he had no doubt the voices were leading him to where Sister Oran's body was found. That fact alone should be warning enough. He should turn around, raise the alarm, and let the authorities deal with it. Everything was pointing towards a cover-up; that Simon Young was innocent and people at the school had conspired – were conspiring – to conceal the truth about Sister Oran's death. He had evidence to support this. And yet, here he was, entirely on his own, without back-up, continuing in the direc-

A Prayer Before Killing

tion of the voices. Why? Because he was concerned Patrick was in trouble, or because he thought Patrick was involved?

He took a step further and the voices stopped. Worried they'd heard him, Colin pressed his body against the frozen wall and held his breath. In the cold, about thirty seconds was all he could handle before letting out a short gasp. By this time, the voices had begun again and he recognised one.

Patrick.

He sounded calm, but Colin still couldn't make out what he was saying. The other voice had fallen silent. Colin's mind raced through the possibilities: was Patrick with one of the remaining Apostles? Had Charlie Murray returned or was it Brother Thomas? Given the height of the figure, he had assumed it was a man, but it had been dark and snowing. Could it be a woman? After all, Caroline was tall and her voice deep.

As Colin edged closer, occasional phrases spoken by Patrick became audible – *not too late, we can make this right, trust me* – but the other person failed to respond.

Ahead, a faint light – either a torch or a candle – began to emerge.

Colin blinked and tried to focus his eyes. Someone stood in silhouette with their back to him, holding a large rubber torch which shone a beam of light on another person who was huddled on the ground, wrapped in a blanket. He drew closer; the person on the ground was Patrick, his cheeks sunken, his face pale.

The standing figure turned and Colin instantly recognised his profile: Matthew.

'Shut up,' Matthew hissed. 'Stop messing with my head.' He sounded angry, frustrated. Any veneer of composure was gone. 'You don't know what you're talking about.'

'I'm just trying to help. Please hear me out.' Patrick's voice sounded weak, pleading. If Colin had to guess, these were not co-conspirators. Far from it.

Matthew turned his back to Colin again and hit the wall above Patrick's head with the end of his torch. 'I said, shut the fuck up.'

Trying to catch Patrick's eye, Colin began to approach, but with Matthew hovering over him, his gaze was fixed firmly on the floor. Whatever was going on, whether or not Matthew's actions were somehow justified, Colin needed to intervene and take control of the situation.

'Please,' Patrick whispered.

Matthew raised his torch, as if about to strike.

Colin sprang out of the shadows. 'Matthew? Patrick? What's going on?'

The brightness of the torch beam blinded him. A sudden force hit his chest, slamming him hard against the stone wall, winding him. Staggering to regain his footing, an arc of light crashed against the side of his head. Then another. And after that, there was nothing but darkness.

CHAPTER 55

Colin opened his eyes, his vision blurred. Around him, lights flickered in the dark, tiny candles illuminating the stone and ceramic murtis, those sacred statues which filled the walls of the Jain temple from floor to ceiling; hundreds of icons to choose from, their eyes glistening like jewels. His head ached and his brain was foggy; he couldn't understand how he'd returned to India so soon. Though it was half a day's hike from the hustle and bustle of Mount Abu, with its honeymooners and travellers, he had no recollection of the journey. But it was good to be back, to feel connected again, to feel peace, to believe – perhaps for the first time – that he was finally on the path he was meant to follow.

A whisper floated out of the darkness. 'Colin?'

He pressed against the ground and tried to raise himself up, but his arms were too weak and he sank back down.

'Colin?'

His eyes snapped open to complete darkness and a cold which penetrated his bones. He lifted his cheek from the frozen floor and with his fingers, explored the side of his head where the pain was most intense. There was a lump and a sticky patch which could only be blood. With a groan, he tried to sit up, fighting against a sudden wave of nausea.

'Colin?'

Though barely a whimper, the voice was recognisable, but he was too disorientated to work out where it was coming from. Or was he still dreaming? He searched in the pitch black for the murtis – all smiling, all knowing – offering him strength and certainty, but there were none. 'Who's there?' he whispered.

Rolling onto his knees, he remembered he'd arrived with a torch. His hands were like blocks of ice, his fingers so numb he could barely bend them. He pulled off his gloves with his teeth and blew on his hands to warm them before searching the ground. He felt something plastic, grabbed hold of a handle and clicked a switch. The entire space lit up.

His head throbbed as he took in the low stone ceiling, the icicles dripping with water, and the walls green with moss. He remembered walking in the snow, entering the tunnel, then Matthew and how his speed and brutality had taken him by surprise.

'Patrick, are you okay?' To Colin's left, the priest lay slumped against the wall, his wrists bound by a rope, threaded through a metal ring fixed to the wall. His lips were cracked, his face a strange pallor. Staring listlessly at the ground, his head drooped to one side.

Clinging to the wall, Colin pushed himself up before falling to his knees again, gagging. He waited until the feeling of nausea had passed before making a second attempt to stand. His head spinning, he staggered towards Patrick and fumbled with the knot at his wrists. Up close, Patrick's skin was deathly pale and his lips colourless. Colin pressed his finger against his neck; he had a pulse but it was very weak. 'Is Matthew still here?' he asked.

Patrick's eyelids slowly flickered open and he shook his head.

A Prayer Before Killing

'Has he been gone a while?'

Patrick nodded, but he appeared distant and very drowsy; everything was pointing towards hypothermia. Colin needed to get him to safety.

The knot finally undone, Colin gripped Patrick close and pulled him onto his feet. He swayed and leant heavily into Colin's chest, almost knocking him over.

'Steady,' Colin said. 'Now, why don't you take my hat?'

'What're you doing here?' Patrick muttered, as Colin pulled his beanie onto his head and rubbed his back, trying to get some warmth back into the man's body.

'We're going for a little walk,' Colin replied. 'Do you think you can do that?'

'Sure,' Patrick mumbled as he pushed the blanket off his shoulders and tried to sit back down.

'Oh no you don't,' Colin said. 'We need to keep you warm and get you moving.' He took off his own jacket and managed to get one of Patrick's arms through the sleeve. Holding him upright, he tied the blanket around them both. 'That's better.'

'Thank you,' Patrick muttered, his head drooping.

'I need you to stay awake,' Colin said gently, trying to stay calm. 'You can sleep later, once I've got you somewhere warm.' Adjusting the weight of Patrick's body against his own, he propelled them both forward. 'One step at a time, that's all we need to do. Do you trust me?'

Patrick nodded. 'Yes.' His speech was slurred, his breathing shallow.

Time was against them.

Colin's muscles ached with the cold and the effort of stopping them both from falling over, but bit by bit, as he got Patrick into a steady rhythm, they made progress down through the warren of tunnels towards the duckpond. There were moments, too, when Patrick became a little more lucid.

'Can you tell me what happened?' Colin asked. 'How did this all come about?'

'I'm sorry.' Patrick shook his head.

'Did Matthew kill Sister Oran?' Colin asked. 'Is that why he tied you up?'

Too focused on the effort of taking the next step, Patrick didn't reply.

Colin tried again. 'Why did you come to the school?'

'My mess,' Patrick mumbled, his energy fading again.

Colin feared he was listening to the final words of a dying man, and he was no closer to discovering why Matthew had been holding him captive. 'Let's say a prayer,' he said. 'How about a Hail Mary?' He started with the first few lines:

'Hail Mary, full of grace,
'The Lord is with thee,
'Blessed art thou amongst women,
'And blessed is the fruit of thy womb...'

'Jesus.' Patrick's voice – barely a whisper – joined him.

Colin lost count of the number of Hail Marys they said before arriving at the duckpond gate, and, had he been a believer, he would have said the effect was miraculous. Patrick remained awake throughout and kept walking, but while he was definitely more lucid, he had begun to shiver uncontrollably. Though Colin had had first aid training as a police cadet, he couldn't remember whether this was a good sign or not.

It was clear Matthew had exited by the gate. The metal bar had been put back into position and a shard of wood was jammed in beside it to prevent it from moving. Colin leaned Patrick against the wall and lay his torch on the ground while he wrestled it back out. He then dragged, and by turns coaxed, Patrick through the opening. Exhausted, they lay outside on the frozen ground gasping for breath. Though the night sky was still filled with clouds, it had stopped snowing.

Clambering to his knees, Colin scanned the landscape. A

luminous white blanket coated everything as far as he could see, but there was no sign of Matthew or even his footsteps in the snow. Colin checked his watch, but it had stopped. How long they'd been in the tunnels he could only guess – an hour, two, longer?

He turned to Patrick who still appeared dazed but was now sitting upright. Colin crawled to him and held him tight, giving his back a strong rub. 'Now, the next bit's the easy part.' He was lying; he'd no idea how easy it would be to get down the hill. The snow was deep and he was physically drained. If Matthew was still about, if he decided to attack them again, he wasn't sure he had the strength to defend them.

He pulled Patrick's arm across his shoulder and dragged them both upright. 'Not far.'

'Wait.' Patrick clasped his hand.

'We need to keep moving.'

'I didn't tell the truth.'

'When?'

'I saw,' he mumbled, his body starting to collapse again.

Colin grabbed his shoulders to steady him. 'What did you see?'

The words came slowly at first, but it was clear Patrick needed to clear his conscience. 'The night Sister Oran disappeared, Matthew left the retreat.'

This corroborated with what Luc had told him but didn't fit with Garr's version.

'But I thought you weren't there.'

'I wasn't.' Patrick gasped for breath.

'Where did you see him?'

'Not far from the school.' Patrick hung his head. 'I've lied about everything.'

CHAPTER 56

THREE YEARS EARLIER – JUNE 1992

Their affair had started at the retreat. Dr Murray had arranged for Davey Baird, the new head chef at the school, to come to Grange Lodges to manage the catering and deliver some outdoor cookery lessons. Youthful and with a sharp wit, he had proved popular with the boys, joining in their games whenever he wasn't working. He was also gay, which Patrick had sensed the first time they met, when Davey had joined the school that Easter. It was hard to tell how he knew, something in the way they exchanged hellos, but once the connection was made, he found it impossible to pass him without showing a spark of interest. And the glances and smiles Davey returned left him with little doubt that he was interested, too.

But, however strong the attraction, Patrick had resisted. He could never act on his desires so close to the school or church; it was far too risky. He compartmentalised that part of himself through occasional trips to Manchester and London, where he could hook up with guys who knew nothing about him, and while these trips left him wracked with guilt, he had resolved they were a necessary evil, a safety valve which enabled him to fulfil his vocation and serve God.

A Prayer Before Killing

The first time they had had an actual conversation was on the second evening of the retreat. Patrick had volunteered to help with the washing up. Alone in the kitchen, they had chatted non-stop for an hour about all sorts of nonsense, the glances between them lasting longer and longer, the smiles they exchanged widening. Davey needed to slip behind him to put the dishes away and each time he squeezed past his body his hand lingered a little more on Patrick's waist.

This led to other moments during that week: long walks in the countryside, their fingers bristling against each other, discussions about their lives, then finally a stolen kiss in a barn a few miles from the lodges. It was exciting and yet chaste.

Immediately after the retreat, Patrick had left for the summer holidays on a study trip to Rome, his head spinning, unsure of where it all might lead. When he returned for the new academic year, they'd not spoken for weeks and he'd rationalised that it was just a silly crush, but as soon as they'd locked eyes again, he was overwhelmed by the same feelings as before.

As dangerous as it was, they began to meet in secret; however, clandestine walks and stolen kisses weren't enough. Davey wanted to take things further, but again Patrick resisted.

'Not here, not now,' Patrick had insisted.

Davey looked crushed. 'When?'

'Soon.'

A few weeks later, they booked into a hotel in Edinburgh. The night had gone better than Patrick had ever thought possible, and in the morning he knew this was a man he wanted to get to know better. So, during the run up to Christmas, despite it being his busiest time of year, they met up whenever possible. It was the happiest he could remember being. But soon, despite best intentions on both sides, cracks began to show.

'I'm totally broke; can't you come round to mine one weekend when my mum's away?' Davey hadn't made many demands up until then. Mostly, he'd seemed content with the pattern they'd settled into.

'This is the best I can offer,' Patrick told him.

'Well, it's not enough,' Davey replied. 'And I deserve better.'

After that, the relationship came to a shuddering stop. There were no more trips away, no more walks, no more furtive glances in the school corridors. Then, in the new year, Davey left his job for a contract on a cruise ship.

Through Davey's mother, Euphemia, who had been brought in temporarily to run the kitchen, Patrick was able to keep track of Davey's movements. While he felt pangs of guilt that she didn't know the real reason for his interest, it would have been too painful for him not to know where he was; that he was safe and happy. Through her, he followed Davey's journey around the Mediterranean and found out he'd returned to Scotland and was back living with her and working in Glasgow.

Any thoughts of getting back together with Davey were finally banished when Patrick left his position at the school to take over St Bridget's in the spring. Becoming a parish priest was the fulfilment of his childhood dream. Vowing he would do nothing to jeopardise it, he recommitted to a life of chastity and celibacy.

However, a few months later, Davey, now working back at the school, called him out of the blue and asked to meet. 'My mum's away on the retreat,' he'd said. 'I'll cook you dinner and we can talk.'

Patrick's heart had leapt at the sound of his voice. 'Only if we stick to some ground rules,' he'd said. 'I have a new life now. Responsibilities. I'll come for an early dinner, but I need to leave by eight.'

The cottage was a few miles from the school, but far

enough for Patrick to not worry about being spotted. A plain, single-storey cottage with white render and a slate roof, it sat alone in a lush garden, filled with flowers and vegetables. He parked a short distance away, under the shade of a large tree, and walked the final stretch in the summer heat, insects buzzing in the air around him.

Beaming, Davey opened the front door as Patrick came up the path. His hair longer and his skin tanned, he looked better than ever.

'Remember, this can only be as friends,' Patrick whispered as Davey hugged him and led him inside.

Davey smiled and took his hand.

Within seconds, Patrick's resolve had failed him and their lips pressed together as they tore at each other's clothes.

A few hours later, he woke wracked with guilt. Mrs Beattie had expected him back by nine, and it was now closer to ten.

Slipping out of bed, he left Davey sleeping and tiptoed around the living room, pulling on his clothes and lacing up his trainers.

'Stay the night.'

Patrick jumped.

Davey stood naked in the doorway of his bedroom.

'I need to go,' Patrick said. 'This was a mistake.' Averting his eyes, he threw Davey's boxer shorts at him. 'Put these on.'

'What the hell's wrong with you?'

'Everything's changed. I can't do this. I can't be this.'

'What? Why not?'

As Davey pulled on his boxers, Patrick threw open the door and hurried down the path. He crashed through the gate and ran down the deserted road, past fields of golden rapeseed, Davey calling after him. As he arrived at his car and fumbled in his pockets for his keys, Davey finally caught up with him.

'Let's go back to the house and chat.' Davey put his arms around him. 'Come on.'

Patrick pushed him away. 'Don't! Someone will see us.'

'I don't care.' Davey drew him back. 'You want this as much as me.'

With the long summer evening light beginning to fade, they stood holding each other. 'It's all too quick,' Patrick said. 'I need time to think.'

As Davey released him, a fast-moving shape turned the corner of the road and hurtled towards him. Stepping back, Patrick locked eyes with the cyclist. As he disappeared from sight, his heart shuddered at the realisation it was someone he knew: Matthew Penrose, a fourteen-year-old boy who was captain of the school football team. 'Christ! Did you see that?' he asked.

'What?' Davey glanced around, but Matthew had disappeared. 'Are you okay? You look like you've seen a ghost.'

In the intervening years, Patrick convinced himself it had been a dream, a vision, an expression of his guilty conscience. Along with the rest of that evening's events, he put it all in a box and locked it away, as if none of it had happened. And though Davey continued to call for several months afterwards, he never met with him again.

CHAPTER 57
WEDNESDAY 6TH DECEMBER 1995

Thankfully, the weather remained calm as Colin helped Patrick down the hill, but the effort of walking through snow, which in places was a foot deep, took its toll on them both. Patrick increasingly stumbled and Colin needed to support more and more of his weight.

Breathless and dehydrated, Colin steered them towards the clearing where St Thomas' spring was located. He sat Patrick on the ground.

Crouching in front of the spring, he cupped his hands beneath the trickle of water and drank. 'You should have some,' he said, turning to discover Patrick collapsed on the ground, his eyelids flickering. 'Stay with me.' Colin held his head and dabbed water at his cracked lips, but there was no reaction.

He was now convinced if he didn't get Patrick somewhere warm – and soon – he'd die. His heart thumping in his chest, Colin went through his options: abandon him and rush for help, which seemed too risky, or try to carry him off the hill. Summoning all his strength, Colin lifted him into his arms. At least he was lighter than he expected.

Staggering out of the forest, he headed in the direction of Sarah and Brendan's cottage. While there was an outside chance they wouldn't be home, it was closer than the school, and if worse came to worst he could break in. They'd understand. The circumstances justified it.

He tacked west across the slope, his feet and hands numb. The terrain began to flatten out and while it was still rough, the snow was less deep. Though every muscle ached from the exertion, he resisted the temptation to put Patrick down even for a second, fearful that if he did, he'd be unable to continue to lift him again. He tilted his head to check Patrick was still breathing.

In the distance, a shadow began to emerge from the snow and the cottage came into view. It was completely dark but that was to be expected; it had to be after midnight. With the destination in sight, he gripped Patrick tighter and tried to speed up. As he stumbled through the garden, he began to call for help, but between gulps of breath, his voice emerged as barely a whisper. Clearing snow from a bench, he sat Patrick down and rushed towards the back door, hammering against the wood and shouting for help. Upstairs, a light snapped on, and he heard footsteps pounding down the stairs.

The door flew open. Brendan, his hair dishevelled and tying a dressing gown at his waist, stared at him in surprise. 'What the hell's going on?'

'We need help,' Colin gasped, gesturing to the bench. 'It's Patrick. We need to get him inside. He's unconscious – I think it's hypothermia.'

As Brendan bounded out from the house, Sarah appeared in her nightdress. 'My God!' she cried. 'I'll call an ambulance.'

Colin joined Brendan and together they lifted Patrick into the kitchen.

'Be gentle with him,' Sarah shouted from the hall. 'Brendan, go and get the quilts and blankets from upstairs.'

A Prayer Before Killing

'I'm on it,' Brendan said, dashing upstairs.

The warmth inside hit Colin like a sledgehammer and he collapsed on the floor beside Patrick.

The phone against her ear, Sarah stuck her head round the door. 'The ambulance is on its way.' She looked at Colin as Brendan returned with bedding. 'Are you hurt, too? Check his head, Brendan.'

He'd forgotten. Raising his fingers Colin felt blood encrusted on his face and hair. 'I'm fine.'

'If Father Traynor's clothes are wet, Brendan,' Sarah said, 'you'll need to get them off before you put the blankets over him. Cut them off if you need to.'

'Aye, aye,' Brendan replied.

Eyes closed, Colin lay on the floor as Brendan attended to Patrick and Sarah spoke on the line to the emergency services.

'Now let's see to you,' Brendan murmured a few minutes later. Helping Colin onto a chair at the kitchen table, he pulled a quilt around Colin's shoulders and sat beside him with a first aid kit.

'How is he?' Colin asked.

'Alive,' Brendan said as he began to clean out the cut on Colin's head. 'What the hell happened?'

Before Colin could reply, Sarah reappeared at the door. 'They're saying ten minutes. It's the weather, the roads are terrible. I've told them to come up the track at the back of here – that's easier than coming up from the school.' She looked at Brendan. 'Once you've got a plaster on that cut, get the fire going and make Colin a hot drink. And check on Father Traynor.'

'I just need a glass of water,' Colin said.

Brendan poured Colin a glass and smiled. 'Sarah's the type you need in an emergency. So, what happened? Did you guys have an accident?'

Colin shook his head. 'We need the police here too. Matthew Penrose attacked me in the tunnels, under the castle. He'd been holding Patrick – Father Traynor – there. Captive.'

'No fucking way,' Brendan said. 'Saz, come and hear this. Colin's saying Matty Penrose attacked them.'

'What?' Sarah returned to the kitchen.

'Matty Penrose attacked them,' Brendan repeated.

She glanced at Brendan. 'Why would he do something like that?'

'Because Matthew's the real killer of Sister Oran,' Colin said.

'No way.' Brendan looked round at his wife.

Sarah shook her head. 'Even in death that bloody woman's still wreaking havoc.'

Brendan reached out to her, but she brushed him off as the sound of a siren could be heard in the distance. 'I'll come with you to the hospital,' he said to Colin. 'That is, if there's space.'

As Sarah opened the back door and peered out into the darkness for signs of the ambulance, Colin could have sworn she muttered 'And don't bother coming back' under her breath. Had they had an argument earlier? He'd noticed relations were often frosty between them but he assumed it was just the nature of their marriage – that it blew hot and cold. Judging by her comment though, Simon appeared to have been telling the truth when he had said Sarah wasn't Sister Oran's biggest fan.

'Can you go with Father Traynor in the ambulance?' Colin asked Brendan as he stood and removed the quilt. 'I've something I need to do.'

'But you're in no fit state,' Brendan said.

'Honestly, I'm fine. If I could borrow a jacket, that'd be great.'

'They're here,' Sarah shouted, blue lights reflecting off her face.

'Where are you going?' Brendan asked, as he helped Colin into a parka.

'The school.' Colin walked to the front door.
'At this time? It's after one in the morning.'
'I need to see if Matthew's there.'

CHAPTER 58

Eddies of snow began to cascade from the sky as Colin made his way downhill towards the school. A vast concrete monolith sitting in a sea of white, it hunkered down in the landscape, dark and foreboding, the glow of emergency lights from the atrium the only indication that pupils were asleep inside. If Matthew was there, Colin was determined to find him. But would he have risked going back? He tried to put himself in Matthew's place. If he was Sister Oran's killer, then why had he not finished him and Patrick off when he had the chance? Why run away?

As he drew closer to the school, he wondered how best to approach the situation. Waking everyone up at once was definitely not the way to go. If Matthew was here, creating any sort of commotion would give him too much warning, would offer him an opportunity to escape. And any direct approach would inevitably involve Brother Thomas; that needed to be avoided at all costs. He'd have no patience to listen to anything Colin had to say, he'd only be interested in removing him from the school grounds. There was the possibility that Caroline might be on house duties – she often covered on a Tuesday or a Wednesday evening – but without

A Prayer Before Killing

access to a phone to ring the housemaster's room, how could he get her attention without waking others? His best option, he concluded, was Sister Helena. He could access the nuns' quarters from the kitchen courtyard and was confident she wouldn't jump to conclusions. She'd proven herself trustworthy in the past; she'd hear him out.

A narrow stairway led down to the paved courtyard which separated the kitchen from the nuns' quarters. Protected from the elements by the surrounding buildings, it was noticeably warmer here and any snow which had fallen had already melted. As Colin skirted past the industrial bins lined along one edge, a security light snapped on. He paused and waited to see if this was going to alert anyone but the school remained in darkness. Crossing to the nuns' annex, Colin gently knocked on the outside door and prayed she'd hear.

He shivered; his body was frozen to the core and he had a thumping headache. Maybe Brendan was right, perhaps he was in no fit state to be out and about, trying to play the hero. He'd been walking in the cold for hours, and it wasn't beyond the bounds of possibility that he had hypothermia too, that he might not be thinking straight. Out of habit, he checked his watch; it was still broken. If he'd left Brendan and Sarah's after one, it must be about one-thirty by now. He wondered where the police were. Surely it wouldn't take them more than half an hour to get here.

'Who's there?' Like the voice of God, Sister Helena's low tones resonated from the far side of the door.

'It's me, Colin Buxton.'

As the door was swiftly opened, the nun appeared in a dark tunic and night cap. As soon as she saw him, her expression changed to one of immediate concern. 'Goodness!' she gasped, ushering him inside and sitting him down on a chair in the living room. 'Are those bruises on your face?'

'I need your help to find Matthew Penrose,' Colin said. 'Can you let me into the main building?'

'Is Matthew in trouble?'

'Yes,' Colin replied. 'I'm almost a hundred percent certain he had something to do with Sister Oran's death, but we need to act quickly.'

Sister Helena stood back for a moment and eyed him up. It occurred to Colin that he must look deranged – a madman turning up on her doorstep in the dead of night, covered in blood and talking gibberish.

'Okay,' she said. 'Give me two minutes to put on my boots and get my coat.'

'Thank you.'

While she disappeared into her room, Colin stepped back outside and listened. There was still nothing to suggest the police were on their way. As he waited, he peered up at the main school building. On the top floor a light came on in a window, then another and another; signs of movement followed. 'Damn it,' Colin muttered.

'What's wrong?' Sister Helena joined him in the courtyard.

Colin pointed to the dormitory level. 'They're up; someone must have alerted them. I need to get to Matthew's room as soon as possible, see if he's there.'

She held up a key. 'Follow me.'

Darting across the courtyard, Sister Helena led him through the kitchens and upstairs towards the refectory. As they approached, the refectory door flew open and the stair landing was flooded with light.

'What the hell do you think you're playing at?' The gaunt figure of Brother Thomas, fully dressed, filled the doorframe. 'Sarah's just been on the phone.'

Before Colin could answer, Sister Helena stepped forward. 'Mr Buxton needs our help.'

Her authoritative tone silenced Brother Thomas for a

A Prayer Before Killing

moment but his anger quickly returned. 'Nonsense,' he said. 'Mr Buxton is determined to spread chaos and division. Nothing more, nothing less.' He turned to Colin. 'You've no right to take advantage of Sister Helena's good nature like this. I demand you leave the school at once.'

'I need to know if Matthew's here or not. He could be a danger to others or even a danger to himself.' The words came spilling out of Colin's mouth and he had to force himself to stop, unsure of how much he could risk saying.

'Sarah's filled me in,' Brother Thomas snapped. 'Of course Matthew's here; it's outrageous that you're even asking. Where else would he be?'

'I don't know. Roaming around the grounds, attacking people?'

Brother Thomas took in Colin's bloodied head and bruised face, and for the first time it looked as if he might relent.

'If you could check whether he's here or not,' Colin said. 'That's all I'm asking.'

'Sarah's told me all about your absurd accusations.' Brother Thomas edged closer. 'Now, I'm asking you, politely, to leave the school and if you refuse, there will be consequences.'

'What? You're going to call the police?' Colin asked. 'Too bad, they're already on their way; I told Sarah to call them.'

'And you think everybody does everything you ask them to?' Brother Thomas sneered.

Colin shook his head in disbelief.

'This man has come to us injured and distressed, asking for our assistance,' Sister Helena interjected. 'It's our Christian duty to help. If you turn him away, I'll be making complaints at the highest level.'

Behind Brother Thomas, in the atrium, there were sounds of commotion. Seconds later, Caroline appeared in a long silk dressing gown and barged past him. As soon as she saw Colin, she pointed to Brother Thomas. 'Did you do this?'

He stumbled backwards. 'Of course not. Why would I—?'

'Caroline,' said Colin, 'can you do me a favour?'

'Yes?'

'Go to Matthew's room and check if he's there. Don't say anything to anyone – or to him, if he's there – just come back and tell me.'

Brother Thomas stood in the doorway to block her. 'You're not going anywhere.'

Caroline sighed. 'Let me pass.'

'Are you disobeying me?'

'I'm doing the right thing,' she said, sidestepping him. 'Something you should have done a long time ago.'

'I don't know what you think you're going to achieve with all this, Mr Buxton. Waking up an entire school in the middle of the night, to make allegations against innocent children? It's ridiculous.'

'It's about getting to the truth.'

'Such as?'

'Who really killed Sister Oran,' Colin replied.

Brother Thomas let out a strangled guffaw. 'You're not still going on about that damned bangle, are you?'

'Simon Young didn't kill Sister Oran.'

'And you think Matthew did?'

'Potentially.'

A group of bleary-eyed boys had gathered behind Brother Thomas. 'Bed! Now!' he barked. As they scattered, Caroline reappeared with a rattled-looking Garr in tow.

'He's gone,' Caroline panted, pushing Garr towards Colin. 'Tell him what you've just told me.'

'A couple of hours ago, I heard Matthew banging around in his room, so I went to see what was going on. He's been kind of down since Johnny's accident, but over the last two days, he's got a lot worse. He was shoving things into his rucksack, saying he had to get away.' Garr straightened his glasses.

'Tell him the rest,' Caroline said.

'He said he'd done a really bad thing, but he wouldn't tell me what.' Garr looked at the floor. 'I could see he'd been crying. I've never seen him like that before.'

'So, you didn't know Matthew was holding Father Traynor against his will?' Colin asked.

'What the—?' Caroline couldn't get the rest of her words out.

'Don't answer that question, Garr.' Brother Thomas took him by the wrist. 'Come with me.'

Garr wriggled from Brother Thomas's grasp, his eyes wide and frightened. 'No, I didn't know, I swear.'

'Did he say where he was going?'

'I thought maybe to his dad's, in Cornwall.'

'Did he have any money?' Colin asked.

'Just what I gave him – less than five pounds.'

'He'll not get far on that,' Colin said. 'What about his mum?'

'She died,' Caroline whispered, 'when he was seven.'

Colin turned to Brother Thomas. 'Can you phone Matthew's father and ask if he's heard from him?'

The colour drained from the monk's face. 'At this hour?'

'I'll do it,' Sister Helena said. 'That way you'll know the job will get done.' She headed towards the office. 'I'll call the police too.'

Colin turned his attention back to Garr. 'Did you notice what he was packing?'

Garr shrugged. 'Just stuff. Clothes, his sleeping bag, his camping stove, some sweets, a knife.'

'Is there anywhere closer he might have gone to hide out?' Colin asked.

Garr shook his head.

'Think about it,' Colin urged.

'We used to have a den at the cove,' Garr said, the hint of a smile playing across his lips.

'Which one?'

'St Fillan's,' Garr replied. 'We'd go there with Sister Oran.'

'I know it,' Caroline said.

'That's where Johnny nearly drowned, isn't it?' Colin said.

'Yes.'

'Can I borrow your car?' he asked. 'Mine's parked miles away.'

'Absolutely no way,' she cried.

'I need to check if he's there. I'm worried about his state of mind. We can't wait for the police. It could be too late by then.'

'I mean, you're not driving my precious car in this weather when you have concussion. I'll drive. I know exactly where it is.'

CHAPTER 59

In less than a minute, Caroline reappeared fully dressed with her car keys in hand. 'Follow me,' she said.

Colin nodded to Brother Thomas. 'I need you to take Garr to the office, and don't let him out of your sight until the police get here.' For once, Brother Thomas didn't argue.

Caroline's pride and joy – her bright red Audi coupé – was parked under cover to the side of the school entrance. They climbed inside and she started the engine; it roared into life.

'Will this be okay in the snow?' Colin asked.

'Please!' she cried, accelerating down the drive. 'It's a Quattro – you know – four-wheel drive? I might be a sucker for a sports car, but I'm a country girl at heart.'

Colin clung to his seat as she expertly whipped the car through the main gates and out onto the main road.

'Can you tell me what's going on?' Her eyes fixed on the road, Caroline switched through the gears with ease.

'How far is it?'

'Normally it's a ten minute drive. In these conditions fifteen, maybe twenty.' She glanced at him. 'So? Are you going to tell me?'

He recounted the events of the night.

'And you're positive it was Matthew?' she asked. 'You couldn't have made a mistake in the dark?'

Colin touched his head, which was throbbing. 'I've no doubt.'

'It's just so out of character.' The car went into a slide as it came out of a corner, but Caroline quickly brought it back under control. 'Oops! Sorry, are you okay?'

He smirked. 'I will be once we get there.'

'You're in safe hands.' She flashed him a smile. 'Years ago, I did the Dakar rally. Sixteen days, over ten thousand miles; punishing terrain and crazy temperatures. Now that's a challenge.' Returning her focus to the road, she switched on the windscreen wipers as snow began to fall heavily again. 'This was always going to end badly. As a teacher, you get a feeling about these things. I'm not just saying this because I didn't like Sister Oran – and I really didn't like her – but there were always red flags. Not just the way she flirted with the boys, but how they followed her around, how they looked at her. It gave me the creeps. She had a hold over them, it was plain to see.' She shook her head. 'I tried to discuss it with Charlie Murray, but he brushed the whole thing off.'

'And what about Simon – Father Young?'

'I didn't get a whiff of anything between them. When he was accused, you could have knocked me over with a feather.' She swerved right to avoid a car which had been abandoned at the side of the road.

'There are still several things which don't add up,' Colin said.

'Such as?'

'Sarah Kenny. I think she lied about seeing Father Young with Sister Oran on the night she disappeared.'

'Really?'

'I'm pretty sure Sister Oran was with Matthew,' Colin replied. 'I mean, I've seen a photo of Matthew from a few years ago; he was practically fully grown. Even then, he must

A Prayer Before Killing

have been a head taller than Simon and twice as broad. It's not as if you could confuse them.' He stared out the window. 'Then tonight, why would she ring Brother Thomas, rather than the police? She could see I'd been attacked.'

'Sarah's a law unto herself. She comes across all "butter wouldn't melt" but she'll turn on you like an alley cat if she thinks you're within an inch of her husband.'

'Has she reason to?'

Caroline raised an eyebrow. 'I don't like to gossip, but there's a wee boy in the village that's the spitting image of Brendan. The mother – a cousin of the Bairds – started in the school kitchens, but then suddenly, after only a couple of months, she was gone. No explanation. Six months later, she was pushing a pram down the main street. Even the boys, who love Brendan, teased him about it.'

Colin flinched.

'He's sex mad,' she continued. 'More than once, he's sidled up a little too close to me and I'm not the only one. Just last year, rumours of another child in Glasgow were doing the rounds.'

'Does Sarah know all this?'

'She'd have to be blind.' Caroline lowered her speed and peered ahead. 'If I remember correctly, you can park at the top of the cliff, then we'll need to walk down to the cove from there.'

'I should go by myself.' He sensed her bristle as she moved to a lower gear.

'I'm coming with you, whether you like it or not,' she said.

'The boy's potentially dangerous. He's already attacked me and who knows what frame of mind he's in.'

'You're not leaving me alone up here,' Caroline insisted. 'Besides, I've taught him since he was four foot nothing and skinny as a French fry. One stern look from me and he'll soften. Trust me.' She swung onto a side road. 'This way, I think. It's been ages.'

'Have you heard anything about money going missing from the school? About Sarah being connected to it in some way?'

Caroline parked beside a fence at the cliff's edge. 'Sarah was involved in that?'

'Are my sources wrong?'

'Well, the rumour is that the real reason Charlie Murray was removed is because of a fifty-thousand-pound hole in the school budget. And it's Charlie who likes the high life. Well, you've met his on-off girlfriend, Hayley. Sarah meanwhile lives in a grotty cottage on the school grounds, and although she wears expensive-looking clothes, they're all knockoffs. I should know – I worked for Dior in the seventies.'

Colin realised he knew practically nothing about this person beside him. How had she managed to keep that fact from him until now?

She opened her door and cold air blasted into the car. 'To get to the cove, we need to scramble down the cliff path,' she yelled. 'It's steep and it'll be slippy, but you can see the snow's not really lying here, not this close to the sea.'

Colin joined her outside. Though the wind howled and the snow tumbled around them, the dominant sound was of waves crashing onto the beach below. 'This way?' he shouted.

Caroline nodded.

Leading the way down the path, Colin brought out his torch. He turned it on and it glowed feebly. 'We'll need to take this really carefully,' he shouted over the boom of the sea. 'Watch your step,' he said, grabbing hold of a rock. 'There's a thirty-foot drop here.' He offered Caroline his hand.

'Thank you,' she shouted. 'Do you really think Matthew would come down here on his own?'

'We need to look.'

Only as they arrived at the bottom of the path and stepped onto the stony shore, did the sea come fully into view: a dark, frothing mass extending to the horizon.

A Prayer Before Killing

'There are a couple of caves down to the left,' Caroline shouted above the wind, 'but I think there's another one to the right.'

'Stay here,' Colin said, shielding his face from the snow. 'I'll check this way first.' He clambered over jagged rocks which jutted out from the base of the cliff and extended all the way into the sea. Behind him, he heard Caroline shout, but her voice was carried away on the wind. When he turned around, all he could see was her luminous yellow beret, a tiny point bobbing along the shoreline, towards the far end of the beach. 'Caroline, wait!' he yelled, but she didn't respond.

He considered following her, but his attention was on a cleft ahead, darker than the rocks around it. As he neared, he could see it was a recess of some description, and potentially an entrance to a cave. He explored the opening with his hands; it definitely went deeper but narrowed quite quickly. He slid himself into it, the surfaces on either side of him pinching his waist. Craning his neck, he felt ahead, peering deeper into the darkness. The merest flicker in the pitch black encouraged him to ignore the claustrophobia which was threatening to overwhelm him and continue.

Seconds later, he tumbled into a tiny domed space strewn with detritus and barely high enough to stand up in. It was lit by a single tealight. Opposite him, crouched in a corner, Matthew stared straight ahead. Instinctively, Colin went to defend himself, but Matthew remained motionless.

As Colin got closer, Matthew released a huge sob and his shoulders began to heave as tears streamed down his cheeks.

'Matthew, I'm here to help.'

'I'm not a murderer,' the boy whimpered. 'I'm not.'

'If that's the case, we can fix this.' Colin knelt beside Matthew and tried to comfort him, but he resisted.

'She was never meant to die. That's not what was supposed to happen.'

'Sister Oran? Are you saying it was an accident? If that's the case, we can tell the police and sort everything out.'

'No,' Matthew said. 'That's not what I mean.'

'I don't understand.'

'She told us she was chosen and that we'd been chosen too; that she'd show us; that a miracle would happen. And it did.'

'How was her death a miracle?'

'The baby.' Matthew smiled through his tears. 'How else do you explain it?'

CHAPTER 60
TWO YEARS EARLIER – MONDAY 14TH JUNE 1993

The heat was unbearable. All day, since the boys had left for their retreat, the temperature had steadily risen, leaving Sister Oran sticky and sweaty. Come evening, she sat in her room by the open window, enjoying the breeze, and placed her hands on her belly; only a miracle would save her now. If the archdiocese were to find out about her pregnancy, she'd lose everything. She'd be banished, cast out of the church, she was certain of it. But she had a plan – a leap of faith – and with everyone away, she needed to act now. However, she couldn't do it on her own, and there was only one person she fully trusted.

She glanced around her tiny room one last time. Everything was neat and in its place; there was nothing to indicate anything untoward. Thankfully, Father Young hadn't returned. Matthew had been right about him; he was weak. She hadn't intended to be cruel, but his declaration of love had been a distraction she could have done without. She needed space to focus.

Saying a final prayer, she laced up her shoes and walked out into the courtyard. Taking the little side stair, she emerged into the gardens and headed for the spot at the foot of the hill where she'd arranged to meet Matthew.

With the school so quiet, it was a relief to be able to move around freely. Usually, Brother Thomas or Sister Helena would be lurking somewhere, ready to jump out and criticise, ask her why she wasn't doing such and such a chore this way or that, finding fault at every opportunity. Sarah clearly hated her, with her, with her caustic remarks. But, she reasoned, that was her cross to bear and bear it she would. After all, she had a higher calling. And at least she had Matthew and the boys. Her Apostles. She drew strength from their unwavering belief in her.

Arriving at the meeting place, the smell of flowers overpowered her senses: the heady scent of roses, the sweetness of lavender, the fresh perfume of gardenias. She loved this landscape. While she waited, she lay on the grass, closed her eyes and took in their fragrance.

On the edge of the forest, at the foot of the hill, she had chosen this spot deliberately. This was where her seducer had found her, two months earlier. She'd had a terrible argument with Sister Helena who had questioned her vocation, suggested she wasn't cut out to be a nun. He'd sat down beside her, made her laugh, held her hand, kissed her fingers. She knew it was wrong, but she'd allowed herself to be led through the trees to a hidden place under the rhododendrons where she had said yes. In that moment, with the cool earth beneath her bare skin, surrounded by the gardens springing into life, she'd meant it. Only afterwards, after he kissed her and left, had the terrible feelings of regret begun to take hold. Matthew didn't realise, but it wasn't only Father Young who was weak.

Was this really God's vision for her?

When she had taken her final vows, she felt the hand of God resting on her shoulder as a real, physical sensation. His grip was strong and firm, and had reassured her as she

A Prayer Before Killing

prayed. The force was so intense that when the superior general first called upon her to open her eyes she couldn't; she was too fearful of what she might see. Head bowed and heart racing, she continued to pray. The sensation only faded when the instruction was repeated. As she felt his hand release her, and as she opened her eyes, God whispered in her ear, 'I have a plan for you.'

She'd told Matthew this story many times, and other stories too: of healing her aunt in Ireland, of the vision she had of St Oran which brought her to Scotland, and the path which led her to the school, and to him. Each time she repeated these stories, she embellished them a little more, but he never questioned their substance. Quite the opposite; he brought Luc, then Garr and finally Johnny to listen and to learn.

So, when she confided in Matthew two weeks previously, told him God's plan was coming to fruition, that a miracle had occurred, that she was pregnant, he didn't question it, and in the telling of her miracle – in witnessing his wonder at the news – she even believed it herself, for a moment, but in her heart of hearts, she knew it could not be this easy, that a sacrifice was called for.

She opened her eyes. Above her, the blue sky was starting to grow pallid. How long had she been dozing? She looked at her watch – Matthew was late, very late. Had something happened? He knew she couldn't do this without him, that he had to escape the retreat unseen. They'd agreed he would pretend to have a migraine and go to bed early. Then, with the boys covering for him, he'd borrow a bike and cycle the forty miles back to the school to help her, before cycling back in time for midnight. 'It's easy,' he'd insisted. 'With my current form, it'll take two hours each way at most. That's plenty.' He'd shown her his muscular legs, then lifted his shirt to reveal how little fat he had on his body. If anyone could do it, she knew he could.

'Is this how you spend your time when we're away? Lazing around?'

Sister Oran sat up to find Matthew approaching, red-faced and wheeling a battered looking bicycle. 'What took you so long?' she asked.

'Turns out, bikes are harder to come by in the country than you might imagine.' He grinned. 'I had to steal this old banger from a neighbouring farm.'

'Oh no,' she cried. 'I didn't want you to take a risk like that.'

'Don't worry.' He gave her a hug and helped her to her feet. 'I'll put it back tonight. No one will notice a thing.'

'You're such a good boy,' she said. Everything about him made her feel better: his handsomeness, his willingness to take risks, his trust in her. Having lost his mother at an early age, he understood the gift of life more than most. When she'd first arrived at the school, he was directionless, angry at his father for sending him away and pushing against authority at every turn. He'd responded to her guidance, though. 'Oh!' She pushed him back. 'You smell awful. You're all sweaty.'

'I know, I went like the clappers. I was worried you might think I wasn't coming.' He touched her belly. 'Was that a kick?'

'Don't be daft,' she said, enjoying the delicate way he placed his hands on her, 'it's far too early. But you know, I get the sense he'll like you.'

'And why wouldn't he? He's the son of God after all.'

Better for Matthew to believe this, she thought. The truth, more mundane, and a lot less appetising, needn't concern him. She needed him to believe in order to follow through on her plan. 'You'll be a true apostle, just like your namesake. How does that make you feel?'

'Like I've been chosen.' Matthew let go of her and hid the bike behind some bushes.

A Prayer Before Killing

With the sun beginning to set, streaks of orange, pink and scarlet filled the sky, making the garden glow, flooding it with an almost supernatural light. Trees and plants which she'd never noticed before radiated with life; around them the flowers and foliage seemed to pulse with energy, as if on fire. From deep in the undergrowth, a hare darted out and paused, staring straight at her, its eyes darkly luminous, accusatory.

'No one can ever know,' she said.

Matthew placed his hand on his heart. 'No one ever will.'

'Not Luc, nor Garr, nor Johnny. Promise me.'

'They don't know I'm here. I swear.' The expression on his face changed to that of a small child. 'They're covering for me because they think I'm spending the night with Alison, the girl that lives on the farmstead a couple of miles from the retreat.'

Part of her felt guilty about luring him here, asking him to lie, but it was all for a greater good. The day she'd taken her vows, she'd committed herself to a life of chastity. Having sinned, she knew there had to be a price to pay. But, she reassured herself, many saints were reformed sinners, and all saints made sacrifices. She hoped the sacrifice she was about to make would bring redemption; she had to trust that the plan which had come to her in her hour of need was God's plan.

Hand in hand, she and Matthew wandered into the forest and climbed the hill. Neither spoke until they came to the beech tree.

She placed her palm against the trunk. 'Never forget, St Francis is always with you, protecting you. That's what the blessing we did here was all about.'

'I know.'

'And in turn, your spirit will always be here, within this tree, protecting me.' She hugged him. 'You, Luc, Garr and Johnny – you're not just my four apostles, you're like four points on a compass, guiding me; like the four elements – fire, earth, air and water. You're giving me strength.' She held his face and smiled. 'Now, we should go.'

'Before I forget.' Matthew took off his backpack and rummaged within it. 'I brought this for you.' He held up a packet of sandwiches.

'What's this for?'

'In case you get hungry.'

'God will nourish me.'

'But what if—' Matthew looked away from her.

'God will look after me. You've got to trust me.'

'I do,' Matthew said, his voice doubtful.

'I tell you what, why don't we place it in your tree? As an offering?'

He knelt and placed it deep in a hollow amongst the roots.

'Let's go.' She noticed tears staining Matthew's cheeks. 'I need you to be strong,' she said. 'Can you do that?'

He nodded.

'Do you remember the story I told you?' she asked. 'About St Oran?'

'I do, but will you tell me it again?'

She smiled. 'Oran was among the twelve who travelled with Columba to Iona and he listened to Columba when he told him that the foundations of the church he was building would not stand until a living man was buried beneath. It was a sacrifice Oran was willing to make in the knowledge that being buried alive would secure the future of the church.'

'Can't I do it instead? To save you and the baby?'

'But *I will* be saved. The baby, too. A miracle will save us. God has shown me the way.'

'But when Columba dug up Oran two days later, didn't he say that there was no great wonder in death? That hell was not what people imagined?'

'Two days was not enough. Forty days is the real test. Just like Jesus in the wilderness.'

'What if things go wrong?' he stuttered.

A Prayer Before Killing

'They won't.'

'But it'll be the summer holidays and we'll all be away.'

'Trust me. You'll know when I emerge.' She held out her hand and he kissed the charms on her bangle, one by one. 'Come on. Follow me.'

Squeezing through the gate, they climbed up the tunnel and deep under the castle. The sounds of lapping water and birdsong fell away as they left the final rays of light behind and plunged into darkness.

'We can turn back,' Matthew said. 'It's not too late.' His voice cracked as he tried to contain his emotions.

She handed him a box of matches. 'Look, I've brought a candle, why don't you light it for us?'

Though his hands were trembling, he managed to do it.

'We should pray,' she said. Coaxing him to kneel beside her on the cold stone floor, they whispered the Lord's prayer together. 'It's only forty days and nights,' she said, opening her eyes. 'Remember, other saints have faced far tougher trials. And at the end I'll rise again. It's been foretold. Neither heaven nor hell will manage to take me.'

'But won't people come looking for you?'

'I'm such a dummy!' She slapped her forehead. 'I knew there was something I'd forgotten to do. When you leave, I need you to write a note saying I've gone home to Ireland and post it under Sister Helena's door. I know it's another white lie, but will you do that for me?'

'Of course.'

'Good boy.' She stood. 'I'm ready.'

She took his hand and led him to the priest hole they'd discovered weeks before. Only large enough for one person, it was perfect. 'You know the drill: tie my hands against temptation, seal the hole with these bits of bricks, then wedge the shards of stones in place to make it all secure. Just like we agreed.'

After he bound her wrists, Matthew grabbed her and held

her tight. She gently extricated herself before stepping inside the hole. She fixed her gaze on him. 'I'm relying on you, Matthew. Remember, in forty days I will rise again and our names will be whispered amongst the legends of other saints. God has told me so.' She bowed her head in prayer. 'Hail Mary, full of grace...'

Matthew positioned the first brick.

She closed her eyes and vowed to not open them again.

Continuing to pray, each brick punctuated her words; she raised her voice to drown out the sound. Soon, she was no longer aware of Matthew's presence. Soon, she was alone in the darkness.

She fell silent and listened to her breathing, conscious of the beat of her heart in her chest, and the pulse of blood at her neck.

This was the sacrifice she was offering to save herself and her baby.

She prayed for absolution.

She prayed for a miracle.

CHAPTER 61
WEDNESDAY 6TH DECEMBER 1995

After taking Matthew to the police station in Dumbarton, Colin stayed for two hours to provide his own witness statement. Over and above Patrick's kidnapping, there was a lot to explain: how Johnny had placed Sister Oran's bangle on the statue in the school chapel, how Sarah had wrongly identified Father Young as the person accompanying Sister Oran into the woods, the role Matthew had in her disappearance and his discovery of Sister Oran's map.

On the drive from the cove, Colin and Caroline had managed to coax a large part of the story from Matthew; he'd seemed relieved to get it off his chest. What was most shocking to hear, however, was how convinced he'd been that a miracle was going to happen. Even when he'd returned from the retreat to find the school and its grounds crawling with police searching for Sister Oran, with all that pressure surrounding him, Matthew had kept his promise to her. Well, almost.

Garr, Luc and Johnny had been sick with worry. Desperate to join in the search, they'd been unable to understand Matthew's reluctance. He'd felt he had no choice but to tell them what he'd done, what Sister Oran had asked him to do. He'd got Luc and Johnny on board relatively quickly, but Garr had been harder to persuade. He wanted evidence but Matthew had none. Other than take him into the tunnel and show him where she was – which, in the circumstances, was impossible – Garr simply had to believe him.

The discovery of her body weeks later had come as a terrible blow, but if anything, it brought the four boys even closer together. In their eyes, Sister Oran's murder at the hands of Father Young made her sacrifice, her suffering, all the more profound. And they continued to believe she would rise again; that she and her child would be returned from death. For two years, they had kept her secret close, tended their faith, operated as a unit. It wasn't until Sister Oran's bangle appeared on the wrist of the statue of the Virgin Mary that things began to fall apart. What Matthew had initially taken to be a sign from Sister Oran, turned out to be anything but.

HAVING GIVEN HIS STATEMENT, Colin staggered outside. It was eight thirty, and the sun was rising on a clear, crisp winter's day. In the carpark, Caroline sat dozing in her car. He knocked gently on the window and she opened her eyes and yawned.

'You shouldn't have waited,' he shouted.

'Nonsense. They only let me go about half an hour ago.' She wound down her window and jangled her car keys. 'Now, where can I take you? Home? A greasy spoon? The pub?'

'I think I need to go back to the school.'

She looked at him, puzzled. 'Okay, if you're sure.'

'I am.'

'Then let's go.'

Caroline pulled out of the carpark and switched on the

A Prayer Before Killing

radio. Though several inches of snow still lay all around, the gritters had been out overnight and the roads were clear.

'It'd be good to find out how Father Traynor's doing,' Colin said.

'He's doing fine,' Caroline said. 'They're expecting to discharge him tomorrow.'

'How do you know that?'

'I have my ways.' She winked. 'When they took you in, I got chatting to a burly young inspector who was kind enough to call the hospital and take my phone number.'

Colin laughed. 'You're incorrigible.'

'I see myself more as an eternal optimist.'

'You sure you don't mean opportunist?' Colin looked out the window as a view of the Clyde, sparkling in the sunlight, opened up. 'I feel bad leaving Matthew at the station on his own. It's going to be hours before his dad arrives and they can start questioning him.'

'What do you think will happen?' Caroline rolled down the window to let in some fresh air. The cold was biting, but it helped clear Colin's head.

'I've said I don't want to press charges for the assault, but it's down to the police. As for the kidnapping, it's a pretty serious offence. I'd be surprised if he got off with just a caution. Perhaps, as it's a first offence, a good lawyer will keep him out of prison, but he can wave goodbye to any idea of joining the church.'

Caroline raised her eyebrow. 'You reckon?'

'Thinking about it, maybe not. The priesthood's not exactly a hotbed of moral piety.'

'And what about Sister Oran's murder? Will they reopen the case?'

'I doubt it. You heard Matthew yourself – he's confessed to helping with her disappearance and withholding evidence, but he's adamant he had nothing to do with her killing and I believe him. As far as the police are concerned, Simon Young still has the motive. She rejected him and, regardless of his denials, they consider him most likely to be the father of her child.' With a yawn, he sat back and stretched his arms.

'Why don't you close your eyes and listen to some music?' Caroline turned up the volume. Christmas songs from his childhood played as she drove – Wizzard, Slade, Mud – lulling him off to sleep.

'That's us arriving,' Caroline said.

Colin rubbed his eyes. Set against the snow, the school looked magnificent in the sun, its windows gleaming like black diamonds captured within a vast wall of concrete. In the distance, a small figure appeared to be sitting on the front steps. He frowned. Surely it was too cold to be out in this weather? As they drove closer, the person jumped to their feet. 'Is that Garr?' he asked, watching him walk towards them. If so, he appeared to be in distress. His blond hair was tousled, his shirt tails hung out over his trousers, and he was frantically waving his arms for them to stop.

'What's he doing?' Caroline parked at the entrance, beside an empty police car and switched off the engine.

Colin could see his eyes were red and swollen, with dark rings around them. 'Garr?' he asked as he stepped from the car.

'What's wrong?' Caroline reached out to hug him, but he recoiled and took several steps back.

The boy's body began to tremble. 'I wanted to say more in the café,' he said, unable to look directly at them. 'But I was too much of a coward.'

'You can tell us now.' Colin approached him carefully.

'I saw Sister Oran on the last day of term,' he stammered. 'And I think you saw something too, Miss Wilson.'

CHAPTER 62
TWO YEARS EARLIER – JULY 1993

'You bricked her up?' Garr still couldn't believe what he was hearing.

'How many times do I need to tell you?' Matthew said. 'She asked me to.'

'What else could he do, Garr?' Johnny's trembling voice rose from the corner of Luc's room. He'd retreated there and wrapped himself in a blanket after Matthew revealed what had really happened two weeks earlier. 'We need to wait for the miracle. We can't let her down.'

'It's not letting her down,' Garr insisted. 'Without food and water, she could die.'

'My money's on a miracle,' Luc said, rearranging his Star Wars action figures. 'She's done it before, when she made her aunt better – don't forget, she was dying – so why not again?' He slapped Matthew on the back. 'I just assumed you were fucking, what with all the secret meetings.'

'What meetings?' Garr asked.

'It wasn't anything, we had a couple of chats on our own before the retreat, to sort out a plan.' Matthew punched Luc in the ribs. 'And you should show a bit more respect. It's Sister Oran we're talking about.'

Garr shook his head. Matthew could be such a hypocrite. How many times had he made his bullshit claims about getting a hand job or a blow job from her on the sly? Matthew was her favourite – they all knew it – but really, Sister Oran just felt sorry for him because he didn't have a mum and his gazillionaire dad was such a fuckwit.

With the three of them against him, Garr had eventually caved and agreed not to say anything to the police, but for the following week, leading right up until the last day of term, he'd lain awake at night, trying to imagine what Sister Oran was going through. Locked away in such a tiny space, she'd be cold, thirsty, hungry. He knew that her faith was strong, that if anyone could do it, she could, but what if she got scared in the pitch black? There could be mice, rats – anything – crawling around down there. Would anyone hear her if she wanted out?

That entire week, he watched the police as they went about their business. They were winding down their search of the school grounds, casting their net wider, looking in the village and surrounding farms. He thought about phoning them anonymously to tell them to look in the tunnels again, but Matthew would have blown his top; he'd have immediately known it was him who'd snitched.

On the final day of term, Garr saw a window of opportunity. The police had scaled back their presence to just a couple of officers at the school gates. The rumour was that the rector had asked them to do this so it wouldn't look so bad to the mums and dads eager to collect their kids. No such eagerness from his own parents, who were such workaholics they always left it to the last minute to fetch him. This year was no different.

Come lunchtime, most boys had gone. Johnny had trotted off to the village to take the bus to his gran's as soon as the final Mass was over, and as usual, Matthew's dad made an early entrance. Keen to make a splash, he drove up in his silver Porsche, like some middle aged saddo, to whisk Matthew away to his Spanish estate, where he'd be dumped on the housekeeper. Likewise, a chauffeur arrived for Luc, spiriting him off to the family chateau in the Loire Valley. If last year was anything to go by, he'd fritter the next seven weeks away, lusting after the head gardener's son.

Alone, and with the coast clear, Garr made his move.

SISTER ORAN WAS OBSESSED with the tunnels and was forever dragging them down there, but they creeped Garr out; they were too dark, too echoey, too smelly. The last time he'd been there was before the retreat, when they'd played the practical joke on Father Young. It still made Garr laugh when he thought about it; what sort of idiot would mistake Johnny for a girl?

A shiver ran down his back; this was the first time he'd ever been in the tunnels on his own and he was scared about getting lost. Just in case, he'd helped himself to a couple of torches from the geography cupboard, plus extra batteries. He remembered a story from when he was small about little kids leaving a trail of breadcrumbs behind themselves so that they wouldn't get lost in the woods. He thought about doing that, then remembered how crows had eaten the breadcrumbs and the kids got lost anyway. What was he thinking? He was being stupid – he needed to banish all negative thoughts. He could do this. He was pretty sure he knew where Sister Oran was. He'd been there the previous month when Matthew and Luc had stumbled across the priest hole, and Sister Oran was so excited about it they'd had trouble pulling her away.

'It's perfect,' she'd said, over and over again.

Looking back, Garr realised she was already hatching her plan.

. . .

MATTHEW HAD DONE SUCH a good job with the wall, you could see how the police might miss it. He almost missed it himself. Matthew must have spent hours putting the bricks together and filling in the spaces between with slivers of stone.

Garr stood motionless in the low stone chamber and listened. The only noise was the hiss of the wind and the sound of the stream in the distance. He put his ear against the wall. Initially he heard nothing, just the pulse of his own blood in his head. He wondered if Matthew was lying after all. Then he began to tune into a faint rhythm which grew more and more familiar. He recognised the soft murmurs of a prayer – a *Hail Mary* – through the wall.

Brick by brick, he carefully began to dismantle it.

'Sister Oran?' he said, but the praying continued, as if she hadn't heard him. 'It's Garr.'

It took half an hour for him to remove enough bricks to be able to peer inside. The stench was awful; he had to hold his breath. Though he could still hear her voice, as he shone his torch around, he couldn't see her. Scrambling up a bit higher, he leaned further into the hole and pointed the beam into the furthest corner. A pair of eyes recoiled from the light, back into the darkness.

'Sister Oran?'

She blinked and Garr began to make out her filthy skin, her emaciated arms and her matted hair. Her entire body seemed withered, twisted in on itself. 'Garr?' Her lips parted and she smiled weakly. 'It's good to see you,' she whispered. 'We should pray.'

Garr clawed at the rest of the wall, pulling out bricks until the opening was wide enough for him to squeeze inside. From his bag, he took out a bottle of water and pressed it to her mouth, but she refused, the liquid dribbling down her chin onto her habit, which sat stiffly away from her shrunken body. 'Please try.' He cupped his hand, filling it with water and holding it to her lips. This time she opened her mouth

A Prayer Before Killing

and allowed some in. 'Sister Oran,' he said, 'I need you to come with me.'

She shook her head and murmured 'No.'

He looked at her wrists and was horrified to see they were tied together with rope. Matthew hadn't told them this detail. He untied the knot; the skin beneath was raw and weeping.

Freed, she grabbed the bottle from him, her skeletal hands pressing it to her cracked lips. For several moments she sipped as Garr supported her head, fearful that she might choke.

'What date is it?'

'The second of July.'

'You go,' she gasped. 'I'll follow.'

'Why won't you come with me?'

'You wouldn't understand.'

From his bag, he took out a packet of crisps – it was all he'd had left in his room – and opened it. 'You need to eat,' he said, offering her a crisp.

'Thank you.' She took it from his hand and nibbled at a corner but spat it out. 'I can't—'

'I'll go and find someone to help. Sarah's still in the office—'

'No,' she interrupted. 'I'll leave myself. In my own time. When you commit to something you need to follow through. It's a tenet of what it means to be divine. One day, you'll learn.'

Garr stood. Maybe it was for the best. If he went and got help, brought someone to help rescue her, the police would find out. They'd discover they all knew where she was, and that Matthew put her there. Yet it felt wrong to leave her. It was so cold and she looked so weak, he wondered if she even had the strength to leave by herself. She could barely hold a bottle. 'Please let me take you,' he said.

She shook her head and began to pray again. It was a prayer he didn't recognise, and after a few seconds, he

419

wondered if the words were real, if she was making them up.

'Try another crisp,' he said.

She nodded. 'I *will* follow. You must believe me.' She took the tiniest crisp from the packet and placed it on her tongue like a communion wafer. Lifting her arm she drew the bangle over her hand and with her bony fingers folded it into his palm. 'Take this,' she said. 'That way you'll know I'll follow. It's far too precious to me to be parted from it for long.'

He looked at the bangle which gleamed golden in his hand.

'God will lead me out,' she whispered.

'I'm not sure God's here,' Garr said.

'God is everywhere,' she reprimanded. 'Don't ever let me hear you say such a thing again. You must believe.'

'I'm sorry.' There was nothing he could do to convince her to come with him. Leaving one of the torches with her, he turned and walked away. As he descended to the tunnel gate, the sound of her praying became more and more faint. He left, hoping against hope he would hear her voice again.

CHAPTER 63

WEDNESDAY 6TH DECEMBER 1995

The walk uphill revived Colin. Garr's confession outside the school was the vital piece of evidence he needed. And the boy was right; what Caroline had witnessed that day was significant and supported his own suspicions.

He approached Sarah and Brendan's front door and rang the bell. Set within the forest, with its snow-covered roof and smoking chimney, their cottage looked like it belonged in a Grimm's fairytale.

'Yes?' Sarah held the door half open. He could see she was getting ready for work; her makeup had been freshly applied and she was almost fully dressed.

'Can I come in?'

'Is this to speak to Brendan?' Her eyes darted about the floor looking for her shoes. 'He's still at the hospital. He slept there last night.'

'No, it's you I'd like to talk to.'

'Oh. Okay. Come on in.' Sarah opened the door and stood aside. 'I hope you don't mind me getting ready.' She went over to a mirror and picked up a pair of earrings, which she carefully put on. 'After all the drama last night, Brother Thomas said I could start at ten. I don't want to be late.'

'I've left Matthew with the police.'

'I can't believe he abducted Father Traynor.' She zipped on a pair of boots which had been tucked underneath a chair and checked her appearance again in the mirror. 'I mean, the boy's just a child. And hitting you, I just couldn't believe what I was hearing.'

'Yes, he's admitted to it all.' Colin glanced around the cottage. He hadn't noticed the decor the previous night; in contrast to Sarah's smart, chic style, it was chintzy and a little rundown. On the wall behind her, a framed embroidery declared *Home is where the love is* and beyond, in the living room, he could see framed photos of Brendan and her arranged on a dark, old-fashioned sideboard.

'That's so sad, ruining his life like that.' Sarah squinted into the mirror and sprayed herself with perfume, the floral scent momentarily disguising the faint, mouldy smell of the cottage. Satisfied, she put on her glasses. 'That's better. I can actually see, now,' she quipped. 'I really need to get to work.'

Colin stood aside as she grabbed a red wool coat from a hook at the back of the door. 'Shall I walk you down?'

She nodded, buttoning up her coat and finishing her outfit off with a handbag and matching scarf and gloves. 'It's such a beautiful morning.'

As she went to open the door, he blocked her way. 'I take it you're sticking to your story that you saw Father Young with Sister Oran the evening she disappeared?'

'Not this again.' She smiled and opened the door. A chill wind blew inside, scattering snow across the hall carpet. 'I know what I saw.'

'And you'd your glasses on, I take it?'

'Yes.' She locked the door behind him. 'I really need to get a move on.'

'Brendan's relationship with Sister Oran – can you tell me if they were close?'

A Prayer Before Killing

Sarah scowled. 'If you mean did they speak to each other during work hours, then yes,' she said.

Colin pursued her down the pathway as her pace quickened. At the end of the path, she mis-stepped and slipped. Colin grabbed her arm to steady her.

'Thank you,' she muttered breathlessly.

'The person you saw walking into the woods with Sister Oran was not Father Young. The person you saw was taller, more athletic, wasn't he? I don't know if you knew it was Matthew or not, it's academic, but you knew it wasn't Father Young. On the day Sister Oran disappeared, you told him things in private which you came to regret, didn't you? In a moment of weakness, you confessed to him.'

Sarah gripped a nearby fencepost. 'Mr Buxton, if Father Young *had* taken my confession, surely that would remain confidential?'

'A formal confession is far different from simply telling someone something in private. Yes, Father Young may have blessed you that day, but what you told him was never within the sanctity of the confessional.' Colin attempted to gauge her reaction, but she turned away from him.

'What's the purpose of all this,' she cried, 'other than to upset me?'

'You knew before she died that Sister Oran was pregnant. Who did you think the father was?'

Sarah remained silent.

'Or let me put it this way, who at the school had a track record of seducing vulnerable young girls? Certainly not Father Young. Did Brendan know she was pregnant?'

She shrugged. 'I didn't tell him.'

'I think it suited you to let people think Father Young was the father, even if that meant they believed he was a murderer too.'

Finally, she looked at him.

'I'm right, aren't I?' he said.

Sarah stared past him, back at her home. 'She betrayed her vows.'

'But what about Brendan? Didn't he betray his, too?'

A Land Rover, its tyres crunching through the snow, approached along the rear drive of the cottage and stopped. Brendan, his face pale from lack of sleep, got out and walked towards them. 'Everything okay?' he asked.

Sarah stepped towards her husband. 'Give me the keys.'

'What? Why?'

'I've a question I need to ask you, Brendan,' Colin said.

Confused, Brendan turned to him. 'What?'

'And it's important you tell me the truth.'

Brendan glanced back and forth between him and his wife. 'Look mate, I've hardly had a wink of sleep. Can't we—?'

'Are you the father of Sister Oran's child?' Colin asked.

Brendan began to laugh. 'What kind of bullshit is this? Sarah—?'

'Your wife thinks you are. Don't you, Sarah?'

She stared at him, then at Brendan.

'Then my wife's wrong.' Brendan reached out to Sarah. 'Honey, what's this about? I swear, I never touched the girl.'

She stepped away from him. 'I've tried to protect you all this time, but no more.'

'Protect me?'

'Tell the truth.' Sarah's voice trembled. 'For once in your life.'

From the school below, Colin could hear a police siren go off. He'd asked Caroline to alert them to where he was going and why. Soon, they'd arrive, but he was sure he was close to a confession. If they appeared too soon, he might never achieve it. And once these two were in custody, who knew what they would say to protect themselves and each other?

'Brendan, you may be the baby's father, but I don't believe it was you who beat Sister Oran to death,' Colin said.

A Prayer Before Killing

'Then who did?' Sarah stared at Colin, disbelief etched across her face.

'You.'

THE INFORMATION GARR had told Colin earlier at the school entrance was key. After seeing Sister Oran on that last day of term, he'd returned to his room to wait for his parents. Staring out of his window he'd seen a lone figure emerge from the forest. Sarah. Garr had reminded Caroline that she was on the driveway at the time, but had been distracted; she'd dropped her bag, and was frantically gathering up the contents. As a result, she hadn't seemed to notice Sarah's dishevelled appearance, but Garr had, and thought it odd.

'What did you say to each other that day?' Garr had asked Caroline. 'Because I saw you speaking to her.'

Caroline had had to think hard but could only recall worrying that she couldn't find her car keys and that she was going to be late for her flight to Rome. 'I can't remember, Garr. I'm sorry.'

'But you gave her something.'

'I did?'

'You picked something off the ground and gave it to her.'

It was then that everything had clicked into place. 'I gave her a plaster. I always have a packet in my bag as I'm such a klutz.'

'Why did you give her a plaster?' Colin had asked.

'Because she had a cut. Right here.' Caroline had pointed to her cheekbone. 'It was only small, but it was bleeding, yet she hadn't noticed. Thinking about it now, it seems strange, but I was in a rush so I—'

'But she looked a total mess,' Garr had interrupted. 'Like she'd fallen.'

'Or been in a fight?' Colin had asked.

Garr had nodded. 'At the time, I assumed she'd had an argument with Brendan.'

Colin had shook his head. 'Brendan spent that day in Edinburgh. I've checked.'

SARAH SNATCHED the car keys from Brendan's hand and pushed him towards Colin.

'Stop!' Colin yelled as he tried to sidestep Brendan and grab her, but Brendan held him back.

'Whatever she's done, she's still my wife,' he hissed through gritted teeth, manoeuvring Colin into a headlock.

'Let me go,' Colin cried, but as much as he pushed and pulled, he couldn't release himself. Brendan was too strong. Instead, he had to watch helplessly as Sarah jumped into the car and revved the engine.

A police siren howled, approaching from the school road, blue flashing lights reflected through the trees. If Sarah was to escape, she had no choice but to turn the four-wheel drive around and leave by the rear track. She threw the vehicle into reverse and it jolted backwards.

'Father Young's the guilty one,' Brendan sobbed. 'They proved it, didn't they?'

Colin felt Brendan's arm tighten around his throat. The strength of the man was unbelievable. Colin's vision began to blur as the police car skidded to a halt yards from them and Brendan dragged him further towards the cottage.

In his mind, Colin began to recite a prayer he once whispered in church as an altar boy. Soft, soothing words that when repeated became a mantra. The pain began to leave his body and all that remained was peace. It felt like he was floating. As he'd been taught in India, he chose to channel the sensation, focus its power. Harnessing all his remaining strength, with one thrust he broke free from Brendan's iron grip.

As he tumbled to the ground, an almighty roar of screeching tyres was followed by a cry and the sound of metal ploughing into something solid. Sarah's piercing scream echoed around the landscape.

Colin opened his eyes, gasping for breath. In front of him was a scene of carnage: Brendan pinned against a tree by the Land Rover, writhing in agony, a police officer trying to open the car door. Gripping the steering wheel, Sarah revved the engine repeatedly, only stopping once the life had drained from her husband's face.

CHAPTER 64

TWO YEARS EARLIER – MONDAY 14TH JUNE 1993

On the day Sister Oran disappeared, Sarah had stayed late at work to make up for her visit to the dentist, going over in her head how best to handle Brother Thomas. The Friday before, he'd more or less accused her of stealing several hundred pounds from the petty cash. She'd put on a show, pretended she was offended, but the truth was she'd helped herself to closer to five thousand pounds over the past couple of years. It had started off with a tenner here and there taken from the petty cash, but the longer Sister Helena had failed to notice, the bolder she became. A tenner turned into fifty pounds taken from the maintenance budget, which turned into a hundred from donations. Her mistake was to assume that Sister Helena would never notice the discrepancy, never bring it to Brother Thomas' attention – that she was too old and senile. How wrong she'd been; she now had less than a week to come up with a plausible explanation.

Given how stressed she was already, she resented even having to think about it; Brendan was her main worry. For several months she'd had a suspicion he was up to his old tricks. He'd cut his hair and trimmed his beard. And he was being too nice to her: paying her compliments, buying her

A Prayer Before Killing

little gifts, helping around the house. It all pointed towards one thing, and one thing only: another woman. But when and where? After the last time, when she'd threatened him with divorce, he'd basically agreed to account for his every move, which he'd been doing. That's what was so confusing and had sent her spiralling, imagining she was going mad; he had no opportunity. She'd warned every woman under forty in the school off him, and he was never allowed into the village on his own.

Over the last few weeks, however, the horror of it all – the complete and utter humiliation – had been revealed. At first, she couldn't believe it – it seemed too far-fetched – but the evidence was all there. It had been there all along if only she hadn't been so blind.

Sarah initially thought Sister Oran had a virus. Like an idiot, she'd asked if she was okay, even offered to go to the chemist's for her, but as Sister Oran continued to appear, day after day, pale-faced and dashing to the toilet to throw up, Sarah put two and two together. This was no bug; with her glowing skin it was clear the girl was pregnant. Sarah had no doubt, she recognised the signs from her own short-lived pregnancy – those eight weeks of bliss just after she and Brendan married, when the future felt like a place of hope and not somewhere to be feared.

And it wasn't rocket science to work out who the father was. It could only be someone from the school, and by a process of elimination it could only be Brendan. She'd considered and reconsidered every other male within a mile's radius – they were all ruled out, either too young, too gay, too uptight, or too decrepit. All the things which Brendan wasn't, with his teasing jokes, his full lips and his muscular thighs.

What was so devastating was that she'd seen them together, multiple times, chatting on the stairs, laughing in the gardens, giggling on the driveway, and had thought nothing of it. If she'd thought anything, it was how Sister

Oran seemed to bring out something paternal in Brendan that she'd never seen before. How could she have been so dumb? Strip the habit from the girl and what you had was exactly Brendan's type: a naïve country girl, barely out of her teens. Precisely what Sarah herself had been when they'd first met.

Sick of thinking about her situation, and her tooth still aching, at eight PM she covered up her typewriter, put her glasses in her bag, and locked up the office. Outside, she slipped off her jacket. It was still warm; heat radiated from the ground and the forest glowed, lit up by the sun which hung low in the sky. Tonight, as Brendan was away on business, she would take her time, she thought to herself, and walk the long way up the hill through the forest.

She'd only taken a few steps when she spotted the figure of Sister Oran up ahead, walking along the path that led into the forest. For days, she'd fantasised about getting her on her own, confronting her. Was this now the opportunity? Sarah needed her to understand how much she'd been hurt, needed to tell her that Brendan would never leave her – his wife – not ever.

Tightly clutching her bag, Sarah picked up her pace, but her heart almost stopped dead in her chest when she realised that Sister Oran wasn't alone. The figure of a man was walking ahead of her. Brendan. The build was right, though she couldn't be certain, as her eyesight was so poor. Struggling to unzip her bag to find her glasses, she accidentally dropped them on the dry earth, forcing her to scramble in the dust to find them, but by the time she stood, fixing them in place, Sister Oran and the figure had disappeared into the shadows.

WHEN IT BECAME clear a few days later that Sister Oran was missing, Sarah had watched Brendan like a hawk. In her worst imaginings, Sister Oran had gone off to have the baby

A Prayer Before Killing

in secret, with Brendan planning to join her once she gave birth.

Over breakfast, Sarah had found the courage to ask him where he thought Sister Oran had gone. He was eating a piece of toast and reading the newspaper. Well, the sports' headlines. He wasn't much of a reader.

He shrugged. 'Dunno.'

'Strange though, isn't it?'

'What?'

'Her disappearing like that.'

He looked up from his newspaper. 'Why are you bothered? You couldn't stand her.'

More than anything, Sarah was shocked by how genuinely uninterested he seemed. He wasn't the greatest liar and there was nothing in his demeanour to suggest he knew, or for that matter cared where she was. But she knew the truth.

As Sister Oran's disappearance quickly developed into a missing person's case, and police officers flooded onto the school grounds, everything changed. With his local knowledge, Brendan became indispensable to the investigation, giving the police information about places where Sister Oran might have got into trouble: the duck pond, the waterfall, the tunnels.

Sarah decided to stay tight-lipped at what she'd seen. After all, Brendan was still her husband. And *he* hadn't gone anywhere.

As the summer term drew to a close, the police search moved on. Prayers continued to be said for Sister Oran, but in private people had begun to express doubts that she would ever safely return.

Sarah prayed this was the case.

ON THAT FINAL DAY, come mid-afternoon, there was little left for Sarah to do in the office. With the police presence minimal, and almost all the staff and pupils having left by lunchtime, she tidied everything up and headed for home. She and Brendan were off on holiday the next morning – a fortnight in Spain, just the two of them – and there was still packing to do.

Outside, the sun was scorching and there was no wind.

She couldn't completely explain why she decided to follow Garr. He was not the sort of boy she would usually take any interest in; with his metal-rimmed glasses and stiff walk, like so many of the students at the school, he seemed old before his time. But the more she thought about it, his actions seemed peculiar. And anyway, she'd some time to kill before heading home to start packing.

As she meandered through the trees, he appeared ahead, striding up the hill in his shorts and shirt, with a plastic bag in his hand. Not only was it strange that he was still there – that his parents hadn't collected him yet – but it was strange to see him on his own, with no sign of the other three Apostles.

Without thinking about it, she changed direction.

Maintaining a safe distance, she kept her eyes fixed on him, increasingly curious about what his destination might be. He walked with such a sense of purpose that it was clear he was going somewhere, but there was a nervousness to his movements – the tilt of his neck and the tight swing of his arm – that suggested deceit. She wondered what sort of secret a boy like Garr could possibly have.

Arriving at the duckpond, he stopped. She stepped behind a tree as he looked around, oblivious to her presence. Rather than take the track which led up to the bridge and the castle entrance, she was surprised to see him cross the marshy ground, where the waterfall joined the duckpond, and disappear from view. A piercing sound cut through the heavy air momentarily, and then there was silence.

Sarah waited ten minutes. Then ten minutes more. When

A Prayer Before Killing

Garr didn't reappear, she decided to investigate. Among the reeds and bullrushes, there was no sign of him, just an entrance to the castle tunnels, with a metal gate across it.

Standing at the tunnel entrance, her body was cooled by a soothing breeze. She placed her hands on the bars and pulled, but it was locked tight. Brendan was in charge of all the keys for the school – could Garr have stolen the key for the gate from him?

Intrigued, she climbed a short way up the rocks to a small grassy area overlooking the tunnel entrance and waited. In the heat, with only the hum of insects to break the silence, for the first time in weeks she felt calm. Wherever Sister Oran was – whatever had happened to her – Sarah was pleased she was gone, prayed she would never return. As for Brother Thomas and his accusations, maybe Sister Oran's disappearance offered an opportunity to muddy the water, suggest she might be the culprit.

Sarah's eyelids had begun to droop when she noticed movement below. Garr pulled himself through a small gap at the bottom of the gate and stood. He held a torch in one hand, but there was no sign of the plastic bag. Grabbing one of the bars, he twisted it; the same sound as before – shrill, like the call of a kestrel – echoed upwards. As he stepped away, the boy appeared to have second thoughts and twisted the bar back, re-opening the gap. Keeping low to the ground, she continued to watch, expecting him to re-enter the tunnel, but instead he turned around and walked off in the direction of the school.

Was someone else in the tunnel?

It couldn't be any of the Apostles – or any other pupil – they'd all left already. Nor Brendan, as he was in Edinburgh, on yet another hunt for parts for the school heating system. Brother Thomas had gone for a meeting with the bishop, reminding her that they still needed to have a chat about the missing money. And Charlie Murray had hurried off to catch a flight to Paris. As for the teaching staff, most had scampered as soon as the final bell had rung. Sister Helena and Miss Wilson were still on site, but she'd left them talking in the atrium.

A thought crossed her mind, but it didn't seem possible – she knew the police had searched the tunnels at least twice – the second time with sniffer dogs. With some difficulty, Sarah manoeuvred herself through the opening. She brushed the dirt from her trousers as she scrambled to her feet. Rummaging around in her handbag, she found a lighter and lit it. The tunnel was damp and smelt putrid. With her free hand, she steadied herself against the wall and ventured deeper.

A gasp of wind blew the flame of her lighter out. As she stood in the pitch black trying to relight it, it occurred to her that perhaps Garr was planning to return. That was why he'd left the gap in the gate. If he did, how would she explain her presence here? What would he think?

The lighter relit, Sarah was about to turn around when a murmur from up ahead reverberated around the curving walls. Shielding the flame, she walked towards it. As she turned a corner, a light glowed. She paused and let the flame of her lighter die.

Someone else *was* here after all.

Sarah's breathing became rapid as she wondered why she wasn't at home, packing their suitcases for tomorrow's flight. She clenched her fists tight to stop her hands from shaking, as a feeling of dread crept over her body.

Her memory was hazy about what happened next.

Sitting amongst rubble holding a torch, a muttering creature – half-human, half-devil – sat on the dank floor, eating a sandwich. As Sarah approached, she saw it had the face and wore the clothes of Sister Oran.

Its eyes dark and vacant, the creature remained still, unaware of Sarah's presence.

A Prayer Before Killing

The closer Sarah got, the more the slow sounds of chewing became amplified, until it was all she could hear. Nausea – an overwhelming feeling of disgust – swept from the depths of her belly to her throat. The idea that this filthy creature was nourishing itself, nourishing the creature growing within it, was too much to bear.

There were no words.

It had to end.

CHAPTER 65

WEDNESDAY 6TH DECEMBER 1995

Annemarie appeared at the front door as Colin climbed out the car. 'Are you okay?' she asked.

'I'm fine,' he replied.

Wide-eyed, Liam squeezed past his mother. 'Is it true?'

Colin nodded.

'It's been all over the news,' Annemarie said.

'I know.' Driving back into the city, he'd caught sight of an *Evening Times* board outside a newsagent with the headline *Hostage Drama at Horror School*.

'They were talking about it on the telly,' Liam said. 'They had a reporter there and everything.'

Annemarie stepped aside to let him into the hallway. 'Is Father Traynor alright?'

'It's been a nasty ordeal, but I'm told he's doing fine.' Colin walked through to the kitchen and pulled open a cupboard. 'He should be discharged tomorrow.'

'I can't believe you rescued him,' Liam said.

'Give your uncle some space.' Annemarie turned to Colin. 'What are you looking for? Take off your coat and I'll stick the kettle on.'

A Prayer Before Killing

'I just need to have a word with Jeanie,' Colin said. 'I see her lights are on.'

'Don't be daft, sit down.' Annemarie held his chin. 'That's some shiner you're going to have. Have you had it looked at?'

'It's nothing.' From the back of the cupboard, Colin grabbed the M&S bag with the empty pill bottles in it. 'I'll be ten minutes.'

HE STARED at the Christmas tree twinkling in Jeanie's bay window and rang her doorbell. It took four attempts before she finally answered. 'Is now a bad time?' he asked.

'No,' she said, her eyes flickering towards the bag in his hand. 'Come on in, son.'

'Have you been away?' Colin asked, entering the hallway. 'I've tried you a few times.'

'Just been busy. It's this time of year.'

Colin followed her through to the living room. Looking round, he could see that the house had been transformed. The piles of boxes and clutter had been removed and a sparkling clean kitchen gleamed from the rear of the house. 'Have you had a clear out?'

'It was about time,' she replied. 'A husband-and-wife team from the church do house clearances, deep cleans, that sort of thing. It cost me forty pounds, but they had it all done in less than a day.'

Colin sat in an armchair on the other side of the fire from her. Christmas cards lined the mantlepiece and tinsel was draped around the mirror above. He held up the plastic bag. 'I was hoping you could help explain this.'

'Explain?' She twisted the tassel of a cushion between her fingers. 'I don't know what you mean.'

Colin spilled the four empty bottles of pills onto the carpet. 'I need to ask you, and I'm sorry if I've got this wrong, but is there something you need to tell me?'

Glancing downwards, she leaned over for a closer look. 'Are those your Mum's?' she asked.

'Some of them.'

She leaned down to pick one up. 'Is this my Alec's?'

'I saw you put the bag in our bin.'

She re-checked the name on the bottle of pills. 'I thought I'd thrown out all Alec's stuff after he died.'

He crossed the room and crouched beside her. 'Did you …?'

'What?' Her eyes widened.

'Did you do something to my mum? Or help her do something to herself?'

Jeanie handed him back the pill bottle. 'Put them away and don't be silly.'

'Did you give her these? Your husband's heart pills would have been much stronger than my Mum was used to.' The way she avoided his gaze told him everything.

'Of course I didn't.'

For a few moments only the mechanical whir of the electric fire could be

heard. Colin finally broke the silence. 'There are too many unanswered questions, Jeanie.'

She stood. 'Colin, I've known you since you were five. What's got into you? Now, I know you've been under a lot of stress recently, so why don't you go get a good night's sleep?'

'Tell me what happened, Jeanie. I promise I'll not judge. But I need to know the truth.'

She hesitated. 'I'll make us some tea. But I promise you I don't know anything about any extra pills your mum might have taken.' She went into the kitchen and closed the door.

Colin stared into the orange glow of the electric fire. If his hunch was correct, Jeanie had somehow played a part in his mother's sudden death. From the start, the timings Jeanie had told about his mother's death seemed suspicious. The disinfected room was another clue. Why had she done this by herself? She could have waited, allowed them to help. Then the bottles of pills rattling in the M&S bag she had on the day his mother died. Finding them empty, discarded in the bin, was careless of her. But leaving her own husband's heart pills amongst them, said it all.

'Jeanie?' he shouted. She'd been away a couple of minutes, and he hadn't heard the kettle boil. Perhaps she was taking a moment to herself, preparing how best to explain.

Suddenly, there was a thud. Jumping up, he rushed through to the kitchen. A knife by her side, Jeanie lay on the floor, wrists slashed, a pool of blood forming around her. 'I didn't know what else to do,' she sobbed.

CHAPTER 66

SIXTEEN DAYS LATER - FRIDAY 22ND DECEMBER 1995

Mrs Beattie helped Colin off with his coat and brushed the snow from it before placing it over a chair beside the radiator. 'It'll be nice and warm when you leave.'

'Thank you. I should have worn something heavier.'

'I'm about to brave it myself.' She shivered. 'The snow's supposed to continue until Christmas Day.'

'A white Christmas? We don't get many of those.'

'It's certainly good for business, brings lots of people to church.' She smiled. 'This way; he's in his study.' Outside the room, she squeezed Colin's hand and whispered, 'Thank you.'

'Is he doing okay?'

She gestured so-so and knocked on the door. 'The break will do him good.'

'Come in!' Patrick called.

'Just me,' Colin said, opening the door.

Standing in the centre of the room, holding several files and surrounded by piles of paperwork, Patrick turned to greet him, laying everything aside.

'You're looking well,' said Colin.

A Prayer Before Killing

Patrick beamed. 'All down to you.'

'I'll leave you two boys to chat,' Mrs Beattie said. 'Remember, I'm popping out to do some Christmas shopping, so if you want tea or coffee, it's all set out for you.' She closed the door and moments later they heard the front door click shut.

'Sit down,' Patrick said. 'That's if you can find a space.'

Colin moved an assortment of folders onto the floor and sat in an armchair beside the window. Outside, in the grey afternoon light, the snow was falling more heavily, covering the lawn and the empty flowerbeds. 'So, you're actually doing it?'

'I've just got these papers to sort through and then I'm off.' Patrick sat on the corner of his desk. 'I say just, but it's going to take another day.' Colin went to speak, but Patrick interrupted him. 'I was so shocked to hear about Jeanie. I still don't know what to think.'

Jeanie's swift and brutally honest confession revealed how she'd assisted not only his mother's death, but also her husband's. She revealed this as they waited for an ambulance, him pressing tea towels to her wrists. Currently she was in a psychiatric ward pending the outcome of a full criminal investigation. He'd visited her once, but she had unravelled, preferring to remember the good times she shared with Alec and Moira. Everything else she'd chosen to forget, and Colin didn't have the heart to push.

'Once she'd made the mistake of confiding in my mum that she'd helped Alec commit suicide, Moira saw an opportunity.'

'It's horrendous.'

'My mother was always a difficult person to say no to.' A recent nightmare placed him in her bedroom on that final day, watching as she swallowed pill after pill, Jeanie on hand to assist and clean up afterwards. If only he'd popped his head round the door that morning, maybe he could have said something to change her mind. But he hadn't, and he would have to live with this.

Patrick got up and stared out the window. 'I'm not sure I'll be coming back to the priesthood.' He smiled. 'The sabbatical's supposed to give me time to work things out, recharge my batteries, but really I think it's the beginning of the end.'

'You're so good at it, though.'

Patrick raised an eyebrow. 'Parts of it; the day-to-day ministry, yes. But there are aspects to the office – what's expected of a priest – which I don't feel I'm ever going to reconcile.'

'Do you have to? The church is full of priests doing exactly what they want.'

'The problem is I believe in it all.' He pointed at his dog collar. 'I have expectations of what a priest should be, how he should live. When I think about the decisions I've made, I realise I'm part of the problem. In my own eyes, I'm failing.' He pulled his collar off and placed it on the desk. 'I'm sorry I made a pass at you; it wasn't my finest hour.'

Colin shrugged. 'Who knows, maybe in a different time and place I'd have kissed you back.'

'Now you're just being kind.'

'I do like you,' said Colin, 'but the whole priest thing – it's a bit of headfuck for me.'

'Wow.' Patrick laughed. 'It must be bad; I don't think I've heard you swear before.'

'Sorry.' Colin grinned. 'At the end of the day, I'm still trying to be a good Catholic boy; it's ingrained.' He sat forward. 'When I was young, all I wanted was to become a priest, and my mum was thrilled, really pushed me to go for it. Then I hit puberty and I began to crave something else. Eventually I reasoned God had chosen me to go in another direction and that's the way I went. It caused a major rift with my mother, which we never quite healed.'

'You do know she was proud of you?'

A Prayer Before Killing

'I'm not sure about that,' Colin replied. 'I was a disappointment. I think the only reason she kept coming to church was because of you: the son she really wanted.'

Patrick shook his head. 'She was always talking about you, and Annemarie and Sean.'

'That's … surprising to hear.'

'She struggled to express her emotions – maybe love in particular? It's something I can relate to.'

'If life's taught me anything so far, it's that it doesn't have to be about regrets and pain and guilt. It can be about joy and acceptance, but you have to discover that for yourself. Other people can't tell you. Or shouldn't.'

Patrick smiled. 'What age are you again?'

'Twenty-eight.'

'Wise words from one so young. You don't think maybe Moira was right after all? That you've missed your calling? There's going to be a vacancy here at St Bridget's shortly.'

'Now *that* would be a turn up for the books.'

Patrick stood and picked up an envelope from the desk. 'This is from Simon. It arrived last week.' He passed it to Colin. 'I'd like you to read it.'

Colin took the letter from the envelope. Neatly written by hand, it contained only a brief paragraph.

Dear Patrick,

As you know, the wheels of justice turn slowly, but I'm hoping to be released soon. There are still parts of me that feel I don't deserve to be out there in the real world, despite knowing I had nothing to do with Sister Oran's death. I may have a long journey ahead of me, coming to terms with everything that's happened over the last couple of years, but I'm grateful to be on it. Without your faith and guidance, I'd still be convincing myself that somehow I was responsible. To know that I'm not, that I never was, feels good.

Thank you,
Simon

Colin handed the letter back to Patrick. 'He's not the only one having to reflect on what's happened over the past two years. I think there's little doubt Sarah's going to jail and Matthew's facing prosecution.'

'Do you think it'll go that far for Matthew, given his age?' Patrick said. 'Surely his father's too rich to let that happen.'

'I don't know. Kidnapping and assault; it's pretty serious. And don't forget the other boys; any one of them could have come forward to the police as soon as Matthew told them where Sister Oran was. I know they've already interviewed Garr and Luc under caution, and with Johnny out of hospital and making a good recovery, it's only a matter of time before they'll interview him.'

'Sarah needs to be punished, but as for Matthew and the rest of the Apostles, I find it hard to apportion blame,' Patrick said. 'Faith was instilled in them from an early age. They'd been taught to believe in miracles, to never question the authority of the church, to abide by its teachings. All those things got mixed up together and somehow distorted. You saw Matthew's face that night in the tunnel, the fanaticism in his eyes.'

Colin understood only too well. People convincing themselves they were doing the right thing, regardless of the suffering of others: the boys' naive pact, Brendan's ruthless attitude to women and the horrific results of that, Sarah's pathological desire to cover things up. If only people could live outside themselves for a moment, be mindful of their effect on others; then, Colin thought, the world might be a better place.

'Why did you arrange to meet with Matthew?' he asked. 'Surely you knew he might harm you?'

Patrick stared at the piles of paper on the carpet. 'Honestly? That hadn't crossed my mind. All I wanted was to protect myself, ensure my dirty little secret with Davey wasn't made public.' He looked up. 'But that secret made me blind to everything else. For that, I nearly got us both killed, and I'm truly sorry.'

CHAPTER 67
JANUARY 1996

In the second week of January, Colin reported to the police station in Dumbarton where there was an awkward conversation. After rapping his knuckles for failing to submit the evidence he'd uncovered sooner, they begrudgingly thanked him for his assistance. Biting his tongue, he resisted the temptation to point out the flaws in their investigation and left.

Outside in the carpark, he sat in his car as rain fell on the windscreen; the prospect of returning home filled him with sadness. Christmas and New Year had passed alone in a haze of sleep, carry outs and late-night TV. Despite invitations from Annemarie and Caroline, he hadn't felt much like socialising. As a result of Jeanie's confession, his mother's funeral had been delayed and Colin found himself in limbo, unable to make any immediate plans. However, with the post-mortem now complete, and – as expected – the toxicology report finding a cocktail of drugs in her system, they'd finally set a date for the following week.

Pulling out of the car park, instead of turning left towards Glasgow, Colin turned right and drove in the direction of the school.

A Prayer Before Killing

. . .

FROM THE TOP of the hill, Colin looked down on the castle ruin, with the grey mass of the school below and the vast Clyde estuary in the distance. Working from memory, he had arrived at what he thought must be the location associated with Garr and St Michael in Sister Oran's map. Stark and leafless, three oak trees stood at the ridge of the hill. As crows reeled in the sky above, Colin explored the area. Pinned to one of the oaks, he found a small wreath. Withered and dry, it had been made by weaving feathers together. Had this been part of Sister Oran's ritual for Garr – feathers from an angel's wings?

Colin felt sorry for the four boys; from his own experience, he knew what it was to be innocent and to believe – how faith didn't always survive when it encountered the harsh realities of life. He wondered about Sister Oran too: had she lived, would she have stayed with the church? Her beliefs, her lust for life, seemed too great, too eccentric, to be constrained by its strictures. Gazing across the landscape, he knew she was right about one thing; it really was magical.

AT THE CREMATORIUM, as Colin stood in line with Annemarie and Sean to shake hands with strangers – some women from the parish and a couple of Moira's former colleagues – he caught sight of Caroline at the very end of the queue. The beads on her distinctive black coat sparkled in the weak Glaswegian sunlight that filtered through the stained-glass windows. He could see people bristle as she chatted to the woman beside her, her confident Home Counties' accent rising above the mourners as they shuffled outside.

'Can we talk?' she mouthed as she drew closer.

'Excuse me,' he said to an elderly woman who was gripping his hand as if her life depended on it. She strained to hear him as he extricated himself from her. 'Thank you for coming.'

He left Annemarie and Sean to thank the last few people and disappeared with Caroline into a side-room.

'Nice service,' she said.

Colin opened a window and took a breath of freezing cold air. 'You think?'

'Maybe a little odd.' She made a face as she closed the door. 'It was strange the person officiating only mentioned your mother's name once.'

'It's all been a bit of a mess. The guy only met with us briefly and obviously he'd never met her.' He grimaced. 'Though maybe that's just as well.'

'And there's no wake?'

He shook his head and sat. 'Given the circumstances, Annemarie and Sean put their foot down. As you'll have seen for yourself, my mother wasn't exactly popular. In fact, the one friend she did have helped kill her, so go figure.'

She sat beside him and squeezed his knee. 'I hate seeing you so down.'

'It's been a weird time, waiting. I think we're all just relieved to get the funeral out of the way.'

'I'm sure. No matter how anyone gets on with their mother, it's always going to be difficult.' She patted his arm. 'I'm sorry, I need to get back to school, but we should meet up for a proper chat. I've time to give you a quick lowdown on what's been happening, though, if you like?'

'Go on, hit me with it.'

She settled herself; Colin could see how much she was savouring this. 'Well, on the first day back, it was announced that Brother Thomas would not be returning this term. The church has relocated him to somewhere in Poland, but the details are sketchy.'

'Has he not been "relocated" before? What's the story this time?'

A Prayer Before Killing

'Financial shenanigans, same as last time. He never made any report to the school board about the money Sarah had been stealing.'

'And why was she? Greed?'

'Apparently, she was paying child maintenance for three children Brendan fathered.' She rolled her eyes. 'I almost feel sorry for her. What a life!'

'Anyway, you were saying about Brother Thomas.'

'Oh yes. The rumour is he was biding his time, skimming money for himself with the plan of making her the fall guy later down the line.'

'So once again he slips through the net?'

'His kind always do.'

Annemarie popped her head around the door. 'So, this is where you're hiding?' She gave Caroline a cursory smile. 'I'm going with Sean and Liam back to the house. The limo's waiting. Are you ready?'

'On you go. I can walk back,' he replied.

'Please, go with your family,' Caroline said. 'I'm just about to leave.'

'No,' Colin said. 'Stay for five minutes.'

'Well, I'll be setting off for Newcastle around three,' Annemarie said, 'and Sean's got a meeting with a client later, so, if you don't hurry, we'll be gone. Remember we've those letters to open.'

Colin looked at his watch. 'I'll be right behind you.'

'Nice to meet you,' Annemarie said to Caroline before closing the door.

'What letters?'

'From my mother. *Do not open until after my funeral* – that kind of vibe.'

'Important, then?'

Colin shrugged. 'Far more likely to be a reprimand from beyond the grave. What else has been happening?'

Caroline sidled closer to him. 'Well, I have some inside

449

knowledge about Sarah's case.'

'You do? How?'

'Remember Tony, the nice inspector I befriended while you were giving your statement in Dumbarton? Well, we've been seeing each other.'

'You're a fast mover.'

'He thinks I'm thirty-nine.'

Colin laughed. 'Don't be absurd. He's a policeman, he'll know exactly how old you are and if you've ever committed a crime.'

'Oh.' Caroline looked disappointed for a split-second. 'Actually, that's rather sweet, don't you think? Anyway, you can't tell anyone what I'm about to say. You need to swear; Tony could lose his job.'

'I swear.'

'Sarah is still trying to pin the blame on Brendan for the murder.'

'It's not a bad tactic; it's not like he's here to defend himself.'

Caroline shook her head. 'Apparently, she was demanding to get out of prison to go to his funeral, desperate to play the weeping widow. But they didn't budge.'

'Quite right. She's as guilty as hell.'

'The good news is the forensic evidence against her is mounting. You're aware they exhumed Sister Oran's body and the baby's?'

He nodded. It had been all over the papers. 'Have they confirmed Brendan as the father?'

'Not only that.' Caroline lowered her voice. 'They found a torch in the cottage which they think is the murder weapon. Plus, there were unexplained marks on Sister Oran's face which have turned out to be a perfect match for that godawful engagement ring Sarah was always waving about.'

'That's really encouraging.'

'They're going to get her – they're determined.' Caroline

A Prayer Before Killing

stood and the beads on her coat caught a shaft of sunlight falling through the window. 'I really need to go.'

Colin walked her to the door. 'If Brother Thomas has gone, who's running the school?'

'Charlie Murray, believe it or not. Having split up with Hayley Falco, he's come back temporarily, but I think the archdiocese are planning to take over the school and turn it into a seminary. So, I may be looking for a new job.' She opened the door. 'And what about you? Are you staying in Glasgow?'

Colin shrugged. 'There's a bunch of stuff to settle, like whether we sell the house or not. Once that's sorted, then I'll decide. I'm not rushing into anything just yet.'

Caroline pecked him on the cheek. 'Stay in touch. You're the best thing that's happened to that school in years. I miss you being there.'

'Thank you. I'm not sure the Catholic Church would agree.'

'That's their loss.' Caroline waved goodbye and strolled through the lobby out into the low winter sunshine.

THE SOUND of the TV blaring in the living room reminded Colin of his mum. He poked his head around the door to find Liam watching a black-and-white Western. 'Thought I might have missed you. Where's your mum?'

'Kitchen.'

'With Uncle Sean?'

'He left in a huff a while ago saying he wouldn't be back.'

'All normal, then?'

They both smirked and Liam turned his attention back to the film.

In the kitchen, Annemarie sat nursing a mug of tea. She looked up and smiled. 'I spoke to Dad on the phone earlier and told him how it all went, how much we love him.'

'How was he? Did he know who you were?'

'Nah. He thought I was Mum.'

Colin joined her at the table and saw one of his mother's letters on the floor, ripped in two. 'Let me guess – she didn't leave Sean all her money?'

Annemarie picked it up. 'Surprise, surprise, her special message is that Michelle isn't good enough for him, that he could do much better.' She scrunched the letter into a ball and tossed it at the bin.

'Just shows how confused she was towards the end.' Colin waited for Annemarie to react, but she didn't. 'Not going to open yours?'

'I couldn't face it.' Annemarie picked up her letter. 'What do you think she'll say? That she loved me, that she's sorry for all the unkindness she's shown me over the years, that she admired me for bringing up a child single-handed without an ounce of support from her or anyone else?'

'Annemarie—'

She thrust the letter towards him. 'You open it.'

'But it's addressed to you.'

'Please, Colin?' Her voice trailed off, too tired to argue.

He took the envelope and ripped it open. 'Want me to read it out loud?'

'Just the highlights. It's going in the bin afterwards.'

He glanced through it. 'Well, thankfully it's short.'

Annemarie stared at him. 'Just read the damned thing.'

'As you know, Annemarie, I disagree with many of your life's decisions, but the one I disagree with most is how you've brought up Liam. The boy needs to come out from under your apron strings and stand up for himself, otherwise he'll be a weight round your neck your entire life. Trust me. Mum.'

'Got off lightly, didn't I?' She took the letter and, as

promised, stood and placed it in the bin. 'There's a bottle of whisky at the back of the cupboard. Fancy one?'

'I'll get it.' Colin took tumblers from the cupboard and poured them each a large measure.

'*Sláinte*,' they said in unison as they clinked their glasses together.

'Your turn,' Annemarie said.

Colin sat and held the crisp white envelope in his hand. He could see that his mother had taken time to write his name in her best handwriting, and if nothing else, this meant something – a small sign of her love. 'Think she's left me everything?' he quipped.

'Her golden boy? I wouldn't be surprised.'

Colin tore open the envelope and had to keep re-reading it as it made no sense.

'What's she said?'

'I'm not sure.' He passed her the letter. 'Read it back to me.'

'I'm sorry I failed you as a mother, but I just couldn't find the words to tell you. Annemarie will explain.'

She looked up at him and her face turned crimson, then white. She threw the letter onto the table.

'What didn't she tell me?'

'I thought she had.' Annemarie took a gulp. 'She told me she had. That you never wanted to discuss it, that's why I've said nothing all these years.' As she put her tumbler down, she accidentally knocked it over. Whisky ran across the table, soaking the letter. 'Shit!'

'Annemarie?' Colin grabbed the letter but was too late; the words were beginning to dissolve, disappear.

She jumped to her feet. 'Here, let me.' With a tea towel she took the sodden letter from him, and tried to dry it, but the paper dissolved. She sat back down and stared at him.

He'd forgotten what a spectacular shade of green her eyes were. As children, he used to envy their colour, so vibrant compared to his own greyish blue. Suddenly, a rush of memories came flooding back, all the good ones: playing in the back garden, going swimming, poring over pop magazines. He loved his sister. She was a pain in the arse at times, but she was a good person and had worked hard all her life. 'You need to tell me.'

'I promise Mum told me you knew.'

'Obviously, she didn't,' he interrupted. 'So, it's down to you.'

Annemarie took a deep breath and stared at the crucifix on the wall. 'I swear that woman was the devil,' she said.

'Just tell me.'

'Okay, here goes.' She clutched his hands. 'Ray, the man you call Dad, isn't your biological father.'

At once, things his mother had said, moments his father had looked at him, pointed references to him being the odd one out, *the foundling*, as Annemarie used to tease, made sense. 'Then who is?'

'If you don't know, then she's taken that secret to her grave.'

'But it's a priest? Am I right?' It was the only thing that made sense. Her obsession with him being an altar boy, working towards a life devoted to the church. From as far back as he could remember, that's all she'd ever wanted for him.

'That was my guess, but she never said.'

Colin stood and poured himself another whisky. He downed it in one and then poured another and did the same. The alcohol burnt his throat and made his chest ache. Crossing to the sink, he rinsed out the glass and placed it on the draining board.

'It changes nothing.' Annemarie was behind him, rubbing his shoulder.

But Colin knew this wasn't true.

'We're still your family,' she whispered.

'Of course you are,' he said and kissed her on the forehead.

Standing in the kitchen, hugging his sister, he thought of all the opportunities Moira had had to tell the truth. No one takes all their secrets to the grave, he told himself. Some might have been buried well, but if you knew where to look, you'd discover things that people imagined were locked away for good.

Nothing stays secret forever.

AVAILABLE NOW

All Mine Enemies, **Book 1** in the **Colin Buxton Series**, is available to buy now.

"A thrilling whodunnit" Amazon reader

"A great read and a terrific debut novel" Amazon reader

"A real page turner" Amazon reader

A remote Scottish island… secrets waiting to destroy… a gruesome killing

What actor could refuse the invitation to rehearse a new play on an exclusive private island?

Two aging actors well past their prime

A young hot-shot whose career is on the up

A jaded ingénue battling the industry

But before a line is uttered, the production's leading man is brutally murdered. And when the fiercest storm in a century cuts the island off from the mainland, all hell breaks loose.

Colin Buxton, a police officer taking a break with his producer boyfriend, is caught off guard, and without back-up, must untangle a web of lies and deceit before the killer strikes again.

And, as the blurring of personal and professional lives threatens to derail an already fraught investigation, Colin asks:

Is the key to solving the murder buried in the past?

Who can he trust to tell the truth?

And might his own partner be implicated?

In this gripping murder mystery, bestselling author CC Gilmartin weaves a dark tale of suspense and revenge that will keep you guessing until the end.

All Mine Enemies is the first book in the Colin Buxton investigative crime series. If you like complex characters and psychological twists, then you'll love CC Gilmartin's page-turning debut.

Perfect for fans of Matt Brolly, Ann Cleeves, CL Taylor and Andrew Raymond.

AVAILABLE NOW

The Look of Death, **Book 2** in the **Colin Buxton Series**, is available to buy now.

"Dark and pacy" Amazon reader

"Brilliant detective story" Amazon reader

"Hard to put down" Amazon reader

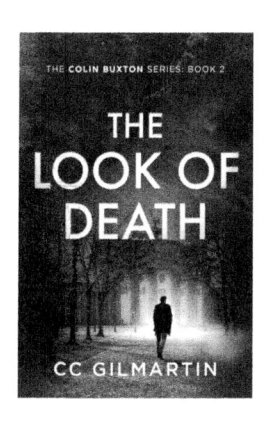

Berlin, summer 1994 … where past and present collide … a serial killer haunts the sweltering city

Colin Buxton arrives in Berlin, which - like him - is facing an uncertain future. And things turn sinister when the bodies of five gay men are found in parks around the city.

Colin suspects there's a serial killer on the loose, and as he delves deeper into the men's lives, evidence suggests it could be someone they've known intimately. But despite the mounting evidence, the authorities seem unwilling to listen. Will it take another victim for them to act?

The Look of Death is the 2nd tense, gripping crime novel in best selling author CC Gilmartin's Colin Buxton Series.

Perfect for fans of Matt Brolly, Alice Hunter, Angela Marsons, Alex Smith, Joy Ellis & M.J. Arlidge.

COMING SOON

Book 4 in the **Colin Buxton Series** will be published in 2026.

AVAILABLE FOR FREE

In the Stillness, a **Prequel** to the **Colin Buxton Series**, is available to download for **FREE** when you join the **CC Gilmartin Readers' Club**.

"An intriguing and insightful prequel" Goodreads

Winter 1984. When Colin Buxton hitchhikes from Glasgow to London with his troubled best friend, little does he know that before they reach their destination, their lives will have changed forever.

Making their way along the busy motorways of the North, Colin is led into a world of casual pick-ups and easy money. Confused but intrigued, he chooses to look the other way.

Until a line is crossed.

ACKNOWLEDGMENTS

A huge thanks to the following people for their expertise and input: editors Shelley Routledge and Mary Torjussen; cover designer Stuart Bache; and website designer Stuart Grant at Digital Authors Toolkit.

Special thanks to the **CC Gilmartin Readers' Club** for their support - especially our **ARC Team**.

ABOUT THE AUTHOR

We're Chris Deans and Coll Begg, and together we write as CC Gilmartin.

If you'd like to know more about our books, please visit www.ccgilmartin.com and join the **CC Gilmartin Readers' Club** for **FREE**. As a member, you'll receive your **FREE** digital copy of *In the Stillness*, the **Colin Buxton Series Prequel**, plus regular updates on the progress of the series, as well as our other projects.

Scan the QR Code below to connect to ccgilmartin.com

We love to hear from our readers. To contact us directly, email: contact@ccgilmartin.com

You can also follow us on social media:

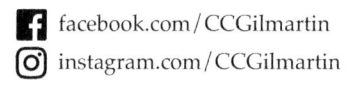

facebook.com/CCGilmartin
instagram.com/CCGilmartin

Printed in Great Britain
by Amazon